TWOPENCE PRESS books are published by
Twopence Press, LLC
P.O. Box 1753
Leonardtown, Maryland 20650

TWOPENCE PRESS

www.twopencepress.com

Cover Design and Interior Format by
The Killion Group, Inc.

ST. CLEMENTS BLUFF

HEART *of* ST. MARY'S COUNTY

BOOK ONE

For Patrick — I hope you enjoy

CHRISTINE TRENT

Raleigh's story!

Christine Trent

For Don
The best thing I never planned

Never wound a snake; kill it.
Harriet Tubman, Underground Railroad "Conductor"
1822–1913

Let us do penance so long as we are still on this earth, dear brothers, for we are like clay in the hands of the potter. So long as the pot breaks or becomes misshapen while the potter is still molding it, he can set his hand to it once more; but otherwise, if he has already put it in the oven, there is no longer anything he can do about it.
St. Clement of Rome
c. 35 AD—99 AD

CHAPTER I

EVERYTHING WAS SURREAL as Raleigh strapped herself snugly inside the co-pilot's seat. She turned to observe the pilot, Captain Grant Bishop, to her left. He was not only the captain of the XC-88J White Lion experimental stealth transport aircraft but also her husband.

His helmet was emblazoned with "Buckshot" across the front in white lettering. As was custom, he had been christened with a nickname by others. Nicknames, once earned, were sacrosanct and completely immutable. Grant's had been given to him on a hunting trip with his compatriots, during which he had been completely unable to bring himself to pull the trigger on an eight-point buck, much to the mockery of his friends.

Their helmets were wonders of technology, with multiple cameras and sensors embedded in them, as well as visors that informed pilots of flight stats such as remaining fuel and altitude. They even provided night-vision capability. Long gone were the days when a helmet was considered merely crash protection and a visor was to shield the eyes from the sun.

This aircraft was a joint effort across U.S. military forces and had taken more than a decade to reach this stage of flight testing. In the way of joint programs, the initial performance requirements for the craft had bloated and stretched beyond all recognition, with star-encrusted navy admirals and air force generals one-upping each other with their latest must-have features for the plane.

The resulting beast was expected to be large enough to transport the military's rapidly miniaturizing drone fleet while flying at a jet fighter's speed to ensure they got to their destinations in record time.

Size and speed tended to work against each other, but the collective work of thousands of GloboCraft International employees had made it possible to bring an early version of the aircraft to fruition for testing.

The array of blinking lights and screens spread in front of them meant nothing to Raleigh, as she concentrated her focus on Grant's confident control of the plane. He was communicating with the jet on the runway next to them. Captained by Avery "Crunch" Sloan, Grant's best friend, it was identical to the jet Raleigh and her husband sat in, except for some alternate landing controls that the Navy was testing. Today's flight would determine which craft had landing controls more readily adaptable to auto piloting.

Grant noticed her looking at him. He winked and flashed her a thumbs-up. There was probably a grin in there, but it was impossible to tell behind his loaded helmet. Any day in the pilot's seat was a happy day for Grant.

He reached out his olive green-clad arm and pressed a button. Raleigh heard a tiny beep in her ear.

The engines revved louder as they prepared for take-off, becoming a roar that enveloped one's body with a sort of tense excitement that was inexplicable to those who had never experienced it. Grant's eyes sparkled with childish joy, and he threw back his head. Now Raleigh was certain her husband was smiling, if not outright laughing. She smiled back at him.

Within moments, they were racing down the runway at Patuxent River Naval Air Station. Employees of the base would frequently gather to watch these take-offs—they were almost as thrilling from the ground as they were from within the cockpit—and today was no exception, even though it was an unusually frosty November morning.

But the onlookers were a blur to Raleigh as both jets tore down the asphalt at speeds unfathomable to the typical commercial air passenger. Grant was competitive, and she knew he was trying to ensure they lifted off before Crunch's aircraft, simply for bragging rights once they landed. Plus, he would make Crunch buy him a beer this evening at the officer's club.

In moments they were in the air, still neck-and-neck with Crunch's plane. It reminded Raleigh of the source of Crunch's apropos nickname, bestowed upon him for totaling his car in a ditch after an idiotic drag race. Long story.

"Can't believe I crunched my car like that," Avery had observed at the time as he walked away without a scratch, earning him mocking laughter and a permanent nickname. He was slated to earn his captain's wings soon, which would make his nickname all the more amusing.

Raleigh had no idea if Grant had won his bet against his friend, for he was now engrossed in the cockpit panel and not flashing her any signs. Listening to his requests and commands through the helmet's earpiece, she responded as he guided the aircraft around toward Solomons Island, a quaint village near the Navy base. Raleigh glanced down to her right, wondering if she could pick out Angler's, her favorite restaurant on the island.

The aircraft gained altitude rapidly, and Raleigh felt Grant's shared sensation of wild elation that came with these moments. This eagle's-eye view of the world, combined with their speed and the knowledge that every experimental aircraft not yet in the Navy's inventory came with a definite level of risk, made for heart-throbbing intoxication. It was like being on a roller coaster with no safety controls, and everything depended upon trust. Trust of the ground crew, the aircraft manufacturer, the software dweebs, and the thousands of other support people who had worked impossible hours to make the White Lion possible.

"No one but us, babe," Grant said into the microphone to her, meaning they were the only ones who had ever flown this particular beast. It was like a dangerously delicious secret.

Raleigh turned back to her husband, intending to give him her own thumbs-up, but something was suddenly very wrong. What was that bang? And why was she lurching forward? Only by inches, of course, as the cross-straps of her harness prevented her from going too far.

She felt dizzy and disoriented. Why was the scenery above them instead of below them? Were they…upside down?

She lurched again and the scenery was properly situated again.

Grant was shouting into his microphone but she couldn't understand him. No, he was merely whispering. It was so difficult to know. Now his gaze was locked onto hers, pleading. Raleigh knew they needed to eject. Why weren't they ejecting, their parachutes carrying them safely downward? Even a river landing would be preferable to whatever hell this was.

Raleigh caught the faintest whiff of acrid jet fuel accompanied by a searing heat as she witnessed an orange ball of light moving upward past them. It felt as though her helmet was being melted against her face. Dear God, it was so hot. She resisted the urge to claw the helmet off, instead staying focused on Grant, whose voice was receding into the background. Or was she fainting? Was this what it felt like to die? Your vision and hearing simply began receding until you no longer had a sense of anything at all around you.

"I love you!" Raleigh shouted into her microphone, unable to hear her own words. "I love you, Grant Bishop! I love you so much! Do you hear me? I love you!" She knew she was babbling the words, but they were all she could conjure up. What was going on on the ground, the incoming messages from flight control—all irrelevant.

Actually, even her words were irrelevant, for it was apparent that Grant couldn't hear her. His gaze was still on her, but it was so…blank. Raleigh reached out her hand to her husband, but in the next instant, he was falling away from her as the cockpit split apart. It was like a roller coaster again—that moment when your car reaches the top of the first hill. You are weightless, as you are neither *clack-clack-clacking* your way up the hill nor are you hurtling downward, screaming your way to the bottom again. Instead, you are suspended, heart in your throat as you wait for what you know is the inevitable plunge.

No, no, no, no, Raleigh implored, her hand clawing upward toward a deity she hoped would save her. *This moment is not real. It is not real. It cannot be real.*

Then she, too, began hurtling toward the river, unable to extricate herself from the instantaneous death that awaited her below.

CHAPTER 2

RALEIGH SAT UP in bed, completely disoriented as usual. She blinked several times in the dark as she regained her senses and forced herself to breathe normally.

She was alive.

She was also drenched in sweat, despite being clad only in one of Grant's old cotton t-shirts and a pair of his dark blue silk boxer shorts. Neither felt particularly good against her clammy skin.

Raleigh looked down to her left at the spot where her husband should be. The bed was still made on his side. Each night, when she reluctantly crawled under the covers, she was careful not to disturb his side, and she invaded his space only enough to throw an arm over his pillow. She had never told anyone, but she was superstitiously terrified that if she were to roll down the covers or otherwise muss them up, his scent would be forever released from the bed, never to be recaptured.

It was why he had been gone months now and she still refused to change the sheets, despite how rank her side was becoming. It would be like throwing Grant into a laundry tub, an unbearable thought.

Instead, she chose to live out this equally unbearable Groundhog's Day, in which she perpetually reenacted her husband's death.

Raleigh was not a pilot and had not been in the cockpit with Grant that day—that seat had been taken by an experienced colleague of Grant's, Mateo Martinez, the flight officer who had also been killed in addition to Crunch and the flight officer of the other plane.

Wasn't it ironic that the impact of two aircraft wing tips touching mid-air was nothing like, say, two vehicle side view mirrors knocking against each other as two cars passed each other on a highway? Whereas the side view mirrors would be demolished, the cars would continue with barely an impact to their forward motion. The aircraft, though, with just a whisper-touch of their wing tips, could spin, crash into one another, and erupt into fiery balls of jet fuel.

Martinez's wife had been a statue at the joint funeral held for all four men at the base chapel. Sofía had hardly spoken to anyone, instead staring straight ahead with one child's hand clutched in each of hers as each man received an honor guard rifle salute and a flyover. Martinez's body was then shipped off to his family's home in Arizona, and Sofía left for her own family in Texas.

She hadn't even said goodbye to Raleigh, which was particularly painful not only because of their shared loss but because test pilot wives tended to stick together.

Raleigh had heard that Jasmine Green, who had been engaged to Crunch's flight officer, was striving to remain part of the test pilot community. She was trying to make some sense of how her rose petal-strewn future path had been destroyed, as if a tornado had violently appeared from nowhere and laid a dystopian waste to it.

Good for her if she could manage to make some sense of it.

Raleigh picked up her cell phone to look at the time. It was just past four in the morning. Too early to get up, too late to get any sort of real sleep before she actually had to get up and start another tiresome day.

Must this happen every night? Couldn't God just for

once be merciful and let her go to sleep so that she never had to wake up trembling again?

Her dreams took different forms. Sometimes she was in her office, reliving the moment that she had received the call, and other times she imagined she was on the ground on Solomons Island, watching the planes' wing tips nick each other. The worst dreams, though, were when she imagined being in the cockpit with Grant as his partner on the flight. Although she wasn't a pilot, Grant had described it all so vividly before that her traitorous mind was able to conjure up the smell, feel, and muffled noise of the cockpit.

The other dreams left her unsettled and crying, but this one went deep into horror territory, mostly because it made her question, for the millionth time, what it was like for Grant when he realized his life was over.

"Accidents happen in the blink of an eye and your husband probably experienced none of the drawn-out terror of your dreams, Raleigh," the therapist had said. "Rest in the comfort that he felt no pain," blah blah blah.

Therapists. How could they possibly understand her pain?

Raleigh hardly remembered the funeral. There were just bits and pieces that periodically passed before her eyes. Sofía Martinez, emotionless and fragile. The pastor offering forgettable words of comfort. The American flag folded tautly by Grant's comrades and offered to her with a salute. Friends asking, "What can I do for you?" to which she wanted to scream, "How do I know? I am just trying to get through the next five minutes!" but instead smiling and accepting their sympathetic, fierce hugs. Her mother and sister, trying desperately—and futilely—to make Raleigh smile.

Then there were Grant's parents, David and Margaret Bishop, so broken themselves they could hardly speak to Raleigh. The Bishops had lived in St. Mary's County since the 17th century and had a proud lineage that stretched back into Merrie Olde England.

The family had had its share of tragic accidents over the centuries, all documented in voluminous heritage scrapbooks, but never anything as high profile and public as this. Raleigh had even had a condolence call from the governor, and both she and Grant's parents had received letters from the president.

As she considered it, Raleigh hadn't talked to the Bishops since last week, when they had suggested she finally open Grant's will and begin taking care of his estate. As Raleigh recalled, she had snapped something about not picking at Grant's corpse like beady-eyed vultures.

Not her finest moment.

So the Bishops had retreated from their daughter-in-law of seven years. Raleigh knew she owed them an apology, but for now, she just wanted to be left alone in her ongoing misery.

Realizing she was fully awake now, Raleigh slid out of bed, her feet gently hitting the oak floor.

Routine and habits—like being quiet so as not to wake Grant when he had been out all hours on night flights—were staying with her.

As if they would ever leave.

Raleigh stretched and yawned, then realized that the bedroom was very chilly. Time to adjust the thermostat, for she certainly wasn't going to switch out for flannel pajamas. Not while she had so many of Grant's clothes to keep close to her skin.

Her cell phone buzzed on the nightstand. It was her boss, Bert Mattingly, Director of the St. Mary's Historical Museum.

Raleigh contemplated ignoring the call, but Bert had been so understanding of her situation—allowing her nearly an indefinite period of leave after Grant's death—that it seemed churlish not to answer.

"Mornin', Raleigh," Bert said with excessive enthusiasm. "Just wanted to let you know that we finally received the state grants for both the new colonial farming display and the Yaocomico village exhibit you applied for last year. You're welcome to start on it whenever you'd like."

Guilt nipped at Raleigh's innards, tearing away at the grief she had been nurturing for so long. "I guess I should think about returning to the office..."

Bert seized on her doubt. "Of course, you should. We haven't touched your office so it's just as you left it."

"That's nice of you," Raleigh said noncommittally.

Bert took it as enthusiasm. "It would be good for you to spend a day or two a week in the office. I hear people say they see you jogging through your neighborhood with your dog, occasionally stopping to pick at a bag of green grapes for sustenance. You need more than that."

"Oh, that," Raleigh laughed weakly. "I don't quite have my appetite back."

Bert was silent for a moment. "After over a year?" he said quietly.

The guilt chewed at her more. "I know, I know. Look, I'll think about it, okay?"

"Okay." Bert sighed in resignation. "But remember that you don't have to immediately come back full-time. Spend Mondays in the office."

"I promise to think about it," Raleigh repeated, now anxious to end the call.

Raleigh glanced back down at the bed. She was fully awake now, but it was tempting to scurry back under the covers and inhale as deeply as she could of Grant's lingering scent, which was all she had left of him.

No, she may as well start the day, such as it was.

Besides, Lindbergh's nails were clicking up the stairs, a sign that he was ready for his morning walk.

Raleigh hadn't wanted a dog, not with Grant's postings so unsure all the time and the time commitment of a pet, but her husband had found their Chesapeake Bay Retriever through a local rescue agency. In no time, Mutt Boy—as Raleigh frequently referred to their water-loving beast—had become Grant's best pal next to Crunch.

Lindbergh sat in the bedroom doorway and glanced up at her with quizzical eyes. "Good morning, Mutt Boy," Raleigh said. The dog's tail thumped twice then he rose and walked over to Raleigh, leaning against her bare legs, another one of his customs. It could be hard to maintain balance against all eighty pounds of chocolate-colored, rumple-furred pooch. She reached down and scratched him behind his ears, to which Lindbergh leaned his head back to more fully enjoy her attentions.

"Tonight maybe, Lindbergh?" she asked the dog. Lindbergh hadn't slept on the bed since Grant had died. Instead, he spent his nights downstairs, curled up on the braided rug by the front door, as if still expecting that his master would be back at any moment. If she thought it might work, Raleigh would have joined him there.

Lindbergh offered no response except a quick whine and two wags of his tail. "All right, give me a minute."

Raleigh brushed her teeth and washed her face, trying to avoid looking into the bathroom mirror, which she knew would reflect red-rimmed green eyes and tousled ash-blonde hair that had once been as straight as a field of straw.

She changed into a pair of gray sweats with the words "U.S. Navy" running down the left leg in large blue letters and the round Navy seal across the sweatshirt front. Then, following her ridiculous superstition, she tucked Grant's t-shirt and boxers down at the foot of the bed and drew the covers up. She could still get more wear out of them before it would be time to open his dresser drawer and pull out a new shirt and pair of boxers, treasuring the smell and feel of them.

What was she going to do when she ran out of his clothes?

Raleigh took a brisk jog with Lindbergh around the neighborhood, thankful that it was still early enough that there were no neighbors out to offer her sympathetic glances or words of encouragement. She and Grant had purchased their home in a new development built to look like a quaint town, despite it having been erected on two hundred acres of fallow farmland that had likely been abandoned when the owner died. Selling farms could result in huge cash payouts to heirs who wanted nothing to do with tilling the soil.

Raleigh had stacks of digitized records at the museum, showing the trend of farm sell-offs that had occurred over the decades. She hated to see the landscape lose its rural flavor, yet she and Grant had also benefited from having this particular farm made over into housing, so it was hard for her to criticize the changes.

Their cool-down was a brisk walk up the driveway to her house with its dark blue siding, bright yellow door, and white trim. Grant had picked the house's shades as a nod to his beloved Navy's colors.

Releasing the dog from his leash inside the house, she fed him some kibble and prepped the coffeemaker with her favorite French roast. Although she had been repulsed by food since Grant's death, she was able to down copious amounts of coffee. She figured that if she loaded it occasionally with sugar and cream, it counted as nutrition for those inquiring minds, like Bert's, who seemed determined to ensure she was eating right.

She poured a little more cream into her cup, stirring it listlessly as she stared out the window at a squirrel raiding the bird feeder. The little thief had chased all of the birds out of their small, fenced-in yard. Raleigh shrugged. It was a dangerous world out there. Sometimes the squirrels won and the birds lost.

Raleigh was like a fledgling baby bird these days, up against a band of squirrels.

She spent the next few hours lying on the couch, idling flipping through channels while she drank more coffee. A sweet Hallmark movie with its true-love-found-against-all-odds theme did little to improve her mood.

Lindbergh hefted his big carcass onto the couch and laid his length along her body, snuffling his snout under her chin. Raleigh wrapped an arm around him and cried silently against his fur. Everything had fallen away from her.

"Everything except for you, Mutt Boy," she whispered, wishing she had something—anything—to lift her out of this constant gloominess. He licked her cheek and huffed before putting his head down for a nap. Raleigh fell into a fitful sleep with Grant's dog—now *her* dog—until late afternoon. At least she didn't have any of her usual horrifying dreams.

Raleigh awoke to Lindbergh whining by the front door. Time to take him back out again.

Was the rest of her life going to be like this? One awful day melding painfully into another, with no relief from the sorrow and the grief? Was she going to withdraw to the point that she completely disappeared? On one hand, it sounded preferable to living without Grant, but the deep, primal instinct of her soul protested the idea.

Perhaps it was time to take Bert's suggestion to return to work and to listen to her in-laws' urging to open Grant's will. That's what she'd do, get a good night of sleep, actually take a shower and wash her hair in the morning, apply a little powder and lipstick for the first time in months, then go to the bank to get the will out of their safe deposit box.

THE NEXT MORNING, she had the large, sealed envelope containing Grant's will in her hands by half past ten. She hurried home with it, deciding that she would read it from bed so that she could feel as though she was reading it with Grant next to her. More ridiculousness, she knew, glad that no one knew about all of her strange behaviors.

Oddly enough, when she sat cross-legged on top of the covers, Lindbergh came clicking into the room and jumped onto the bed for the first time since Grant had died. He immediately curled up in a giant ball and stared up at Raleigh expectantly.

"Shall I read it to you, Mutt Boy?" she asked, breaking the seal on the envelope and removing the document. Lindbergh whined and reached out a paw to her. Feeling silly, she took the dog's paw, as if she could draw strength from it.

Raleigh Bishop began reading her husband's will. The words were utterly inconceivable... *To my beloved wife, I leave —*

CHAPTER 3

IT WAS FUNNY how they did things in movies, where the reading of a will was some big production in a lawyer's office, with relatives expressing shock or elation in turn at whatever surprise the deceased had left behind for them. Then there was the periodic video of the deceased, telling off those relatives who had been particularly greedy or nasty to him during his life. More expressions of shock and elation, with threats of contesting the will.

The reality was so much more mundane than that.

They had gone to the lawyer together to draw up their wills. The lawyer had recommended the two documents be mirrors of each other's and suggested that they revisit them every two years or so to be sure all was still as they intended. She had also told them to come right away if at any point they decided to have a family, as that would change their estate significantly.

How Raleigh wished now that she and Grant had chosen to work on having children sooner so that she might now have a living reminder of him. *Water under the bridge*, she told herself, wiping away a familiar hot tear that had spilled down her cheek.

Anyway, they had tossed copies of their wills into their safe deposit box a few years ago and she had never considered them again. Nevertheless, she expected his to read just like hers, since they were each leaving the other all of their worldly possessions, and in the event one predeceased the other, most of their goods would be distributed to charities.

Except that Grant's will had a strange addition to it. When had he changed his will? And why had he done it without her knowledge?

The words blurred before Raleigh's eyes. She had to re-read them three times before they began to make sense.

Even though there was much of the same phrasing from her own will, there was one particular paragraph that stood out to her.

Also, for my beloved wife, Raleigh Moore Bishop, I leave the property named St. Clements Bluff, located in Compton, Maryland, which contains a home and various outbuildings along St. Clements Bay. I request that she caretake this property for the rest of her life.

An exact address and plat location were also provided, as well as instructions on where to find the deed and key. What was this property? She'd never heard about it before.

Raleigh's eyes watered again at the words "for my beloved wife." Had he executed those words casually upon paper, never imagining how soon she would be reading them?

But there were larger questions. How could Grant have possibly saved the money to make a purchase as large as a *home* without Raleigh knowing about it? Moreover, why would he secretly buy a house, then just as covertly change his will to leave it to her?

It made no sense at all.

If it was some ancestral Bishop home, he should have left it to his brother, Trey. After all, Trey was the elder son and the most logical one to inherit anything in his immediate family.

Of course, this raised another question. If it was an ancestral home, how and when had it even passed into Grant's hands?

Raleigh gently squeezed Lindbergh's paw and released it, trying to decide what to do next.

Well, first things first, as they say.

With a sense of purpose she hadn't had in weeks, Raleigh rose from the bed. "Want to help, Mutt Boy?" she asked as she made her way downstairs to the garage, following the mysterious directions from the will.

Lindbergh padded down the stairs behind her, his tags jingling on his collar as his nails clicked on the stairs.

Raleigh opened the door leading from the kitchen to the garage and paused before taking the two steps down onto the concrete floor.

This had been Grant's retreat for working on his old Triumph Thunderbird motorcycle, which sat gleaming atop a spread-out tarp in one bay of the two-car garage. Unlike most garages Raleigh had ever seen, the Bishop garage was as neatly arranged with tools and as sanitary as an operating room. Not a drop of oil or dirt anywhere, and Grant had installed banks of metal cabinets and counters for everything from his golf clubs to his woodworking tools.

Raleigh managed to muster a wry smile at that thought. Grant had purchased countless saws, chisels, and cans of foul-smelling stains and goos, all with the intent of pursuing a woodworking hobby. It had only ever materialized into a tool-collecting hobby, but everything was tidily kept in drawers and on wall hooks.

It took mere moments to figure out which floor-to-ceiling cabinet held her husband's golf clubs. Seeing them there, standing erect and proud in their green and tan leather bag, caused a large lump to form in Raleigh's throat. Grant and Crunch had had several favorite charity tournaments they played in together each year.

In their competitive way, the two men would always place silly bets against each other despite playing on the same team. The loser typically ended up beating a club against a tree at the humiliation of having to spring for drinks in the clubhouse.

Grant would never pick up these clubs ever again.

Lindbergh whined next to her, then padded over to the motorcycle to sniff at it. "Careful, Mutt Boy," Raleigh said. "Your human wouldn't want to see his bike tipped ov—"

Again, that catch in her throat.

Best to take care of matters and not linger in here.

Raleigh pulled the bag out of the locker-style cabinet, and it landed on the ground with a dull thump. She knelt and ran her hand down the worn leather to the zippered pocket at the base of it. She unzipped it, slid her hand in, and her fingers quickly found a folded sheet of paper and a small metal ring with several keys on it. The keys were old, although not so old as to be old-fashioned skeleton keys. The paper was the deed to this mysterious home she now owned.

She rose and put the golf bag away, closing the cabinet door softly, feeling inexplicably guilty for shutting them away again.

Raleigh Bishop figured she was facing two decisions: she could either drive straight to the property to check it out, or she could detour first to Grant's parents' home to see what they knew about this.

"Well, there's a third decision, isn't there, Mutt Boy?" she asked the dog, who had lost interest in the motorcycle and was sitting next to her. "And that's to just go to bed until tomorrow and forget this ever happened."

Lindbergh looked at Raleigh blankly. His repertoire of words generally consisted of "potty," "breakfast," "dinner," and "chew toy." He also knew "Lucas," the cat next door who periodically came to the living room window to peer inside and taunt Lindbergh until he was hysterical and frothing at the mouth.

Raleigh sighed. "I guess you're probably ready to go potty, aren't you?" she said to the dog, realizing she'd been having far many more conversations with the dog over the past year than with other actual human beings. Lindbergh didn't offer her sappy advice or compassionate looks. He simply wanted his normal life back, just like Raleigh did.

She took him for another quick walk, and by the time they had returned, Raleigh's curiosity had gotten the better of her and she no longer planned to go to bed. Instead, she would forego a stop at her in-laws' house and drive straight out to see Grant's unexpected gift to her.

RALEIGH WAS FIRST struck by how well-kept St. Clements Bluff's grounds were. The only marker to the property was a short section of freshly-painted white fencing upon which hung a nearly unnoticeable sign stating "St. Clements Bluff, Est. 1823."

Everyone in the county knew that St. Clement had been an early pope. The Romans had been none too fond of the church leader and ended up executing him by tying an anchor around him and throwing him into the sea. Thus, he was the patron saint of mariners and his name was given to the local body of water known as St. Clements Bay.

And, apparently, to this house.

Raleigh entered the long, rutted gravel driveway, which was lined by old cedar trees. It made her feel as though she was entering an antebellum plantation.

On the front passenger seat, Lindbergh was alert and

excited, his goofy big head extended out the window as he barked happily into the cold afternoon air. Was this familiar territory for him?

"Have you been here before?" Raleigh asked him, slowing down and a reaching a hand over to scratch his ears. Lindbergh offered a low woof and licked her hand in return.

"I wish you could talk," she told him. "You would be able to clear everything up in an instant for me, wouldn't you?"

Lindbergh licked her again and Raleigh resumed driving down the graveled path. The tree line ended as the road curved off to the right, and St. Clements Bluff came into full view a thousand feet in front of her.

Raleigh stomped on the brakes of her Toyota SUV so hard that Lindbergh yelped as he scrambled to stay upright.

"Sorry, Mutt Boy," she said absentmindedly, trying to grasp what it was she beheld before her.

Under a typically gloomy winter sky and with its back to a placid river sat an old, white, abandoned farmhouse, the kind used in teenage horror movies. Everyone knew they shouldn't enter, but libido and alcohol destroyed all reason, so they barged right on in to be taken in turn by knives, machetes, chainsaws, and other devious murder weapons.

Except…St. Clements Bluff appeared to have experienced some sort of regular care. A circle drive encompassed the front and was flanked by a trimmed lawn. In the center of the driveway was an old concrete statue of the Virgin Mary that must have been scrubbed clean of algae and mold at some point in the past few years. It still had traces of blue and red paint on it. The black shutters, while not exactly gleaming with fresh paint, were intact and hanging properly on both sides of each of the windows.

But there were definitely places where the white paint was peeling off the house, particularly near the roofline, and the covered porch had certainly seen better days.

Scattered trees on the property were in a winter state, devoid of their leaves, but there was no evidence of decay—no fallen rotting trunks, nor any that were vine-choked.

In the distance were a variety of sheds, a red barn, and a couple of outbuildings that looked as though they might be guest houses or little studios. All were coated in peeling white paint.

Raleigh was startled by the sudden buzzing of her phone in its car holder. She glanced down. It was Mom again, no doubt seeking an update on what Raleigh was doing to get out of the house, meet new people, and resume getting on with life.

Raleigh pressed a button and sent the call to voice mail. She'd deal with Mom later.

Instead, she contemplated Lindbergh as he panted expectantly in the seat next to her. It gave her an idea. She put the vehicle in park, stepped out, and waved to Lindbergh. He leaped cleanly over the driver's seat and out of the car.

Raleigh watched carefully to see what he would do. After a minute or so of bounding back and forth in front of the house aimlessly with his breath condensing in a cloud around him, he finally began sniffing intently near the set of steps leading up to the wrap-around porch.

Raleigh quietly approached Lindbergh, wondering whether he truly recognized the place or if he was just being a dog.

Clarity came as Lindbergh became obsessed with a spot next to a—what was that? Raleigh moved closer to inspect the structure partially obstructing her view of Lindbergh who now appeared to be digging his way to the Antarctic.

Two large wooden doors were set at an angle to the ground. They were painted white to match the house, making them blend with the wrap-around porch behind them.

Raleigh supposed this was an old food storage cellar. No doubt opening the doors would reveal a set of rickety stairs disappearing into a dark space lined with shelves, crates, and baskets full of root vegetables and canned jams. Or perhaps it was only full of cobwebs and crickets.

There was a lock securing a chain looped through both iron door handles. Removing a glove and holding it between her teeth, Raleigh dug the key ring out of her front jeans pocket and examined them. Did one of them fit this lock?

Lindbergh barked excitedly and dug furiously next to the cellar, an easy job since the ground had not yet frozen for the season. She shoved the ring back into her pocket and put her glove back on.

"Mutt Boy, what is it?" Raleigh asked, knowing that her car was going to be a mess once his meaty paws got finished depositing dirt all over the seats.

Lindbergh yelped once and ran off with something in his jaws.

"Idiot," she said affectionately to his retreating figure. She let him run a few moments until he tired of his triumph. As was the retriever's nature, he pranced up to Raleigh, never desiring to be too far from his human for very long.

He dropped his bundle at Raleigh's feet. She felt that familiar twist in her stomach. Lindbergh now recognized *her* as his human.

Raleigh bent down to pick up Lindbergh's find. She held the soggy, dirt-encrusted item between a thumb and forefinger. The dog had unearthed one of the special hickory-flavored dental bones that Raleigh and Grant had found on a specialty pet website. It wasn't likely that this had been buried decades ago and Lindbergh just happened to catch the scent of it. It belonged to him.

She dropped the bone, which must have been of no interest any longer, for Lindbergh ignored it.

Grant, what is this place?

Raleigh imagined an interior filled with old antebellum furniture, covered in ancient dust cloths. Perhaps a photograph of Robert E. Lee in a frame with cracked glass hanging in the entry hall. A sweeping walnut staircase leading to second and third floors. Maybe even some old gasoliers hanging from the ceiling, draped in thick cobwebs.

The kitchen would no doubt be an afterthought, a knit-together space taken from other rooms with tiny old 1930s style appliances and an old sink that may or may not have water taps attached to it.

Surely the bedrooms would be arranged for a large family of at least a half-dozen children. Multiple beds in each room, including a cradle in the parents' bedchamber. All covered in dust cloths, of course.

There would also be wood-mantled fireplaces and multiple layers of floral wallpaper in every room. Raleigh imagined big pink and white cabbage roses against an emerald green background as the final layer of paper covering.

It was ironic that Raleigh's crushing grief for Grant was being interrupted for the first time by Grant himself. It was both a momentary relief and a guilty burden.

Well, there was nothing to do now but enter the house.

Raleigh climbed the steps to the front porch with Lindbergh at her heels.

Once more she removed her gloves, shoved them into a coat pocket, and pulled out the key ring.

Which key?

She randomly selected one and approached the door, which was a faded red. The doorknob was relatively new and modern, with the brass still maintaining a bright finish.

Raleigh examined the keyring again and selected what seemed to be the newest key on it. It slid into the lock and turned easily. Raleigh pushed open the door, which protested mildly on creaking hinges.

She and the dog stepped inside. Raleigh had had an overactive imagination as to what the interior would look like. It wasn't done in antebellum style. It wasn't decorated in any style whatsoever.

The house was empty.

It was also nearly as cold inside as it was outside. Raleigh tossed the ring onto the floor in the entryway and sought her gloves again.

"Well, Mutt Boy," she said, her voice echoing against the entry hall's high ceiling. "Shall we look around for some sort of clue about this place?"

She moved through the first floor quickly, given that there was nothing to see. It seemed as though someone had taken great care to ensure that not a crumb of evidence remained of any previous owners, other than a particular odor of staleness that might have been old pipe tobacco. The kitchen was more modern than she had expected. She estimated that it dated from the 1960s, based upon the hideous walnut-colored appliances, the liberal use of Formica countertops the fake brick linoleum, and the orange, yellow, and brown psychedelic wallpaper.

It was all in reasonably good shape, though. Like a frozen snapshot in time. How many families had spent time here over cake mixing bowls, boiling pots of crabs, and rolled pie dough?

And were those families all Bishops?

"Whew," Raleigh said, looking down at Lindbergh. "The decor is just a bit much, isn't it?"

The dog just sat and stared at her. "You're useless, Mutt Boy," she said, patting his head with her gloved hand as she moved back out into the main part of the house. "No interesting conversation at all with you."

Had she just had a moment of humor? It was such an odd feeling that she couldn't quite be sure.

Raleigh opened every door she could find. Everything opened into empty rooms or empty closets. There wasn't a scrap of anything to suggest who had lived here.

She moved to the staircase, placing her hand on the newel of the curved walnut banister. "Shall we?" she said, beginning to feel ridiculous talking aloud in an empty house to a dog who couldn't understand her.

The treads were grooved at the center of each uneven step, another reflection of centuries of families walking, running, and bouncing up and down them. The staircase didn't creak as much as she anticipated it would, but maybe she was lost in her teenage horror movie delusion again.

The landing at the top of the stairs appeared to intersect the house in half, with a corridor to either side and glass-knobbed doors lining both hallways.

She had no idea where to start but her feet seemed to naturally move to the left, so she obeyed them. One room seemed to follow into another here—probably an ideal setup for a mother who needed to move quickly from chamber to chamber checking on her children. All were nearly identical, with long-unused fireplaces tucked in corners, small, shelved closets near those fireplaces, and the walls covered in either vertical wood wainscoting or some sort of wallpaper.

The entire floor was just as spotless as the downstairs and shared the same chilly, stale air.

She walked back along the corridor down to the other side right of the staircase. It was nearly a replica of the other side.

Back at the center of the house, the stairs continued up to another floor, but the stairs were not wide and sweeping. Instead, they curved up and back over her head. Raleigh held the banister as she climbed up the next set of stairs.

These steps were even quieter than the main staircase. Across from her was another banister, over which she could gaze down upon the other staircase and the entry hall.

She could almost imagine a candlelit ball being held in the home, the owner's wife or daughter sweeping down in a wide-hooped confection of lace and silk to the applause and gasps of admiration of the onlookers.

Raleigh decided she would investigate this floor by heading to the right, in the other direction from the previous floor. That was essentially to the left again, given that the stairs had ended up on the opposite side of the hallway than they had before.

Once again, she passed through a series of rooms, but this time just three of them, with entry doors to the right, the end, and the left sides of the hallway. It was all very basic. And empty.

It was when she went to the other side of the landing that things became vastly more interesting. Here the corridor was very short, with a door at the end of it. The doorknob wasn't glass here but was instead something from long ago. Raleigh tried depressing the iron latch, but the door didn't budge. She applied some force to the door, thinking it was perhaps stuck, but as she put her strength to it she quickly realized it was actually locked.

Why was this lone door sealed? What lay behind it?

Now she wished she hadn't tossed the key ring to the floor by the door.

She moved to head back downstairs, but Lindbergh was far ahead of her. He began barking hysterically as he scooted past her on the rounded staircase. He was on the ground floor before she could even reach the second-story landing.

"What's the matter, Mutt Boy? What do you hear?" It was hard to know sometimes whether Lindbergh had heard a burglar testing a window or a leaf skittering across the porch.

Raleigh held firm to the banister as she headed to the entry hall, to ensure she didn't lose her footing on the unbalanced stairs. By the time she reached the key ring on the floor next to the entry door, Lindbergh was in a fever pitch of hysteria.

She peered out the nearest window and realized that there was a woman next to her car, walking around it and peering into the windows. At the driver's door, she tried the handle. Raleigh hadn't bothered to lock the door, and the woman swung it open wide, then just stood there with her eyes closed, as if absorbing whatever energy might be inside of it.

CHAPTER 4

RALEIGH POINTED TO her foot. Lindbergh rose and fell quietly into step with her, quiet except for his panting. Both Raleigh and the dog made breath clouds as they moved toward the woman, who still stood motionless next to Raleigh's open car door.

"Excuse me," Raleigh began, breaking the woman out of the reverie caused by whatever was of such great interest inside the vehicle.

Raleigh didn't get any further than that, for the woman looked up with a start and scowled, first at Raleigh, then at Lindbergh. "Who are you?" she demanded.

A fine question coming from the person invading Raleigh's vehicle, she thought. Raleigh estimated the woman to be in her fifties. Short and chunky, she had frizzed gray-streaked white hair that likely hadn't felt a comb's touch in quite some time.

More remarkably, although the woman wore an old puffed ski jacket of baby blue with ski tags still dangling from the zipper, she also wore khaki cargo shorts and brown Birkenstocks.

How was she not freezing to death? And how did she have enough sense to put on a coat, but not long pants?

"I'm Raleigh Bishop. That's my SUV," Raleigh said, drawing closer to examine the invader. The woman wore no makeup of any sort and had unfortunately large pores on her nose. Her cheeks were reddened and chapped. She really would benefit from a little powder. "And you are...?"

"Bishop!" the woman exploded, not answering the question but responding with another one of her own: "You're one of them Second District Bishops?"

Raleigh had no idea what a "Second District" Bishop was. Why was she the one on the defensive anyway? She was the one whose car was being invaded.

As if realizing her rudeness, the woman shut Raleigh's car door. "I guess you're alright to be here then. I'm Magda Raley. A neighbor. My family's been here almost as long as yours. I like to walk through the woods along the bay. Keeps me in fighting form." Magda whistled and a yellow Labrador retriever, who wasn't quite as stocky as Lindbergh, came bounding out of nowhere.

The dog ran right up to Lindbergh, who reacted to the newcomer with great joy, and the two of them chased each other in gleeful circles.

"My dog knows yours," Raleigh observed.

"Yes," she said. "He and Jacky are great friends. But I've never seen you with him. He's usually out by himself."

"Have you met my husband, Grant?" Raleigh asked her, knowing she had phrased it as if he were still alive.

"I've seen a man about your age here, keeps to himself. Very proper, military looking, and not hard on the eyes at all."

That was Grant. Raleigh supposed there was no harm in telling Magda about him.

"Apparently he owned the place," Raleigh began.

"Apparently? You don't know?" Magda asked, crossing her arms as though once more suspicious of Raleigh.

Lindbergh and Jacky had found the scrap of hickory bone again. Each had one end in his mouth as they play-growled and entered an earnest tug-of-war session.

"I—" Why did Raleigh feel embarrassed to explain this? "My husband died awhile back and he—" Her voice cracked on the word "he" and those unwanted hot tears formed in her eyes.

They were uncontrollable, like a breached dam during a relentless summer of rain.

Magda reacted unexpectedly, immediately launching herself onto Raleigh in a bear hug. "There you go, girl," Magda said, pounding on Raleigh's back in what Raleigh supposed was meant to be comfort. Raleigh had to refrain from coughing from the beating she was taking.

Magda smelled of stale frying oil and wood smoke. And sweat. It wasn't entirely unpleasant—it was the odor of a woman who labored hard. Raleigh wondered who Magda was other than a neighbor.

She managed to extricate herself from Magda's clutches and stepped back. "Thank you," she said, imagining she would be putting the heating pad beneath the covers tonight when she slipped in next to Grant's fading essence.

"My husband's—" Her voice cracked again but she quickly recovered, unwilling to be enveloped in Magda's overwhelming embrace again. "My husband's will contained this house, which he left to me."

As if seeing Raleigh's distress, Lindbergh left Jacky to sit next to her, leaning against her leg. He never understood how powerful he was and that his mere weight could topple a small tree. She leaned down to scratch behind his ears, missing the warm contact that wasn't possible through her gloves.

"And he had bought the house without your knowledge?" Magda guessed, nodding sagely. "Worried that he was hiding a cheap little something here?"

Raleigh started in shock. Everything was all so new that such a thought had not even remotely occurred to her. "No! Grant would have never done that!"

But a week ago she would have never dreamed that

he would have bought a home without her knowledge. Had she not ever known her husband at all?

Raleigh felt as if the ground were shaking beneath her and she was an ice sculpture out in this frigid air, delicate and ready to crack and crumble if she couldn't get some stability beneath her sneakers.

Magda was gazing at her sadly. "Of course, I'm sure you're right, my girl. So, now you have a house. Will you be moving in, then?"

So many questions Raleigh hadn't considered. Her brain was still foggy even after all this time, and she was unable to consider much more than whether to crawl out of bed in the morning to ensure Lindbergh didn't starve to death.

"I don't know. It's empty. And the kitchen is very dated." *Grant asked you to caretake it for the rest of your life.*

"Shouldn't be afraid of a little work," Magda replied. "It's good for the soul."

"Are you a widow as well?" Raleigh asked, not even sure why that question had popped into her head.

"Me? No. Never been married. Most men are afraid of an independent woman like me. Well, that and afraid of old Jacky here. Right, boy?"

The dog wagged his tail. Raleigh doubted he could frighten a cat, much less a grown man intent upon pursuing a woman.

Magda herself was a little intimidating, though.

"We already have a house," Raleigh told her, thinking of the familiarity of the bed, of the location of the coffeepot on the granite countertop, and even of the hooks near the front door where Lindbergh's array of leashes hung. How could she uproot herself from all of that intimacy with Grant in order to live in this cavernous old home that probably leaked, creaked, and wasn't up to any sort of modern wiring and plumbing codes?

"Lots of people already have houses and move into other houses," Magda argued. "Be nice to have someone next door. Well, a coupla acres over. Of course, this place has always been—" Magda stopped, considering. "Has always held secrets, I suppose."

"What do you mean?" Raleigh asked, becoming convinced that she absolutely did not want to live here, despite Lindbergh's happy canine frolic with Jacky.

"Maybe I shoulda said that the *family* has always had secrets. Some peculiar blood runs through their veins. No disrespect intended."

Magda glanced to either side of her. "Freezing out here," she observed, clapping her bare hands together. "D'ya think we could talk inside?" She nodded her head toward the house.

"It's not much warmer in there than it is out here," Raleigh said, unsure if she wanted to let this stranger in. It felt as though she would be permitting a trespasser to violate Grant's secrets.

But Magda was looking at her expectantly, and it seemed rude to not invite her in. So, the two women and their dogs made their way up to the house.

"Nothing here!" Magda pronounced in wonder, her voice like a barking echo in the empty space.

"Have you been inside before?" Raleigh asked.

Lindbergh and Jacky traipsed toward the kitchen as if it were familiar territory. Had Grant called them in there for treats? Would Raleigh find a bag of Carnivore Crunchies in a drawer?

"Been a long time," Magda said, following Raleigh toward the kitchen. "Back when Old Man Billy Bishop was still alive. Guess he's been gone, oh, about twenty years."

Raleigh realized that even though she had been married to Grant for almost seven years, she knew little about his extended family or ancestors. She'd only ever met his parents and his brother, Trey.

She'd even asked him once about other family members. Grant had shrugged and said, "We Bishops have been here since the Dove sailed over with colonists. I'm related to half the people in the county."

That may have been true, but Old Man Billy Bishop appeared to be a tangible member of Grant's family. Why had Grant not mentioned him? And if Billy Bishop had died twenty years ago, who had lived here since then?

One question that seemed to be answered was whether Grant had purchased the property. It seemed much more likely that he had inherited it. From someone.

Her in-laws might know more, of course. She'd need to seriously think about dropping by their place to ask them.

"Who lived here after Old Man Billy?" Raleigh asked as she began opening cabinets and drawers, searching for dog treats. She'd already seen the hickory bone, and Grant wasn't one to let Lindbergh go too long without a treat. If they had spent time here together, there must be a stash somewhere.

Raleigh realized that the cabinets were made of old metal. Drawers and shelves alike were lined in old contact paper in a yellow, orange, and white daisy pattern. It was peeling, cracked, and rubbed away in most places, revealing rusty metal beneath.

Magda leaned an elbow on top of a counter, crossing her thick legs as she watched Raleigh.

"It was Old Man Billy's boy, William. Everyone called him Junior. Nothing like his father, who was a mean old cuss and always fighting with everyone. Postal lady even stopped delivering to him when he threw a bottle of beer at the mail truck because he'd received a property tax notice he didn't like. Junior kept to himself but was pleasant enough if you kept a proper distance. Had a big collection of lawn jockeys in the yard, but it didn't hurt anyone, did it? Like I said though, the family's always been peculiar. Junior's been gone a few years now."

Raleigh realized that Lindbergh and Jacky were sitting near the old brown icebox, which was at least a foot shorter than she was. She found success when she pulled open a drawer next to the icebox. Inside were several packages of Carnivore Crunchies.

She should have known that the dogs would guide her.

Lindbergh was practically quivering at the sight of one of the bags in her hands. She opened it, then tossed a treat to Lindbergh, who caught it expertly with a single snap of his teeth.

Raleigh held up the package to Magda, who nodded. Raleigh threw another Crunchie toward Jacky. Lindbergh intercepted it for himself.

"Hey, no fair," Raleigh admonished him, this time holding a treat out directly for Jacky to slobber out of her hand.

"Good boy, Jacky-Jack," Magda said to her dog.

Raleigh focused her attention on this new neighbor once again. "When did you first meet my husband?" she asked.

Magda shrugged. "Probably two, three years ago? Not long before Junior died, actually. I noticed your husband much more frequently after Junior was gone."

Raleigh had no recollection of the death of Grant's relative. He'd said nothing about it. "Was my husband at the funeral?"

Magda lifted her shoulders again. "Musta been a private affair. Didn't know about it until I saw the obituary in the *Enterprise* newspaper."

Raleigh's mind was awhirl with questions that perhaps Grant's parents could answer.

CHAPTER 5

DAVID AND MARGARET Bishop expressed pleasant surprise at finding Raleigh on their doorstep, minus Lindbergh whom she dropped off at her house, and warmly ushered her inside. They lived in an old rambling one-story near Leonardtown on Breton Bay. Raleigh wasn't particularly good at geography, and she wondered now how far from St. Clements Bluff the Bishops' home was and if the two properties were easily accessible to one another by boat.

She would have termed this home a cottage if it weren't so sprawling, having been built in stages over the past seventy-five years. Every bedroom had its own en-suite bathroom and morning kitchen, and they were connected by a series of sitting rooms full of overstuffed chairs and lap blankets, paneled studies lined with bookshelves, and cozy dens with roaring fires topped by mantles crammed with family photos. Going through the house was like wandering through a long, comforting maze, except that to one side were always windows overlooking the bay.

It was a maze that always smelled like a bakery. Grant's mother was famous for her donuts, which were wonderfully crispy on the outside and consisted of moist tender yellow cake on the inside. Raleigh's mother-in-law perpetually experimented with unusual toppings, too, and the results were artfully displayed under dome-topped pedestal cases in her kitchen.

Today the house also had the lingering scents of

cinnamon and peppermint, likely the aftermath of Grant's mother attempting some normalcy during the Christmas season. A Christmas enthusiast, she usually continued baking until well into January and left decorations up until early February. But, just like last year in the aftermath of Grant's death, there was no evidence of holiday decorating having occurred here. Only the fragrance of holiday baking hanging in the air offered any proof that Christmas had made a brief appearance.

And Raleigh hadn't even returned her in-laws' call on Christmas Day. In fact, she hadn't even risen from bed that day to do more than go to the bathroom and brew the next pot of coffee.

"Pop," Raleigh said to her father-in-law, accepting his loud smack to the cheek before shrugging out of her coat and hanging it on their coat rack. "Hi Mutzi," she said as she hugged Grant's mother. Although David Bishop, Jr., was called "Pop," as he had called his own father, Margaret Bishop had always been known as "Mutzi" for reasons that no one completely understood, something about a pony she'd once had as a childhood pet. She even insisted Grant and his brother call her that when they each turned twelve years old.

"It's good to see you out and about," Mutzi said carefully. Raleigh felt an instant pang of guilt. She had not been particularly kind to her in-laws over the past year, and now she was here to essentially interrogate them about their dead son.

"To what do we owe this visit?" Mr. Bishop said.

"Davey!" Mutzi exclaimed. "Let the poor girl breathe. How about a little treat, dear? I've just made a batch of Nutella doughnuts."

Raleigh's favorite, followed closely by Mutzi's pumpkin cheesecake doughnuts, which Mutzi typically reserved only for her fall baking extravaganzas. She actually felt her stomach growl at the thought of one of Mutzi's confections. She couldn't remember the last time she'd felt anything remotely akin to hunger.

"You know I can't say no to a Nutella," Raleigh said, offering her mother-in-law a wan smile. In moments she was sitting on a Windsor-style counter stool in their expansive kitchen.

Grant had preferred his mother's Boston crème doughnuts, which would always become an unholy mess of custard and chocolate in his hands. He would unabashedly lick his fingers of the sweet stickiness and down it all with gulps of chocolate milk.

Raleigh's smile widened briefly at the sweet memory. A red dessert plate with two doughnuts topped with chocolate glaze and chopped hazelnuts on it was pushed across the granite countertop and now rested in front of her.

"Cider? Regular milk? Chocolate milk?" Mutzi asked, opening one side of her stainless-steel refrigerator and pausing to look back at Raleigh.

"Regular milk, please," Raleigh said. The doughnuts smelled heavenly, but she doubted her ability to finish one of them, much less two. Surely her stomach had shrunk to the size of a peanut.

David and Mutzi sat on the remaining stools at the kitchen counter and waited politely for Raleigh to sample the doughnut. It was, as expected, marvelous, but she was filled after just one bite so she put the remainder back down. She washed the mouthful down with a gulp of milk and opened the conversation as delicately as she could think to do.

"Pop, Mutzi, I want to apologize for my—for not being more communicative since—since—" Why couldn't Raleigh ever finish a simple sentence containing Grant's name?

Mutzi saved her by clasping both of Raleigh's hands

in her own. When had Mutzi's hands developed liver spots and bulging veins? Her mother-in-law's diamond wedding ring had twirled around to the bottom of her finger and dug into the palm of Raleigh's hand. Mutzi used to joke that her ring fit like a soaked wet suit and was as much a part of her as the skin to which it had melded. Raleigh was reminded that she was not the only one who had suffered from Grant's death.

"It's fine, dear. Think nothing of it. We're just happy to see you again. Why don't you stay for supper, and we can have a long visit? We could even invite Trey and his new girlfriend, Barbara. She's a cancer nurse at the hospital. Isn't that interesting?"

"I don't know. Lindbergh still gets anxious if I'm away from home for too long," Raleigh said, fibbing a tad. This visit was hard enough. She wasn't sure she could drag it into dinner, which would be accompanied by wine, which would likely be followed by a long, maudlin session of reminiscences about Grant. She wasn't ready for it.

"Of course," Mutzi said. Her tone was gracious, but she pulled her hands away from Raleigh's. As for David Bishop, he had lifted what looked like a lemon-glazed doughnut from under the dome and was gobbling it without a plate, the crumbs spilling onto the counter. If he were eating anything other than one of Mutzi's creations, Raleigh might have thought lowly about his manners.

Raleigh started again.

"I opened Grant's will," she said, picking at some of the chopped hazelnuts on one of her doughnuts, a way to occupy her hands now that they were free. "I was... surprised by it."

The Bishops said nothing at first, merely waiting for Raleigh to continue. As she struggled to do so and the yawning silence became uncomfortable, Pop finally said, "Were you pleasantly surprised or surprised in a bad way?"

Raleigh considered the question. "I suppose it's both. You see, Grant left me something in his will that I had no idea he even owned."

Raleigh's father-in-law rose from his stool. Doughnut crumbs trickled down the front of his red and black flannel shirt like a landslide of buttery yellow nuggets. He stood behind his wife, whose chair faced Raleigh, and put a protective hand on her shoulder.

They both gazed at Raleigh not only expectantly but as if bracing themselves for bad news.

"He left me a house," she said simply.

The expression of relief on both of their faces was tangible. "Well, of course, he wanted you to have the house you shared," Mutzi said, reaching a hand up to pat that of her husband's, which still rested on her shoulder.

Raleigh had the sense that it was a motion of reassurance.

"No," she replied. "Grant and I own—owned—our house jointly. I mean that he left me a house I knew nothing about. One that is apparently a Bishop homestead. Do the names Old Man Billy and Junior Bishop mean anything to you?"

Mutzi shook her head in puzzlement, but the color drained from Pop's face like it had when Raleigh had relayed Grant's death to her in-laws.

"Pop, did you know them?" Raleigh probed.

David Bishop cleared his throat. "I know the names. Indeed, I do. They were from the Second District side of my family. We haven't communicated with them in years. Old Man Billy died a long time ago, I believe. Are you saying this house belonged to one of them?"

"Yes, first to Old Man Billy and then to Junior, who died a couple of years ago. It would seem that Junior left the house to Grant," Raleigh said, faintly suspicious that she had to explain Bishop history to Grant's parents, particularly to Mutzi. Or was this just her grief expressing itself in a different way?

Grant, if only you were here to tell me the whole story.

"Mutzi," she said patiently. "Do you still have those old scrapbooks? The ones you showed me during Grandpop's eightieth birthday party?"

Raleigh remembered Mutzi dragging out a series of old black leather scrapbooks, stuffed with old sepia photographs, newspaper clippings, letters, and postcards, and having everyone in attendance go through them. For many decades, members of the Bishop family had documented the family history—births, deaths, weddings, and other events of interest—although in recent years there was no one particularly leading the charge and so they were simply stored here. Raleigh remembered being politely interested at the time—after all, these were Grant's long-dead ancestors and there were dozens and dozens of them. Only a dedicated genealogist could have kept them all straight. Although Raleigh's career had kept her deeply involved in—and fascinated with—Maryland's history, she found the examination of twisting, intertwining family trees an exhausting exercise.

"Well, of course, I do," Mutzi said. "Do you want to see them?"

Raleigh nodded and slid out of her chair. "Lead the way."

She followed Mutzi and Pop through the maze of rooms until they ended up in a room near the rear of the Bishop home. As with most of the rooms, one wall consisted of windows. The long wall opposite was full of white built-in bookcases, and in front of it was a long sofa and coffee table.

"Davey, how about a fire if we're going to spend time in here? It always gets so cold this far back in the house," Mutzi said, shivering for emphasis. A small brick fireplace sat empty on one of the short walls next to one of the room's two doorways. The iron log holder sitting on the floor between the fireplace and one end of the bookcases was empty.

Pop nodded and left the room.

"I don't remember which of them might have anything about this house you're talking about," Mutzi said, bending down to a lower shelf and removing the familiar old volumes. She stacked them up on the coffee table, then sat companionably next to Raleigh to go through them.

"Oh, this is Teeny Bishop. He was married to Pop's great aunt. Or was it his great-great aunt?" Mutzi said, pointing to a bear of a man in an old photograph. He stood in knee deep water wearing waders and was holding up an old square crab trap while grinning wolfishly at the camera. Inside the trap was a gargantuan blue crab. Even if the photo didn't date itself by its spotty edges, Raleigh would have known it was old because crabs just didn't get that big in Maryland waters anymore. Highly prized for their sweet, succulent meat that required no seasoning but upon which locals applied Old Bay spice, butter, and vinegar in liberal doses, they were now heavily trawled. They were still plentiful but didn't have a chance to become as old as the captured crab in the picture.

Raleigh made an appreciative noise and began examining the scrapbook she had placed in her own lap. She quickly flipped past numerous stiffly posed family photographs, glancing at them only long enough to see if the words "Billy" or "Junior" popped out. Or perhaps by some miracle there was a photo of the house itself in one of the books, with some sort of inscription that might give Raleigh a clue as to why Grant had had possession of it.

Raleigh ignored her mother-in-law's exclamations and sighs as Mutzi went through the Bishop scrapbooks and perpetually made comments about this cousin or that. There were at least a dozen scrapbooks to potentially go through and it might take all night if Mutzi were not faster about it.

But soon Raleigh was pausing and sighing to herself as she saw Grant's features reveal themselves on his ancestors who had worked, loved, and fought through the centuries. It was as if he had suddenly appeared in the room with her to offer a bit of comfort that there were—and would be—many Bishops to echo his life into the future. Raleigh felt a flicker of hope in that.

Pop returned with an armful of seasoned split wood and some kindling, paying the women no attention as he worked expertly to get a fire going in the brick firebox. Soon it was burning and crackling merrily.

"So where is this house that Grant left you?" Pop asked her, the crackling sound of his poking about aimlessly in the fire filling the air of the cozy room.

"It's in Compton," Raleigh replied without looking up. "I'd be happy to show it to you." She didn't offer to do so right away, though, as she felt a need to understand it herself first. If David and Mutzi Bishop didn't already know about the house, then perhaps Grant hadn't wanted them to know about it. Raleigh wanted to be very selective about whom she let into the house—Magda Raley notwithstanding—until she felt more comfortable with its very existence.

"Oh, here we go, dear," Mutzi said, handing over the volume she was going through and pointing to the right-hand page. "Is that the house?"

Raleigh eagerly took the scrapbook and peered down at the fragile old newspaper clipping. It was from the *Saint Mary's Beacon* newspaper. The article was dated Saturday, March 15, 1913, and the headline beneath the old photo of the house read, *St. Clements Bluff Celebrated as Stop on Underground Railroad.*

Pop stopped playing with the fire as Raleigh read the article aloud.

On the sad occasion of Mrs. Harriet Tubman's death on Monday, the Beacon's community reporter decided to commemorate her life with a visit to St. Clements Bluff, one of many properties—or stops—on Tubman's so-called "Underground Railroad." This network of homes in states as far flung as West Virginia, Ohio, Indiana, Illinois, Michigan, and Missouri, were secret stopovers for slaves escaping to the North prior to the late War of Northern Aggression.

Tobacco plantations were plentiful in St. Mary's County then as they are now, but powered by involuntary labor rather than the farming families of today. The children and grandchildren of many boys lost during the war continue the proud tradition of tobacco production today.

Mrs. Tubman was born into slavery as Araminta Ross on the Eastern Shore in 1822. She married a freedman, John Tubman, in 1844, and changed her name to Harriet. When her enslaver died five years later and she was set to be sold, she escaped. One hundred dollars was offered for her capture, but instead of remaining in hiding, she spent the next ten years making trips back into Maryland to rescue friends and family and deliver them to freedom via her secret Underground Railroad.

The prominent journalist and abolitionist William Lloyd Garrison, gone now these past 36 years, called Tubman "Moses," and the name stuck.

Mrs. Tubman's exploits as a wartime spy, nurse, scout, and cook, as well as her friendships with Frederick Douglass, John Brown, and Harriet Beecher Stowe, are well known to citizens everywhere. Less well known is the role that St. Clements Bluff played in her efforts to spirit escaping slaves out of the South.

Although only thirty-four men, women, and children have been officially documented as having stayed at St. Clements Bluff, it is estimated that at least three times that many may have done so. Records are naturally scarce.

The home has never passed out of family hands and the current owner, Walter Bishop, showed this reporter a ledger listing a series of several slaves' names, the state where they had started from, the state where they were headed, and the slaves' signatures, most of which were denoted as an "X."

As Raleigh read this paragraph, Pop drew in a sharp breath.

"Is something wrong?" Raleigh asked, looking up at him.

"No, no, just a little twinge in the knee is all. Bent down funny-like picking up firewood." Pop reached down and squeezed his right knee for emphasis. Raleigh concluded the article.

Mr. Bishop also provided a look at some of the secret hiding places on the estate, including an old abandoned shallow well, a storage shed with a false wall, and an underground icehouse.

This reporter was impressed by the stark evidence of what a determined individual is willing to endure in the name of freedom.

St. Clements Bluff is certainly a fascinating landmark in Maryland's history and a worthy stop for all St. Mary's County residents. Mr. Bishop accepts visitors on Wednesdays, Fridays, and Saturdays, provided he is not out oystering or crabbing.

Raleigh closed the scrapbook, impressed by the significance of the property. She wondered about the outdoor cellar entrance. And all of the outbuildings. Were some—or all—of them part of the property's involvement in the Underground Railroad? The article wasn't specific.

"Well that explains it all now, doesn't it?" Mutzi said, rising from the sofa and beginning to gather up the stacked scrapbooks.

"What do you mean?" Raleigh asked, holding her volume tightly in her lap. She wasn't ready to give it up yet. Pop had returned to jabbing at the flames, his back to both of them.

"It explains why Grant left you the house. Who could appreciate its history more than a museum exhibit expert?"

That was true, but hardly an explanation. "It still doesn't tell me why Grant hid the ownership of the property from me," Raleigh insisted.

Pop had finally finished playing around in the fire. He put the poker in its stand and turned back to Raleigh. "Perhaps he was making repairs and fixing it up, and intended to surprise you with it, not knowing he would soon be—" Pop paused and cleared his throat. "Not knowing he wouldn't be able to finish the work."

Was the answer really that simple? "But he didn't tell you about either?" she said.

They both shook their heads no.

"Do you think he may have told Trey?"

The Bishops glanced at each other. "Maybe," Pop said with doubt in his voice. "The boys were close unless there was something competitive involved. Would have depended on whether Grant viewed the property as something Trey would want for himself. So where is this house that Grant left you? Wouldn't mind seeing it."

Raleigh looked at her father quizzically. "In Compton, remember?"

"Oh, right, right." Pop frowned as Mutzi's cheeks flamed.

"Davey, don't tease the girl like that," Mutzi admonished. "She isn't ready for it."

Raleigh's father-in-law still looked puzzled but responded obediently. "Of course. Sorry about that, m'dear."

After a few moments of uncomfortable silence, Mutzi attempted to take the scrapbook from Raleigh but Raleigh resisted. "Please, may I keep this awhile longer?" she asked, not sure what other information she thought it might offer but wanting to take it home and go through it again.

"Of course," Mutzi said. "Keep it as long as you like. I'll also give you a few Nutella doughnuts to take home."

Raleigh nodded her thanks and yawned. She realized that today had represented the most activity she'd undergone since Grant's death, and she was thoroughly exhausted. Perhaps Pop was as tired as she was, hence his forgetfulness.

Maybe she wouldn't be so exhausted if she returned to the normalcy of her job.

Raleigh left her in-laws, the old scrapbook, and a plastic box full of bakery treats clutched to her chest. She intended to take it to the St. Mary's County Historical Society to see if someone could help her find other records or newspaper clippings concerning the St. Clements Bluff's role in the Underground Railroad. She also planned to show it to Bert. Maybe he could guide her in seeking out more information about the estate as well as wartime. Mary's County in general.

Raleigh would get resolution on how the house had come into Grant's hands, then she could decide what to do about it.

CHAPTER 6

THE NEXT MORNING, Raleigh woke early, walked Lindbergh, and fed him. He wolfed down the bowl of kibble before she had even clipped the bag closed and put it away. "Okay, just a little bit more," she told him, pouring a handful into the stainless-steel bowl. He chomped the nuggets only marginally more slowly this time.

She left him licking at the empty bowl, his efforts resulting in the bowl being pushed around the kitchen.

With Lindbergh thus occupied, Raleigh decided to spend some time going through Grant's desk to see if there was anything among his papers that would shed light on how he had come into Junior Bishop's property.

Raleigh and Grant had turned one of their three bedrooms into a shared office. Ironically, it was Raleigh who appreciated the streamlined look of a glass and black metal desk, whereas flyboy Grant had loved the warm feel of an antique oak roll-top desk. Paired with an old rolling banker's chair, it had made Grant look like a country lawyer—or maybe an innkeeper—when he sat there tapping away at his laptop.

A glance at the black leather chair behind her own desk was a reminder that she really would have to put attention to more than just paying bills at some point. Envelopes, catalogs, magazines, and unopened sympathy cards were stacked up in a tottering pile on the seat. Raleigh turned away from them.

She eased her way into Grant's chair and momentarily

just sat there, conjuring him in her mind behind closed eyes. The chair didn't have his smell imbued in it the way the sheets did, but the smooth feel of the leather reminded her of Grant sitting here, excitedly tapping the arms as he described the results of a big flight test day at work. She opened her eyes and found herself smiling as she wheeled her way closer to the desk, pushing up the tambour roll top.

Grant's desk was much neater than hers, but in her defense, her desk was a sheet of glass whereas his was full of drawers and cubbyholes, making it much easier to organize. Raleigh opened all of the drawers, which were filled with the usual supplies of any desk, then poked and prodded in an attempt to find any of those secret drawers that were frequently hidden in old desks.

She was pleased when her fingers found two such secret compartments, but there was nothing in either of them, other than an old fragment of a yellowed newspaper dating from the 1950s advertising a Buick Roadmaster wagon. The car appeared to be larger than Raleigh's first apartment.

Her search led her to a bottom drawer down the right side of the desk. Inside, she found a boot box. Raleigh remembered this pair of black leather boots from the sketched picture on the side of the box. They had been his first pair in test pilot school. She pulled the box out and set it in her lap, lifting the lid. She sighed at what she saw there.

The box was filled with photographs of her, her and Grant together, and a myriad of cards and letters she had written for him over the years. Grant had never struck her as being this foolishly romantic, and it nearly made her heart burst in a combination of pride in him and overwhelming wistfulness.

How did the old saying go? *Better to have loved and lost than never to have loved at all?* She supposed she should be glad that she had been so well-loved once in her life.

With the box in her lap, Raleigh went through every scrap of paper. It represented the most important years of his life—their lives—including photos of them together during their dating days—cuddled up in front of a Pennsylvania ski lodge fire, on a friend's boat on St. Mary's River with their Rockfish catches dangling from lines, and standing in front of the Bishop family Christmas tree in matching sweaters with Raleigh holding up her hand to show off the diamond that had just been placed on it minutes before. The memories were cathartic in an odd way.

She remembered that day as the one she had goofily practiced writing down what her new name would be, since, at the time, she had the then-monumental decision of whether to use her maiden name as her new middle name.

Raleigh Susan Moore's mother had been a big fan of the 19th century reforming nurse, Florence Nightingale. Florence and her sister, Parthenope, had been named after the cities in which they were born while their wealthy parents were on a two-year tour of Europe. Thus, Raleigh's mother decided to name her own two daughters the same way, over the objection of Raleigh's father.

Raleigh's older sister, Salem, had been born in Oregon thirty-three years ago, with Raleigh following in North Carolina three years later. Raleigh figured she had had the better end of the naming deal because children on the playground always asked Salem if she were a witch. Salem still lived in North Carolina but had threatened to move to Maryland to stay with Raleigh and bring her "back to life."

Raleigh glanced down at her left hand. Her hand hadn't aged, but her engagement ring was starting to roll around on her finger, wasn't it? Heaven help her if

Salem found out she had lost so much weight. Worse, it was to the point it could fall off and be lost. She couldn't stand to lose another piece of her life with Grant...

She placed the Christmas tree photo back in the box and replaced the lid, but remained there with the closed box in her lap for several minutes, thinking. Then, with tremulous resolve, she slowly pulled the loose ring from her left hand, opened the box lid, and placed the ring gently on top of the memorabilia in the box. Safe, now.

Putting the lid back down over her memories, she put the box back in its resting place and firmly shut the drawer.

Although there were no clues in the desk as to why Grant had possession of St. Clements Bluff, Raleigh felt as though she had accomplished something important, and that put her spirits in another place. A place they'd not ventured to for a long time.

CHAPTER 7

THE SINGING PERSISTED relentlessly as Raleigh emerged slowly from sleep. She had been dreaming that she was a member of the Yaocomico tribe and was harvesting vegetables to be laid up for the winter. The dream was vivid and had imbued her subconscious mind with ideas for the new museum exhibit. Except now there was singing interrupting those sleep-induced plans.

She couldn't figure out where it was coming from. She reluctantly pushed Grant's pillow away and looked around. Lindbergh was no longer on the bed.

The singing was now somehow familiar. Raleigh sat up and rubbed her eyes, hoping it would serve to rub away the musical earworm. It only served to make her realize the sun had already risen pretty far.

She realized it wasn't singing she was hearing, it was the stupid doorbell and the bonging of Westminster Chimes that was about to drive her insane. Whoever was at the door was insistent about getting in.

She slid out of bed, straightened the t-shirt down over the boxer shorts, and went to the window, peering out between the blinds at whoever was below.

It was her brother-in-law, David Bishop III, known in the family as Trey. He was with an auburn-haired woman wearing her hair in a ponytail and a knitted ear warmer-headband accenting her casual look. That must be Barb, the nurse.

"Raleigh Bishop!" Trey shouted, now banging on the door in addition to pressing the doorbell repeatedly. "I know you're home because you never leave. Open the damned door. It's past noon, woman."

Noon! Was it really that late? Poor Lindbergh, he hadn't been walked in more than twelve hours.

She unlatched the window but left the blind down so that she couldn't be seen. The frigid air that blew into the room nearly knocked her backward. "I'm here. I'll be down in a minute," she called out to her brother-in-law.

She shut the window and latched it again, then retrieved a coral-colored terry cloth robe from the closet. It was bleach-stained and threadbare, but it was her largest one, so it covered her completely.

She made her way to the door, where Lindbergh sat just inside, thumping his tail against the ground. "Really?" she said to him. "Not even the slightest bark to protect me from all of that racket? What if had been a serial killer standing out there?"

Lindbergh merely whined. Poor boy had to go. Raleigh had an inspiration. Grabbing his collar and leash from the hook, she stood behind the door, opened it wide enough to let Lindbergh out, and handed Trey his leash. "Walk him, will you, while I get ready?" she said, not inviting her visitors in. "I need about twenty minutes."

"Honestly, woman," Trey said, his trademark statement for any female who defeated him in conversation. "C'mon, boy, Uncle Trey and Miss Barb will take care of you."

Raleigh waited until she heard them move off the porch before shutting the door and retreating back upstairs to take a quick shower, tie her hair up, and dress in serviceable jeans, a cobalt blue tunic sweater, and tennis shoes. She did a critical examination in the mirror. The tiny flat mole along her jawline probably needed makeup, and the bags under her eyes weren't going away any time soon, but she was passable enough for a living human being to keep Trey from asking too many penetrating questions.

She was downstairs starting a pot of coffee when she heard the front door open and Lindbergh's nails clicking in the foyer. "Rals?" Trey called out, using his nickname for her.

"In the kitchen," she replied. She could hear Trey helping his girlfriend hang their coats. Trey had spent considerable time at their house and was perfectly comfortable with making himself at home here.

They entered the kitchen as Raleigh was pulling out cups and spoons. She left what she was doing for introductions.

"Raleigh, may I present Barbara Costello to you? Barb, this is my sister-in-law, Raleigh." This was as formal as Raleigh had ever seen Trey behave. This woman must be a serious contender for his heart.

"Pleased to meet you," she said, shaking the other woman's hand. It was rough and chapped with short, clipped fingernails. "I understand you are a nurse," Raleigh said, returning to coffee preparation and covertly appraising Trey's new girlfriend.

Lindbergh's nails clicked on the ceramic tiles as he also entered the kitchen and then curled up on top of a floor vent next to the rear French door. The dog had learned as a pup how to take full advantage of heat sources.

"Yes," Barb said. "I work with cancer patients at the infusion center." She was quite a beautiful girl, with intelligent blue eyes and a wide smile. Strands of hair had already fallen out of her ponytail, no doubt partly because removal of her headband had caused their disarray. The effect was quite charming. Raleigh knew she looked like she'd been run over by a speedboat by comparison.

Raleigh asked a couple of polite questions about Barb's

work as she served them coffee at the kitchen table. Barb chatted pleasantly about her work at the hospital and how much she enjoyed helping people who were suffering and needed comfort. Trey soaked up every word she uttered with a goofy, besotted grin.

Raleigh's gaze drifted off through the window as she cradled her warm cup in both hands. She appreciated that Trey still thought enough of her to bring over his new girlfriend for inspection, but Raleigh wondered why Trey seemed to need her approval. As a substitute for Grant's thumbs-up, she supposed.

"What is in this, Rals?" Trey asked, making a face. "I mean, I like it as strong as the next person, but this stuff could start a jet engine."

Raleigh blinked and turned her attention back to her brother-in-law. Really? This was his metaphor? "Oh, I guess I've been grinding a stronger bean lately. And using more in the filter." She took another sip from her cup. Perhaps it *was* a little too strong.

Barb, meanwhile, surreptitiously reached for the sugar container and poured liberally from it.

"So." Trey shifted in his seat, signaling a change in subject. "Mutzi and Pop said you came by the house. Something about a house Grant left you."

So that was it. He's the eldest wondering why the house had gone to his younger brother.

Raleigh wasn't sure she wanted to discuss the house yet, but it made no sense to keep it from Grant's brother. "It's in Compton. It's an old Bishop estate from the 'Second District' side of the family." She used air quotes. "There isn't a stick of furniture in it but a sign on the property suggests it was built in 1823. It has obviously been updated, but not recently. It's large and on beautiful waterfront acreage."

Trey nodded. "And it has a history?" he prompted.

"Yes. We found an old newspaper article that showed

the house was a stop on the Underground Railroad. Maybe it belongs on the National Register." That thought occurred to Raleigh for the first time. Maybe there was a way to divest herself from it in a beneficial way that would have made Grant proud. It could be a beautiful house museum. She imagined docents in period attire escorting people up the staircase. Of course, there would need to be provable hiding locations in the house. Were the places mentioned in the old newspaper article still in existence? She needed to look more closely at the scrapbook she had brought home.

"Maybe," Trey said. "Or maybe it belongs to future generations of Bishops."

Raleigh shrugged. "Perhaps Mutzi can dig through the scrapbooks and figure out who the nearest living relatives to Junior Bishop are. He was the last one to live there."

Trey drained his cup and returned to the coffee maker himself for more. "What do you imagine the place is worth?" he asked as he sat back down, picking up the sugar container.

Raleigh had not yet considered this. "It's waterfront property, so quite a bit, I would imagine. And the house isn't the typical old clapboard cottage that would be burned down to make way for new construction. It's very habitable, although the kitchen needs a serious makeover."

"It sounds dreamy and romantic," Barb murmured, pulling on her ponytail.

Raleigh mentally rolled her eyes. It was historic. It was a significant property. But "romantic"?

"I suppose," she replied, wondering if Barb would one day be part of the Bishop family.

One family member goes, another arrives to fill the void.

Silence ensued for a few moments, and Raleigh found

her attention wandering to the outdoors where a dry leafless branch dropped from one of the oak trees in the backyard. So much wet weather was bound to make that happen.

"Rals," Trey said. "Don't make me beg. Aren't you going to invite me to see it? After all, it's part of the Bishop heritage—even if it's the family on the other side of the tracks."

Raleigh frowned. "Yes, I can show it to you. Sometime," she added vaguely.

Trey held up a palm, a sign of withdrawal from the discussion. "Well, at least I know you've got your head above water and are doggy paddling along—with Lindbergh's help, right boy?" Trey held out a hand to the retriever, who thumped his tail but was too warm and comfortable to even consider lumbering up and padding over for some attention.

Raleigh rose from her seat and went to the treat drawer located in the kitchen island, pulling out a bag of Carnivore Crunchies and tossing it silently to Trey. Lindbergh was sitting in front of Trey in mere seconds.

Grant had taught the dog a series of ridiculous tricks, none of which Raleigh had kept up on. However, Trey was familiar with them all and began putting Lindbergh through his paces. "Gimme five," Trey said, and the dog responded with a paw against his open palm. "On the back side," he added, flipping over his hand. The dog tapped his paw again and was rewarded with a treat.

"Bang!" Trey said, pointing a finger gun at Lindbergh. The dog scooted back several times, then fell over, even going so far as to loll his tongue out to the floor.

"Oh, how adorable!" Barb exclaimed, clapping her hands together. "He's so smart."

"Watch this," Trey said, standing up as Raleigh continued to watch from behind the island. "Back from the dead," he commanded Lindbergh, raising an arm straight up in the air. The dog, following Trey's leading, rose up in the air until he was balanced on his two back paws. Trey laid a Crunchie on his snout, and it was promptly gobbled up as Lindbergh descended back on all fours.

Raleigh was both impressed that Lindbergh remembered his repertoire of tricks, as well as struck with guilt that she hadn't bothered to interact with him enough to run through them with him. He deserved better than Raleigh.

He deserved Grant.

She inhaled sharply as Grant's face rose in her mind's eye, laughing as he threw a tennis ball for Lindbergh to run barreling after. Man and dog were completely devoted to one another. Actually, Grant was completely devoted to everyone he loved. He was like a human blanket, warm and protective.

Trey misinterpreted her reaction. "He's still got it, doesn't he?"

Barb was busy leaning over, nuzzling Lindbergh's neck and rubbing his back. He happily accepted her adoration.

"Yes, he does," Raleigh said, clearing her throat as she shuttered the sweet memory. "I think if you don't mind now, I have some work to do around the house. Barb, it was a pleasure to meet you." Raleigh came out from around the island.

Trey nodded and soon they were all at the front door. He put a hand on her shoulder. "Rals, if there's anything I've learned in life, it's that cobwebs need to be swept out on occasion. I know how hard this is. We're all suffering, Mutzi especially. But we can't lose you to a broken heart. Think about what needs a broom handle taken to it in order for you to at least return to work." He kissed her cheek. Trey always wore a musky cologne and it enveloped Raleigh now.

Raleigh smiled as she broke out of his embrace, then she quickly hugged Barb. "Look forward to seeing you again," she told the other woman, who seemed pleased by Raleigh's implication that there would be a next time.

After more pleasantries, Raleigh was finally able to shut the door behind them. But Trey's words clanged in her head, and she again thought about returning to her job and spending time with her co-workers again.

But as the day went on, it occurred to Raleigh that maybe her own cobweb sweeping should include Grant's property. Rather than let St. Clements Bluff linger in her life, she should bat at it with a broom so that she could quickly forget it had ever existed. Perhaps doing so would give her a real sense of closure. Tomorrow she would investigate whether it would be faster to donate the property to the county or state or to simply outright sell it.

Live in it she would not do, despite Grant's request that she take care of it for the rest of her life. As far as she was concerned, turning it over to someone better equipped to improve the property *was* caretaking it.

She then remembered that she had never investigated the locked room in the house. It was most likely as empty as the rest of them, but she should check it out just to be sure.

So that was it. Check out the final room, then get rid of the property as fast as possible, despite how disappointed any of the Bishops—or Grant's spirit—might be.

CHAPTER 8

BY MID-MORNING THE next day, Raleigh was back at St. Clements Bluff, standing in front of the locked room on the third floor again. She'd left Lindbergh at home despite his vocal protest against being left behind. She wanted to do this as fast as possible and having Lindbergh along would no doubt lead to protracted interactions with neighbors and other dogs.

She pulled the key ring from the front pocket of her jeans, grateful it was warm enough that she didn't actually need gloves indoors today.

Before trying out a random key, she knelt and looked at the lock. It had a very long aperture from top to bottom. It made it easy for her to find the key to match. She wasn't sure how far back it dated. It wasn't an old skeleton key, but it wasn't particularly new, either. Raleigh might work for a museum, but she was no expert in a specialty like keys. The key seemed to be made of pewter and was very thick, even though it had the overall resemblance of a modern key.

The lock clicked twice as if it had two different mechanisms in it.

She pushed open the old, worn oak door. It protested with a groan but acquiesced to Raleigh's pressure against it.

She blinked in disbelief. What was this?

Unlike the rest of the house, this room was not empty. In fact, it reminded her of many a historic house museum setup, with furniture precisely placed along walls and draperies artfully folded and pleated against windows to delight the visitor's eye.

It was decorated as a bedroom, but it might have been transplanted from the Palace of Versailles, based on the exotically carved furniture displayed.

Every piece—the bed's headboard and footboard, the massive armoire, the dressing table, the escritoire, and even the chair pulled up to it—were of some dark wood inlaid with various colors of lighter wood painstakingly cut and set in scenes. Like ancient figural Greek vases.

It was breathtaking.

In fact, each piece was so filled with these scenes, ranging over every square inch of it, that it quickly became confusing. Was this just a display of the cabinet maker's extraordinary talent? Did the scenes tell a cohesive story? If they did, Raleigh had no idea how she would be able to decipher it.

Bert Mattingly would be very interested in this suite of furniture. The value was probably incalculable.

The thick Turkish rug in the middle of the herringboned floor, as well as the formal draperies topped with cascading, ball-fringed valances, were done in shades of salmon and pale green. The draperies coordinated exquisitely with the muted floral wallpaper. There was no bedding nor even a mattress inside the bed's frame.

After soaking in as much as she could from the door, Raleigh entered the room. She did so reverently; there was something special about this room that she could not even begin to fathom.

She approached each piece of furniture, lightly running her hand over the inlay as though it might speak to her through osmosis. The inlay was so expertly done that there were no rough places where one wood joined another; it had all been sanded down and lacquered to smooth perfection.

Raleigh decided to pick a random starting point at the extravagantly scrolled headboard, which probably reached up seven feet at its curved apex. Stepping over the bed's rails into the center of the rectangle created by the bed's entire frame, she knelt in front of the headboard and examined the carvings critically. They just seemed like rows of figures, plants, animals, and buildings. As if she were staring at a Rosetta stone made of wood.

Well, that hieroglyphic code had eventually been cracked, so surely this could be, too.

With only a patch of denim separating her knees from the floor, Raleigh quickly became sore and readjusted herself into a squatting pose. It was only marginally more comfortable, but at least there wasn't hard oak pressing against her kneecaps.

Soon, though, she was able to make out some rhythms to the marquetry in the headboard. At first glance, the scenes seemed to all run together, but it became apparent to her that there were actually narrow division lines between them. Upon realizing that, she rose and went to the top left corner and attempted to "read" across the headboard.

After several minutes of this, she took a step backward, still standing inside the bed frame in order to look at the entire headboard again.

Many of the scenes seemed to be agricultural in nature. Men sowing, hoeing, and plowing. The detail of a horse's mane in one vignette was extraordinary. There were also depictions of various plants, such as wheat, corn, tobacco, and the like.

In days past, tobacco had been to Maryland what rice had been to South Carolina. It was no surprise to see a motif of the wide-leafed plant in the furniture. It convinced Raleigh that the furniture had likely been made locally.

Of interest was a scene about halfway down the headboard. To the left was a building—possibly this house?—with a path connecting it to a tree, which towered up as if twice as large as the house. On the path was a male figure, walking toward the tree. In his hand was a book, no, it was some sort of document.

Raleigh wondered if it was meant to represent the path to a hiding place on the estate. If the furniture dated as far back as the house's involvement in the Underground Railroad, perhaps this was some sort of commemoration of it. All of the agricultural symbols might also be reflective of the home's heritage as a farm and plantation.

George Washington's Mount Vernon had such symbols as part of its plaster ceiling decorations. Raleigh would have thought that such a practice would be relegated just to extremely prosperous plantation owners. But maybe this side of the Bishop clan had once been quite wealthy.

Another scene near the lower right corner of the headboard—which would presumably be covered up by mattresses and bedding—was more disturbing. Again, there was a large tree, with several people observing it. From a large branch hung a body. Raleigh shivered. Had someone been hanged here on the estate? Her imagination ran wild, conjuring up an episode whereby the owners were discovered harboring escaped slaves and vigilantes hanged a member of the Bishop family.

Or did the scene mark an event that had occurred elsewhere?

The other remarkable vignette on the headboard showed someone walking into the house's front door. Next to that was what looked to be the same figure standing in a room, with a small crowd of people, hiding behind a wall where they couldn't be seen. Dear God, was this a display of a slave hunter entering the home and looking for escapees? Raleigh recalled that there had been good bounties paid for slave retrieval in the mid-19th century.

She stepped outside of the bed's rails as if doing so would get her away from the thought of what might have gone on here so many years ago. She went to the footboard and examined it. It was full of the agricultural symbols of the headboard, as well as baskets of fruit and flowers. The detail work here was just as exquisite as on the headboard. But it was on the footboard that Raleigh caught her first clue. To the lower right, the name "Joseph Jonson" was inlaid in script. The narrow little bands of wood used here were some different species than what was used anywhere else. It suggested that the artisan had been very proud of this work and wanted to be sure his name was seen.

The cabinet maker had every right to be proud.

Joseph Jonson. The name wasn't familiar to Raleigh, but just because she worked with the museum didn't necessarily mean she knew every family name associated with the county. However, with a name in hand, she could do some research on who the cabinet maker was. What information that would lead to she could only guess.

She walked over to a window that overlooked the rear of the estate. Adjusting the draperies minimally just so she could take in the view outside, Raleigh looked out over what the inhabitants of this room would have seen. The house sat upon the top of a slope that gently rolled down to St. Clements Bay. A rocky retaining wall had been built along part of the shoreline, but the rest was succumbing to centuries of tidal action. Jutting into the water were the remains of an old pier.

The property was mostly an expanse of cleared land punctuated by trees and seemingly random outbuildings. Some were obviously much older than others. One was next to an enormous tree stump that had been sawn off close to the ground. It was large enough to be a dining table.

Raleigh's imagination ran wild as she thought of the possibilities. Could some of the buildings be old slave cabins, particularly the one next to the tree stump? Had the stump served a purpose? Could a slave cabin even withstand years of abandonment?

Some of them would have had other uses, too, like a kitchen, a wash house, a smokehouse. And didn't the newspaper article refer to an underground icehouse? Perhaps it was worth taking a walk around the property to explore all of the buildings.

She thought about how the landscape would have changed over the years. Some of these larger trees would have been merely saplings. There had perhaps been trees that were cut down for furniture or firewood. There would have been large plantings of tobacco and other crops.

As she envisioned the past, she could almost see tall-masted ships sailing by, ferrying goods up and down the Maryland shoreline. Where would have been the nearest docking for unloading barrels of whiskey and crates of cloth?

Raleigh got so caught up in creating a picture of the past that for several long moments she forgot about Grant.

In the distance, though, heavy gray clouds began forming at the horizon. Yesterday's snow had quickly melted but were they due for more? Raleigh hardly paid any attention to weather forecasts these days. She debated whether she should attempt to explore the buildings now or come back the following day.

She turned back to the room again, letting her glance take in the ostentatiousness once more before making her decision.

The furniture was of far greater interest to the history

of the home and what lay behind Grant's purpose in hiding it from her. She would research what she could on the Jonson cabinet maker first.

RALEIGH WAITED UNTIL after dark to make a clandestine visit to the museum, letting herself in through the back employee entrance. It took her several moments to even remember the entry code, but she absolutely had not wanted to come in through the front door during operating hours and have to answer all of the "How are you doing?" questions and endure the endless sympathetic gazes.

It felt surreal to be back in her office. It was exactly as she had left it the day she'd gotten the news and dropped everything to go speeding down to Patuxent River Naval Air Station. The only difference was the pile of mail on her chair, just like at home. At least someone had been thoughtful enough to put it all in a box. She put the box on the floor without so much as a glance at the heap of envelopes and sat at her computer.

A quick search through the museum's archives and several online genealogical resources gave her the answers she sought. Joseph Jonson had come to St. Mary's County as a young man in the early 19th century via a slaver. The exact date was unknown. It appeared that he had ended up in the ownership of a wealthy cabinet-making family named Jonson. Joseph eventually managed to purchase his freedom and later married a woman named Ruth, of whom there was almost no information.

Copies of both Joseph's and Ruth's handwritten manumission papers—those critical documents that proved a slave had been legitimately freed—were both available online. Joseph must have managed to save enough to buy Ruth's freedom, too. Presumably he had learned cabinet-making skills from his master, and he must have learned them well to have made so much money.

There were numerous Jonsons still listed as being residents of St. Mary's County, and Raleigh found websites for Jonsons who owned home construction businesses and handyman shops, and one had even hung out a law shingle. Finally, she found a website for Jonson Custom Furniture. That was her best starting point for discovering the origins and meaning behind all of that bedroom furniture.

Raleigh put the box of mail back on her chair and ensured that her office looked as it did when she had arrived, then slipped quietly out of the building.

Unfortunately, by waiting so late to come to the museum, she would have to wait until tomorrow to visit the Jonsons. At least there had been no snowfall.

It proved to be another sleepless night, but instead of the cause being a nightmare, it was due to a sense of anticipation. Raleigh hadn't been acquainted with that sensation in far too long.

CHAPTER 9

JONSON CUSTOM FURNITURE was located in an enormous red barn next to a modest old farmhouse. Raleigh's tires crunched on the blue-chip gravel drive as she slid into an open spot in front of the barn.

Inside was a hub of activity, as the front of the shop was full of display pieces, wood and stain samples, and numerous bookshelves filled with dusty books on every aspect of woodworking imaginable. A middle-aged couple was examining an unstained oak dining room hutch. It had been built in a traditional country design except that the upper part contained multiple cabinet doors of various sizes and paint colors, some with glass inserts and some of solid wood.

It had a whimsical, Dr. Suess quality to it. A sign next to the hutch read, *In your choice of stains or paints.*

Other display pieces ranged from early American Windsor chairs all the way through the centuries to modern highly polished ebony entertainment centers.

Behind the sales counter was a long wall separating the showroom from what was the workshop. A single door led to that mysterious world, from which came the high-pitched but muffled sounds of table saws and drills.

"Help you?" came a voice from behind her.

Raleigh whirled around. Standing there was a tall, lanky man with smooth chocolate-brown skin and eyes. His tightly-cropped hair was grayed at the temples and he had several tiny moles at the corners of his eyes.

She estimated him to be in his late forties, despite his wrinkle-free countenance.

"Yes," she said. "I'm looking for Mr. Jonson."

He smiled. "Which one? I'm Derrick. My brothers, William and Toots, are in the back, and my father is in the loft working on the books." He pointed up. Raleigh's gaze followed his outstretched arm and she saw that there was indeed a set of stairs on one side of the building leading up to a platform where an elderly man sat behind a desk, scowling at a computer screen.

Raleigh introduced herself and explained that she was looking for information regarding the intricately designed set of furniture at St. Clements Bluff and how she had come across the Jonson name.

"Don't think we have records that far back, miss. But you should talk to my dad, Ezra. If anyone knows, it's him. Come," he instructed, guiding her to the stairs leading up to the loft.

The elder Mr. Jonson stood politely as Raleigh entered his working area. He didn't stand fully erect, and Raleigh wondered if he had back troubles. Although his desk was relatively clean, there were boxes piled high all around the floor, and file cabinets so crammed with papers that many of the drawers didn't fully close. But what else would Raleigh expect from a business that had existed for so long?

"Dad, this is Mrs. Raleigh Bishop. She's looking for info on a piece that was sold a really long time ago."

Mr. Jonson appraised Raleigh with a weary gaze as if he had seen war at some point in his life. "So, you're a Bishop," he said. Raleigh wasn't sure if this was a statement or an accusation.

"Yes sir," she responded, inexplicably nervous at his examination. "By marriage. My husband is—was—Grant Bishop. He was a test pilot."

Ezra Bishop nodded, and Raleigh noticed that he had

the same tendency toward moles under the eyes that his son did and showed his age much more clearly. "Read about that. Sorry 'bout your man. So, he was one of the rough-n-tumble Bishops."

Whatever that meant. How many Bishop sects were there? "I guess so, yes. Turns out my husband left me an old home that I didn't know about. In the house, I found a bedroom suite signed by a Joseph Jonson. It is not only beautiful but is heavily inlaid with scenes that seem to point to slavery on the estate." She let that dangle, hoping Ezra would pick up the story. His response disappointed her.

"And you want to know how much was paid for it?" he asked, seemingly uninterested in the find.

"Well, more so, I wondered if you have any information on your ancestor and his other work. And who, exactly, bought the suite."

Ezra Jonson grunted. "'S'pose I might have something. Derrick, dig out that drawer, will you?" Ezra pointed to the bottom drawer of the file cabinet farthest away from his desk. Unlike the many metal ones surrounding his desk, this one was made of dark wood, parts of it blackened with age.

The drawer creaked uncooperatively, but with some strength and mild cursing, Derrick was able to remove it from its shaft and place it on his father's desk. Ezra went shuffling through the drawer's papers. It would have been too kind to call them filed, as they were just haphazardly tossed inside. As he dug further down, Raleigh could see that the papers were turning yellower, then browner, and the handwriting became more illegible.

She wondered if the Jonsons had a paper receipt for every sale made since Joseph Jonson had earned his freedom.

"This might be it," Ezra proclaimed, pulling out a

thick piece of paper and unfolding it. He laid the page on top of the drawer's contents for Raleigh to inspect.

It was a bill of sale.

Jonson Fine Furniture and Coffins
Redgate, Maryland

Sold to: Mr. and Mrs. Francis Bishop, September 20, 1845
One group of walnut furniture for a bedchamber: bed, two armoires, escritoire, lady's chair
To be inlaid with design of the customer's choosing
For a period of ten years, Jonson's will carve updates to furniture as per customer's request

The Bishops had agreed to a price of a hundred dollars for the furniture, no doubt a princely sum back then.

Most of the furniture listed here was still in the room, although one of the armoires was gone now. Or missing from the room, at any rate. Time was generally unkind to both houses and furniture alike unless special care was taken of them.

"Isn't it strange that there would be a long period in which the maker could be summoned to add carvings to the furniture?" Raleigh asked, this being just one of a hundred questions already popping into her head.

"I 'spect Joseph Jonson was happy for any work he got, no matter how foolish his customer's demands. Those was tough times in St. Mary's County. The war made it worse, but it was hard even before, 'specially for folks like us. Family had to turn to coffin-making to survive. There's never any end to people needing their final piece of furniture."

Raleigh thought rapidly. "So, this order would have been a great boon to the Jonson family business. And the Bishops must have been quite wealthy to have afforded it. I wonder if they were involved in more than just agricultural concerns. Maybe shipping? Some sort of technological invention?" she mused aloud.

The Jonson men didn't respond to her rambling thoughts. "I just wish I knew what Grant had been doing..." she said.

"Sounds like you're wanting to dig up old family history, Mrs. Bishop," Ezra said to her. "And why would you want to do that?"

Raleigh shook her head, puzzled. "What do you mean? Why wouldn't I wish to know? Family history is important, right?"

Ezra gave her a penetrating look as though she had just uttered the stupidest statement ever. The man made Raleigh very nervous for no explicable reason.

"Would you like to see the furniture?" Raleigh offered. "It's not too far from here."

"Yes ma'am, I'd like to see it," Derrick spoke up.

To her surprise, the elder Jonson declined. "Don't need to see it. What went into someone's house a hundred years ago ain't none of my business," he said, sitting back down at his desk and waving at the file drawer. As Derrick put it away, Ezra added pointedly, "Don't see a reason it's any of our business, son."

But the younger Jonson did not take his father's hint. "I'll follow you over," he said to Raleigh.

WITHIN TWENTY MINUTES, Raleigh had pulled up to the house again, Derrick Jonson close behind in his old Arctic blue Chevrolet truck. It had to be thirty years old yet was in pristine condition. As he clambered out, he reached back into the cab and pulled out a pair of vinyl gloves, which he tucked into the back pocket of his khaki pants as he walked up to the front door where Raleigh waited for him.

She escorted him up both sets of stairs to the third floor. Derrick commented on the quality workmanship throughout the house, running his hand along the banister, the wood paneling on the wall, and the various paneled doors.

His reaction at seeing the furniture suite was much like her own, a gasp of amazement. He, too, examined the scenes that had been inlaid on them, but went further, putting on the vinyl gloves and lying on his back to reach under the furniture and examine it from a cabinet maker's perspective. He grunted several times as if making discoveries.

Finally, he emerged from beneath the escritoire, talking as he peeled off his gloves and shoved them back into his pocket.

"Mrs. Bishop, this may look like it's one complete set of furniture, but I can tell by the joinery work that the pieces were made in different periods. I'd say the bed was made in the early to mid-nineteenth century—it's nowhere close to being a standard bed size of today—while the machine dovetailing on the desk drawers tells me it was made in probably the early 1900s. Machine-cut joints were introduced earlier, but most fine cabinet makers continued fitting joints by hand until the turn of the 20th century. Our shop included."

Derrick walked over to the armoire and opened one of the doors. "See the raised design on these hinges?" he asked, pointing inside where the door met the frame of the piece. "These are Stanley hinges. I'd say they date to the 1940s."

Raleigh was confused. "So, you're telling me that this furniture was built over the course of a hundred years?" That didn't seem to fit her idea that a wealthy couple purchased the set, nor did it coincide with the bill of sale.

Derrick nodded and scratched his head above his right

ear. "What's even stranger is that the inlay was done at different times on the pieces. If you look closely at each one, you can see where some of the inlaid areas have a yellowish cast to them. Shellac was applied thickly there. But in other locations, someone applied a thin coat of varnish. Varnish is clear and a much better choice for this kind of furniture. The changes to these pieces went on for far more than just the single decade that the sales order said. In fact, I would say that one or another piece was revisited at least once a decade for a very long time."

"Over the course of more than a hundred years," Raleigh repeated flatly.

Derrick Jonson nodded. "What do you plan to do with it?"

"I—" Raleigh was at a loss. "I don't know. I'm so confused as to why this furniture remains when the rest of the house is empty. And it seems to have its own very colorful history."

"Well, I don't mean to muck up your thoughts more, but I'd like to make you an offer for it. Would be nice to bring it back into the family, give it a proper place of honor in the shop. And if some granddaddy of mine from way back was making scenes of slavery on the furniture, that makes it even more special."

He named a low figure. Nevertheless, Raleigh wanted to say yes to him in order to return it to the Jonson family, but an invisible hand stayed her. Didn't the house—and its contents—really belong as a preserved historic property? "I'll think about it," she told him.

Derrick didn't push the idea and soon left to return to his family's shop. Raleigh watched from the front porch as his pale blue truck made its way down the driveway, puffing the faintest amount of smoke from its tailpipe.

Raleigh went back up to the third-floor bedroom and put a hand against the armoire, as if willing it to speak to her. It did no such thing.

It did occur to her that perhaps she should contact the Harriet Tubman organization. Perhaps they would want to be involved in the home's preservation as a part of the Underground Railroad.

As she continued to stand in the room, her hand on the armoire, another thought came to her. It was so simplistically logical that she couldn't believe she hadn't considered it before.

Were the scenes on the furniture some sort of indicators for slaves passing through here? Pictorial explanations or warnings for people who had not yet necessarily learned to read or write? And perhaps the later iterations of construction and inlay were intended to cover up the Underground Railroad history of the furniture as if to forget that sordid piece of the past.

Raleigh was warming up to this theory. The bed was the oldest piece and had the greatest number of what could be interpreted as slave scenes on them. The other, newer pieces were far more dominated by agricultural and floral motifs.

If Raleigh was correct, didn't the other Bishops deserve to keep the furniture—and the house—in the family? After all, they may have single-handedly saved many poor souls trying to escape wretched lives.

Maybe this was what Grant was attempting to do. Preserve this important family history. Maybe he was even researching it and was waiting to come to a formal conclusion before showing it to Raleigh. She could imagine him doing so, saving up this explosive and powerful information to shower upon her with a blindfolded visit to the estate on her birthday or their anniversary.

As Raleigh stood there, contemplating how Grant must have intended to present her with news of St. Clements Bluff, she heard a sharp crack, followed by a sickening thud.

The noise had come from outside. Raleigh raced out of the bedchamber and down the stairs. She was about to fly out the front door when she realized that she didn't have Lindbergh with her today and...hadn't that sounded awfully like a gunshot?

She glanced down at her long burgundy wool coat. If that had just been a hunter going after geese, was she bright enough to avoid being a target?

Raleigh took a deep breath. It may have just been a car backfiring somewhere or the sound of any number of things that happen on rural properties every day.

She calmly opened the front door and went outside. All was frigidly motionless out here. She rubbed her bare hands together and stepped lightly down the steps into the front yard. Doing so reminded her of the storm cellar to her right. She really should investigate it, in addition to the other outbuildings.

For now, though, Raleigh wanted to discover what the source of that noise had been. She stepped quietly around to the back of the house and stopped, observing everything around her again. Still nothing unusual.

On this side of the house, though, she could hear the water gently breaking against the riverbank. It was rhythmic in stillness, almost lulling her to a standing sleep as if she were a horse settling in for a quick nap.

She decided to head down for a closer listen to the waves lapping against the rocks. She would inspect the pier while she was down there and try to determine if it was salvageable. Weren't piers expensive to replace? Would just tearing it down make the place look more attractive to a buyer?

A large elm tree with two trunks and numerous long, thick branches stood proudly near the shore. Raleigh imagined it created a wonderful canopy of leafy coolness during the humid Maryland summers. She continued walking toward it, stumbling once over a stray root.

"Sorry," she said aloud, apologizing out of habit and immediately feeling silly for doing so to an inanimate object.

As she neared the tree, she realized that the loud crack and thud she'd heard earlier were from a substantial branch that had broken off and now lay on the ground, the base of it freshly splintered, and the wood's fragrant scent drifting over to her.

The tide was out, so about ten feet of riverbank showed. Raleigh made her way past the elm and on toward the pier, walking along the hard dirt path that separated the grassy lawn from the retaining wall. As cold as it was near the house, it felt at least twenty degrees colder here, what with the wind blowing in from the river. Raleigh shivered and reached into her coat pockets for her gloves. They helped ward off some of the chill.

She bent down and gazed up at the underside of the pier from a distance. There were many broken and rotted planks, but the vertical posts themselves seemed solid enough. Perhaps it wasn't too expensive a reconstruction effort.

Had Grant already considered whether to repair the pier? How would he have kept that expense a secret from her?

Raleigh shut her eyes, willing away the thought of Grant and attempting to just let the lulling sounds of wind and water working together wash over her like a freezing cocoon. The more the wind numbed her cheeks and lips, the more she was able to forget everything. This house, the bizarre furniture, her waiting job, Lindbergh, the perpetually voiced concern of others… everything that suddenly felt like an albatross around her neck.

She was nearly insensible when the distant yowl of an animal jolted her into reality. It sounded like a tomcat. He'd probably come upon another cat in his territory.

Raleigh blinked several times and closed her eyes again, trying to bring back the sensation of blankness. It wasn't working. Maybe if she just moved closer to the water…

She picked her way from the pier across the rocky barrier and sat down along the edge of the low wall where it reached into the river, sticking her feet in the water.

She grunted at the shock of feeling the freezing water against her feet. The water penetrated her sneakers almost instantly. Raleigh shut her eyes again and gritted her teeth, determined to become used to the cold water. It took surprisingly less time than she imagined it would, and soon she was numb from her mid-calves down.

Her thoughts drifted further into darkness and into her nightmares. She was strapped in the aircraft's passenger seat, plunging helplessly down to the watery depths below. Here she was now, at the edge of those watery depths.

Sitting here was not a good representation of that, was it? Raleigh slid off the rocks so that she was upright in the water. She was surprised that she could even maintain her balance given how numb she was, but she managed to take a couple of steps forward. The freezing water was easier to deal with in each successive step. She wondered how far she could go before it became intolerable.

Ah, going under would be so much more comfortable than being above the water line. Her extremities were quickly numbing, and she hardly noticed them. Underwater there would be no criticism of her withdrawal from society, no mysterious house to contend with, no responsibilities, no pain…and she might even see Grant again.

Was it a sin to kill yourself if you did so to rejoin loved ones that you found it impossible to live without? She knew it was, but she toyed with the question anyway.

Raleigh had no time to contemplate it further, for she was suddenly flailing in the water, trapped in her big coat and unable to find the bay's soft sandy floor. Had there been a serious drop-off in land depth right here? She thrashed about, instinctively knowing it was the wrong thing to do, yet feeling out of control of herself. Maybe she didn't really want to walk into her own watery grave. Maybe she wanted to live. For the home she shared with Grant. For her family. For her job. Even for goofy little Mutt Boy.

Raleigh attempted to regain her footing in the river's mud, but her legs were too frozen to do it. She reached in every direction she could with her arms, as though she might find a bit of flotsam or something solid to cling to for support. There was nothing. She had wandered just a little too far from the shoreline and fear now prevented her from thinking clearly and making any sort of rational decision.

Unable to stay afloat any longer, Raleigh plunged completely beneath the icy surface.

CHAPTER 10

KIP HEWITT SHUT off the single outboard engine of his small trawler as he consulted with his electronic fish finder to determine whether there were any swimmers below him. He didn't typically wander into St. Clements Bay since there was no commercial fishing permitted there, but today he was out just for himself.

"Nothing," he muttered to himself as he floated in the still waters of the bay. The frigid air didn't bother him after so many years as a waterman. In fact, Kip enjoyed having many parts of the area's rivers and bays to himself during the winter.

Kip was about to switch the engine back on to trawl another part of the bay when his attention was caught by activity a couple of hundred feet away along the shoreline.

Was that a woman wading into the water? Hard to tell at this distance but it sure did seem like a female form. "Damn," he said softly. While Kip didn't mind cold air, he sure as hell wasn't about to dive into this icy body of water.

He tossed the fish finder into the boat's lock box, his attention now fully riveted on whatever it was the woman was doing. She would move forward a little, then stand there as if getting used to the cold, then step forward a little more. What was her purpose in this? Was the woman seriously planning to take a swim? In a winter coat?

Suddenly, the woman disappeared from view. Now not sure whether he had simply seen an apparition and not an actual human being, Kip opened the locker again and retrieved his binoculars. Quickly focusing them on where he was certain he had seen the woman, he scanned back and forth across where he was certain he had seen her.

A hand reached out from beneath the smooth surface and briefly clawed at the air before going down again.

Raleigh wasn't sure how much time had passed. Based on the fire searing her lungs as she refrained from breathing in water, it must have been hours in the icy flow.

How did swimmers and divers stroke and kick their way for more than a few seconds?

It was too late for her. Her instincts were screaming at her to draw in a breath, in direct conflict with her brain lecturing her not to do it.

Perhaps she wasn't as interested in dying as she'd thought she was.

How ironic, since she was now going to have to take a big gulp of—

A hand grabbed the collar of her coat and yanked her effortlessly out of the water then tossed her unceremoniously across the edge of a small fishing boat. It was made of the highest quality fiberglass available, based on the thumping her head and shoulders took as she struck both the built-in bench seat and then the bottom of the boat beneath it.

"You going to make it?" A deep male voice spoke gently to her.

Raleigh was still too paralyzed from fear and cold and nearly drowning to do much more than cough violently.

It didn't take long before she knew she sounded and looked like a barking seal.

Whoever owned that male voice didn't seem concerned about her condition, as he was letting her bark and gasp to her heart's content.

Raleigh's choking subsided, and she fumbled to get herself into a seated position.

A pair of arms assisted her onto the boat bench.

Raleigh's breath still crystallized in the air, but at least her coughing had subsided.

Her rescuer remained silent, so the only noise was that of the boat gently sloshing back and forth in the water.

Raleigh finally ventured a glance up at her rescuer and had to prevent herself from recoiling in fear.

Looking at her in concern was a man with dark hair—everywhere. He wore a knitted cap, but it did little to contain wild, curly hair that reached to his shoulders.

His beard was thick and full, too, giving an overall impression of a lion's mane sprouting as a halo around his face, with just a pair of concerned blue eyes disabusing her of the notion that she shared these quarters with a wild feline.

How very disconcerting.

"Did you decide to go swimming in these temperatures?" he asked as he moved to center himself on the bench directly across from her. It was impossible to tell how old the man across from her was. With all of that beard growth covering his features, he might have been anywhere from twenty to eighty.

Raleigh refrained from a biting retort to him, her irritation exacerbated by being deeply chilled after nearly drowning. The man had rescued her, so he was probably entitled to a little snark at her expense.

"No. I was..." Raleigh stopped. How should she explain what she was doing in the water? She was shivering uncontrollably now just wanting to get back to the warmth of her home.

"I...I thought I saw something in the water, and I was trying to reach it," she offered.

"I see," the man replied. He clearly didn't.

Nevertheless, he leaned forward and popped open a built-in cabinet beneath his seat. He produced both a life jacket and a bright blue wool blanket.

"I'm not sure which of these you need more," he said, not unkindly. "Here."

Raleigh held out her arms as he fitted the life jacket on her. He whistled softly as he did it, but in the winter air, the sound carried and seemed to ricochet off the shore to envelop Raleigh in companionable comfort.

With the orange life jacket strap securely fastened around her waist, the man opened the blanket and draped it over her shoulders.

"It's not much, but it's the best I can do. Not used to rescuing people in shallow waters in the middle of February," he said. "You live there?" he nodded toward St. Clements Bluff.

The breeze caught his beard and the point of it gently moved across his face. Now he really did remind Raleigh of a lion.

"Yes," she replied. "Well, no," she amended, shaking her head.

He raised an eyebrow. "You aren't sure?"

At this, he turned a key on the boat's dashboard, and the engine sputtered to life. With his hand on the tiller, he guided the boat the short distance to her crumbling pier.

Up close, he eyed the structure and, apparently deciding it wasn't to be trusted, he hopped out of the boat and pulled it just far enough ashore that it lodged into the bank.

He held out a hand for Raleigh. "Come," he said.

But she was regaining all of her senses and became

hesitant. Who was this man? How had he appeared out of nowhere to ostensibly "rescue" her?

She stared at his outstretched hand. It was large and calloused. This was someone who was no stranger to manual labor.

Finally deciding that it was irrational to imagine that someone who was working so hard to help her could possibly be untrustworthy, Raleigh took his proffered hand.

It felt as rough as it looked, and it was as icy cold as hers, but the man was strong and easily helped Raleigh out of the skiff and onto the shore.

She stood still for a moment, realizing that mere minutes ago she was contemplating her own demise and now she just wanted a mug of steaming hot French roast.

The man dropped her hand. "I don't think you need this anymore," he said.

In what seemed like one fluid motion, he slipped the blanket off Raleigh's shoulders, unhooked and removed the life jacket, then wrapped the blanket around her again.

He tossed the life jacket back toward the skiff, where it landed with a lighter thud than Raleigh had.

"You need to be inside where it's warm," he said. "I'll walk you to the door."

Raleigh automatically obeyed him, falling in step alongside his stride. She was tall for a woman, but he was much taller. Between her frozen clothing and near-brush with death, she struggled to keep up.

He must have sensed it and slowed down as they made their way across the rear of the St. Clements Bluff property toward the house.

Raleigh was finally regaining her senses, despite being soaked through. What was she thinking, permitting this stranger to accompany her to this sanctuary of Grant's? Why, she didn't even know his name.

Raleigh's mind was still awhirl as they walked in companionable silence. She continued to lead him around to the front of the house, desperately trying to decide if she should invite her rescuer inside.

As they reached the first wood tread of the steps leading to the door, the man paused. "You'll be alright now. I'll leave you to it, then."

He stepped back and stood there, his hands behind his back like a sentry.

Raleigh almost sighed in relief that he was not going to pursue her further. She would have to immediately leave, anyway. It was nearly as cold inside the house as it was out here.

"Name's Kip," he said, holding out his rough hand again. "Kip Hewitt. I live down the road a piece. Just doing some personal fishing but there's nothing biting this late in the day."

Raleigh was puzzled as she moved toward him and clasped his hand briefly again. "Kip? That makes me think of Rudyard Kipling. You know that author?"

The man named Kip rolled his eyes. "Of course. My mother was a fan of *Captains Courageous* and named me after him."

Raleigh found herself smiling, despite how anxious she was to get out of her freezing wet clothes and curl up on her own couch in a thick robe with a steaming mug in her hands.

"My name is Raleigh Bishop. Raleigh after the city in North Carolina where I was born. My mother adored Florence Nightingale."

Kip looked at her quizzically.

"Florence was born in Florence, Italy," Raleigh explained.

Kip's teeth flashed in an understanding grin beneath the beard. He seemed much younger in that moment.

"Sometimes our parents love us so much, they curse us," he said. "Have a safe day, Raleigh Bishop. Stay away from the bay until spring."

With that, Kip Hewitt sauntered back around the house toward his boat.

Raleigh felt a confusing mixture of guilt, relief, disappointment, and a strange sense of hope.

She also still had Kip's blanket around her shoulders.

CHAPTER 11

"...AND I WAS just wondering if you'd found anything of interest in the scrapbook," Mutzi said after apologizing for calling so early.

"I'm happy to hear from you," Raleigh said in reply. Really, she had to make an effort to see her in-laws more often.

Mutzi's voice brightened. "Always a pleasure to talk to you, too, dear. Oh, wait, here's Dad."

There was shuffling and muttering, then Mr. Bishop's booming voice came onto the line. "How's our girl doing? Ready to come by for more doughnuts? Mom bought some sort of newfangled sprinkles she says taste like apples. Or is it cherries? Which is it?" David now turned his attention away from Raleigh as he sought to confer with his wife over what flavoring the sprinkles were.

While her in-laws debated, Raleigh sat on her couch, dressed in her U.S. Navy sweats as she flipped carefully through Mutzi's scrapbook, hoping to find a missed clue about the Bishop family that might help her in figuring out why Grant has been in possession of St. Clements Bluff. Lindbergh lay curled up in a tight ball next to her, his rear end against her thigh as he dreamt his doggie dreams.

As usual, Raleigh had a thermal carafe of French Roast on the end table next to her. Why disturb Lindbergh by constantly arising for more coffee pours when she could just sit in place for hours?

David returned to the call. "Mom says they taste like strawberries. I knew it was some sort of fruit."

"Sounds good to me. Name the day." Raleigh hadn't told anyone about her near drowning, having felt too mortified by her own contemplations to share them with others. Besides, her in-laws would have become insanely worried. Mutzi might have even insisted that Raleigh move into their house so they could keep an eye on her.

Nothing was going to budge Raleigh from the home she had shared with Grant. She and Lindbergh were quite content here together.

She reached over and scratched the dog's lower back. He grunted happily without opening his eyes.

Mutzi returned to the call after more shuffling and background discussion with her husband. "Dad says you should come today for doughnuts. I know you're too busy to come that soon. Anyway, what have you found in the scrapbook?" she asked.

"Truthfully, I'm just now going through it," Raleigh said.

"Oh." Mutzi sounded deeply disappointed that there was no point of conversation to be had.

"I'm sure I'll find something before we have doughnuts again, and I'll immediately call you when I do."

Mutzi seemed satisfied enough with that, and Raleigh was able to end the call. After a few more moments of raking her nails across Lindbergh's backside, Raleigh returned to the scrapbook. Lindbergh grunted again, but this time it was an irritated tone.

"Okay, Mutt Boy, sorry to have offended you," Raleigh said, returning to scratching his backside while managing the scrapbook on her lap with one hand.

She flipped another page and came upon a two-page spread consisting of an old, yellowed newspaper article on the left side and two photos on the other. The article was dated 1915 and was titled, *Leonardtown Man Wins Museum Award.*

It detailed how Thomas "Teeny" Bishop had been honored by the St. Mary's Historical Museum—Raleigh's own workplace—for donating an old lantern with a giant ring attached to the top of it. A grainy photograph of it was cut from it and taped down on the right-handed page, along with a clipped photo of two men—one in a suit and the other an enormous man in dungarees—shaking hands. The photo caption was missing, but Raleigh imagined the man in the suit to be the museum's director at the time and the other to be Teeny Bishop. The museum considered the piece a significant historical artifact.

Raleigh frowned. Had she ever seen this piece? She mentally skipped through all of the museum's collections and shook her head. It definitely wasn't on display anywhere. Raleigh wondered why it had been removed. Likely it was now in storage, so she made a mental note to look for it, wondering what made it special.

The following two pages were even more interesting. A longer article from the *St. Mary's Beacon* had been cut out and placed on the scrapbook pages in sections. Without reading the text, Raleigh knew this was a disturbing find. The headline blared:

Walter Hewitt Arrested for Attempted Murder of Francis Bishop

Hewitt was the last name of the scraggy-faced Kip. That was a strange coincidence.

Of course, Hewitt wasn't an uncommon name in the county.

With a hand massaging a very happy Lindbergh, Raleigh read the article, which was accompanied by an old black and white photo—now just in sepia tones—of a young man in a suit and derby hat, with his hands behind his back and a lawman leading him toward a

Model A police cruiser with an enlarged rear box for holding prisoners.

Raleigh scanned the article. Apparently, Mr. Hewitt was accused of trying to kill Mr. Bishop with rat poison for having attempted to lay claim to a property that Hewitt said belonged to him. Apparently, there had been some inter-family marriages and then finally this particular land had been left without a clear heir.

Oh, and Bishop had seemingly been keeping entirely too much company with Hewitt's wife.

Everyone involved had protested their innocence, but Hewitt had been duly arrested.

Raleigh quickly flipped further into the scrapbook. There was no other mention of the incident. She wondered what sort of sentence Hewitt had served or whether—

The doorbell rang, bonging the first half of Westminster chimes throughout the house.

She patted Lindbergh's rump and went to answer the door.

"Hi, Sisso, miss me?"

At the door was Raleigh's sister, Salem, with two bright magenta rolling luggage cases next to her.

"You're running the risk of a sparrow trying to nest in there, Sisso," Salem said with a laugh, pointing a forefinger at Raleigh's mouth. "You should shut that and open up to let me in."

So many questions raced through Raleigh's mind as she mutely obeyed her sister's request, pulling the door back wide as Salem wheeled in her two suitcases. Raleigh embraced her sister, noting that Salem's return hug seemed perfunctory. Otherwise, she was still Salem: cool, confident, lean, outgoing. And with all of that, also the prettier of the two of them, in Raleigh's opinion. Salem's hair was the type of multi-toned blonde that the best salon in the world couldn't replicate. She wore it long and seemingly carelessly, producing an enviable, casual-glamour effect that was beyond Raleigh's talents to pull off.

Grant has always said that Salem had a lot of crazy buried beneath the blonde, undoubtedly his way of assuaging his wife that her sister wasn't perfect.

Raleigh and Salem shared the same blue-flecked green eyes and athletic frames, though, and in that, no one could mistake that they were related.

Lindbergh padded out from the living room. He offered a half-hearted bark as he went to inspect the intruder but quickly realized this was a friend, not a foe to be dispatched with menacing growls and bared teeth.

"Hey, Lindbergh," Salem said, letting go of her suitcase handles and kneeling next to him. The dog sniffed at her coat pocket. Salem laughed again. "You got me, pal," she said, reaching in and pulling out a dog biscuit, which was gone in a single chomp, accompanied by a powerful butt wag.

"He remembers you," Raleigh said as she led her sister to the kitchen, wondering what would have driven Salem to show up unannounced.

Raleigh's hands automatically reached for her bag of coffee and her dwindling stack of filters.

"Caffeine still your drug of choice?" Salem asked as Raleigh continued with her ritual.

"The better question might be what brings you back to St. Mary's," Raleigh replied, as she pressed the brewing button on the coffeemaker. Within moments, the unit started its customary and comforting gurgling noises as it brought water to its proper temperature.

Salem's sunny disposition dimmed. "I thought you'd be happy as a hare to see me, Sisso." Salem was forever mixing up her metaphors. "After all, it's been almost a year. I'm here to help you."

Raleigh was on guard. Surely Salem couldn't have

known anything about recent events. "Help me?" she asked cautiously.

"Yes. Mom says you've been too withdrawn. You hardly respond to her calls and e-mails and you aren't back to work yet. I'm going to lift you out of your doldrums, Raleigh, with a liberal application of shopping, pedicures, and Mai Tais. Is the Rose Garden still open this time of year?"

The Rose Garden was an ironically named local bar, located on a sandy strip of land with no rose bushes, flowers, or even a semblance of a garden in sight. However, it overlooked the Potomac River and was renowned for its oysters prepared twelve different ways and its powerful Mai Tai drinks. It also didn't close up during the winter, as many places did.

"Yes, it's open." Raleigh's voice was flat. She appreciated the local ambiance of the place but wasn't sure she was up for an evening of being surrounded by loud raucous laughter and blaring music. She hadn't even finished scratching Lindbergh's backside yet.

"Great!" Salem said brightly. "Let me get unpacked and then we can go out for drinks and oyster stew. I haven't had oysters in ages."

Without waiting for Raleigh's concurrence, Salem picked up one of her bags and headed for the stairs. Raleigh stared at her sister's retreating figure for a moment, wondering how to tell Salem that she was in no mood for oyster stew, or Mai Tais, or even leaving the confines of her home. Besides, Salem wasn't exactly an invited guest.

She did no more than wonder though, before picking up the other bag and following her sister, Lindbergh lumbering up the stairs behind them.

Until now, Raleigh had staved off her sister's ongoing threat to move in and take "care" of her.

Salem was still unmarried, having spent every moment

following college pursuing her high-flown finance career. Raleigh doubted that her sister had any intention of trading her high-rise city condo in Charlotte for a spare bedroom in rural Maryland, so the threat of moving in was an empty one.

She supposed she shouldn't be too hard on her sister, who had adored Grant upon meeting him during her extended visit to Maryland while Raleigh was working for the historic Chase-Lloyd House museum home in Annapolis. In fact, they had double dated a few times with a classmate of Grant's at the Naval Academy during Salem's visit. That relationship had gone nowhere, but it had been two weeks of memorable sailing trips, seafood restaurants, and pub tours for the four of them.

Their most frequented pub was the Rams Head Tavern, where Raleigh and Grant had first met. Raleigh had been there with some co-workers, where they were planning out the following year's special events schedule over specially made Fish House Punch drinks. The museum staff always tried to drink colonial-period beverages when they had off-site meetings. "For inspiration," the museum's director had said.

Grant had come in with some fellow midshipmen from the Naval Academy for fish tacos and craft beers. Midshipmen were always recognizable by their clean-shaven looks and trim physiques, as well as their love-of-life joviality. Grant and his friends had seated themselves noisily at the next table, and soon Raleigh found herself more focused on the laughing, dark-haired guy with the buzz cut sitting twenty feet away than on the printed lines of school groups who wanted special visits during the upcoming school year.

So fascinated was Raleigh by Grant that she hadn't been paying attention to the wiry man in a stained jacket who sidled up to her chair and lifted her purse by its strap from the back of it.

The museum director had noticed it first. "Hey!" she shouted, causing Raleigh to turn and realize that it was her purse the thief was taking off with. Raleigh had instinctively jumped up and yelled, "Stop him! He has my purse!" then proceeded to wildly chase him out of the restaurant, knowing there was no way she could run fast enough to catch him. He was already out the door and running down West Street, a cute walking district of shops and restaurants.

The man Raleigh had been admiring sped past her with ferocious speed, nearly flinging the pub's door off its hinges in his haste to go after the purse thief. Raleigh continued to pursue them both, and by the time she caught up with them, completely out of breath, Grant had the other man face down on the brick sidewalk as he sat on top of his back and dialed the police from his phone. The thief was howling protests of his innocence.

Grant initially introduced himself to her as Prince Charming and winked as Raleigh stood there and tried to act as though she wasn't winded. "I believe this is yours, my lady," he said, reaching next to the thief's body and handing up her purse. It was an old, battered black vinyl purse, as much as she could afford on a docent's salary in an expensive area like Annapolis.

"Thanks," she said, trying not to grimace at the sorry bag he was handing over to her. Surely, he thought it had hardly been worth risking his life over.

"I'm Grant Bishop," he said, reaching up a hand for her to shake from where he sat on top of the thief, who was now shouting epithets at both Grant and Raleigh.

"Raleigh Moore," she replied, enjoying the feel of his strong paw clasping hers even while feeling ridiculous about introducing herself to a man who was literally sitting on top of a criminal.

The police arrived to take statements and to haul away the thief, who was now hollering about his rights and how his brother was a big-time lawyer. When they were gone, Grant offered to walk Raleigh back to the Rams Head.

They never went back to the pub. Their walk had taken them all over the Annapolis waterfront and ended with them holding hands at McGarvey's while they shared a dish of fried oysters.

Raleigh's life had never been the same.

Grant hadn't been tops in his classes, but the Bishops knew their Congressman and thus he had gotten a recommendation to the naval academy in Annapolis. Ironically, it was there that he fell in love with studying. After graduation, he had gone back home to St. Mary's County to go to test pilot school, with a plan of serving in the Navy for twenty years and then switching out into the commercial world.

He had spent most weekends in Annapolis visiting Raleigh, and it wasn't long before she was picking out a dress and flowers and agreeing to move to a tiny town in Maryland she'd never even heard of.

But it had quickly become home, particularly once she had found the job with the St. Mary's Historical Museum as a docent and had eventually worked her way into exhibit design.

Now, Salem had worked *her* way back to Maryland with some vague offer of "help."

OVER STEAMING BOWLS full of plump oysters, sherry, and cream, Raleigh and Salem talked together for the first time together since Grant's funeral. Actually, Salem chattered while Raleigh silently ate her soup. Raleigh wasn't surprised to learn that her sister had been through all sorts of drama over the past year.

"...so, I told Todd that he was suffocating me. Can you imagine getting a gold bracelet for your second date?"

Salem shook her head, as though every woman should sympathize with her plight of receiving an expensive gift from someone of such short acquaintance. Raleigh nodded impassively.

"I shouldn't have kissed him, that was a huge mistake. It made him think we had something. But I was the first woman he had dated since his divorce, and I didn't want to be his rebound." Salem took a bite of a Captain's Wafer, a buttery-tasting cracker that added the right amount of salty flavor and crunchy texture to a thick concoction like oyster stew.

Crumbles fell to the brown kraft paper that served as a tablecloth. Salem glanced down at her mess and brushed the crumbs into one hand then dumped them into her empty soup crock.

"Did you return the bracelet?" Raleigh asked, taking a sip of sweet tea to wash down the last of her stew.

Salem looked at her sister incredulously. "It was a gift," she said.

Raleigh made no comment as she put her glass down. Salem had always experienced no end of suitor offerings.

"Anyway," Salem said brightly. "It's just as well that Todd drove me away because it gave me the idea to come spend some time with my favorite sister."

Raleigh felt a twinge and was certain she could hear alarm bells in the distance. "How much time?" she asked, hoping her tone was neutral.

"Oh, I don't know. Until my Sisso is feeling more like her old self. Oh, they're about to start." Salem nodded toward the makeshift stage, which was really just a blocked-off corner of the restaurant containing two bar stools and a couple of floor microphones.

Raleigh turned in time to see two men who appeared to be in their early thirties, wearing flannel shirts over blue jeans sit down behind the mikes and prop guitars on their laps. There was a smattering of laughter and applause as one announced that they were The Two Mikes, back by popular demand…the demand of their mother that they get out of the house for the evening.

The musicians were not only competent but very entertaining, telling self-deprecating jokes as they moved through their set of classic rock numbers. Salem seemed entranced, particularly by the Mike who had a dusting of dark beard on his face and what even Raleigh had to admit were twinkling blue eyes.

Patrons began moving into the open area to rhythmically move to the beating music. "Let's dance," Salem said to Raleigh, not taking her eyes off Blue-Eyed Mike.

Raleigh sighed. As usual, this was turning into far more than she wished. "You go," she said. "I'm sure your intended will enjoy watching you gyrate." She took another sip of her Mai Tai, which was sliding down much easier than was probably wise.

Salem tore her gaze away from the guitarist. "No, I'd look ridiculous up there by myself. Come with me. Just for one song, I promise." Salem slid off her stool as though the decision was already made.

Raleigh knew that this wouldn't be for just one song.

It wasn't.

Raleigh half-heartedly joined her sister on the dance floor for four songs. When the duo switched up to a ballad for slow dancing, Raleigh couldn't get back to their table fast enough.

Now sweaty and with any effects of the Mai Tai gone, Raleigh requested ice water from the server, while an unflappable Salem merely ordered a plate of grilled oysters, a Rose Garden specialty.

"All of that exercise made me hungry again!" Salem exclaimed.

Raleigh quickly downed her glass when it arrived and was glad the server left behind a full pitcher of water so she could continue refilling her glass herself. When the oysters arrived, Salem attacked them with gusto, moaning in delight at the flavor.

Between the oysters and the fact that The Two Mikes were taking a break and had disappeared from the stage, Salem was finally able to concentrate on Raleigh again.

"What do you think? Shopping or pedicures first thing tomorrow?" Salem asked as she inserted an oyster knife in between two rough shell halves and split them open. Using the knife's flat blade to dig out the oyster, she held the juicy morsel on the blade with her thumb and lifted it to her mouth, chewing a couple of times and swallowing.

Raleigh didn't reply because she couldn't decide which activity was less appealing.

"Oh, for cripe's sake, Sisso, I know you're hurting but you simply cannot just sit in that tomb of a house all day long and drown yourself in Folger's or espresso or whatever it is you drink." Salem tossed aside an empty oyster shell and reached for another in her bowl. "Surely there is *something* that interests you. I can't tell Mom I bombed out with you this quickly."

Raleigh mentally rolled her eyes. *Of course,* the visit was actually about Salem scoring points with their mother. However, Raleigh did have the issue of St. Clements Bluff on her mind and no one with whom to really discuss what had happened. Salem might be a pain, but she was also smart and analytical.

Thus she shared with her sister everything surrounding St. Clements Bluff, beginning with the will and ending with Kip Hewitt. Raleigh was certain that it would be Mr. Hewitt upon whom Salem would focus her laser attention, but to Raleigh's surprise, her sister expressed tender concern for her safety.

"Sisso, I can't believe you kept all of that to yourself. You might have drowned if not for Captain Grizzly rescuing you." Salem reached out a hand and placed it over Raleigh's. "You have to be more careful. And you can start by taking me to St. Clements Bluff so I can see for myself everything you've told me."

Raleigh nodded, feeling more relief than she imagined she would. It was actually good to share all of her anxiety over Grant's bequest to her. Perhaps getting her sister's take on it all from inside the old home would help her come to better conclusions.

"Well, then, time to get home and get to bed," Salem exclaimed, dropping down money for their as-yet unmaterialized check. "We have a big day tomorrow."

Raleigh rose from her bar stool once more, but she wasn't able to leave with her sister until Blue-Eyed Mike came by and obtained Salem's phone number with a promise to call her.

THE NEXT AFTERNOON, Raleigh pushed open the door to the locked room at St. Clements Bluff. As expected, Salem gasped upon taking in the magnificent suite of furniture while Lindbergh whined once and padded back downstairs.

Raleigh's sister went straight to the bed. Removing one mitten from a hand, she brushed her fingers over the footboard's ornate carvings. "Your description didn't do it justice. I've never seen anything like it," she breathed.

"My thought exactly," Raleigh agreed.

Salem stepped around the bed and over the rails to examine the headboard more closely. "I can't even fathom how your flyboy was able to keep this a secret. I feel like I'm in the middle of some quest-for-a-treasure movie. Except we don't know what the treasure is."

Salem turned back to Raleigh. "The draperies are spectacular. They almost look new. How is it that they aren't completely dry-rotted and hanging in tatters?"

Raleigh shrugged. "Excellent question. The rest of the house shows its age, but this one room seems to be impervious to the ravages of time. I don't understand it, either. My next step was to examine the outbuildings and the root cellar. I wondered what their conditions are."

Salem nodded absentmindedly as she stepped back over the bed rails to walk around the room, removing her other yellow knitted mitten and stuffing both into a coat pocket as she did so. She reached out to touch the draperies, the armoire, the walls, and everything else in the room, as if hoping they would share some sort of secret knowledge with her.

She went to the windows and, using her hands—perfectly manicured with glossy red polish—to shield her face from the sun, peered outside at the grounds, then returned to examining the interior of the room. It was amusing for Raleigh to watch Salem go through nearly the same motions of drinking it all in as she had.

Except that Salem noticed more.

With both hands on her hips, Salem turned to Raleigh and cocked her head to one side. "Does it seem to you that the proportions of this room are all wrong?"

Raleigh frowned. "What do you mean? What size should it be?"

Her sister shook her head. "I don't mean the size, exactly, but the configuration. Doesn't the fireplace seem to jut way too far into the room? Look." Salem led Raleigh to where the fireplace mantel met the wall. "See the depth between the back of the firebox and the wall? There's something like five feet of chimney behind here. That's crazy."

Raleigh tried to conjure up what she knew about 19th century fireplace construction and came up blank. "Maybe that's how they were made back then. Or maybe it was a poor construction job. Or the room was an add-on around an exterior chimney."

"Maybe," Salem said doubtfully. "Didn't you say this may have been a stop on the Underground Railroad? Maybe there's a hiding spot behind the fireplace."

Salem knocked in random locations along the wallpapered wall with her ungloved hand. "Does it sound hollow?" she asked. "I don't know what 'hollow' sounds like."

Raleigh took a couple of steps backward, examining the entire fireplace and its position on the wall. Could there be an entrance behind the firebox into a hiding place? It made sense that it would have been long plastered over, she supposed, once slavery was eradicated and there was no need for a reminder of those tragic days.

Raleigh noticed that the mantel of the fireplace was very thick and made of multiple layers of wood versus just a single piece hewn from a solid block of wood. Was that unusual? Raleigh made a mental note to ask Derrick Jonson about it.

In fact, maybe the carpenter would be able to tell whether there was an open space behind the wall without tearing it out. The preservationist in her didn't want to destroy anything unnecessarily.

"Let's go explore the outbuildings," Raleigh suggested. "I'll bring an expert later to determine if there is a hiding hole back there."

Salem looked positively enthusiastic. "Great idea! Surely there is a sledgehammer or crowbar somewhere around here that we can use to dig into the wall." She made a pounding motion in the air next to the wall. "I bet Mike would be able to do it in a single swing."

Raleigh grimaced. "It can wait. I shouldn't tear out any walls if I don't have to."

Salem's expression went from joyful to incredulous.

"Are you kidding me, Sisso? It's *your* place. You can tear out a wall if you like. In fact, you could burn the whole damn thing down if you wanted."

But Raleigh was resolute in not causing damage to Grant's mysterious house.

She led Salem out of the room, locking the door behind them. Salem grumbled the entire way down the staircase but by the time her feet hit the first floor where Lindbergh was patiently waiting, she was already chattering about what they might find in one of the outbuildings that connected St. Clements Bluff to the Underground Railroad.

Raleigh thought it made sense to visit the cellar first since it was steps away from the front door. She went through her key ring, trying out keys until she found one that worked on the storm cellar's lock. The shiny new metal chains around the door handles had been well wrapped and it took time to undo them. Raleigh's hands were numb by the time she finally freed the double doors.

Lindbergh jumped down the wooden stairs into the murky depths below them.

"It's like he knows the place," Salem observed, waiting for Raleigh to find her footing on the stairs before following.

"Yes, he does seem to be familiar with this house," Raleigh replied as she reached blindly for a rail, eventually finding one and using it to ensure she didn't stumble down the stairs. As her eyes became accustomed to the dark, she realized the open cellar doors provided enough light to maneuver around, and she soon landed on the packed earthen floor.

Raleigh took a deep breath. It smelled earthy and musty down here but was warmer than it was above ground. There was shelving along the old brick walls, some of it in good repair, and some of it appeared to date back to the building of the house. Like the interior of the house, it was mostly empty, with just a few old cans of used paint and some bins lined in burlap marked "onions," "turnips," and "potatoes" offering any indication of the cellar's past life.

"Whew, I'm glad I didn't have to climb up and down those stairs every day to live here," Salem said, stepping onto the compacted floor. "Can you imagine that in a long dress and hoop skirt?"

Raleigh shook her head. "If you were someone with the money to wear a hoop skirt, you weren't likely to be someone who spent time in a cellar," she told her sister.

Salem shrugged. "True enough. So, what's down here?"

Raleigh had just noticed one end of a shelving unit pulled about a foot away from the wall to her right. The shelving itself had nothing on it.

Without responding to her sister, Raleigh made her way to the shelving. Salem and Lindbergh followed obediently.

Raleigh edged her way behind the shelving and inspected the brick wall behind it. It was darker further into the cellar and the daylight did not penetrate as well.

Too bad I don't have a flashlight.

Behind her, Salem sneezed violently in three bursts. "Whew!" her sister commented at her own outburst. "This place is as dusty as my makeup table at home."

Lindbergh also sneezed, causing Salem to laugh and then dissolve into another sneezing fit.

While her sister and dog amused themselves, Raleigh continued her inspection, feeling along the wall to determine why the shelves would have been pulled away.

Her hand connected with a small metal ring. She pulled the ring toward her. Nothing. Raleigh started fiddling with the ring, twisting and pushing against the wall where the ring was attached.

Lindbergh whined as she did this. Raleigh noticed that Salem surreptitiously slid a treat from a coat pocket directly into Lindbergh's mouth. The dog was magically distracted from Raleigh's efforts.

Suddenly, there was movement. A two-foot-wide section of the brick wall moved backward with a groan that was deafening in this underground space.

Salem jumped and squeaked in reaction to the noise. Lindbergh was unfazed, likely still in euphoria from the dog treat.

The wall section moved back about two feet and then appeared to hit another wall. Raleigh let go of the ring and observed that she had unveiled a small space that she wouldn't quite call a room, although a couple of chairs might fit in it. It had the same compacted earthen floor as the rest of the cellar but the walls here were not brick, just more tightly packed dirt.

"A hiding spot?" Salem asked from behind her.

What other answer was there? "I think so," Raleigh replied. She stepped completely into the space, observing the dark area to the best of her ability, running her hands along the brick wall on one side and the earthen floor on the other. Tiny niches had been dug out of the dirt wall, mostly at her shoulder height.

"Well?" Salem demanded impatiently. "What's in there? Anything dead?"

Raleigh smiled at her sister's ridiculous question. "Not that I can tell. There are these strange little cutouts in the wall—oh." Raleigh's hand came across something protruding from the wall. She desperately wished she had a flashlight for what was turning into a Nancy Drew investigation.

"I think I've found a..." Raleigh continued feeling. "It seems to be a hanging lamp. And it seems to—"

Raleigh found a latch on the lantern and opened it, "—it seems to have, yes, there is a taper candle in it."

"So, it really *is* a hiding spot!" Salem exclaimed. "Let me see!"

Raleigh could think of no other purpose for the hidden space. Perhaps the niches were for messages or food. She slipped out of there and allowed Salem in.

Lindbergh whined and thumped his tail against the ground as Raleigh exited. "Sorry, boy," she told the dog. "I don't have anything for you."

Salem returned in a few moments with the candle in her hand. It was brittle and cracked and burned down to just more than a nub. "This is amazing, Sisso. I bet there are lots of these hiding places on the property. The owners of this place were risking a lot to hide all of those slaves, weren't they? Couldn't they have gotten in a lot of trouble for it?"

Raleigh nodded as she, her sister, and Lindbergh made their way back to the stairs leading out of the cellar. "Not just legal trouble, but they could be ostracized from society for it. To be shunned was a serious trial in a day where generations of a family stayed in the same area and didn't move much."

Raleigh now had so many questions about St. Clements Bluff. Starting with why Grant had hidden it from her, all the way back to whether it was the Bishops of many generations ago who had hidden slaves on the property or some other previous family.

Once they had all exited the cellar into the nippy air, Raleigh rewrapped the chain around the handles and affixed the lock again. "Why don't we next try looking at the—" Raleigh began, but got no further, as Lindbergh started barking and prancing wildly.

In seconds, they were confronted with Jacky, Magda Raley's yellow lab, who was as overjoyed to see Lindbergh as Lindbergh was to see him. The two dogs ran alongside each other, barking and playfully snapping at each other, their breaths intertwining in their happiness.

Raleigh waited, but Magda did not make an appearance. Perhaps Jacky had made an unintended escape.

"This is the neighbor's dog," she told Salem. "I think he may have wandered off from her. We should probably see him home."

"But..." Salem glanced longingly down the front of the house. "What about the outbuildings?"

"We can come back right after. I'll introduce you to Magda, Jacky's owner."

"Weird name," Salem said, pulling her mittens out of her coat pocket and putting them back on. "How did you meet her?"

"I told you. She appeared when I first visited the house, remember?" Raleigh pulled out her own gloves. "She said she had met Grant but didn't seem to know as much about him as she did the rest of the Bishops." Raleigh rubbed her covered hands together. How much more frigid it was along the river than it was in town.

"Mutt Boy, come!" she commanded. Lindbergh loped up with Jacky close behind. Both seemed oblivious to the cold.

Raleigh bent down and scratched Jacky behind the ears. "Let's get you home. Do you know the way?"

Jacky wagged his tail and sat down.

Raleigh shook her head. "That's not very helpful. Let's go." She began walking away from the house. Salem joined her and in moments both dogs had raced in front of them, still unconcerned by the frozen ground beneath their paws.

Jacky seemed to figure out that it was time to go home. He put his nose down to the gravel as if sniffing for the right path. He apparently found it, as he started moving forward confidently off the gravel path and toward the woods located across the lawn on the left side of the house.

"I hope there are no crazy axe murderers out here," Salem said as their feet crunched dead leaves and fallen branches.

"I believe they fly south for the winter," Raleigh said, holding up a low-lying tree branch and pausing to let her sister pass under it.

Salem laughed and grabbed Raleigh's elbow. "Sisso! Did you just make a joke? There is hope for you yet."

Raleigh extricated herself from her sister's grasp and lowered the branch as she passed under it herself. Even though her sister's visit was an unwelcome surprise at first, Raleigh was feeling more whole already having Salem near.

As they trailed behind Jacky and Lindbergh, progressing further into the woods, Raleigh was grateful that it was winter, and thus the house behind them wasn't obscured by the thick foliage of summer. It would be easy to get turned around and lost in here.

Jacky made a right turn, and a path through the trees became apparent, despite the leaf-covered floor. It opened onto a one-story, yellow clapboard cottage with trees growing nearly up to the front door.

The cottage itself wasn't completely dilapidated, although the roof shingles were moss-covered, a couple of red window shutters were missing, and the quaint, white-railed front porch running along the front of the house was in serious need of paint. An old, rusted Toyota truck sat in the driveway.

However, none of this held any importance compared to what Raleigh saw on the front porch. In one of the several rocking chairs that were haphazardly placed along the porch was Magda Raley, slumped over and unmoving.

CHAPTER 12

RALEIGH BARELY HEARD Salem ask, "Is that Jacky's owner?"

Racing and practically leaping up the three steps to the front porch, Raleigh knelt next to her neighbor. Magda's head lolled backward against the chair and her mouth hung open in an awkward grimace.

Raleigh placed a hand over Magda's. The woman was still warm to the touch despite the cold, so she couldn't have been gone long.

Salem had also hopped up the steps and was peering over Raleigh's shoulder. "What do you think happened? A heart attack? A stroke? I hope someone didn't do this to her!"

With a hand still on Magda, Raleigh turned her head back to her sister. "What in heaven's name could this poor woman have done to someone else to have caused *this*?"

Salem was gazing anxiously at Magda's body. "I don't know. Maybe she knew something spooky about St. Clements Bluff."

"'Spooky?' Seriously?" Raleigh said. But she was becoming unnerved herself. She had never been this close to a fresh corpse before and although she thought about looking for a pulse, she couldn't bring herself to it. Even with Grant, his body had been located by search and rescue crews and spirited off to the funeral home before his commanding officer had come to their home to deliver the blow. The funeral director had recommended a closed casket and she had acquiesced to that, and every other suggestion made to her at the time, which saved her from having to think about what was happening.

But now Raleigh was alert and focused on the deceased person before her. There was no blood anywhere, nor did Magda seem bruised or beaten.

Salem's suggestion of a heart attack seemed as good a guess as anything, although Magda had seemed so robust when Raleigh had met her just a few days ago.

What else did the detectives in the procedural crime television shows look for when solving their tidy little mysteries? Wasn't there always some subtle clue at the scene that the detective picked up on that revealed whether a death was suspicious?

But other than the rocking chairs, there was nothing else on the front porch. Perhaps if they had gotten here earlier, Magda's death could have somehow been prevented.

"Sisso, we need to call the cops, pronto," Salem urged. "They need to take care of this, and soon. The longer we wait, the more it will look like you might have had something to do with it." Salem turned and went down the steps, walking until she was at the base of the walking path again.

Raleigh quit watching her sister's retreat and looked once more at her gruff neighbor, wondering if they might have eventually become friends.

"I wish I'd noticed Jacky sooner," Raleigh murmured, reaching up with her free hand to brush some of Magda's hair away from her face. "If I had, and we had walked over earlier, maybe I—"

At that moment, Magda emitted a great *wooooosh* from her mouth and her eyes flew open, although she seemed to stare at nothing.

Raleigh fell backward onto the porch, emitting an

embarrassing squeak of terror. She remained frozen, unsure what had happened. Is this what the dead did?

From somewhere behind her in the yard, Salem also shrieked and then began mumbling, "Oh my God, Oh. My. God. Oh my God."

Ignoring her sister's babbling, Raleigh slowly got to her feet. With her heart pounding mercilessly, she again approached Magda, whose eyes were closed again. Raleigh tentatively bent over and brushed at Magda's hair again. She had the strangest emotion welling up in her, sort of a ball of light and strength that she hadn't known in a long time. The two combined into a great desire to protect and care for Magda in death in a way she hadn't been able to do for Grant.

"I realize I didn't know you," she whispered. "But I am indeed sorry for—»

A hand grasped Raleigh's wrist. "What do you think you're doing?"

The voice was Magda's, raspy and demanding.

Raleigh tried scrabbling away again, but Magda held her tightly. "What is the meaning of you disturbing my nap?"

"You're napping outdoors in the middle of the winter?" Raleigh asked.

But Magda ignored Raleigh, looking past her to where Salem stood.

"Jacky?" Magda called.

The dog came loping up to the porch and Magda released Raleigh, who was fairly certain the thumping in her chest could be detected from several miles away.

"Hey, boy," Magda said, reaching down to pat her dog on the neck. Jacky sat down and thumped his tail. Lindbergh, who seemingly had no interest in Jacky once he went off to his owner, was sniffing the ground near Salem, who was rooted to one spot with her mouth hanging open. Raleigh had to close her own mouth, as well. She put a hand to her chest, as if doing so would somehow stop it from pounding uncontrollably.

Once she was done with the dog, Magda lumbered up from her chair. "I suppose you came by and thought I was dead," she said.

Raleigh nodded. "I'm surprised that you aren't. But quite relieved," she added quickly.

Magda stepped heavily down from the porch. "You're not the first one to catch me in a deep nap."

Deep nap? Why couldn't they see her breathing? Maybe this was what narcolepsy looked like. Raleigh was still unnerved but squared her shoulders and followed Magda off the porch.

"Who's this?" Magda pointed at Salem and peered at Raleigh's sister as though she were a hairy insect to be inspected.

Raleigh introduced the two women. Salem said, "Hiya," and stuck out a hand toward the older woman, who sniffed once and reluctantly took the proffered hand for a moment before stepping away.

"So, what brings you both here? Did Lindbergh run off to find Jacky?" Magda asked.

Raleigh shook her head. "The opposite. I found Jacky in the yard and followed him home."

Magda was still looking at Salem with a look of suspicion on her face. "Well, you may as well come in."

Raleigh, Salem, and the dogs followed Magda into her cottage, which was simply but neatly furnished in a style at least forty years out of date. The heavy smell of spices hung in the air, the by-product of some recent cooking spree. Raleigh detected notes of Old Bay crab seasoning and something smoky. Paprika, perhaps?

Magda led them through her small living room into a narrow galley kitchen with yellowed cabinets and appliances. An old, enameled cast-iron sink held a stack of dirty, mismatched dishes. The kitchen connected the living room to a sunroom with floor-to-ceiling louvered windows along two walls. The windows were sealed shut.

The third wall was brick and featured a Franklin-style wood stove on a raised hearth. This room was cozy-warm despite the wall of glass. Magda invited them to sit down on an old burgundy floral couch while she took an olive tweed recliner with a lamp table next to it and Lindbergh and Jack extended themselves on the linoleum near the stove. On the lamp table was a round tray with a bottle of sherry and several small stem glasses on it.

Magda uncorked the wine and started pouring. She held up one of the glasses in inquiry. Salem nodded in agreement for both of them. Raleigh accepted her glass, surreptitiously twisting the stem in her hand so that she did not bring the chipped part of the rim to her lips.

She grimaced at the taste. The sherry had turned and now resembled something akin to vinegar. By the expression on Salem's face, it would seem that she, too, was underwhelmed by the drink.

"How is it?" Magda asked, pulling a frayed throw pillow from behind her back and tossing it on the floor.

"Just fine. Thank you for your hospitality," Raleigh said, wondering if there was a houseplant nearby that wouldn't shrivel up too much if she watered it with the contents of her glass. There was nothing, so she tamped down her revulsion and took another sip.

Raleigh decided to broach the topic of the furnished room at St. Clements Bluff. "While we're here, I was wondering if I could ask you a question about my house."

Magda set her half-consumed glass down on the tray and settled back in her chair, her fingers laced across her stomach. "Sure. Shoot."

"There is a bedroom on the third floor of St. Clements Bluff that is…odd," Raleigh began. "Maybe you know something about it."

"Not just odd," Salem volunteered. "Downright spooky."

Magda ignored Salem and kept her attention on Raleigh. "You got a spirit or something living there? I told ya Old Man Billy was a mean old cuss, so if anyone was planning to come back to haunt a house, it would be him."

Raleigh shook her head. "Nothing like that. It's just that, well, while the rest of the house is empty—as you yourself saw—this particular room is beautiful. Draperies, wallpaper, oriental carpets, and fine old carved furniture. It's nothing like the rest of the house." Deciding to risk seeming ungrateful for the drink, Raleigh set it down on a table at the end of the couch.

Magda seemed to take no notice but instead leaned forward, her hands on the arm ends of her chair. "Maybe your man was fixing the house up to surprise you with it one day soon. And that was the intended bridal suite." Magda winked exaggeratedly at Raleigh.

Raleigh sat up straight at this suggestion; that was what her in-laws had suggested to her. Could that be what Grant was doing with the place? Preparing it as an eventual surprise to her, knowing how much she loved history and might appreciate an old home. Maybe he had done work to collect the old pieces of Jonson furniture and bring them together in the room.

Still, it seemed as though Grant's way would be to present her with the house to let Raleigh fix it to her heart's content. She mentally dismissed Magda's idea.

"Perhaps," she said to the woman. "But there's more. My sister observed a space that seems to exist in the wall behind the fireplace. I read an old *St. Mary's Beacon* article indicating that St. Clements Bluff was a stop on the Underground Railroad. Maybe it's an old hiding spot for escaping slaves?"

Magda became thoughtful. "I remember Old Man Billy once saying that there were secret places in the house. Wait, or did he say that he owned many secret houses? Maybe I don't remember so good—it was a long time ago." Magda wrinkled her nose and looked upward, as if trying to pull the thought down from above. Finally, she shrugged. "Whatever it is, it is from before Old Man Billy's time, because he surely would not have done anything to help anyone. I guess the Underground Railroad would have pre-dated him, anyway."

Magda's words sparked a thought for Raleigh. "But it could have been Old Man Billy who enclosed the space, right?"

Magda's expression was a mixture of pity and curiosity. "Maybe. Or perhaps you've got an old house that has had walls torn out lotsa times. You might just have yourself a servants' staircase behind the fireplace that goes down to an old kitchen in the basement. Tho' it's way too low here for there to be a basement. It'd be awash with every tide."

Except it wasn't. "No, there's a storm cellar under the house. We explored it earlier and found what seemed to be a secret little room behind a wall panel," Raleigh said.

"Are you sure?" Magda asked doubtfully. "It might just be a dry storage pantry."

Salem stood. "We should have a look at the fireplace again. Now," she insisted.

Magda rose heavily as well. "I'd like to see it myself," she said.

She looked down at Jacky, whose tongue lolled to one side as he snored next to the wood stove. "Don't be troubled boy, we'll be back shortly." She grabbed a thick glove hanging on a wall hook near the stove, grabbed the metal handle on the front of the stove, and swung it open. "Eh, just embers. It will be fine. Let's go."

Their impending departure seemed to have no effect on Jacky, but Lindbergh opened an eye and dragged himself yawning to his feet. He snuffled over to Jacky and bit the other dog gently on the ear. Soon three women with flashlights, mallets, and two dogs were making their way back through the woods to the house and its mysterious fireplace.

Salem sneezed again once they were inside, but it was far less explosive than what had happened down in the cellar.

"Allergic to the county, are you?" Magda observed as they all went upstairs. "You'll be happy when you go home, I'm sure."

Raleigh avoided looking at her sister, knowing that Salem's expression would be one of disbelief at the other woman's comment.

"Here we are," Raleigh said brightly as she opened the door to the bedchamber, letting the other two women in to have a look.

"We have to tear the wall out," Magda said, her arms crossed as she stood at the fireplace, her mallet resting on her arms. "No choice if you want to know what's going on behind here."

Salem gave Raleigh an I-told-you-so look. Giving up, Raleigh gave them permission to do what they needed to do.

Fortunately, they had left the dogs playing together outside so they wouldn't interfere with the work being done. Presumably, they would generally stay put and not wander back to Magda's. Or anywhere else.

While Magda and Salem busied themselves with walloping the wall with their implements, Raleigh removed herself and stood in front of the fireplace and its strangely stacked mantel. Why would anyone have created a mantel so thick and deep with so many wood layers to it? It made no sense.

Maybe it was made from old cabinet boards stacked one on top of the other. Perhaps the number of boards was symbolic, much like numbers in the Bible. If this had been a stop on the Underground Railroad, perhaps the number of boards provided travelers with some sort of information.

Raleigh cocked her head to one side, her heart pounding with a new thought. Maybe the boards were actually removable. If she could slide them off individually, she might find that each board had some sort of story to tell.

Raleigh approached the mantel, which had been painted multiple times in the way that was common in old houses. She attempted to insert a fingernail in between the top two boards. The layers of paint eventually gave way, and she was able to run her nail across for several inches.

She needed a knife or flat-head screwdriver to really get in there.

Before she could ask Magda if she could borrow an implement, the other two women shouted in triumph. "We're in!" Salem said excitedly.

Raleigh abandoned the mantel to see what they had done. Plaster bits and scraps of wood lathe lay at their feet as the older and younger woman lifted their flashlights to peer into the space.

"Holy crap, Sisso," Salem said. "There *is* a staircase here."

Raleigh looked over their shoulders. An impossibly narrow staircase began about three feet behind the edge of the fireplace and reached down into inky blackness.

"Alrighty then. Who's first?" Magda asked.

Salem's only reaction was to shiver and say, "Spiders."

Magda nodded. "Looks like I'm to clear the way."

"I'm right behind you," Salem assured her, which only earned her an eye roll from Magda.

Raleigh pulled up the rear. As she entered the confined space, she cast her flashlight around the wood lathing that remained as well as on the ceiling. The space was surprisingly warm. There were plenty of cobwebs and old, unidentifiable nests in between the thin wood slats. Raleigh paused and sniffed the air as Magda and Salem muttered their way down the stairs about the dangers of life in previous centuries. It was musty, as was to be expected, yet there was also a hint of something else. It was almost as if Raleigh could smell the terror experienced by whoever had journeyed behind the fireplace. She stood transfixed for several moments as she breathed deeply of the past.

Salem called up, breaking Raleigh out of her reverie. "Sisso, get down here! You won't believe it!" Her voice came from a great distance.

Raleigh made her way down the stairs, feeling her way along a wall and sweeping the flashlight beam back and forth to illuminate her path. The narrow set of steps was uneven and went on and on. She imagined she was making her way down two stories.

Eventually, though, the air became warmer. Was she below ground?

At the bottom, Salem waited excitedly for her, while Magda was nowhere to be seen inside what seemed to be just a large, dark closet containing nothing but a simple pew bench.

"Look!" Salem said, swinging her flashlight beam. Raleigh swung her own in the same direction. Illuminated before her was a narrow opening about five feet high and the width of the staircase.

"Magda's already gone in to see where it leads. I swear, I'm starting to feel like a junior detective! Let's go." Salem cast her light into the tunnel and stepped in. Raleigh swept the walls with her beam to see if there were any treasures hidden along these walls, but they were all just packed earth.

Salem's voice floated back to her. "Light up ahead. Can you believe this thing? We're almost out to—ack! What's this?"

Raleigh almost stumbled into her sister, who had stopped suddenly in the passageway. It only took a moment to realize why Salem had stopped. They stood in a couple of inches of water. It wasn't frozen but was cold enough to remind Raleigh of the bay, which was undoubtedly where the water had come from.

"I think I have frostbite," Salem groused, lifting one gold-buckled leather boot and then another before taking tentative steps forward again. "I am going to be so mad if these things are ruined. They are definitely not waterproof."

Raleigh's mind was decidedly not moving tentatively but was instead racing. This tunnel was headed toward the bay. Images of pirates and smuggling ships were popping into her head. Maybe St. Clements Bluff had had multiple lives. A smuggler's den, an Underground Railroad stop…and now a candidate for a haunted mystery novel.

Her imagination of St. Clements Bluff's past dissipated as they came to the end of the tunnel, where Magda was grunting as she climbed straight up an old metal ladder.

Salem climbed up behind Magda and Raleigh pulled up the rear, thinking as she did so that it was strange that the ladder was metal, not wood. Did metal ladders exist in the mid-1800s? Something else to research.

Magda grunted from above them and Raleigh heard a great thump, as of wood against wood.

"Hah!" Magda exclaimed as she disappeared off the ladder.

In moments, Raleigh and Salem had joined her. "What is this?" Salem asked, looking around. They were in a small, octagonal building with a creaky wood floor. In reality, it was just a room, perhaps twelve feet in diameter. They had entered along the edge of one wall, and a cut-out section of the floor that Magda must have thrust into the room lay next to that opening.

The walls had actually been plastered at some point, but now it was cracked, peeling, and in some areas the plaster was gone altogether, exposing the wood lathing behind it.

There were no windows, but natural light filtered down to them through the ceiling. Raleigh swept her flashlight upward, showing that the ceiling tapered upward into a hole. It reminded Raleigh of the old medieval huts that contained such ceilings to enable fires to be lit in the center of them by having the smoke drift upward.

However, this hut's previous use was evident by a wall of old rakes and shovels hanging from randomly placed iron hooks on one section of the octagon.

"Just a gardener's shed," Magda observed. "Except someone went to the trouble of putting up real walls."

Salem shook her head. "It can't be just a gardener's shed. Why would it connect to the bedroom?"

Raleigh glanced back up at the opening above them, which she estimated about fifteen feet up, then back down at the section of flooring that had been pushed aside. "I think this may have been both the gardener's shed and a hideout."

"So, the gardeners would have been in on the secret?" Magda asked.

"That or this was simply meant to look like a gardener's shed," Raleigh mused. "Slave catchers probably wouldn't think much of this little building."

Salem frowned and crossed her arms. "What I think is

that I'm cold and there seems to be no way out of here except for back down into the tunnel."

Raleigh glanced around again. Salem was right, there was no obvious exit. Except…

She went to the wall of the octagon where the tools were hung in a haphazard manner. She could see a thin vertical slit in the wall, running from the floor to a point just about three feet off the floor. This part of the plastered wall was in better condition than everywhere else, likely because the old tools afforded some protection from the elements.

Kneeling down and pushing aside some of the tools, it became apparent that the top of the slit made a left turn down to a certain point where there was what looked like very cleverly constructed hinges.

"Eww," Salem said from behind her. "There could be black widows hiding back there. Don't get bitten by a black widow."

Magda seemed to understand what Raleigh had discovered, for she began removing implements from their hooks and tossing them aside.

If there had been a handle on the wall, it was long ago lost. Raleigh tried pushing against this section of wall. It didn't budge. Perhaps it was meant to swing inward, but there was nowhere to grab.

Maybe she should just try tearing out plaster here to get a grip on the wood slats behind it so that she could pull this hidden door open.

Raleigh discarded the idea, deciding instead to keep pushing on it first. Using both palms against the wall, she thrust against it as hard as she could given her awkward positioning.

It didn't budge.

She tried again with no result. Perhaps there was just too much overgrown foliage on the other side of it.

Magda knelt next to her and wordlessly put her palms

against the wall next to Raleigh's. Together they shoved against the old wall. The sound of a splintering crack filled the small space, and the section of wall gave way.

With a little more effort, Raleigh was able to fully extend the old door outward. Feeling foolish, she crawled outside on all fours with Magda and Salem following close behind.

Raleigh rose and massaged smarting palms together while waiting for the other two women to emerge as ungracefully as she had.

Looking around, she realized that they were actually in a section of woods between the rear of the house and the water and that the small structure was hidden behind a small berm in the landscape. Not an ideal location for a gardener's shed, but who knew what the grounds looked like back then? Perhaps it had been farmland.

Salem's expression suggested that the excitement of discovery had worn off and she was not happy to be standing among the broken branches and brambles, but Raleigh ignored her as she stepped completely around the shed. From the exterior, she could see that there had once been a regular door in one of the sides that faced the house, but it had long ago been sealed up.

Her imagination ran wild with how this building must have been part of slave escape operations. Escapees must have come to the house for rest and to be victualed for their trip, then sent through the tunnel and through the shed to wait for the boats that would take them from St. Clements Bay to the Potomac River and eventual freedom.

Raleigh felt the stirrings of excitement, a feeling that had been suppressed for so long that it seemed to cause tremors in her.

If what she imagined were true, this property should be placed on the National Register and opened to the public so that future generations could be witness to the bravery of the escaped slaves and those who helped them. Didn't that newspaper article discuss various buildings on the grounds being part of the underground system? They needed exploration. Raleigh needed to talk to Bert Mattingly, her boss at the museum, to see whom they could get to do a dig at St. Clements Bluff to discover any other existing tunnels and building foundations, thus establishing exactly how the property had been used. There could be maps made and busloads of schoolchildren and history enthusiasts could make their way—

"Sisso, where are you?" Salem interrupted her thoughts. Raleigh's sister had slipped her mittens back on and was stamping her feet. "Let's go find some hot coffee and come back tomorrow. I think it's supposed to be a little warmer tomorrow."

Magda contradicted Salem. "I can see this interests you. Let's walk the grounds now." She shot a poisonous glance at Salem, who seemed bewildered by it.

Why had Magda so quickly formed an ill opinion of Salem?

Raleigh chose the middle ground between the two women. "I could definitely use some coffee. Why don't we head to the Leonardtown Cafe for takeout cups and then come straight back?"

Salem clapped her hands together and they made a muffled sound beneath the knitted fabric. "Works for me."

Jacky and Lindbergh came loping up happily, skittering in the dead leaves as they stopped before the women. "Hey, Jacky Boy," Magda said. "Why don't we go home and get back to our wood stove?"

Jacky wagged his tail and scampered off again. Lindbergh ran next to him and attempted to chew his ear while running.

"You two go on. You don't need me slowing you down," Magda said.

Raleigh wasn't sure whether she should just accept Magda's bowing out of their little adventure or if she should convince the older woman to stay with them. Salem started walking toward the house, so Raleigh went back to the opening in the shed to close the cracked door as best she could.

Magda once more bent down to help and they quickly had the wall looking more or less like it had before. Magda rose again, placing a hand against the shed's wall for support as she did so. "You don't need me for the rest of this. I'm going to go have a little nap."

"Magda, is something wrong? Have we offended you somehow?" Raleigh asked. "You seem out of sorts."

"Nah. Sometimes I get a little sensitive. Oh, I don't mean like my feelings get hurt." Magda began walking toward the house, and Raleigh fell in step with her. "No, I mean that I get annoyed with people who are rude, especially when they aren't from the county and think they're better than the locals," she said, casting a glance at Salem's retreating back.

CHAPTER 13

ONCE RALEIGH AND Salem got to the coffee shop, their plans changed again. Salem had noticed a day spa on their drive through town and insisted that they go for pedicures after picking up coffee.

Now fully topped off with a French Roast shot with a little hot milk and some caramel flavoring at Salem's insistence that she try something new, Raleigh sat in a pedicure chair in the Spa Company shop. Oddly, the half-dozen luxury chairs were located in the shop's front window where passers-by could glance in and watch people's toenails being clipped, buffed, and polished.

However, the foamy water in which she and Salem had sunk their feet was gloriously hot after so much time outside, causing Raleigh to not even mind that they had abruptly ceased their exploration of St. Clements Bluff.

She lay against the headrest, allowing the chair's massage rollers to knead into her back while an aesthetician named Sandi worked on her feet. Raleigh suppressed a moan of pleasure.

"So," came Salem's voice from next to her, causing Raleigh to unwillingly open her eyes to listen to her sister. "I was thinking about something you said last night," Salem said, lifting her lidded cup with *Coffee Counts As Breakfast!* imprinted on the side of it. Raleigh's cup assured her that *Not Drinking Enough Coffee Can Cause A Latte Problems.*

Salem took a sip of her mocha and put the cup back

down. "You said that this bearded man, Kit, rescued you from the water."

"Kip," Raleigh corrected. "For Rudyard Kipling. His mother is from the same newborn naming school as ours."

"Kip, Kit, whatever. So, this hairy-faced waterman just happened to come along as you were flailing in the water the other day and possibly drowning. That was terribly convenient, wasn't it? Maybe he was pushing you under. Ahhh," she added as the nail tech apparently worked magic on Salem's feet.

Raleigh hadn't confessed that she had made a half-hearted attempt to drown herself, instead merely telling her sister that she had been at the water's edge, suddenly slipping and finding herself beneath the surface.

"Maybe," she said, hoping the doubt was evident in her voice. "However, if he was trying to push me under, why would he then rescue me?"

Salem held up a hand to tick off the reasons. "Guilt. Fear of getting caught. Remembering that he had to take his mother to a doctor's appointment."

"But what reason would he have to kill me?" Raleigh asked, even though she had speculated the same thing when she worried about him walking her to the house. "I am a complete and utter stranger to him. You think he was trolling the frigid waters of the bay looking for a victim? That's ridiculous."

Salem contemplated Raleigh's response and ventured another opinion. "Maybe he's a fisherman by day but at night he goes into town looking for victims. You just happened to be a convenient 'catch' while he was out."

The aesthetician, who thankfully wore earbuds and was paying no attention to the sisters' conversation, finished scrubbing and rinsing Raleigh's feet and flipped a lever to let water drain from the bowl.

"I guess that's possible, but it seems like a stretch, doesn't it?" Raleigh said.

"How old is he?" Salem asked, changing directions.

Raleigh shook her head then emitted a soft "oooh" as Sandi began massaging her calves. "I don't know. It was hard to tell beneath the beard and layers of clothes. Somewhere between thirty and seventy is my guess."

Salem rolled her eyes. "Now you're just being ridiculous. So, either he's a vicious young killer or a crazy old man."

Raleigh stared at her sister. "Or most likely he's neither. What has you so worked up with this idea?"

"Because believe it or not, I'm concerned about you. You aren't yourself, and I don't think you would recognize ill intent around you. Take that Magda Raley. Now there's an odd character if I ever saw one. I bet she would beat you to death for accidentally forgetting to switch off an overhead light."

Raleigh felt her feathers ruffle. "Salem, stop. Magda is just a local who might be set in her ways. She's harmless and I suspect she has a heart of gold." Raleigh recalled Magda roughly grabbing her in a bear hug after hearing about Grant.

Salem jumped once more to her previous track. "I think I'd like to meet this Kip character," Salem said. "If he lives anywhere near you and is some potential serial killer, we need to know."

Raleigh could still feel Kip Hewitt's blanket around her shoulders as he walked her to the house. "He was very polite."

More eye rolling. "So was Ted Bundy. I'm serious, Sisso. I need to know that you're safe living here, especially if you might move over to St. Clements Bluff. We need to find this guy."

Raleigh couldn't think of anything she wanted to do

less. "I don't really know where he lives," she lied. "I'll just avoid the water if that makes you feel better."

"Except that *he* knows where *you* live, right?" Salem picked up her coffee cup and tipped it to her mouth, finishing off the contents. "Well," she declared, tossing the cup over to an open garbage can and hitting it square in the middle of the bin. "If you don't want to clear his name, so to speak, I think I will have to extend my visit to protect you."

Raleigh immediately agreed to look for Kip Hewitt.

THE NEXT MORNING, Raleigh drove Salem back to St. Clements Bluff. Lindbergh panted and paced in the rear of the SUV the entire ride to the estate.

In the car, Salem made Raleigh swear solemnly that she would look for "this Kip character." Raleigh did so in hopes the subject could soon be over.

First, though, Raleigh insisted they finish inspecting the grounds of the house.

As Salem indicated, the day was warmer than the previous one, even hinting at spring around the corner. They wore light jackets but left their gloves stuffed in their pockets, which made carrying flashlights much easier.

Lindbergh leaped happily out of the vehicle and sniffed around on the ground. He seemed to realize quickly that he wouldn't have Jacky's company today and resigned himself to staying near Raleigh.

Raleigh and Salem headed back around the house onto the rear grounds once more. They spent a couple of hours poking around in outbuildings, flashing their lights into as many crevices and openings as they could. Some buildings were collapsing, some were in surprisingly good condition. None of them seemed to be anything other than what they obviously were: a smokehouse that still smelled faintly like hickory wood and had enormous hooks dangling from the ceiling, an icehouse evident by its partially submerged structure with an A-frame roof, a long saltbox-style poultry house, and so on. They even found remnants of an old outhouse.

Raleigh had seen enough slave cabins from plantation tours to recognize them when she stumbled upon a cluster of four shacks in a row that were in remarkably good shape. She and Salem went through all of the one-room buildings, each of which contained a brick fireplace on one wall and a ladder up to a small loft on the opposite wall. There was no evidence of secret doors, tunnels, or hiding spaces in any of them.

"So just the one outbuilding was involved in the Underground Railroad," Raleigh observed, switching off her flashlight as they walked back to the main house. "I guess that kept everything as inconspicuous as possible."

Salem nodded, also turning hers off. It took several moments for their eyesight to adjust from the dim interior. "Escapees had a single route to remember. Of course, if the slave catchers had discovered that one path through the gardener's shed, the whole gig would have been up. There wouldn't have been any other paths to follow."

"The home's owners would likely have been arrested and the estate sealed off," Raleigh said. "Additional routes out probably wouldn't have mattered."

"Hmm, maybe you're right," Salem said as they made it to the front of the house. "Hey, what's this?"

Standing in the driveway was a strange man who had a tight grip on Lindbergh's collar and was talking earnestly to Raleigh's dog.

CHAPTER 14

RALEIGH WAS INCENSED. With her brain settling into white-hot anger, she marched over to the stranger. "What the hell do you think you're doing?" she demanded. Her outburst startled the stranger enough that he released Lindbergh, who licked the man's now-empty hand and padded happily over to Raleigh as though nothing had happened.

"Oh, hi," the man said. He flashed Raleigh a smile that was somehow both warm and aloof at the same time. He wore a khaki-colored baseball cap with a crab embroidered in a Maryland state flag pattern on the front panel. That cap-covered dark hair that curled at the nape of his neck and framed a familiar face containing twinkling eyes edged in laugh lines. Blue jeans, an untucked black and navy buffalo check flannel shirt, and well-worn work boots completed him. Behind him was an old Mustang convertible, an incongruous accessory for someone who looked like he should be in an old Chevy pickup.

Raleigh tilted her head to one side, not quite believing whom she thought stood before her. Was this man actually—?

Salem walked right up to him and stuck out her free hand. "Hi. I'm Salem Moore. Visiting my sister here in St. Mary's County. You live around here?"

"Sorta," the man replied noncommittally as he briefly grasped Salem's hand. "Down a-ways. Off Herring Creek in Tall Timbers."

He had undergone a total transformation. Gone were the full beard and layers of rough outdoor clothing. Standing before her was someone…normal.

Salem had a particular way of flashing nearly all of her teeth in a winsome expression that took full advantage of her dimples. Men were powerless to resist her when she did it. She turned this charm on the man that Raleigh had realized was Kip Hewitt.

"What are you doing here?" Raleigh asked, keeping a hand on Lindbergh and stroking his ears to prevent anyone from noticing that she was shaking. Kip Hewitt had been a witness to her doing something she now completely regretted, and Raleigh was mortified over it.

"Just thought I'd see how you were doing," Kip said. When Raleigh didn't respond, he added, "You know, after the—" He gestured toward the bay.

As he pointed, Lindbergh broke away from Raleigh and went back to Kip, jumping up to his outstretched hand and licking it again.

Kip's laugh lines deepened as he turned his attention to the dog. "You smell the rockfish I was gutting this morning, huh, big man?"

Raleigh roiled with multiple emotions. Watching Lindbergh react so joyfully to another man made her miss Grant. But Lindbergh had clearly put his slobber of approval on this Kip Hewitt, and that made Raleigh a little happy.

Longing, happiness, nausea—Raleigh squared her shoulders and shook it all off. After all, Salem no longer seemed suspicious of Kip Hewitt at all. In fact, Salem was blasting the man with a gust of charm that Raleigh knew few had ever withstood.

"My sister was widowed and inherited this house. It's full of amazing secrets we are investigating. There's even a secret staircase, just like in a Nancy Drew story," Salem said, placing a hand on Kip's flannel-sleeved arm and chattering on about their finds in the upstairs bedchamber as well as the tunnel and shed.

Ignoring the flirt, Kip flashed Raleigh a look of sympathy, which only made her feel worse.

"We could sure use some strong male help in moving furniture and exploring the upstairs. Interested in helping a couple of damsels in their distress?" Salem winked at him.

Without moving his gaze from Raleigh, Kip nodded. "I'm always ready to help those in need. A secret staircase, you say?"

Salem tucked her hand into Kip's tucked elbow and led him to the house while Raleigh followed behind with Lindbergh, feeling like an intruder upon the little scenario Salem was creating.

They walked through the empty downstairs living areas and the antiquated kitchen, then walked upstairs. The moment her foot touched the top step of the staircase, Raleigh heard the sound of gravel crunching outside, signaling that someone had entered the driveway.

She left Salem and Kip to go through the second floor and headed downstairs. The traitorous Lindbergh didn't move from Kip's side. Raleigh shook her head at the dog's perfidy as she reached the ground floor and opened the front door.

Standing there with a fist poised over the door was Derrick Jonson.

"Mr. Jonson," Raleigh said in surprise. "Please, come in."

"Mrs. Bishop," Jonson said, pulling folded papers from his jacket as he removed his leather coat, revealing that he wore a thick ivory-colored cable-knit sweater. He followed Raleigh into the house where she took the chocolate-colored coat and draped it on the staircase newel.

"Thought I'd stop by and give you these." He offered Raleigh the papers. "Dug through Pop's stuff and found them in an old McCormick's pickling spice tin he had."

Raleigh placed her flashlight on the bottom stair and unfolded the brittle, yellowed pages. They appeared to be bills of sale. She motioned him to follow her to the kitchen, where she spread them out on the Formica counter.

They were old bills of sale, their dates ranging from the 1820s to the turn of the 20th century. They were for various suites of furniture, but all were billed to people named Bishop. Jeremiah Bishop, Barton Bishop, Paps Bishop, and Boots Bishop.

Jonson tapped the Boots Bishop invoice with a roughened, nail-chewed forefinger. "Believe this Bishop was a member of the Second District Bishops. Dad says they were the Baloney Bishops. Always involved in some con game or other. Made a lot of money."

This was the second time Raleigh had heard that term. "What's a 'Second District Bishop?'" she asked.

"Someone from the second voting district in the county. I guess you haven't been here very long." Jonson said this as an observation, not a criticism.

Raleigh smiled. "So not a part of the 'rough-n-tumble' Bishops?"

Jonson didn't seem to get the joke. "No," he said flatly. "Boots here ordered a fifteen-foot-long dining table and twelve chairs. Either the man had a lot of parties or a lot of young 'uns."

Raleigh looked at the bill of sale. Apparently, the Bishop-Jonson relationship went way back.

Raleigh heard Kip and Salem come downstairs, with Salem chattering vivaciously as they entered the kitchen.

"So, this is what's keeping you down here," Salem exclaimed, looking back and forth between Raleigh and Derrick Jonson in curiosity. "I didn't even have a chance to show Kip the secret staircase before I heard another voice down here."

Raleigh made introductions, adding to Salem, "Remember I told you I had found the furniture makers who created the furniture upstairs? Mr. Jonson is part of that family."

"Please call me Derrick," he said. "Only my dad is called 'Mr. Jonson' at the shop."

He gestured toward the papers again. "Anyway, thought you might like these as part of your family records. Besides, my father doesn't need to keep every single piece of paper drafted since the company was founded. I can give you boxes of documents if you want them." Derrick flashed a smile. Now he was the one making a joke.

Raleigh thanked him and briefly explained the discoveries she had made on the property. She finished by asking if he would like to see the secret staircase entrance.

With Derrick's enthusiastic assent, she led the group back upstairs, remembering to grab her flashlight on the way up. Lindbergh was laid out in the space that would have held a mattress, as though he didn't realize he wasn't actually on a bed. He opened an eye at the intrusion and went back to sleep.

He is very comfortable in this place, she thought. *If only he could tell me its secrets.*

As Salem gushed over the opening behind the fireplace with the two men looking on, Raleigh stepped back, again examining the front of the hearth. There was something about it that bothered her. That clunky, thick mantelpiece wasn't in keeping with the ornately carved furniture. They were likely from vastly different eras, but why would that awkwardly stacked mantel have ever even been constructed in such a beautiful home, no matter the era?

She put a finger to her lips, studying, then approached the mantel once more and touched it, as if it might transmit a message to her if she did so.

It didn't.

When Salem suggested they all head down the secret stairs and through the tunnel, Raleigh demurred, wishing to remain privately with the puzzle of the mantel. Maybe later she would show it to Derrick to see what he thought.

As the others' voices slowly faded away, Raleigh contemplated the block of wood further. Did other mantels in the house look like this? An excellent question.

She walked out of the room and quickly assessed the rooms located everywhere else in the house. On all of the other fireplaces, which totaled nine by her count, mantels were either missing or were styled in the typical fashions of previous centuries. Some had corbels attached to the wall on either end for support, others had more elaborate legs connecting the mantel to the hearth.

None of them had the strangely stacked mantel with no visible means of support.

Raleigh returned to the bedroom and went to the window to check on where Salem and the men were. They had not yet made it outside. However, standing here confirmed that the gardener's shed itself was not visible from the house, given that she was at the highest point of St. Clements Bluff and had the best view of the property's rear.

With that piece of information tucked away, she went back to the mantel and placed a hand against the front of it. Maybe the mantel somehow signified to those looking for it that there was a secret staircase behind it. But a large mantel like this had to be well-anchored into the wall, didn't it?

Hmmm. Raleigh went to the stairway opening and trained her flashlight on the wall behind the fireplace. She hadn't noticed in her previous quick assessment that there were vertical iron pieces roughly a foot long each running along the length of the wall. The plaster was still fairly good here, perhaps because the iron straps had held it together.

She clicked off the flashlight and went back out to the fireplace. That answered how the mantel was being supported, but why was it so different?

She suddenly had an idea. Scurrying down the interior stairs and going outside, she opened the passenger door of Derrick's truck. As hoped, there was a toolbox on the passenger seat floor. She pulled it to the ground, grunting at the weight of it. Unlatching the hasp on the front of it, she pulled open the lid. A stack of cantilevered trays opened out with the lid.

Raleigh nodded and searched for the largest flat-head screwdriver she could find, tucking it into the back pocket of her jeans and racing back into the house.

Once more in front of the mantel, she did something that was unthinkable just yesterday. Gripping the screwdriver handle with one hand, she wedged the tip in between two of the apparent wood layers and attempted to create an opening.

Layers of paint and age were not cooperative with what she was attempting, but Raleigh kept at it, moving the screwdriver tip down along the various horizontal lines of the stacked mantel and jamming it in where she could, and twisting it. Paint chips dropped everywhere.

Eventually, she heard faint cracking as the wood layers began separating. With that encouragement, she worked more furiously at releasing the layers.

Once she had decided the screwdriver had provided as much service as it could, Raleigh tossed it to the floor.

"OK," she said to the mantel. "Show me what you've got."

She got as good a grip as possible at the top of the mantel and started tugging on it. It was very resistant as Raleigh continuously pulled and found different gripping points in an effort to remove the top layer of wood. She had just started to think she might need the others to help her when the mantel moved, nearly sending her flying backward.

She kept her balance, though, and continued gently pulling the ledge toward her. The top ledge was followed by the second ledge staggered beneath it and then the next and the next.

Raleigh's jaw dropped in amazement that her guess was correct. The mantel opened toward her in the manner of a toolbox with cantilevered drawers. It was almost like a magical staircase pulling toward her, except instead of stairs they were shallow boxes.

Those boxes were full of old items. Mostly folded-up papers and letters, but also items like brooches, lighters, cigarette tins, and old ballpoint pens.

Obviously, not everything here was from the 19th century. What had Raleigh stumbled upon?

She heard voices outside behind the house. She quickly pushed the mantel back into place. It had obviously been tampered with, but perhaps no one would notice. Raleigh didn't want to share this find with anyone yet, instead, desiring to come back and go through it all by herself.

Smoothing back her hair and brushing old paint flecks from her jeans, she grabbed the flashlight and screwdriver and headed back downstairs to meet the others, Lindbergh on her heels.

He sat in front of her in the kitchen, whining. "So, you think after all that I'm going to reward you with a treat, Mutt Boy?" Raleigh admonished before doing exactly what the dog wanted to by retrieving the bag of bone marrow treats.

She was continuing to half-heartedly lecture Lindbergh, who sat through it with an air of boredom, when the three others piled into the kitchen.

"Thought I heard you in here!" Salem exclaimed breathlessly.

Raleigh nodded as she fed Lindbergh his fourth and final treat. "Little piglet," she said under her breath as Salem chattered about how surprised the men had been to pop up in the woods near the water. Lindbergh thumped his tail against the floor in response and padded back over to Kip Hewitt, no doubt attracted to the lingering odor of scales and entrails.

Retracing her steps through the tunnel and into the gardener's shed had obviously been pleasant for Salem, whose eyes were shining brightly as she recounted their adventure.

When Salem was done, Raleigh handed Derrick his screwdriver. "This is yours. I'm afraid I rifled through your toolbox to find it in order to open a stuck drawer I found here in the kitchen." She was surprised at how the lie rolled off her tongue. Why was she hesitating to show him the mantel? "Now the toolbox is sitting open in the driveway because it weighs as much as a small horse, and I couldn't pick it up after I dragged it to the ground."

Derrick laughed. "Most people take everything when they steal tools, they don't just remove a cheap screwdriver. Don't worry about it. However..." He hesitated as he glanced at Kip and Salem, as if unsure whether to proceed in front of them.

Seeming to decide that it was fine to go ahead, Derrick continued. "I was just wondering if you'd thought more about what you plan to do with the bedroom suite our family made for yours. It'd be mighty special sitting in our shop and would demonstrate to folks that our family's been making fine furniture for centuries. I talked to my dad, and we'd be willing to increase our offer by twenty percent."

Raleigh wanted to consider agreeing to Derrick's proposal, but she instinctively knew that the pieces had relevance to St. Clements Bluff's history. She couldn't part with it. Not yet.

"I don't think I'm ready to let anything go, I'm sorry," she said.

He pressed on. "Wouldn't mind taking it off your hands for you. Can bring a couple of boys from the shop to get it out of here. The money would go a long way to helping renovate this place."

What a curious statement. His offer for the furniture would hardly take care of replastering a few walls. Did Derrick Jonson not realize that? Or did he think Raleigh didn't realize it?

She shook her head. "Sorry, maybe at some point. This was my husband's house, and right now I want to keep it intact."

Derrick scowled at her and was silent for several moments. Then his expression cleared, and he flashed a smile. "Well, can't blame me for trying. You might just change your mind sometime soon."

Derrick left the house, leather jacket over his left arm and the screwdriver in his right hand. Raleigh walked to the front of the house and watched as he effortlessly tossed the toolbox back into the passenger side of his truck and threw the jacket in after it. He climbed into the driver's side, still holding the screwdriver, and Raleigh observed him suddenly snarl and jam the screwdriver into the top of the dash.

Now wasn't that interesting.

CHAPTER 15

KIP HEWITT STOOD on the screened-in back porch of his mother's old, white-framed ranch home along Herring Creek. It was a convenient place for taking care of his hauls, as she not only had a pier with a boat lift outside, but her porch contained an old farmhouse sink with plenty of counter space to either side for working. That counter space was currently covered in newspaper and prep instruments. He thought of it as his personal surgical table.

The porch reeked of generations of watermen taking care of their catches in here. Oysters, crabs, rockfish, perch…untold numbers of full nets and cages had come through here to be cleaned, scaled, and boiled.

Kip liked the odor, which was briny and distinctive. He turned on the hot tap, knowing it would never actually get hot, and waited for it to conclude its squealing and banging as it protested the work of forcing water upward.

With water flowing, he put on rubber gloves and reached into one of the two ice-laden white buckets next to him, pulled out a rockfish, hooked two fingers behind its gills to hold it upright, and rinsed it clean.

He tossed the fish onto one side of the counter and reached into the bucket for another.

"Didn't hear you come in," came his mother's voice from the back door. "Do well this morning?"

Kip finished rinsing the second fish and added it to

the first one before turning off the tap and facing her. "About twenty large ones."

Doreen Hewitt nodded. "Not bad. Morris Point Restaurant should be happy."

She wore her old yellow-flowered, ruffled pinafore apron over a three-quarter length white shirt, tan cotton pull-up pants, and thick-soled sneakers. It had been her indoor uniform since Kip could remember. The apron only came off if she went somewhere, which hadn't been often since the death of Jason Hewitt eight years ago.

Kip turned the water back on and continued rinsing the remaining fish while his mother remained at the doorway, watching him. He felt her gaze linger on his back. She did so regularly these days. It used to bother him, but he was used to it now. Mother didn't do much anymore other than roast, bake, and fry for family and church events, so she didn't really have a lot to talk about and needed others around her to provide her with diversions.

Kip was routinely expected to fulfill the role of son, news anchor, and entertainment.

"Went over and saw the new owner of St. Clements Bluff the other day," he said casually. He hadn't mentioned to his mother what had occurred in the river prior to that.

His mother perked up. "Didn't know anyone had moved in there. Another Bishop or some D.C. transplant?"

"A Bishop by marriage," he said. "Widowed by a Bishop."

His mother nodded knowingly. "Naturally. Some fool Bishop get into a bar fight? Ride a motorcycle into a telephone pole?"

"Something like that. Killed in a plane crash." With

all of the fish completely rinsed, Kip began the task of gutting them. Picking up a knife with a long thin blade that curved at the tip, he pulled a fish toward him, laying it on its side with its belly facing him.

"Oh. Poor woman. Nothing worse than someone being yanked from you suddenly."

"Yup," Kip replied. With one hand on the fish, he placed the knife tip just below the fish's head and drew a slit down the length of the body. Putting down the knife, he scooped the entrails out and dumped them onto the other side of the counter. They'd freeze well and could be used in a couple of months as crab bait. Crabs were bottom feeders. The nastier the food offering, the better for attracting them into traps.

"Why'd you pay a visit to the widow?" Doreen asked. "She need help getting along? I can make her a stuffed ham. Or I can dig some crab out of the freezer and send over some crab cakes. Or does she need some help with taking her meds or cleaning her house? I can—"

"Nah. She's not that kind of widow. She's...young. Her husband was a pilot in that new White Lion they were testing on base." Kip used the knife to slice off the fish's head in a single swift movement and added it to the bait pile. The prepped fish went back into the iced bucket.

"I remember that. His wing tip touched a second plane's. Killed several of them." His mother seemed to be reaching through her memory banks for information. "There was some sort of investigation, but the Navy declared it an accident."

"I think that's right." He pulled another fish toward him to gut.

"So, what made you go over there?" Her voice was entirely too neutral to be genuine and Kip knew she was very curious.

"Happened to see her as I was piddling along over on

St. Clements Bay. Wondered if the old place was being restored."

"Restored," his mother repeated flatly. "You're not going to go after the place, are you?"

With the second fish finished and in the bucket, he turned to her. "Why would you say that?"

Her features tightened. "Leave well enough alone, son."

He turned back to his work. Pull. Cut. Scoop. Toss.

"Don't need to worry about me," he said with finality. His mother remained in the doorway, continuing to watch his movements.

He dressed the final four fish of the load differently. After gutting but before removing the heads, he rinsed his hands and put on gloves. Picking up a different knife, he used short, firm strokes along the scales from the tail to the head. The fish's scales scattered in a shower around his hands, but the gloves protected him. Damned scales could be razor sharp.

Kip only scaled fish that he thought would be prepared and eaten quickly. Scales protected the fish and kept it fresh. Although edible, most folks didn't like the taste or texture of them. He would scale the remainder tomorrow and take them to Morris Point. Today he had other tasks to accomplish.

Kip gathered the four fish in a piece of newspaper and handed them to his mother. "For you," he said.

"I thank you, son. I've got some crab meat laid up in the freezer. Could stuff a couple of these for you if you want to come for dinner."

"You know I can't say no to stuffed rockfish." He pointed to the section of counter heaped with fish entrails. "Make me some crab bait?"

"Of course." She went inside briefly and returned without the fish. She moved onto the porch to begin her work of portioning out the entrails into piles that would fit comfortably inside a crab trap's bait compartment. No one could separate it all and stuff it into freezer bags as quickly and efficiently as Doreen Hewitt.

While his mother took his place at the counter, Kip lifted the pail full of fish and dropped it near a free-standing, commercial ice maker. Another of his father's improvements to the place. He opened the door and grabbed the wide-mouthed scoop from inside, digging it into the crushed ice and repeatedly pulling it out and dumping it over the fish to keep it fresh.

"I'll put this in the freezer," he said to his mother as she scooped entrails with her bare hands and guided them into small freezer bags, sealing them, then flattening them so that the bags would stack on top of one another.

She nodded but didn't turn around from her work. "You remember what I said, Kip. Leave it alone."

Kip grunted in response and headed out through the screen door and walked a worn path to drop off the bucket of fish in the freezer kept in the barn, then hopped into his Ford long bed pickup.

The next morning, Salem arrived downstairs while Raleigh was working on only her second cup of coffee at the kitchen table. She airily waved off Raleigh's offer of some.

"I'm thinking of running out to pick up some cereal. And some eggs and bacon. You definitely need some solid food around here. Actually, just *any* food would be good. No need to come with me—I'll take care of it all and then later we should go to Toot's Bar. Do you know the place? I understand that The Two Mikes are playing there tonight." Salem hummed something light and nonsensical as she reached into a cabinet and pulled out a box of toaster pastries. She examined the box.

"Good heavens, Sisso, these things expired two

months ago. I'm going to clean out your cabinets when I get back."

Salem was becoming very irritating. "My cabinets are fine and don't require inspection."

Besides, the toaster pastries were Grant's favorite on-the-go breakfast fare. He regularly grabbed a foil-wrapped package of two iced strawberry tarts on his way out the door for work.

"Hmmm," was all Salem said in response.

Once her sister was off running her errands, Raleigh decided to pour more coffee and curl up on the sofa with a blanket and the old scrapbook that Mutzi had loaned her.

Lindbergh joined her, snuffling as he nosed his way under the end of the blanket. His head and shoulders were covered while the rest of him was exposed.

"Idiot," Raleigh said affectionately. "Do you think I can't see you under there?"

Lindbergh thumped his tail twice.

Avoiding the dog's concealed head next to her, Raleigh opened the scrapbook on her draped lap.

The volume was heavier than she had remembered it being. In fact, it was heavier than any of the old hand-sewn map books in the museum's archives.

A pang of guilt shot through her. *I really should call Bert.*

Raleigh glanced through the earlier pages she had already seen, this time looking them over in more detail for any clues it might give her about St. Clements Bluff's past.

There were the usual award-type articles. There was a Bishop who had won a businessman of the year plaque and another Bishop who was recognized for an expansive victory garden that had fed local service members' families.

A larger spread contained an amusing story of a circus that had come to town in 1947 and sought a place to house its menagerie of lions, bears, and even an elephant, during its sojourn alongside the County Fair at Leonard Hall.

The circus owner had approached the owner of St. Clements Bluff for permission to use the property's many outbuildings for housing the animals away from the public during off-hours to keep the animals calm and rested.

The request had been flatly denied by Philip Bishop, the property's owner at the time. The article went on to quote from its interview with Mr. Bishop, who stated that, "...an established old estate in the mother county of Maryland wasn't to be treated like some zoo enclosure. I don't care how much money the drunken sots offer me."

Raleigh could only imagine the incident being both outrageous and uproariously funny.

Another article showed that a Charles Bishop had died as the result of his plane being shot down between the French and German borders during a bombing raid on an aircraft factory. His body had been brought home for burial and his service had been attended by hundreds.

She was more than halfway through the scrapbook and its brittle old newspaper articles, photos, and other ephemera when she landed on a fascinating two-page spread.

It was a community-interest type of story, dating to 1935 and offering photos and blurbs about some of the well-known historic properties in the county. An inset offered a recommended driving route to see the properties.

This was written after the Civil War and American involvement in World War I, Raleigh thought, but before World War II. The date was in the middle of the infamous oyster wars, that series of violent disputes between oyster pirates and legal watermen in the waters of the Chesapeake Bay and the Potomac River from the end of the Civil War to the late 1950s.

The thought made Raleigh pause.

The properties listed alongside grainy photos in the article were all located in various places fronting or adjacent to the Potomac and Patuxent Rivers, which sandwiched St. Mary's County. Calvert County was the next county over, and it, too, was bordered on both sides by water—the Patuxent River and the Chesapeake Bay. None of the homes mentioned in the article were in Calvert.

Raleigh traced the driving route with her finger. It was a loose oval around the county, connecting sites with the names of St. James Hill, St. George Manor, and, of course, St. Clements Bluff.

So what? she thought. *It didn't mean anything, did it?*

She tried to remember details about the oyster wars, which Bert Mattingly had waxed about in great detail when she was first hired.

The oyster wars were between legitimate watermen and those who were unlawfully harvesting them, though. It had nothing to do with hiding slaves. Except that these wars started at the tail end of the Civil War. Could the secret rooms, tunnels, and staircases have shifted their use from saving slaves to saving...oyster pirates?

What a ridiculous thought. *You should write fantasy movie scripts,* she admonished herself.

She was interrupted from her thoughts by her cell phone's melodic ringtone. Closing the album, she reached over for the phone, which lay next to her untouched cup of coffee. Caller ID registered "Eleanor Moore." Raleigh sighed inwardly. No doubt Salem had sparked this call from their mother.

"Hello, sweetheart. How are things? Been doing

anything interesting lately?" Raleigh's mother was bright and chirpy.

Raleigh rolled her eyes. "Mom, you are fully aware that Salem is here. Is she saying bad things about me?"

"Raleigh Moore Bishop!" her mother exclaimed. "What a terrible thing to say about your sister. She's only trying to help you."

Raleigh rolled her eyes again and took a deep breath. "I'm sure she is. She's out running errands at the moment, and I'm in the middle of something, so—"

"Salem says you're uncovering a bit of a mystery. That Grant left you a house, and it's full of secrets. It must be quite the distraction for you." Eleanor Moore's voice was dripping with curiosity.

There was no point in trying to avoid an explanation. "It has been interesting. St. Clements Bluff has apparently belonged to various members of the Bishop family, and it came to Grant through an uncle; I'm not exactly sure why. Salem and I—along with a neighbor—discovered what we think was a slave escape route to the Potomac River."

"Fascinating. I imagine your boss is quite taken with the find."

Raleigh paused. "Well, he doesn't know about it."

Her mother was silent for several moments. "Why haven't you told him? Imagine the publicity for the museum when it gets out that one of its own employees inherited such a fantastically historic home."

Raleigh really had to stop being so irritated, lest her eyes get stuck in the back of her head. "I haven't gone back to work just yet. I haven't been ready."

"Raleigh..." Her mother sighed faintly in the background. "All right, I understand. So, what do you think?" she asked, making her tone light again. "Will you move in? Could be an exciting project to bring an old home back to life. Researching how to bring it back to period glory is right up your alley."

Raleigh didn't have the heart to tell her that she was actually considering having it taken over by a historic trust.

"Maybe," she said noncommittally.

Eleanor Moore changed the subject. "I think visiting you is just what Salem needed, in addition to being such a good help to you. I can hear happiness in her voice that I haven't heard in a long time."

"Do you mean happiness from the musician or the fisherman that Salem is flirting with? At least, I think all she's doing is flirting." Raleigh couldn't help herself from biting out the sharp words.

At his mistress's change in inflection, Lindbergh crawled his way back out from under the blanket and slid to the ground, padding quickly toward the kitchen.

"Raleigh, don't take your heartache out on your sister. You've spent a long time flopping around in misery. You know your sister is someone who fundamentally wants to be happy, and I think she wants the same for you. You should appreciate that. It's time to *choose* to be happy."

Raleigh knew she was being properly chastised. Was it time to at least pretend to be happy? Maybe pretending would lead to reality.

After some more small talk, Raleigh clicked off the call and continued to hold the phone in her lap, thinking.

In a few minutes, she made a momentous decision. She went upstairs, stripped the sheets from the bed, and threw them into the washer.

Raleigh then decided on a short nap on the sofa. Lindbergh crawled up with her and stretched out tight against her so that the idea of getting up was futile anyway. Her sleep was blessedly peaceful, interrupted only by Salem bursting through the front door.

"Guess who I ran into at Target?" Salem said, standing at the entry to the family room with her arms full of shopping bags. "Mr. Kip Hewitt. And you wouldn't believe what I learned."

CHAPTER 16

RALEIGH FELT PINPRICKS up and down her spine. "What do you mean?"

Salem smiled, dropped her bags dramatically, and placed her hands on her hips. "I do believe the unassuming waterman is quite rich, my dear."

Raleigh laughed in relief. "I thought you were going to tell me you learned he had a criminal record of some sort."

Salem airily waved a hand. "Oh, I'm quite certain now that he's clean."

"Because...you think he has money? Why, by the way, do you think this? I'm guessing he didn't say hello and immediately announce that he had secret offshore accounts."

"No, he didn't do that," Salem said, rolling her eyes. "However, he did tell me that his family supplies seafood to many of the local restaurants in this county. I'm pretty sure that's profitable. So, he might stink of fish during the day, but I bet he's wonderfully fragrant of hundred dollar bills at night." Salem struck a seductive pose and waggled her eyebrows up and down.

Raleigh couldn't help but laugh at her sister. "You're an idiot."

"*I'm* an idiot?" Salem replied. "*You're* the one who got saved, then received a post-rescue visit from him. Maybe you should be friendlier."

"What? You're the one who was insisting just days ago that he might have been trying to kill me."

Salem pursed her lips. "Yeah, but I've changed my mind about him. Seriously, Sisso, that man is a catch. Oh! That's a pun. Get it? He's a rugged fisherman who is a catch?"

"Again, you're an idiot," Raleigh said.

"Maybe," Salem said. "But I think I might be a little smarter than you in this."

Raleigh's phone buzzed again. This time it was Mutzi Bishop.

"I thought you might like to come for dinner Thursday evening," her mother-in-law said. "Trey and Barbara are coming."

Raleigh thought back. How long had it been since she'd actually had a meal with her in-laws? Or spent more than just cursory time with them? Guilt flooded through her.

"I would love to," she said, trying to project a little joy through the phone. "Salem is visiting me. All right if I bring her along?"

Raleigh could hear the happiness in Mutzi's voice when she said, "Of course. We'd be delighted to see Salem again. We haven't seen her since—well, she's welcome to come. The more the merrier, as they say."

Raleigh clicked off the call. She had heard from both mothers in under two hours. Interesting.

"Dinner at the Bishops' on Thursday. Want to go?" she asked her sister.

"Sure! I bought a cute little sweater today. Dinner gives me a perfect opportunity to wear it." Salem was as chipper as always.

Once Salem had taken her bags upstairs to sort through her purchases, Raleigh was blessedly left alone once more.

Her coffee was cold, but instead of dumping it and pouring more as she would typically do, she let the contents drain down the sink and put the mug in the dishwasher. Perhaps it was time to lay off so much caffeine, although the resulting caffeine headache would be hell to endure.

With her thoughts still swirling from what she had read in the Bishop scrapbook, Raleigh decided that now was as good a time as any to return to St. Clements Bluff to look at the mantel's contents by herself.

With a sense of purpose she hadn't had in months, Raleigh tossed the sheets into the dryer, then grabbed her keys and the scrapbook. She softly said, "C'mon, Mutt Boy," and headed for the door. She'd text Salem from the car that she was off running errands.

It was time to find answers to St. Clements Bluff, and without question, that mantel held at least one of them.

WITH LINDBERGH ONCE more curled up in the space where a mattress would be but watching her attentively, Raleigh dislodged the mantel from the wall again, holding it firmly with her gloved hands as she helped it make its unique waterfall drop and reveal its contents.

The compartments weren't as full as he might have hoped, but there were some old treasures to examine. The compartments were of varying widths and many still had traces of old burgundy felt lining.

Raleigh gently lifted an old pipe from a drawer. It wasn't made of clay, as she would have expected from something made before the 20th century. She ran a finger around the bowl. It seemed to be made of some sort of molded material. Bakelite, perhaps? She sniffed at the bowl. It was redolent of old tobacco with a hint of cherry.

She replaced the pipe. Another compartment contained beeswax candles that had been burned to near nubs. She wondered if they were kept here and given to escapees so that they could make their way through the tunnel and on to the other side.

Other compartments held a metal folding utensil set like those a soldier from years past might carry, a tiny brown medicine bottle with a worn, unreadable label, and a pair of wire-rimmed spectacles. Raleigh examined each in turn, wondering how each little treasure came to make its way into this elaborate memento box. Nothing seemed to be of such great value that it required a special hiding spot.

She had a sudden thought. Perhaps the mantel simply amounted to a sophisticated supply box for the slavery escapees, made completely undetectable to any authorities. She nodded in satisfaction. That made complete sense and fit with the types of items the folding box contained.

A small, folded piece of newsprint caught Raleigh's attention. She removed her gloves and lifted the paper, brown and brittle with age, from its compartment. Carefully unfolding it, she realized it was just a torn scrap from an old newspaper.

ROOM TO LET
Second floor in quiet farmhouse on large, private property
Rent payable the 1st of each month
No animals; zookeepers inappropriate; sobers ONLY
Telephone Compton 4—3104, ask for P. Bishop

Raleigh laughed aloud, causing Lindbergh to momentarily lift his head to see what was going on. Seeing that nothing was amiss, he went back to sleep, completely oblivious to the chill in the air.

Raleigh was amused to find this link back to what she had seen in the scrapbook. She refolded the paper and put it back in its compartment.

She also discovered an old, shabby pocketknife. A couple of its implements had snapped off over time and its wood handle was worn from use.

Interestingly, near the pocketknife was a traditional stubby oyster knife with a short, flat blade ending in a rounded point. Its bulbous wood end, shaped so that the user could get a good grip on it to maneuver the bladed end for prying open reluctant oysters, was cracked but still sturdily attached to the blade. The flat metal blade itself was rusted, but the prying tip was sharp.

Did this give credence to her idea that St. Clements Bluff had something to do with the oyster wars? Raleigh touched the tip to her forefinger again. She realized that if she applied any sort of pressure, she would definitely break the skin. Oyster knives were not to be underestimated, despite their innocuous appearances.

"Hmmm," she mused aloud, twirling the piece in her hand and thinking. If this place had gone from helping slaves to helping wronged watermen reclaim their oyster beds, then the property's history was remarkable.

Raleigh then noticed that there were several oyster knives in the mantel, each one tossed into different compartments. They all seemed to be from the same set.

So what? she thought. Practically every home in St. Mary's County had specialty knives for oysters, fish, and crabs. Finding them here couldn't possibly be meaningful.

"I just don't know what to think, Mutt Boy," she said aloud. "Why would anyone hide these worthless items? None of it makes any sense."

She folded the mantel back up into its resting position.

"Come on, lazy," she said to Lindbergh, who grudgingly arose and stretched before following her down the stairs. He headed straight for the kitchen. "Yeah, I know, I'm sure you're starving to death without a bone marrow treat."

As she gave Lindbergh treats in return for going through his repertoire of tricks, she mentally went over everything that had happened that day.

Her mother had mentioned Mr. Mattingly. Perhaps it really was time to get his take on everything. He could at least tell her whether her oyster wars notion had any merit. He could probably show Raleigh archives that would give her a greater historical perspective on St. Clements Bluff than she could get from family scrapbooks, too.

She would also get his thoughts on turning the property over to a historical trust.

Her thoughts turned. She had managed to forget her grief entirely while she was here going through the mantel. It felt...good.

An image of Grant rose in her mind. His will stated that she should take care of St. Clements Bluff for the rest of her life. Turning it over to a trust would fulfill that wish, wouldn't it? Surely he didn't mean that she should physically work the property herself.

She hoped.

As she shifted into gear and began rolling down the gravel drive to the road, it occurred to her that the home should have a mailbox. Was there still mail being delivered? If so, it might contain valuable correspondence or bills to give Raleigh more information.

She actually felt a little excited as she reached the end of the driveway. The house itself had no free-standing mailbox. "That's okay, Mutt Boy," she said to Lindbergh, who was busy licking the passenger window glass for some reason understood only by dogs. "I bet there's a bank of old country mailboxes somewhere nearby."

Raleigh turned left out of the driveway and drove for almost a quarter of a mile without finding anything. She entered a random driveway and backed out, heading in the opposite direction. After passing St.

Clements Bluff again on her right, she found exactly what she was looking for about five hundred feet away on the left. It was a long row of mismatched mailboxes, crammed together on a wooden structure. Most had house numbers on the front of them and she was able to quickly pick out the St. Clements Bluff box, which was one of the larger ones in the row.

Raleigh stopped her SUV next to the box. "Here we go," she mumbled to the dog as she pressed the window button to lower it. Despite the cold air she was perspiring a little.

Calm down, she thought. *What, do you think something's going to jump out at you?*

Raleigh pulled the metal tab on the mailbox door toward her. The mailbox was stuffed full of envelopes, flyers, and periodicals. Clearly, this box had not been opened except by the mail carrier since Grant died. It made her realize that of all the tasks she hadn't accomplished after Grant's death, she had at least taken care of shutting down his personal accounts and subscriptions.

She slowly pulled out sections of the mail and tossed them onto the back seat. It took a couple of minutes to dislodge everything from the box. Although tempted to park the car and go into the back seat to sift through it all, she refrained until she arrived home.

The house was quiet despite Salem's car in the driveway, so Raleigh assumed her sister was asleep upstairs.

It took several trips, but she finally lugged all of the mail into the house and spread it over the kitchen table. Her next steps were to sort the mail into related piles. Most of it was the usual postal onslaught of repetitive catalogs, warnings that an automobile warranty was about to expire, and announcements of CLEARANCE! ONE DAY ONLY! sales, along with a few utility bills addressed to Grant that Raleigh set aside for payment.

Lindbergh quickly became bored with supervising her and padded off.

Raleigh was nearing the end of her sorting task when she found a regular white envelope. It contained no return address and the mailing address was handwritten.

It was addressed directly to her.

Raleigh was puzzled. Beyond the Bishops, her own family, and Magda Raley, who would be aware that she was here? Moreover, anyone she knew wouldn't know to write to her at the St. Clements Bluff address.

Maybe it was some sort of welcome-to-the-neighborhood note.

She ripped one of the short ends of the envelope and withdrew the single sheet of paper. Its typed contents were astounding.

> *Mrs. Bishop,*
>
> *So, this is now your home. You realize your husband didn't come by it honestly, right?*
>
> *You know that he covered up what happened there, don't you?*
>
> *You don't seriously plan to live there, do you? If so, don't be surprised if it accidentally burns down one day soon.*

The short note ended with, *"A Friend."*

What sort of "friend" would send such a thing? Raleigh was filled with a nauseating mixture of disgust, anger, and trepidation. It couldn't possibly be true that Grant Bishop had done something so offensive that a person was ready to burn the home down over it. It especially couldn't be true that Grant had done something dishonest.

Could it?

Raleigh then remembered that Derrick Jonson and Kip Hewitt also knew that the home now belonged to her. But what difference would this make to them?

It briefly passed through her mind that Derrick Jonson had seemed anxious to own the furniture upstairs, thus he had a tangential interest in St. Clements Bluff—but why would that lead to his sending her a letter like this?

Raleigh decided to ignore the note and its insinuations. She didn't think she was being naive by doing so—this wasn't New York City after all. This was just small-town Maryland. She doubted she needed to worry about someone taking action on it. No, this was all to scare her because of some apparent goings-on in her inherited home.

So, in God's name, what could have happened at St. Clements Bluff that was so terrible?

CHAPTER 17

KIP HEWITT SAT in the driver's seat of his pickup truck in front of the Valley Lee post office, quickly sorting through his mail, which included the usual assortment of marine-related catalogs and bills, plus a couple of postal delivery confirmations for important letters he had recently sent and notice of an upcoming boat show in Annapolis.

Nodding in satisfaction, he started up the Ford. He let his vehicle idle as he sat in silence, contemplating the past and trying not to allow himself to get swallowed by his disappointments.

Becoming irritated with the utter quiet and stillness beyond the truck's engine rumble, Kip flipped on the radio to the local station so he could listen to the tail end of the weekly morning program, "T-Bone and Heather."

The morning radio team, consisting of a husband and wife, was a staple in St. Mary's County. They were an ingrained part of the community and were everywhere, it seemed. Kip had met them on more than one occasion, at the County Fair, the Oyster Festival, and other local events.

Listening to their banter made him forget everything that was wrong and instead believe that he was at a bar with a couple of close friends.

Kip had friends, of course, but they were all busy in their lives. Responsible jobs on the naval base, wives, kids, coaching youth sports…all activities that left most of his buddies too busy to casually grab a beer together during the week.

He didn't blame his friends, but he sure did envy them, imagining their full and laughter-filled lives.

Doreen Hewitt tried to encourage Kip as best she could, but her bitterness had left her ravaged with open emotional wounds. Sometimes it was just difficult to be in her presence, what with her suspicions about everyone.

Raleigh Bishop's face rose unbidden in his mind, and Kip remembered her shivering beneath the blanket after he had pulled her from the water. Her expression had held a strange curiosity. Of course, he knew he had looked practically like a yeti that day. He'd been doing a lot of hunting, fishing, and work outdoors, basically spending a lot of time on his own, so he hadn't shaved or bothered to trim his hair in over a month. Yeah, he admitted, he had to have looked scary.

His memory shifted to encountering Raleigh again at St. Clements Bluff with her sister. That day Raleigh had seemed almost angry to see him. What the hell was that about?

She is not your friend, he reminded himself.

At his age it, was hard meeting people anywhere, let alone in a rural place where everyone is in everyone else's business. But this was where his life was, and he'd almost had a family and future once, too, but fate had mercilessly taken back the cards he had been dealt. Life was funny that way.

Kip shifted his truck into reverse and pulled out of the post office parking lot. Yeah, he could use a friend right about now, but he wasn't likely to find one in this neck of the woods.

Raleigh arose early the next morning, having been disturbed all the previous night by restless thoughts of

St. Clements Bluff and imagining what sort of dark, vile event might have once occurred there.

Exhausted from a lack of sleep but determined to get to the bottom of what was wrong with her new home, Raleigh showered, walked Lindbergh, and quickly made her way through half a pot of coffee, not yet willing to take on the caffeine withdrawal headache. With Salem's snoring audible all the way downstairs, there was no need to have a conversation with her sister about her plans. She simply left a note on the kitchen table that she would be back in a couple of hours.

Raleigh drove to the St. Mary's County Museum, surprised to find that she was actually looking forward to seeing her boss. Bert was a lifelong resident of St. Mary's County, tracing his lineage back to the original settlers that had arrived from England in the 17th century on the Ark and the Dove sailing ships.

His pride in his heritage as the descendent of an English servant had led him to write a book on the county's history twenty years earlier, which had then led to a series of positions culminating in his present position as the museum's director. No one had a greater passion for local history than Bert Mattingly.

"Raleigh!" he exclaimed, grabbing her hand and pumping it up and down with fervor. "Good to see you, good to see you. Your office is just as you left it, and we can meet later today to discuss an exciting new acquisition that—"

Raleigh extracted her hand from Bert's grip. "Thanks, Bert. I'm here just to…I just had a couple of questions for you about Grant's will."

He frowned in consternation. "Questions about a will? I'm not sure I can be of much help with legal matters. Although I hope you'll reconsider coming back soon. We miss you, and there is much to be done. Well, come on then."

Raleigh followed Bert, whose large frame nearly filled the hallway that led to his office. The staff called this the "panic hallway" because it was cleverly concealed behind a life-sized display of the 17th century English queen, Henrietta Maria, wife to Charles I. The devout Catholic King Charles had granted the seven million acres that would become Maryland—named for his queen—to George Calvert, the first Lord Baltimore. However, St. Mary's County, Maryland's first county, was actually named for Mary, the mother of Jesus.

Bert loomed in his office as much as he did in the hallway. He was so tall that even seated across his desk from Raleigh he towered above her. The stacks of papers and journals on his desk weren't quite as tall as he was, but were imposing nonetheless.

It made Raleigh realize that she needed to clean out the mail from her office very soon, lest she be swallowed whole by it all. The world had gone digital, yet it seemed like there was more paper than ever to sort through, categorize, file, or discard.

Bert pulled a door latch in the credenza behind his desk, revealing a small refrigerator. He opened the refrigerator and pulled out a bottle of cold brew white mocha coffee and a bottled water. He handed the water across his desk to Raleigh.

"Presume you still can't stand anything but piping hot java that can practically walk on its own?" he asked.

"You haven't forgotten me at all," Raleigh replied, raising the water bottle in toast to him as he unscrewed the cap on his cold brew. "Coffee was never meant to be drunk cold." She shivered for effect.

Bert laughed and took a sip. He didn't seem to notice that a couple of milky drops clung to his goatee. "How is it that I can help you with Grant's will?" he asked, taking another swig. This time he pressed the backs of two fingers to his facial area—which was oddly salt-

and-pepper gray in contrast to his still mostly-brown hair. The dabbing caught the lingering coffee droplets.

"Grant left me property," Raleigh began.

"Of course," Bert said. "Your house and cars."

Raleigh shook her head. "No, it's another house. One I didn't know about. I'm hoping you might know something as the house is quite old."

He put the bottle down and leaned forward, lacing his fingers together, his cold coffee forgotten. "How old? Who built it?"

"It was built in 1823," Raleigh replied. "I don't know who constructed the home. It's located on St. Clements Bay, and I believe it to be in very good condition for its age. It has been owned by Bishops since at least the early 20th century."

"Is it a named property?"

"Yes, it's called St. Clements Bluff, but I don't know when it started being known that way."

Bert leaned back in his leather chair, now moving his laced fingers from the desk to the top of his expansive belly.

"St. Clements Bluff?" he repeated. "I know that place. Let me see..."

Bert hefted himself up from the desk and promised to return momentarily. He came back with a thick, board-bound book. As he opened the tome on his desk, Raleigh saw that it was full of browned pages containing ledger entries in old, spidery handwriting.

"Let's see," he mused again, flipping pages near the front of it. "This contains the property deed recordings in the county from its beginnings until we started automating in the 1980s. After it all went digital, the land records office put this on permanent loan to us for preservation."

Raleigh sipped water while waiting for Bert to make

a discovery. It wasn't long in coming. He stabbed at an entry with a thick, nail-bitten forefinger.

"Here we go!" He exclaimed in triumph. "Just as I thought. That's one of the estates built by Roger Thoroughgood, an early 19th century speculator down here. I know that he built four places in St. Mary's County along well-traveled river routes. They were all constructed nearly identically. Legend has it that his sister proposed the layout as amenable for both raising families and entertaining friends. Thoroughgood simply took his sister's word for it that it was an ideal floor plan and erected them all at the same time. One burned down rather quickly when the new owners' cat knocked over an unattended candle while the owner was out."

Raleigh's thoughts raced faster than she could keep up. Her primary question was whether these other homes had the same furniture set in them, as well as the hidden escape route behind an upstairs fireplace. She needed to see another of these properties. "Do the other two still exist?"

"Pretty sure they do." Bert continued through the ledger, flipping gently back and forth through the pages. "Looks like one of them is—or at least was—sold to a family named Abell and promptly named St. George Manor. It's over in the Tall Timbers area. The other one, hmm…" Bert frowned.

More searching, but this took longer as Bert marked a few pages with scraps of paper and referred back and forth between the markings.

"Looks as though the second property was sold to someone named Price. No record that the property itself was given a name. Then twenty years later, in 1843, it was sold to the Bishops. But interestingly, in 1861, it was sold to an entity called 'Maritime Shippers.'"

Bert turned the ledger around on his desk so that

Raleigh could see the transaction for herself. She ran a finger along the entry as she read it. "Is that a normal transaction?"

Bert was hesitant. "Typically, no. During that period families worked hard to not only hold onto, but to expand, their holdings. Wealth was still primarily in property here in the South. Selling it to a shipping company, hmmm..." Bert glanced up thoughtfully. "It suggests there may have been some desperation in the family. Likely a financial crisis of some sort."

Raleigh thought on this. "Maybe there was no heir to take it over?"

"Maybe. As you know, families weren't as transient in those days as they are now and six children or more was common. I would expect there to have been plenty of extended family in the area. You could be right, though. However, with the sale occurring at the start of the war to a business called 'Maritime Shippers,' I do wonder if the property didn't go to a highly profitable blockade runner. They were making money when everyone else was financially devastated, so possibly could have easily afforded to make the purchase."

Raleigh was intrigued by that interesting idea.

Bert returned to his ledger. "Now, let's see, from Maritime Shippers the property went to..."

He was turning pages again. "Huh. So, it was sold to a Henry Bishop in 1866. The date is interesting, if I'm correct, in that it had been owned by a blockade-running enterprise. The end of the war would have created a turnabout for the blockade runner's fortunes, and he may have needed to sell to raise money to get out of prison. I don't see anything else in here, so presumably St. Clements Bluff was just transferred down through the family after that. You could check with land records for any more recent transactions."

Raleigh knew the answer to that was probably in one of the Bishop scrapbooks.

She needed to inquire about something else. "This may sound strange, but—the date that the sale to Maritime Shippers took place. That would have been during the oyster wars, right?"

"Sure, some of the oyster pirates also served as blockade runners. Is there some connection?"

Raleigh paused. "I hope this doesn't sound foolish, but—»

She proceeded to tell her employer about the secret tunnel and the cleverly constructed mantelpiece, as well as the ornately carved furniture in the bedchamber.

Bert sat rapt, not interrupting at all but waiting patiently until Raleigh was done. Afterward, he sat in silence for several moments, absorbing her story. "And you think it's possible that the tunnel may have originally been constructed for escaping slaves and was then later converted to secreting oyster pirates."

"Is my theory crazy?" Raleigh bit her lip.

"I'm surprised so often by what I learn in history that I'm no longer ever surprised. There are, however, two problems with your idea." He drank from his coffee bottle then put the lid back on it and placed it off to one side. "First and foremost, I can't imagine that anyone on the St. Mary's County shoreline would have been sympathetic to the oyster pirates. They were destroying the livelihoods of the honest watermen who had worked along the shores for generations and people were getting shot in the Potomac River. Second, how exactly would the house be used to 'hide' an oyster pirate? In other words, where exactly would he be traveling to after docking at the pier? That said, absolutely anything is possible. What would you say to letting me have a look at the house?"

"Of course. Truthfully, I'm sort of thinking that I might want to turn it over to the historical society if they are interested in such a thing."

"I'm sure I don't need to tell you that the house would be a very important acquisition for them," Bert said evenly. "But you should think on it. When you're ready, I'm happy to discuss it."

Raleigh appreciated her boss's circumspection on it. She thanked Bert for his time and rose to leave, then sat again as he held up a hand to stop her. "You haven't told me how it is that Grant willed you a property that you never knew about."

Raleigh sighed inwardly, wishing she had a comforting cup of French roast in her hand. "It appears to have been a home that has been in his family for a very long time, and Grant simply never told me that it had been willed to him. I really don't know any more than that."

Bert looked at her with something that looked like disbelief mixed with sympathy. While that sort of expression had been making Raleigh's stomach churn with irritation until now, at this moment she was experiencing something else.

I don't want anyone looking at me like that anymore. But what was she going to do about it?

"I see," Bert said. He clearly didn't but changed the subject. "Have you given more thought to coming in and starting work on the farming and tribal village displays? Why don't you stop by a couple of hours a day to plan out and oversee that refurbishment?"

Raleigh was silent, again feeling that little flicker of—what was it? Hope? Excitement? that pirouetted in her chest. Watching Bert's expectant expression, she was overcome by guilt that was quickly replaced with grief as an image of Grant rose unbidden in her mind. But the grief was like a strange wave that passed over her in just one overwhelming instant but was now crashing somewhere behind her on the shore, no longer drowning her like before.

"Yes," she said, nodding at her boss, who blinked in astonishment at her agreement. "I'll be here Monday."

CHAPTER 18

AS SHE SAT at the Bishops' dinner table, Raleigh was inexplicably furious.

Maybe not furious, but extremely irritated.

Irritated enough that she slammed one of Mutzi's dinner rolls onto her plate after removing it from its cloth-lined basket. Realizing she had done so, Raleigh attempted to act as though she had done so accidentally.

Salem chattered away happily, completely oblivious to Raleigh's annoyance. Actually, everyone seemed oblivious to her simmering peevishness.

Pop was at the head of the table to Raleigh's left. Salem was to Raleigh's right. Next to Salem was Barb Costello, Trey's girlfriend. At the other end of the table, across from her husband, sat Mutzi, smiling, even if it was unsteady and tremulous.

Trey sat across from Barb, then there was an empty chair. Directly across from Raleigh sat Kip Hewitt.

Salem had gaily announced that she had invited the waterman as they were pulling up to the Bishop home as if seeing his truck in the driveway didn't make it obvious enough.

In response to Raleigh's grunt of annoyance as she pulled her SUV into the driveway, Salem had said, "Sisso, I know you're enjoying being morose, and I wish you well with it, but damn, some of us want to live. You've got to let us do it."

Salem had never spoken this way to her, and it was unsettling. "I don't begrudge you if you *live*. I just find it a bit disturbing that as you carry on with Mike, you find Kip—the same man you thought might have tried to kill me—to be a romantic prospect for you now that you think he has money." Raleigh had spat the words out, seemingly unable to control these freshly recovered emotions.

"But I changed my mind. Now that I've met him, I don't think he has a mean bone in his well-formed body."

"You changed your mind only because you think he's attractive," Raleigh said.

"So what?" Salem countered. "What if I do think Kip Hewitt is handsome and worth pursuing? Why does that matter to you? It's not as though *you* like him. And I'm not exclusive with Mike. I'm keeping my options open."

Raleigh had no answer. She started to open her car door, but Salem pressed the button to lock the doors from the passenger seat. "I know that the past year has been horrible. What you've endured is beyond awful, and I am so sorry for it, I really am. But Raleigh, sometimes you act as though you're mad *at me*."

"No, I'm not." But Raleigh knew she just sounded petulant. She supposed she should be glad that she was having such a wide range of emotions all of a sudden, but it had been puzzling why she was mad at her sister for inviting Kip Hewitt. The words "green-eyed monster" had appeared in her mind, but she had summarily dismissed them.

It was now fourteen months and twelve days since Grant's death, and she felt like things were slipping away. First, she had washed the sheets of his smell, then stuffed some of his clothes into garbage bags for the Salvation Army. She was sleeping through the nights, and her mind was no longer pining day and night for something that could never be.

Was she healing or forgetting the love of her life? Maybe both.

Her appetite had been improving. Raleigh filled her plate from a tantalizing array of dishes containing Caprese salad, homemade lasagna, roasted green beans, and the just-slammed yeast rolls before her. Yet another sign of her healing, but what scared her was she didn't know if she was ready for it. Ready to join the living, and on Monday she'd start working again.

Meanwhile, Salem was at her sparkling best. "Tell me more about these 'poor' crabs," she was saying to Kip. "They sound delicious, but you say they shouldn't be eaten. Why not?"

"They're females. You've got to leave them alone so they can do what they do best, which is to make millions of babies. If the female population gets too low, the state puts in regulations declaring that all females have to be thrown back. But it's just a good idea to leave the females alone in general so they can reproduce."

Raleigh had to admit that Kip Hewitt had again cleaned up well, and he was dressed very respectfully for dinner. He wore a Black Watch plaid flannel shirt tucked into black denim jeans. Mutzi was fluttering over a small bouquet of cellophane-wrapped hothouse carnations that she showed off to Raleigh and Salem as having been presented to her by Kip. Was Mutzi blushing? For his part, Pop was nodding approvingly over Kip's gift to his wife.

Salem had immediately taken possession of Kip by taking his arm and leading him into the family room to introduce him to Trey and Barb.

Now, at the dinner table, Raleigh's sister continued to shine.

"Fascinating," Salem gushed. "I'd love to try a poor crab."

Kip shook his head and cut through a small piece of lasagna with his fork. Steam rose lazily from it. "No crabs right now. They keep themselves buried in mud during the winter and won't be running until around April."

"Gives me a reason to come back in a couple of months, then," Salem said. Raleigh knew her sister was baiting Kip for a flirting response.

Kip's expression was neutral. "Everyone loves crab season," he said with a shrug.

Salem wasn't able to school her features as well but covered her disappointment by taking a sip of merlot before changing topics to St. Clements Bluff, chattering on about the unusual furniture, the secret staircase behind the fireplace, and how she, Kip, and the cabinet maker had explored the tunnel.

Grant's family sat in rapt attention to the story.

"So, it was a stop on the Underground Railroad?" Trey asked. "What an interesting family we have."

With Salem's knowledge now exhausted, Raleigh was able to fill in more details, particularly concerning the 1861 sale of St. Clements Bluff to a "shipping company" that may have been a blockade runner.

Salem seemed to have recovered from her disappointment enough to return to her previous subject. "I have an idea. Perhaps we can have a grand crab feast right here come April."

Pop nodded. "It would be nice to have a bunch of you young folks here for a party. But we might want to wait until May or June for crabs to be plentiful. What do you think, honey?" he said to his wife.

Mutzi's smile became more genuine. "I agree. We could get out the cornhole boards and have a tournament. I'll make some pork barbecue, too."

Pop nodded again. "I'll ask Grant to set up the badminton net in the yard."

Everyone froze in place. Even Raleigh was unable to continue moving her fork to her mouth.

"Oh, honey," Mutzi laughed nervously. "You meant you'll have Trey set it up."

Raleigh's father-in-law blinked a few times before seeming to understand his mistake. "Right. Of course, I meant Trey. Sorry, dear," he said, glancing sheepishly at Raleigh. "Anyway, it sounds like we need a tour of Raleigh's house before we have a crab picking, eh?" he suggested with false heartiness.

Soon the table was a cacophony of voices shaping this picnic event at least two months in the future. "I'll bring my Sea Ray around, and I can take people tubing," Trey offered. "Have you tubed before, Barb?"

Barb twisted her ponytail with one hand as gazed at him with the same dreamy expression he had for her. "Never. You can teach me."

Trey grinned goofily at his girlfriend. "I'll teach both you and Raleigh." He turned his attention to his sister-in-law. "I seem to recall tubing near Myrtle Point and you falling off and drinking half of the Patuxent River the last time we all did this, Rals."

It had been ages ago. Grant had been a wonderful husband, but he was not a patient teacher. He had taken the controls of Trey's boat that day and driven at a high rate of speed in a zig-zag pattern, causing the inflated round tube Raleigh was lying on to whip back and forth like the tail of a snake.

She had held on to the tube's handles with all she had, but her limited strength was no match for the wild motion caused by Grant's driving. Raleigh had flown off the tube and then swam back to it multiple times, to Grant's constant explanation from the back of the boat as to what she was doing wrong and how to improve her grip. It had been exhausting.

It had no doubt been Grant reverting to the disciplined way he had received experimental aircraft flight training so she couldn't be too angry with him, but still.

It wasn't a happy memory. What happened later that evening was.

"I seem to recall you being the biggest loser at holding your Mai-Tai's," she retorted. "Didn't you end up face down on your parents' bedroom floor that evening, requiring everyone to drag you out to spend the night snoring on the family room floor?"

Trey grew sheepish while everyone else laughed. "I had had too much sun that day was all," he protested but joined in the amusement over it.

Raleigh had to admit, the laughter felt good. It reminded her that she had been a happy person before tragedy had upended her life. Time heals all wounds, right?

Maybe I'm healing.

"We need a new family competition," Trey suggested. "Something anyone can do."

Salem pushed her empty plate away. "I know! How about a poker game?"

Barb wrinkled her nose. "Do we have to smoke cigars and drink beer?"

"Not in my house!" Mutzi exclaimed. "Smoking outside only. You can drink whatever you want, but we will keep an eye on Trey."

More laughter.

Kip had been quiet throughout but now he spoke up. "Anyone here like pool? We could play in teams. Losing team buys a round of drinks." He raised an eyebrow at Raleigh.

"I'll take that bet," Salem said, challenge in her voice. "What's the best place for shooting pool around here?"

Kip shrugged. "I usually go to Back Road Inn. They don't have regulation-sized tables, but it's laid back and they have good music."

Raleigh grinned. Like Salem, she, too, was happy to take that bet.

CHAPTER 19

BACK ROAD INN was a place that might have been called a honkytonk if it had been located somewhere in Texas. A loud country music band, sticky floors, and cheap drinks constituted its entire range of attributes.

But it did have a large area with three pool tables far enough away from the band that conversation could be had while playing.

They broke into two teams, the men against the women, with the women each alternating turns at play. "It just doesn't seem right for Kip and me to have this much advantage over you three," Trey joked.

While Salem wriggled provocatively lining up a shot during a game with Kip, Trey carried three glass mugs of beer to the small square table where Raleigh and Barb sat watching the proceedings. Trey placed a mug before each woman before sitting down across from Raleigh with his own. A thin trail of foam head ran down each side of their mugs and puddled on the table, the result of hastily pulled orders from the keg.

Raleigh sipped at the amber liquid, trying to remember how long ago it had been since she'd had a beer. Wine and cocktails were typically her drinks of choice.

The three of them watched Salem and Kip in silence until the band took a break. "Everything going okay, Rals?" Trey asked casually, putting a foot up on the empty chair next to Raleigh. "That's quite a story you told about the old Bishop house."

Raleigh nodded. "I'm still trying to absorb it all myself."

Trey took a gulp of beer. "And you say Grant never said anything to you about the place? I can't understand why he wouldn't have taken you to see it and suggested that you live there together. He should have at least mentioned it."

Raleigh shrugged. "That's my eternal question."

Barb again smoothed her ponytail. "Did you have a birthday or anniversary coming up? Maybe he planned to surprise you with it."

The game ended with Kip victorious. Raleigh's sister playfully smacked Kip on the arm before retreating to the bathroom.

"My turn," Barb said, abandoning her half-drank beer and rising.

"Go get 'em, killer," Trey said in encouragement.

With Barb at the pool table chalking a cue stick and Kip racking up balls, Trey moved around to Barb's seat so that he was sitting next to Raleigh.

"You remind me of a peanut butter cup these days," he said.

"A what?" No one had ever made such a comparison to her before.

"You know what I mean. You're still sweet on the outside, but it covers up a pretty gritty interior."

Raleigh couldn't help it. She laughed at her brother-in-law. "I suppose I should be glad you aren't telling me that I remind you of a bobcat. Or a porcupine."

"Or a warthog." Trey nodded sagely.

"Indeed. I hear that in addition to being vicious creatures, they have awful fleshy wattles that hang from their faces," Raleigh said, playing along with Trey.

He grimaced exaggeratedly and swallowed more beer. "Actually, while we are alone, I wanted to talk to you about something serious."

"Shoot."

Trey lowered his voice conspiratorially. "I'm thinking of doing it. Of giving Barb a ring."

Not a surprise. "I figured this was coming sooner or later. You're like an intoxicated teenager with her."

He swept his gaze downward but had the goofy grin back on his face when he looked at her again. "I suppose I am. She's just perfect, Rals. I've been hesitant to mention anything to you because I know you've been so sad for so long. I didn't want to make it worse for you. And I miss Grant, too. But I just want to live again, and I want to share living with Barb."

There was that phrase about wanting to live again. What she had thought earlier in the evening for herself too. Suddenly, Raleigh felt very guilty over how she must have been appearing to her entire family over the past year.

"Of course, Trey. You *should* live. And you should be very happy. I'm sorry if I have wallowed for so long that it has made you uncomfortable. Barb seems like a wonderful woman and I'm glad for you. Really." She reached over and squeezed his arm in assurance.

It was all Trey needed to begin gushing over his plans for a surprise proposal in the near future. He described the perfect diamond ring he had selected and the perfect romantic restaurant where he planned to propose and the perfect cruise he wanted to take the new Mrs. Bishop on for a honeymoon.

Salem returned from the bathroom, her makeup freshened and her skin fragrant with newly-applied perfume.

"Who's winning now?" she asked, sliding into the chair Trey had vacated, her gaze solely on the action at the pool table.

"Don't know," Trey said. "You should probably go supervise them."

"I should!" Salem immediately rose from the table.

"Your sister is as subtle as a warthog," Trey observed as he watched Salem flirting with Kip. "What do you know about that guy?"

Raleigh decided maybe it was time to open up a little. "Not much, except that one day at St. Clements Bluff I was in some…distress…in the water, and he came by and saved me."

Now Trey's full attention was on her. "What do you mean, 'distress'? Why were you even near the frigid water in the middle of winter?"

Raleigh became uncomfortable. "I, um, thought that I saw something under the pier and accidentally fell in while I was investigating. I got caught up in something and couldn't get out. Kip happened to come by while fishing and, well, fished me from the river."

"You decided to walk down to the pier and step into the icy water, and he just *happened* to be there to save you?" Trey's disbelief was palpable. "Do you realize what I'm thinking right now? What the hell is he doing at our family functions?"

"Salem thinks he is a decent guy." Raleigh knew that was a ridiculous endorsement. "And it's not as though he had some motive to kill me if that's what you're contemplating."

"Humph." Trey turned his attention to the pool table for a few moments, then rose and went to the bar. He returned with two more mugs of beer.

"Sorry, Rals, to be suspicious," he said, placing another mug in front of her and moving her empty one to one side. "You know we are all just very protective of you."

Raleigh nodded. "I know. And I appreciate it."

Trey took another swallow and frowned, seeming to be gathering courage to say something. "I'd like to talk to you about something else before your sister mauls Kip to death and Barb wins by forfeit."

Salem was lightly raking Kip's shoulder with her brightly painted fingernails as he bent over the pool table. She leaned over to whisper something and giggled at whatever she had said. Kip missed his shot.

Raleigh turned her attention back to Trey. "Hopefully we won't need to call a coroner. What's up?"

Trey set his mug on the table and tapped his fingers against the glass. "I want to give Barb everything she deserves," he began hesitantly.

"Of course you do." Why was Trey stating the obvious?

"You know I've never been, well, serious enough to buy my own place. But I want Barb to have a home that is worth someone like her. So, I was wondering if you might consider selling St. Clements Bluff to me so I can give it to her as a wedding present."

"Oh." Raleigh was startled by his proposal and wasn't sure how to respond.

Trey took her silence as an opening to make his case. "I think we would start having children right away, and it sounds as if there would be so much room to grow there. Plus, I can take care of the place and make improvements for future generations."

Raleigh hated to disappoint him. "I had been thinking that I would turn it over to the historical society as a place of great significance. I envisioned it opening to the public for tours and thus it being preserved for future generations."

Trey was warming up to his own pitch, though. "But my plan keeps it in the Bishop family for future generations. Isn't that what Grant would have wanted?"

Raleigh's breath caught in her throat. Grant had asked her to care for the home for the rest of her life. Had he thought Trey would simply never be mature enough to care for it? Would he have happily turned it over to his brother now that Trey planned to be married?

She wasn't ready to commit to anything. "I need to think about it."

Trey blushed. "Of course. I'm sorry, Rals, I didn't mean to pressure you. We can talk about this when you're ready."

Raleigh nodded. "I'll get back to you soon. You should probably know that there is someone else who is, shall we say, *interested* in St. Clements Bluff."

"What do you mean?" Trey asked.

"I received a letter in the mail at the house suggesting that something bad happened there."

"You mean related to people passing through on the Underground Railroad? Who sent it?"

Raleigh shrugged. "I don't know on both counts. It was just signed 'a friend' and made reference to something that had occurred there that had been covered up."

"Covered up? By whom?"

Raleigh was pained to say it. "The letter said that Grant covered it up."

"Grant!" Trey exploded. "That's crazy. He was a total straight arrow. Who the hell is running my brother through the mud like that?"

Raleigh put out a hand to calm her brother-in-law. No need to attract attention over this. "I have no idea. Maybe it was just a weird prank of some sort. Please keep this to yourself. I'm not ready for anyone else to know about it."

Trey responded with muttered curses about what he would do to whomever was besmirching Grant Bishop.

Kip won his game against Barb. They shook hands across the green felt and Barb returned to the table.

Trey nodded at Raleigh. "Your turn. Show him how it's done."

Raleigh went to the pool table, where Salem was still standing, ostensibly continuing to cheerlead Kip.

Kip racked the balls. "Care to make it interesting?" he asked.

"I thought we had already agreed that the losing team was buying drinks."

Kip shrugged. "Sure, but this is between us. Winner of this game, let's see…" He rubbed his smooth chin thoughtfully. "Loser takes the other out for a drink."

Salem's reaction was one of pure shock, and it made Raleigh uncomfortable.

"You mean, the loser buys the winner a drink here after the game?" Raleigh asked.

"No, I mean the loser buys a drink in the kind of place that doesn't have sticky floors and greasy walls."

Although Raleigh was sure he was just teasing her, and she was ready to give back in kind, Salem's venomous expression made her pause.

Mistaking her hesitation for nervousness, Kip raised an eyebrow. "Sure you aren't afraid of losing? I'll take it easy on you so you have a fighting chance." He grinned at Raleigh.

That was all Raleigh needed to hear. "You're on," she said, going to the wall and pulling down a cue stick. Picking up a chalk cube from the pool table's ledge, she rubbed the blue chalk against the business end of the cue stick, the length of which was wrapped with a Coca-Cola logo.

Kip nodded at the table, indicating that she should break.

Raleigh set the solid white cue ball to one side at the other end of the table, her favorite shooting location. Taking careful aim, she leaned over, the forefinger and middle finger of her left hand creating an inverted "V" on the table's green felt as she practiced guiding the cue stick through the V opening with her right hand. Once she felt she had the exact right aim on the cue ball, Raleigh pulled back on the cue and then pushed through with controlled strength.

The cue ball hit the assembled group of striped and solid balls with a very satisfying smack. Even more gratifying was that two striped balls dropped into pockets.

Kip crossed his arms. "Not bad," he admitted.

From there, it was easy for Raleigh to make her way around the table, lining up shots and sinking her remaining five striped balls. When she followed up by gently tapping the eightball in, Kip nodded in defeat.

Raleigh almost felt guilty. She had been shooting pool for years. Before Grant's death, they would occasionally head out to local bars for a few games on a Friday or Saturday evening. Grant would joke that he should quit the Navy and just earn money betting on her.

"I think I've been tricked," Kip said. "I wasn't expecting that." But then he shrugged and grinned again. "I wasn't going to win either way," he said. "I'll meet you tomorrow afternoon around five o'clock. How about Social Coffeehouse?"

Studiously avoiding her sister, Raleigh nodded in agreement.

Kip placed his own cue stick in the rack and went to join Trey and Barb. Salem wrinkled her nose in disgust at Raleigh and trailed behind Kip.

Raleigh fished balls out of pocket nets and placed them back into their triangular holder as she waited for Trey to come to the table to challenge her.

"Lawdy, girl, what are you doing here?" came a strong, familiar voice. Raleigh looked up to find Magda standing at the opposite end of the table, holding up a quarter in one hand and managing what looked like a glass of whiskey in the other.

Magda slapped the quarter down on the table's ledge.

"Saw what you just did to that man," she said. "Let's see if you're that good, or he's that terrible." She took a long drink from her glass.

Raleigh smiled at her new neighbor. "Sure," she said, nodding at the table that Magda should break.

Magda refused. "Oh no, let's see if you can repeat what you just did twice in a row."

And so Raleigh did. This time when she broke, both a striped and a solid ball went into the pockets. She selected solids to play and proceeded to sink six more.

The band reassembled on the makeshift stage at one corner of the bar and started playing again, leading off with their own raucous tune about best friends teaming up in a bar fight.

To Raleigh's surprise, Magda began singing along at the top of her lungs.

And I asked the girl to be mine
But she said it weren't the right time
Next thing I knew
She was walking out with Drew
Now I know that
Bar fightin' for love
Only leads to another shove
To your heart-line

Magda was surprisingly agile as she bopped in place with a drink in her hand.

Raleigh leaned over and sank the eight ball again, but Magda no longer cared as she drank from her glass and cheered on the band.

Raleigh was amazed to see her neighbor like this, having assumed—completely incorrectly—that Magda was just a loner who rarely interacted with people.

Putting her cue stick away and scooping up Magda's

quarter, Raleigh signaled to Magda as well as she could over the band's noise that she should join them all at the table.

Magda secured another whiskey before joining them. The group dragged another small table over to allow for six chairs. It was nearly impossible to hear over the music—particularly with Magda continuing to sing along and then whistle, clap, and hoot at the end of each song. Thus Raleigh just kept her hands wrapped around her glass and observed the world around her.

Trey and Barb were leaning into one another, talking as though the world around them didn't exist. Raleigh wondered how they were even able to make themselves heard to one another. Salem sat next to Kip, morosely staring into her glass while he leaned his chair back on two legs, observing the band.

Raleigh had to admit the man was handsome. He looked so very different from the grizzled waterman that had pulled her from the river. He was…solid. Sure of himself. Like someone who could easily handle trouble and worry.

As if reading her mind, Kip glanced across the table at her. She wasn't able to turn away in time so that he didn't know she had been staring. Hoping her face wasn't flaming red, Raleigh offered him a weak smile, which he returned with a wink before finally paying attention to whatever it was Salem was now shouting at him over the music to grab his attention.

Magda elbowed Raleigh's side from next to her as the band took a break once more.

"Well, I guess you're just that good," Magda said with a wink, seemingly unoffended by Raleigh running the table. "I've got my eye on you now."

Raleigh smiled. "Most people don't expect me to play well."

"It can be good to be something that others don't

expect," Magda replied, draining her glass. "No one should ever know what you're really up to." She put the tumbler down with a thud. "Ain't no one else's business what you can and can't do, nor what you do or don't want to do. Remember that." She yawned. "Well, that's more than I drink in a month. That's about it for me."

To Raleigh's surprise, Magda folded her arms on the table, put her head down, and was asleep in seconds.

Kip glanced at Magda in concern. "She okay?"

Before Raleigh could respond, Salem piped up. "Oh yes, she's just Raleigh's oddball neighbor. I'm sure she's fine."

Raleigh bristled, suddenly protective of this "oddball" neighbor.

"Magda is a neighbor to St. Clements Bluff," she told Kip.

He nodded. "I've seen her at places before. Car shows, the crab festival. She's been around a long time." That seemed to be a seal of approval on Magda. "She probably needs a ride home. You or me?"

"I'll take care of her," Raleigh said.

This seemed to please Salem, who leaned over and whispered in Kip's ear. He responded with a shrug and a nod.

Within a few seconds, Salem rose, beaming once more as she playfully tapped Kip's arm. He, too, stood. "Until tomorrow," he said to Raleigh with a nod.

Raleigh watched their retreating backs with a mix of emotions. She had to admit that jealousy stood out among her other feelings, but she wasn't sure whether it was jealousy over Kip himself…or over seeing Salem happy. That left her unsettled. Surely Salem had never begrudged her sister happiness with Grant, which made Raleigh wonder why she had these very conflicted feelings.

It required some contemplation.

Raleigh drove Magda home, thankful that the poor sleep-disordered woman managed to stay awake for the ride home. Later, Raleigh was stretched on the couch with Lindbergh, flipping back and forth between two cooking shows on the television when Salem finally came in around one o'clock in the morning. Lindbergh slid away from Raleigh to go greet her, leaving her chilled where his body had been.

Salem was entering the house with the stealth of a rhinoceros, so Raleigh simply called out to her, "I'm in the living room."

Salem walked in with Lindbergh, her mascara smeared and her complexion blotchy. "That Kip Hewitt is simply awful. I don't know what you see in him," she said in an accusing tone.

Raleigh was incredulous. "*I* don't see anything in him. You're the one who has been flitting around him like a moth." She took a deep breath. There was no point in arguing with Salem. "What happened?"

Salem collapsed in a recliner as Raleigh sat upright and clicked off the television. "I had proposed we go have coffee together. You know, to be sure neither of us was too inebriated from the evening."

Raleigh cut in, "You didn't seem concerned about that for the rest of us." She immediately regretted her resolve not to have an argument.

Salem offered her a glare in return as she clutched the arm ends of the black leather recliner. "Anyway, he agreed to meet me at a diner. We had coffee and pancakes. He likes them with pecans. He also puts way too much sugar in his coffee. I thought we were having a good time, but then I noticed that he wasn't asking questions about me, only about the house."

"You mean St. Clements Bluff?" Raleigh asked, sitting straighter on the sofa. "What sort of questions?"

Salem waved a hand. "I don't know. Things like who the previous owners were, when the modern kitchen was added, how old we thought the tunnel was, that sort of thing. Who cares? He had *me* in front of him, and all he cared about was a *house*?"

Raleigh didn't know how to comfort her sister, as she also found it curious that he wanted to question Salem over St. Clements Bluff. Why so much interest? "Maybe he likes architecture? Or he's a history buff?" she suggested.

"Yeah, just like *you*," Salem said, leaning forward.

Raleigh had said the wrong thing again.

"Kip had questions about you, too," Salem returned her head to the back of the recliner.

"Me?" Raleigh hoped she hadn't sounded panicked. "What about me?"

"How you came into ownership of the house, whether you planned to move into it and when, what renovations you intended to make. Questions about you, but really about the house. Oh, except that he asked how old Lindbergh was. That was weird. I told him Lindbergh was five years old. That's right, isn't it?"

Raleigh didn't know what to make of Kip's interrogation of her sister. "He's four. Not that it matters. What happened next?"

"When I didn't seem to know anything else, he tossed down some money for the bill, walked me to my car, shook my hand, and that was the end of it. As if I were just some realtor he was meeting with to discuss the purchase of a piece of property." Salem shook her head in disbelief.

Raleigh knew that Salem's primary problem was that her ego was bruised. She wasn't used to men not responding to her charms and beauty. Perhaps she needed distracting. "What about one of the Mikes you were interested in?"

Salem brightened a little at that. "I'd almost forgotten about him. Maybe we should go back to the Rose Garden this weekend."

The storm was passing. "Sure. Maybe this time we can try some of their oyster fritters."

"Definitely!" Salem was almost smiling now. "You know they say oysters are good for the love life."

Although Salem's ire was dissipating, Raleigh was discomfited. Kip Hewitt had been making intrusive inquiries about her and her inherited home, and she was scheduled to see him later in the day to collect on the bet made at Back Road Inn. She was glad they were meeting at a public place so that she could leave if it got uncomfortable.

But for now, her curiosity was up, and she intended to do some questioning of her own.

Salem rose from the recliner, yawning and stretching. "It's late, time for bed," she said.

Watching her from the floor, Lindbergh yawned, too. Salem started to walk out of the room but turned back and casually said, "Oh, by the way, Kip asked where you live when you're not exploring St. Clements Bluff."

Raleigh froze. "What did you tell him?"

"I told him you live in Leonard's Hundred."

"What were you thinking?" Raleigh demanded, once more incredulous over her sister's behavior.

"Well, it was before I got mad at him for being focused on the house. I figured he would eventually be coming over to see me here anyway. Sorry, Sisso."

Raleigh watched as Salem retreated up the stairs. Lindbergh started to follow Salem but seemed to realize that Raleigh wasn't going with her, so he yawned once more and climbed back onto the couch for a snooze.

Raleigh was torn between rage and panic over Salem's perfidy. Perhaps her sister had overstayed her welcome and needed to return to her namesake city.

CHAPTER 20

THE NEXT MORNING, Raleigh fled the house on a neighborhood jog before dawn to avoid seeing Salem, fearful that she might snap at her sister. What was done was done, and, as Salem had said, Kip Hewitt was likely harmless.

Besides, it was essentially impossible to remain anonymous and all Salem had done was make it a little easier for Kip to learn where she lived.

Firmly resolved that she would inform Mr. Hewitt that he was not to make any unannounced visits at her home, Raleigh felt more at peace with Salem's inadvertent blabbing about their location, although she was still irritated with her sister's carelessness.

By daybreak, Raleigh sat at her kitchen table, steaming cup of coffee in hand, contemplating how to spend her day before meeting Kip.

Reviewing the myriad of events from the previous few days in her mind, she realized that she had done little to investigate the "other" side of the Bishop family. She had a scrapbook full of pictures and articles, but maybe she needed to talk to someone who had actually known some of these people, at least those who had been alive in the last century.

She arrived on Pop and Mutzi's doorstep at nine o'clock, the scrapbook she had borrowed under one arm.

Mutzi expressed delighted surprise at her arrival. "How nice to see you again so soon, dear. I was just cooling a batch of pumpkin spice doughnuts."

Raleigh gave her a quick hug and ventured the questions.

"Sit with me while I make my glaze and I'll answer what I can, although I think David will know more than I do. He went to pick up his chainsaw from Milt's but should be back soon. He's been waiting a few weeks for it to be repaired and ran out as soon as the shop opened."

Raleigh followed her mother-in-law to the kitchen, quickly becoming enveloped in the aroma of cinnamon, cloves, and nutmeg. She assumed her regular counter stool spot and opened up the scrapbook on the counter as Mutzi continued working.

Raleigh flipped the pages until she reached the article about Francis Bishop, the headline of which she had forgotten but now it was like a glaring neon sign.

Walter Hewitt Arrested for
Attempted Murder of Francis Bishop

Raleigh read the article again, once more absorbing the details of Hewitt's attempted murder of Bishop for trying to appropriate a piece of Hewitt's property, as well as for having had an affair with Hewitt's wife.

"Did you ever hear of a Francis Bishop?" she asked Mutzi.

The older woman was pouring maple syrup into a mixing bowl. "That's a pretty common name," she said. "I'm sure there have been dozens of Francis Bishops."

Mutzi moved to another bowl, where she dumped in confectioner's sugar from a box. A small white cloud *poofed* up from the bowl. "He would have been alive in 1915," Raleigh told her, going on to read the article to her mother-in-law.

As she listened, Mutzi added water to the bowl of powdered sugar and used a whisk to blend them together.

"Rat poison?" her mother-in-law asked. "Sounds awful. I guess maybe Francis deserved it, though."

The sound of the front door opening caused Mutzi to call out, "Hon?"

David Bishop appeared in the kitchen as his wife was pouring the sugar and water mixture into the maple syrup. He was clad in worn, frayed clothing, suggesting he planned on hard, messy work with his repaired chainsaw.

"Do you know about a Francis Bishop who was almost murdered by a Hewitt at the turn of the 20th century?" Mutzi asked without preamble.

Pop raised an eyebrow at Raleigh. "What in heaven's name have you been discussing this early in the morning?"

Raleigh smiled at her father-in-law. "I'm just doing some research on the family and came across this article." She turned the scrapbook around so that he could read it for himself.

Her father-in-law stroked his chin thoughtfully. "Yes, I remember talk about this old scandal. There had been fighting over a house. Walter Hewitt had gone down south somewhere to take care of some business matters, and while he was gone, well, Francis Bishop sort of moved himself into Walter's bedroom. Walter had actually married a Bishop girl, although I don't think she was any sort of close relation to Francis. But it set the gossiping to full throttle."

Mutzi was now sprinkling various baking spices into her glaze and tasting after each addition.

"They were fighting over the Hewitt home?" Raleigh asked.

"Yes, it had been built in the previous century. There was something about it, let me think…"

Mutzi now drizzled her glaze over the cooling doughnuts. Pop gave them a longing glance.

"How are you related to Francis Bishop?" Raleigh was having a hard time focusing herself with the irresistible aroma surrounding her. Mutzi really was a wizard at baked goods.

"Not sure. He's from the other side of the family. The Bishops split so long ago and went their separate ways that it's hard to know when and where it happened."

To Raleigh's dismay, Mutzi picked up the platter of doughnuts and started walking away. "Hey!" Pop said. "Where are you going with that?"

Mutzi paused. "They have to go into the refrigerator for just a few minutes so my glaze can harden. Don't worry, it won't be long."

Raleigh shared her father-in-law's angst over the round treats' disappearance.

Pop reluctantly returned his attention to Raleigh. "Where was I? Oh yes, the other Bishops. The side of the family that moved down county seemed to drift into bad ways. Petty crimes, hanging with bad elements, shady business enterprises. Not all of them, mind you, just…a few."

An uncomfortable thought seeped into Raleigh's mind. "Do you think St. Clements Bluff belonged to someone that—of whom, Grant was perhaps not proud?"

Pop considered this. "Maybe. Have you checked the county records on it?"

"Actually, yes, the Bishops obtained the property in 1843, although later it was bought by an entity called 'Maritime Shippers.' My boss thinks it may have been a blockade runner as the property was purchased in 1861. By 1866, St. Clements Bluff had reverted back to a Henry Bishop."

Mutzi opened the refrigerator door to check the doughnuts, and Raleigh's stomach rumbled in response. Had she regained her appetite?

Mutzi pulled the doughnut tray from the refrigerator. Raleigh was ready to fall on it like a rabid hyena, and Pop looked like he was ready to join her.

"Not so fast, you two," Mutzi said, wagging a finger. "Presentation is everything."

Raleigh's mother-in-law made them wait until she artfully arranged the doughnuts on the glass pedestaled tray. Then they had to wait even longer while Mutzi got out plates, knives, and napkins, and poured glasses of milk.

Is this what it felt like to be Lindbergh, waiting for a doggie treat?

Finally, with two place settings out and drinks poured, Mutzi offered the tray to her husband and Raleigh.

Raleigh lifted one doughnut from the tray while Pop immediately took two. The first of his was downed before Raleigh had an opportunity to cut hers in half.

She asked her next question, the one that was truly bothering her. "Has there been any sort of long-standing feud between the Hewitts and the Bishops?"

It took Pop a moment to respond as he was busy gathering the crumbs from his first doughnut, presumably to ensure he didn't waste anything before moving to the second one. He finished the crumbs before responding.

"Don't think so. Last feuding I know of down here was during the oyster wars. But that was watermen against pirates, not local families against each other. Besides, isn't Hewitt the name of the young man Salem invited over the other night? He doesn't seem to have any problem with us."

"True." Raleigh focused on her doughnut while contemplating what Pop had said. Funny that he had brought up the oyster wars to her.

"About that," she said. "Do you think there may have been people along the St. Mary's shoreline who were sympathetic to the oyster pirates? Those who may have seen them as somehow romantic or rebels to be hailed?" Bert Mattingly had already shot down the idea, but she thought she'd ask someone whose family had been here for ages.

Pop gazed at Raleigh as if a third eye had popped out on her forehead. "Absolutely not. The watermen here were outraged by what was going on. It would have had to be an absolute traitor to our way of life if someone had supported the pirates."

Raleigh nodded. "I'm sure you're right, Pop."

"I'm always right," he replied with a grin before turning his attention to his wife. "Mutzi, I've got to go pick up my chainsaw from Dave's Engine. I'll be back shortly."

Mutzi stopped what she was doing at the sink, a soapy plate in her hands. "What do you mean? You just got back from that."

David Bishop frowned. "Right, right. I'm just testing you to see if you're paying attention, woman." He followed this with a jovial laugh.

The expression on Mutzi's face gave Raleigh concern. Had grief impacted her father-in-law far more than she had ever imagined?

It bore heavily on her mind later as she drove away from her in-laws' home.

Kip sat nervously in the coffee shop, willing himself to stop tapping his right sneaker against the floor. Fortunately, Raleigh arrived a few minutes later at the Social Coffeehouse where Kip had arranged their meeting.

He rose to greet her when she entered, his smile genuine. It was unnerving, how she made him feel.

"How was traffic?" he asked as they both sat down. Kip had a glass of water next to him, a lonely sliver of lemon floating in it. The cafe was humming with activity, as usual, with a line of patrons six deep wanting their afternoon mocha lattes to keep them going until bedtime.

Raleigh shrugged. "It's the county. Just the usual slowpokes, plus an Amish carriage and a combine harvester to go around."

"A combine? In February?"

"I suppose it was a little unusual." She shrugged again. "Perhaps the farmer was moving it to another location?" The tractor wasn't really all that interesting a topic.

Kip shrugged, too. "Sounds reasonable enough. So, I owe you this one. What's your pleasure?"

Kip followed Raleigh's cue and glanced up at the chalkboard that served as the coffee shop's menu. It was alive in multiple color chalks, which a talented artist had done up in swirls, hearts, and stars surrounding the offerings of hot and cold drinks, as well as sandwiches and salads.

"Hmm," she said. "Since this is penance, I suppose I should have a large coffee. French Roast, please."

Kip looked at her quizzically. "That's it? Just regular coffee?"

Raleigh put a hand to her chest as if in mock horror. "*Just* regular coffee? Didn't you hear me say that I wanted a large cup of French Roast, the finest style of bean ever produced?"

Kip rolled his eyes. "Alright then. How about something to eat?"

Raleigh frowned. "No, I'm fine with just coffee."

Kip joined the long line of patrons to secure their order then rejoined her at their table, which was clearly made from reclaimed wood, with unpretentious gouges and nicks in the darkened, aged stain.

It went well in the cafe, which was popular in the

county because it almost had the atmosphere of a cozy wine cellar instead of a brightly lit restaurant.

Once her lidded cup and his smaller one were served—along with a plate containing two chocolate chip cookies for him—Kip sat back in his chair and observed Raleigh with a bemused expression. "So, where did you learn to shoot pool like that?"

"I had a boyfriend when I was a teenager who was very serious about the game. He played every weekend and most weeknights after school, so I learned that if I wanted to spend time with him, I better learn to play. Turns out I was good at it. Better than him, even. He dumped me when my ranking went above his in the league we were in together." She laughed as though it was a pleasant memory.

Kip drank from his cup. "You should always expect your student to surpass you, and be glad of it," he said. "For it means you have improved the next generation."

Raleigh laughed again. "You sound like a fortune cookie."

"I'm probably more about cookies than fortunes. Especially warm chocolate chip ones. Perfect on a cold day." He held one up before taking a bite, then asked, "Sure you don't want one?"

"Thank you, but no." Raleigh's expression turned serious. "How long has your family been in the county?" she asked.

Kip took another bite and put the cookie down. "Long time. At least as long as the Bishops. I mean, we aren't so illustrious that I have ancestors who came over on the Ark or the Dove from England, but we go back to at least the late 1700s. Why?"

"Just wondering," she said. "I've been doing so much research since—acquiring—St. Clements Bluff, and I find it interesting how many families settled here ages ago and still have land holdings."

Kip nodded. "My family doesn't have a lot of land holdings. We are just simple folk, as they say. Actually, my father sold some waterfront acreage quite a few years ago and made a tidy sum on it. Used to be that only poor people and watermen lived on the water. No self-respecting rich person would have dreamed of living in a place overlooking crab traps, stinking of briny air, and in perpetual risk of ruin from storms. Now, though, everyone wants to live by the water if they can." He polished off his second cookie in a few bites, leaving a single chocolate chip on the plate.

He gingerly picked up the dark morsel and handed it to Raleigh, who instinctively put her hand out to take it. "They were great cookies. I could buy you one to take home if you'd like."

Raleigh gave him a wry look. "Thanks." She popped the chip in her mouth and drank more coffee.

Kip pushed both his plate and his coffee aside. "Speaking of houses, I'd like to show you something. A house."

"What do you mean?" Raleigh said. She looked wary now and that was certainly not his intention.

"My family doesn't have a lot of land holdings, as I said, but we do have a particular house that might interest you."

"Are you trying to sell it? Because I'm not—"

Kip held up a hand. "Definitely not. I just think you might be interested in the layout."

A faint light of understanding dawned in her eyes. "Is it…is it a replica of St. Clements Bluff?"

He nodded. "After I had the tour of your house, I recognized it as being just like St. George Manor, but there are, shall we say, significant differences."

"No secret tunnel?" she asked.

He didn't answer, not wanting to reveal too much

at once. Instead, he just said, "You need to see it for yourself."

Raleigh hesitated and he knew she probably didn't quite trust him yet. And he couldn't blame her. She didn't know him, not really.

"Tell you what," he said. "I'll give you my largest filleting knife, and you can slice me open if I behave in an untoward manner at any point. Okay?" By not taking any offense to her hesitation he hoped to calm whatever reluctance she had.

It worked, for Raleigh agreed to ride with him to St. George Manor. They finished their coffees and stood. Two other patrons sat at their table before they had even reached the shop's front door. "Sure you don't want that cookie?"

Her smile was sweet but tentative when she answered him. "Next time."

And, for some reason, Kip felt warmth spreading throughout his torso.

CHAPTER 21

INSIDE KIP'S TRUCK bed was a wire crab trap, several fishing poles, and a large tackle box. For the first time, he noticed that the cab's interior was heavy with the smell of salt. All they needed was a hurricane to sweep through to make the picture complete.

He opened the passenger door and lifted a couple of dog-eared wire-bound notebooks from the bench and tossed them to the floor. Then he held out a hand to help Raleigh up into the seat before coming around and sliding into the driver's seat.

Once they were underway and driving down Route 5, Kip said, "Your brother-in-law is a bit older than you, isn't he?" He kept his tone casual, hoping Raleigh wouldn't hear the great curiosity he felt.

"Yes, he was the eldest over Grant by three years. That's an odd question. Why do you ask?"

Kip shook his head. "No particular reason. Just curious about the family. He seems very taken with Barb." In addition to changing the subject, he flipped on his turn signal and made a right off Piney Point Road.

"I suppose he should be. He plans to propose to her. I've never seen him so absolutely gaga before."

Kip turned to observe Raleigh's profile in the fading light. She was disturbingly attractive. He frowned and focused his attention on the road before them.

"I hope they are happy together," he said, immediately realizing that his words sounded sarcastic.

He had no time to worry about it. Raleigh gasped next to him as they pulled up in front of an old, white clapboard house that looked just like St. Clements Bluff, down to the water visible in the distance behind the house and even the same circular driveway with the lawn jockey in the center of it.

"Here we are," he announced. "St. George Manor on Herring Creek. This property originally included around two thousand acres as part of an old land grant. It was built by a Roger Thoroughgood around 1820. Same guy who built your place."

Kip let his truck idle as they sat parked in front of the house, knowing that Raleigh would need a moment to take it all in.

"It does look similar."

"Yep, look closer," Kip said, finally killing the engine. "Even down to the shutter, colors, gravel drives, and little painted iron men."

He opened his door and jumped down. Raleigh did the same. He walked up to the front porch and on the same steps painted in the same white as St. Clements Bluff.

Raleigh followed him inside and, in what was no surprise, gasped again at the layout which was an exact replica of her own home. What was different about St. George Manor, of course, was that this home looked lived in, with its old furniture pieces and fringed carpets strewn about. Both landscapes and portraits of long-dead relatives hung on the walls.

The kitchen here was about as old as the one at St. Clements Bluff but done in an awful palette of lime green and aqua. Intent on staying true to his word, Kip pulled open a drawer and pulled out a boning knife, which he handed to Raleigh. "Kindly don't use it if I tell a bad joke."

He could tell she felt silly the way she took it from him. "Thank you, I think." She wrinkled her nose in an endearing way.

They continued walking through the downstairs. "It's laid out just as the long-ago builder would have done with the other houses he built on speculation," Raleigh said, as she now stepped behind Kip up the staircase.

"Hmmm," he replied noncommittally. He went straight to the top floor and into the bedchamber mirroring the one at St. Clements Bluff. This room didn't have the ornately carved furniture that hers did, of course, but did have a perfectly serviceable walnut bedroom suite in it.

"What's different in here?" Kip asked with an air of challenge as he crossed his arms and waited for her answer.

She looked around the room, which was approximately the same length and width as the bedchamber at St. Clements Bluff. The windows were situated in the same way and appeared to be roughly the same height. He refrained from smiling as Raleigh's gaze moved to the fireplace and she nodded in understanding.

"There is no space for a secret passageway behind the fireplace," she said. "That's what is different. This home was not likely a stop on the Underground Railroad."

"True enough. But follow me." Kip led her out of the room and down a flight of stairs to where the other bedchambers were above the first floor.

He pushed open the door to one of the rooms and waved Raleigh in. This room also faced over the back of the property with a view of Herring Creek, like the upstairs bedchamber. "What do you see now?" he asked. He didn't have to wait long for her reply.

"The fireplace," she said simply.

He nodded. "What of it?"

Raleigh walked over to it. She splayed a palm against

the wall, which was covered in floor-to-ceiling wood wainscoting. "Is this what I think it is?" she asked.

"It is. Watch." Joining her at the wall, Kip felt around until he appeared to find a location he sought and pressed against it. There was an audible click and then Kip was able to easily push the section of wall inward. She looked inside and then turned to him, her expression one of amazement.

"How is this possible? That both of these homes have secret spaces? Were all four of them built this way?"

"According to what little I could dig up, Thoroughgood's sister, who came up with the floor plan, thought these places were not only 'amenable' for families but provided secure hiding from the British, who were regularly rampaging a bit too much for most Americans' comfort, I expect. I don't know about the other one still existing, and, of course, the fourth house burned down, so we will never know whether it did or not. Ready?" he asked.

Raleigh nodded as she followed him down the rough staircase. As with St. Clements Bluff, it led down into a tunnel. This tunnel wasn't as wet as that of St. Clements Bluff but still moved toward the direction of the water.

Where they exited was into a meagerly outfitted guest house, with a bed, a clothing armoire, a small table and chairs, a wood stove, and some kitchen pots, pans, and utensils. It was cool inside but not unbearable.

Raleigh's expression was confused. "Are we in a fancy slave cabin?"

Kip smiled sadly. "I'm afraid not. Let me tell you a story."

He sat down at the table and Raleigh joined him. He suddenly wished he could offer her a cup of coffee to cradle in her hand, for he knew she wasn't going to like what he was about to tell her.

"My father, Nelson Hewitt, purchased a commercial

walk-in cooler a few years before he died. He placed it in the detached garage of our house, where it shared space with lawnmowers, crab traps, crab pots, nets, and fishing gear. Basically, the garage held everything but cars." Kip sighed, remembering his past.

"Dad's foresight on the cooler was admirable. Offering fresh, locally-picked crabs to the area's up-and-coming 'fusion' and 'locally-sourced' restaurants had been just the start of our family-run business. Soon, my father and I were in the water every day seeking out fresh catches of all sorts to supply restaurants in the local area. I learned more about government red tape with regard to commercial crabbing and fishing licensing and about seafood supply regulations than I could have ever imagined knowing."

Raleigh was silent but listened intently as Kip continued.

"Suddenly, my father was gone from a heart attack—one of those widow-makers that fells a larger-than-life man who has barely turned fifty—and I was now in charge of the business. I do love it, despite the long hours and the uncertainty of what haul I'll be able to get on any given day, and despite stinking to high heaven." He turned to look straight at Raleigh. "And also, despite not knowing whether I will come across damsels in distress."

"That's not fair. I—" Raleigh started to protest.

He held up a hand and winked, again trying to set her at ease. "Just teasing. Anyway, here's where the story gets a little darker. Like you, I inherited this house from my father. Also like you, I had no idea of the home's existence until after my father's death. Strange how many parallels there are, right?"

Raleigh nodded. It was downright eerie.

Kip breathed deeply. He had no desire to say the next part. "When I told my mother I had found this secret staircase, she said—and I quote—'So that's how the old dog did it.'"

Raleigh looked puzzled. "How he did…what?"

Kip stood and began pacing in the small room. "Mom told me that at some point in their marriage, my father became interested in a woman who ran Fenwick's General Store. It no longer exists. Anyway, Dad suddenly needed to run out nearly every day to pick up bait, hooks, potato chips, whatever. Mom was certain Dad was having an affair but couldn't figure out how he was managing it. Not many hotels here in that day, plus everyone knew everyone else's business even more than they do now. Nowhere to hide, you know?"

"But why did your father need a house with a secret staircase and tunnel to an outbuilding? Why not just meet her in the house?"

Kip smiled sadly. "You really don't understand rural life. Doesn't matter where you live, you don't want your car and that of your mistress parked together in one location. *Someone* will notice, and the blabbing will begin. This place would have enabled one of them to come by boat and the other to go through the tunnel to their secret nest. The house never had to have any of their belongings in it. Turns out the home had been originally built with the staircase and tunnel in it. My father was just able to take advantage of it."

Raleigh blinked several times and Kip thought he saw tears well up in her eyes, but they were gone in an instant. He hadn't intended to make her sad, nor to feel sorry for him. Why couldn't he ever say anything properly?

"I read about another Hewitt in one of my mother-in-law's old scrapbooks," Raleigh said. "He, too, was apparently dallying where he shouldn't have been, and it nearly got him killed."

Kip offered a wry smile. "Old Francis Hewitt. Yes,

he's one of our historical black sheep. But assuredly he and my father don't represent the rest of the men in the family."

Kip stopped pacing and placed himself directly in front of her. "My family has had its share of pain, more than you know."

Raleigh lowered her voice to a whisper. "I can't imagine how difficult that would have been for your mom to discuss."

"Yeah, well. I'm not sure why I told you about my family history. It's just that all of these homes have weird compartments of sorts. I guess it was the nature of the design back in those days for whatever they were used for."

Raleigh pushed her chair away from Kip, and he knew she was breaking whatever connection they had in this moment. He was almost relieved. She definitely made him feel things and he needed to regain his breath and bearings.

"Sorry if I've said anything stupid. Friends?" He stuck out a hand.

Raleigh glanced down at his proffered palm, and for the first time, he felt embarrassed by how roughened it was from many years of hard work. Then she said, "When you rescued me, I guess we can call it that, I remembered your hand and the roughness of your skin…I, ah, liked it."

Kip smiled at that. That day kind of freaked him out, but he was glad he was there to help her. Maybe fate had a hand in that, then he smiled broader at his pun.

She tentatively held out her hand and he clasped it firmly.

"Of course. Friends," she said albeit hesitantly. "It may take me a while to actually be one," she added with a wan smile. "I'm afraid I'm still healing."

"I understand. More than you know." He needed

to lighten things up. "Hey, I have an idea. Feel adventurous?"

"More adventurous than discovering a second old home with a potentially dark past?" Raleigh's tone was teasing. Thank God for that.

"I'm definitely not proposing anything else dark, gloomy, or depressing. Have you ever been to First Friday?"

First Friday was an event held the first Friday of each month in the town square of Leonardtown. Shops, restaurants, and other venues participated with special pricing, meals, and fun activities to draw locals into their establishments.

"I've been once or twice, but only in the summer when there are bands playing in the square."

"Definitely no bands outside in February, but there's still plenty to do. If you feel up to walking in the cold, that is?" He posed it as a challenge.

"It beats cobwebs and musty smells," she said. "Let's go."

Because it was winter, the event was not as crowded as it would be in the heat and late sunsets of summer. After finding parking, they walked to the center of the town's square and went in and out of shops offering everything from locally-made chocolates to whiskey to artwork using reclaimed wood from area barns.

There was something relaxing in just forgetting everything for a few minutes and just immersing himself in the pleasures St. Mary's County had to offer with this woman by his side.

Raleigh purchased a small box of milk chocolate-enrobed graham crackers from the chocolatier. "For my mother-in-law," she explained.

"Hungry?" Kip asked. "It's been a long time since those chocolate chip cookies for me."

Raleigh nodded at Kip, and he led her to the nearby

Rex Restaurant. Unlike the shops, this place was hopping with patrons. Many sat at the bar, trying out the First Friday special, written on a board as a Town Square Mule, made from cinnamon whiskey, ginger beer, and apple cider, and accented with a cinnamon stick. It sounded perfect for a chilly evening.

Kip led her past the bar to a booth and they both slid in across from one another. With drinks and an order of nachos served a few minutes later, Kip watched Raleigh in amusement as she dug into the food with gusto.

"Been on a deserted island recently?"

Raleigh dropped the meat and cheese-laden chip she was holding, her cheeks suddenly aflame.

"I guess it has been a long time since I've been interested in eating," she said. "I've lived on coffee since Grant died." She tore the loaded chip in half and popped the piece in her left hand into her mouth. "And I must tell you, this blend of spiced meat, cheese, sour cream, and cilantro is total goodness. Grant really loved nachos and—"

She abruptly stopped and grew quiet.

Kip understood her completely. "I know all about loss," he said, lacing his fingers in front of him on the table and ignoring the nachos.

"You do?" Raleigh asked. "Do you mean beyond losing your father?"

He nodded. "Yes, that was difficult enough, especially after I discovered what my mother had been keeping secret about him. When someone you've loved and respected turns out to have considerable flaws that are difficult to overlook, well, it becomes confusing."

"Who else did you lose?"

Now Kip became interested in the nachos. He pulled a towering section of them toward his appetizer plate and let it fall over onto his dish, then pushed some of the nacho mixture onto a chip and took a bite.

His gaze locked onto hers again. “I’ve never been married. But I almost was once. I had a girlfriend, Helen, about ten years ago. Well, she wasn’t just my girlfriend, she was my fiancée. We were planning to marry over Christmas, her favorite time of the year.”

CHAPTER 22

KIP KNEW HIS tone was almost emotionless, but that kept him under control. Raleigh said nothing as she waited expectantly.

"Helen had a pet greyhound that she had gotten from a rescue group. She loved that thing beyond all reason. I was even a little afraid that the greyhound might end up being the third person in our marriage. But I was willing to consider Petey a part of the family."

Lindbergh probably meant the same to Raleigh.

"Just after Thanksgiving that year, she learned of another greyhound that the rescue group wanted to save from some sort of abusive owner. The dog was in Pennsylvania, just across the Maryland state line. I couldn't go with her as I had promised my mother I would help fix a leaky pipe under her kitchen sink that day, and Helen didn't want to wait to snatch the pup from its owners and give them a piece of her mind."

He took a drink from his glass, postponing the next part of the story for just a moment.

"Helen called me after she had retrieved the dog from its tiny, filthy pen. She had let the owners have it, verbally lashing them until they begged her to just take the dog and leave them alone." Kip smiled at the memory. "She told me she'd be home in about three hours, and that was it."

Raleigh looked at him quizzically. "What do you mean, 'that was it'? Are you saying you never heard from her again?"

"No, it wasn't that. She got on the Capital Beltway and was heading south when it started raining. It had been an unusually cold November—almost as cold as it is now—and it quickly turned to freezing rain. Have you ever experienced the Beltway up near the Mormon Temple in Kensington?"

"Yes. It's a winding, nerve-wracking, raceway-like strip of road, designed as though the civil engineer had been inebriated the day he planned it out. You need great intestinal fortitude to get through it."

"Helen certainly had fortitude, having just made two people wish they had never been born. I suspect she was so rushed on adrenaline from the encounter that she didn't realize how slick the road was getting. When she got into that patch of road, she lost control of her car. It was too difficult for her to regain control what with the road curves. The investigators estimated that the car rolled at least four times and that it was a miracle no other car was involved. And so…she was gone."

Kip caught Raleigh's gaze and they stared at each other for long moments, food and drink completely forgotten and the noise of the restaurant fading into a distant buzzing in Kip's ears.

She finally broke the silence between them. "I know how inadequate words of condolence are."

He shook his head. "It was a long time ago. I should warn you, though, that grief has a way of popping back into your life at the very moment you think you've buried it for good. You think you've buried it, planted grass, and installed a headstone. But grief rises out of the ground, grabs you by the throat, shakes you, then tosses you to the ground, leaving you gasping for air."

"Morbidly poetic," Raleigh observed.

"Not at all. I just want you to know that although life will seem to make progress back to normal—like regaining your appetite and venturing out to shoot pool—there will still be very bad moments."

Raleigh smiled wanly. "Grief has been a close friend of mine, and not one I'm willing to completely part with yet. Do you still have bad moments?"

"Only rarely. They usually appear after having a nightmare in which I'm in the car with Helen and can't convince her to slow down as she's driving. Then I live the accident with her, still screaming at her to take her foot off the pedal."

His statement caused more tears in her eyes. This time they did not disappear quickly. "I understand that," she whispered.

Kip took a deep breath. "Okay, enough of this. It's First Friday, and a 'first' anything should mean renewal. Looks like there's a band setting up over in the corner." He indicated a place somewhere behind Raleigh.

She stood and turned around to get a better view and quickly sat down again. "Oh my, it's The Two Mikes. Salem has started dating one of them."

Kip laughed. "Am I forgotten so quickly, then? Actually, I'm glad to hear that she has an interest in someone. But she lives in North Carolina, doesn't she? Long-distance romances can be tricky."

"You don't know my sister," was all Raleigh said, which was good enough for Kip.

They spent time just listening to the music, which was quite good. The other patrons seemed to think so, as well, as much of the energy in the place was directed at the Mikes, with people shouting out song requests and a few couples wandering onto the floor to shake and wriggle to the music.

The Two Mikes eventually changed it up to a soulful, romantic song. "What do you think?" Kip asked, holding out a hand.

Raleigh stumbled. "I—I don't know if I can—I'm not ready—"

Kip took her hand in his other one and placed it in his open palm, closing his strong fingers around hers. "Raleigh Bishop, haven't you figured out yet that I am fall—that I don't mean you any harm? You're jumpier than a trout trying to shake an angler's hook. Relax for just a few minutes around me. Please."

Her hand relaxed in his and she nodded as if making a decision. "I will. Or at least I promise to try."

With a wry smile, he replied, "I guess that's as much as I can expect from an independent, coffee-swilling pool shark."

They laughed as Kip led her to the dance floor and found a spot next to a couple that may have indulged in one too many Town Square Mules, as they seemed to be propping one another up. Raleigh soon forgot about them as Kip slid an arm around her waist and pulled her close. Her perfume reminded him of a fresh river breeze in April, promising warmth and sunshine in the summer to come.

It was both intoxicating and terrifying at once.

Kip instinctively bent down and pressed his head against the side of hers, humming along with Mike's words, dreading the moment the song would end and burst this cocooned moment.

But it did, and The Two Mikes announced that they were going to take a ten-minute break. It required all he had to move away from Raleigh, but he did so with a very gentle kiss on her forehead. "Thank you," he whispered against her skin.

He thought she whispered, "You're welcome" as he led her back to the table.

They sat again. How could he make this outing last longer? He had an idea.

"I bet the Old Jail is open late," Kip said. "Want to visit? Oh, wait, you're involved in museums, so that's probably old news to you."

To his surprise, she quickly agreed to his suggestion. "No, let's do that. I tend to be very focused on my own work and rarely get out to go visit other locations in the community. I've only been to the Old Jail once and don't know that much about it."

Kip could hardly believe his luck.

They walked about five hundred yards to the Old Jail, which Raleigh took to mean the structure that existed prior to the building of the modern, well-secured facility that had been around since at least the turn of the 21st century. She tried to stay focused on where they were going and not on his presence next to her as they walked. The dance had left her breathless, and she was still recovering from it.

She had enjoyed dancing with Kip, surprised she could do it without falling on the floor in a heap of tears thinking about Grant. But it had been…easy. In fact, she had even felt what she could only describe as an internal nudge when Kip had encouraged her to join him on the dance floor. Could it be Grant reaching out, letting her know it was ok? She was getting ridiculous with all her machinations. Perhaps it was time to stop.

As they approached the building, she saw that the Old Jail was hardly bigger than a standard, two-story house, although it was interestingly built of both brick and stone, with the first floor made of unevenly cut stones and the upper story facing containing old red brick. There was a single, white-painted door entrance to the jail and the paned windows across the front were all flanked with black shutters.

It had to have been the tiniest museum Raleigh had ever entered, but what she learned there was astonishing.

The downstairs had served as the living quarters for the county jailer and the jailer's family. Up a narrow set of stairs were three cells, one larger than the other two, and each containing a few rough bunks and buckets for defecation. At different points, they had held anywhere from ten to thirty-five prisoners at a time.

Raleigh couldn't imagine that many people spread across the three spaces.

Constructed in 1876, the building was the sixth jail constructed in the county and had replaced an even smaller, one-story structure that was reputedly easy to escape from.

There was one piece of information, though, that was extraordinary enough to almost make her forget Kip's presence.

"Look," she said pointing to a placard entitled, *Freedom Seekers in Leonardtown*.

> *The Old Jail is a site on the Underground Railroad Network to Freedom. Many freedom seekers and those who aided them were detained at the jail.*
>
> *Two women were convicted of "harboring a slave." One, a white woman, was pardoned. The other, a formerly enslaved, free black woman, served a four-year sentence.*

The information was accompanied by a map showing the Railroad's network in Maryland.

Raleigh's mind was swirling.

"What's going on in there?" Kip asked, leaning close to her and gently placing a hand on the back of her head.

"There's something significant here, but I don't know what it is," Raleigh said.

"You think that a Bishop was harboring slaves at St. Clements Bluff and then, what? Ended up in jail? What would that have to do with Grant hiding the property from you?"

Raleigh's thoughts were even more confused. "You're right, of course. And there are many branches to the Bishop family. Including, apparently, a good side and a bad side. I wish I knew more. Maybe there is a list of everyone who ever served time here."

But a quick check downstairs with the museum's docent on duty indicated that records that far back were a little sketchy as compared to modern times. The only Bishop on record for having served time in jail was an Ernest Bishop, who spent thirty days there for "total drunkenness and depraved destruction of a bicycle not his own" in 1892.

Raleigh and Kip returned upstairs to where the cells were. They were alone on this floor of the museum. Discreetly placed ceiling lights illuminated the exhibit signs, but with only moonlight outside it was evident how very isolated a prisoner would have felt here. To have been imprisoned for a noble act, like helping someone to freedom, and then to be crowded in with thieves, rapists, and murderers in nearly total darkness would have been terrifying. Had one of Grant's ancestors ended up here for using St. Clements Bluff as part of the underground movement?

Raleigh shuddered.

"You okay?" Kip asked, putting an arm around her shoulders.

"I'm fine." Kip's arm was comforting, but he kept it there only briefly before sliding it off and putting his hands in the pockets of his jeans.

Raleigh instantly missed his touch.

"Still feeling adventurous?" he said, tucking his hands in his jacket pockets. "I can't promise to unearth more Bishops, but we can do some more local history. Have you ever visited the Moll Dyer rock? I never have, even though Moll Dyer is infamous around here. I only know she was rumored to be a witch."

"I have. The rock was named for St. Mary's County's famous 17th century witch, and her name was on the cinnamon whiskey they put in our drinks."

Kip raised an eyebrow. "I see you really do know St. Mary's County. Even if you're just a transplant," he added with a wink.

Raleigh was secretly pleased with his praise. Meanwhile, the evening with Kip was not yet over and she was pleased about that, too. They began walking away from the jail. Their hands brushed together and he reached out to take hers in his. This time she didn't protest.

It's time to choose to be happy, her mother had said.

"I suppose witch trials went on in more places than just Massachusetts," he said. "Although those were the most famous ones."

"I wouldn't exactly say Moll Dyer had a trial," Raleigh said. "She was supposedly living in seclusion in a hut in the woods below Leonardtown. She had no husband nor children, so townspeople viewed her with suspicion."

At "no husband nor children," Raleigh felt a small pang but was relieved that it quickly dissipated, especially with the warmth she was experiencing with her hand tucked in Kip's.

"So naturally, during a particularly harsh winter where many were suffering, a mob decided it was the fault of the 'witch' Moll Dyer," she continued. She blew out a breath and it made a cloud in front of her face as it crystallized in the cold.

Raleigh's pang was back, only this time because she knew what Moll Dyer's fate was.

"They marched down to her little hut, presumably just to chase her out of town, but who knows what the mob may have truly had in its mind. Moll fled her hut and disappeared into the woods. The mob, not completely content that they had forced a woman out into the freezing weather, burned her decrepit home to the ground before returning, satisfied, to their own houses." Did that sound too sarcastic?

Kip stopped. "Did Moll return to see her destroyed hut?"

Raleigh shook her head and continued walking. "No, she didn't come back. A couple of days later, a local boy went into the woods, seeking a cow that had wandered away from his family's farm. The story holds that he found Moll frozen to death on the ground, lying prone against a rock and clawing up at the air with one hand."

"What was she clawing at?" Kip asked.

Raleigh shrugged. "God? Her tormentors? Who knows?"

"Maybe she was raining down a curse on them," Kip suggested.

"Maybe." She paused the story as she stopped next to Tudor Hall, another historic county landmark just two hundred yards from the Old Jail. "Here we are."

Raleigh pointed downward with her free hand at a rock that was maybe a foot across. It was cordoned off by chain roping and had a spotlight on it. The placard stating that it was allegedly the rock upon which Moll Dyer died was larger than the stone itself.

"Oh." Kip sounded deflated. "The way you told the story I thought the rock would be more…substantial."

Raleigh laughed and blew a cloud of vapor from her mouth. "I think most people feel the same way when they see poor old Moll's death place."

He released her hand to check his watch. "I guess it's getting late."

Was that a note of disappointment in his voice?

Kip drove in silence back to Raleigh's car at St. George

Manor. Once there, he jumped out of the driver's seat and came around to let her out.

"Thanks for an interesting evening," he said as she climbed out of the truck. He leaned down to hug her and placed a kiss on her forehead before breaking away and going to her vehicle and opening the driver's door for her.

Was Raleigh relieved or disappointed that he had kept it so platonic?

"Hang on a minute," Raleigh said. She went to the passenger side of her car and unlocked the door. She reached in, pulled out a bundle, and brought it around to Kip.

"I have no idea whether you've even missed this or not, but—well, it's clean." Raleigh handed over the blanket Kip had wrapped around her the day he had pulled her from the river. "Thanks for saving me," she said, wondering if her own words had a double meaning.

"My pleasure," Kip said, his voice catching. He cleared his throat. "You know, I never believed you when you said that you were trying to reach something in the water that day. But I didn't like to think that you had perhaps...intentionally...been under the water."

His words provided a vivid reminder of what had happened that day. It seemed a lifetime ago that she had gotten caught up in the freezing river. It seemed almost ridiculous now that she had desired to do anything like that.

With a final goodbye, Raleigh slid into the driver's seat and started the engine. It took her a few moments to pull out while she sat there, thinking.

Had she just been out on a date?

CHAPTER 23

WITH HER BRUISED ego recovered, Salem was out with Mike on Saturday evening, so Raleigh had her house to herself. It struck her as funny that as much as Salem annoyed her, it was already a little lonely without her around.

She and Lindbergh had just settled in to watch some old comedy reruns when the doorbell rang. Lindbergh woofed softly and slid off the couch, waiting for Raleigh to rise so that he could escort her to the front door. She was glad that she was at least in her Navy sweatshirt and pants and not in her ratty bathrobe.

It was Trey. "Where's Barb?" Raleigh asked as she stepped back to let him in.

"At some community theatre thing with a friend of hers. I told her I wasn't sure I could endure one more variation of *A Midsummer Night's Dream.* The guy has been dead for centuries. Can't we let his stuff rest and do something newer with language that a mere mortal can understand?" Trey shrugged off his jacket and hung it on a hook next to Grant's flight jacket.

Raleigh smiled. "You were never one for the arts, were you?"

Lindbergh snuffled at Trey's hand. "You got me, buddy," he said, slipping a bone-shaped treat to the dog, who flopped to the floor to down it in two bites.

"Coffee?" Raleigh asked as she led her brother-in-law back to the kitchen.

"Sure, why not? I'm going to need some milk to cut it down."

"Amateur," Raleigh said as she began grinding beans.

As they sat down together, Raleigh noticed that there was a cobweb lightly blowing beneath the heat register in the ceiling. She grimaced. The house needed a thorough going-over. St. Clements Bluff was probably cleaner than this.

Trey tasted the coffee put before him and grimaced. He picked up the milk carton and poured it in until the coffee threatened to spill over the lip of the cup. He gingerly picked it up and drank from it.

"Too strong?" Raleigh asked.

Trey rolled his eyes. "No, not at all. Doesn't everyone want coffee that makes them ready to do a couple of laps on the Indianapolis Speedway without the benefit of a car?"

Raleigh lifted her cup to Trey and then downed half of it.

"Showoff," he said good-naturedly. "Listen, I have a plan for proposing to Barb in April and I need your help."

While they drank coffee together, he went on to describe his plan, which involved rounding up some of her fellow nurses to meet at the Lighthouse Restaurant on Solomons Island. Trey planned to be there and to propose in front of her co-workers who, in Barb's words, had become her family.

Trey needed Raleigh to invite Barb out for lunch, ostensibly just to get to know each other better. Trey and the nurses, and, of course, David and Mutzi, would be waiting at the Lighthouse.

"It was where we had our first date," he explained.

Raleigh agreed to her task, then approached an uncomfortable topic. "I know that you're interested in St. Clements Bluff but, truthfully, I think the property rightfully belongs to the public. I think it has a past way beyond what any of us can imagine and I also think Grant would have wanted others to have a peek into its history."

Trey nodded in resignation. "I realized at Back Road Inn that you didn't want to sell. What would you think about letting me get married there? One final Bishop blowout before the property moves into other hands?"

Raleigh considered this. She could imagine an arch and chairs next to the water for a ceremony, and a white tent on the rolling landscape for a reception. "Sure, we can have your wedding there. Provided she says yes, that is."

Trey beamed. "Once she hears we can get married there, I will be utterly irresistible. And maybe you can sell this house to me one day when you go off to marry the waterman who is clearly besotted with you. Salem never had a chance with him."

His statement left Raleigh speechless, but she let the comment slide as she walked him to the door. She wasn't ready to share any details of her evening with Kip Hewitt.

Trey paused with his hand on the front doorknob then turned back to her. "Rals, I really didn't want to tell you this because I don't want you hurt any more than you already are, but you're basically my sister, so I guess I have to do it."

Raleigh's insides tightened. Even Lindbergh seemed tense as he sat there, gazing intently at Trey.

Trey seemed to be considering his words carefully. "Grant told me several years ago that he had found an investment property that he wasn't ready to tell you about until it had shown that it was profitable. I thought he meant some sort of newfangled fund or business venture. Grant was always much smarter about that sort of thing than I've ever been."

"You think he was planning to renovate St. Clements Bluff and then sell it?"

"Not exactly. We have—or had—a great granduncle named Peter. He was known as Peetie. Uncle Peetie was involved in some sort of get-rich-quick scheme. Something to do with subdividing acreage he had gotten cheap that had been contaminated by a hazardous spill that had never been recorded by the authorities. He planned to sell off the parcels to unsuspecting out-of-towners who think St. Mary's County is the perfect setting for a summer cabin." Trey looked down, as if embarrassed to say more. "Uncle Peetie was from the other side of the family."

What preposterous thing was this? "Are you saying Grant was part of this scheme to dupe people? That's crazy. He never would have done that, under any circumstances."

Trey looked pained. "Not exactly," he repeated. "Grant finally confessed to me that he was offering up the property as a location for Uncle Peetie to hold his 'interest seeker' meetings of people who wanted to buy land. Uncle Peetie thought the house provided the right sort of...ambiance...for convincing out-of-towners to buy the land. The house made it look like he was from old money, and he was able to spin a tale about the family falling on hard times, taxes spiraling out of control, bad farming equipment investments, and so on."

"You're wrong," Raleigh said flatly. "Grant wouldn't have been involved in something like this, and I'm sorry Trey, but I don't want to hear any more about it."

Her voice must have risen an octave, for Lindbergh whined. "It's okay, Mutt Boy," she said, bending down to scratch his ears.

"Do you really *not* want to hear more?" Trey's tone suggested that he was ready to drop the topic and bolt out the door.

Raleigh let long moments pass. Her evening with Kip had caused her to feel some actual sparks of joy for several hours. In fact, she'd even slept decently last night. If she listened to the rest of what Trey had to say, she would no doubt have the jet crash nightmare again and spend the next three days unable to crawl out of bed.

But it would be even worse to not listen to him. Raleigh needed to live inside reality, not outside of it in a protected film of platitudes and false encouragements.

With Lindbergh now leaning against her—a comforting feeling—Raleigh told her brother-in-law, "You're right. I should know. You may as well come back in and have more coffee."

Trey shook his head. "No, I've got enough in me to power around Budd's Creek Raceway on my own two feet. But let's sit down."

Again, seated on the sofa and with Lindbergh's head in her lap, Raleigh braced for the rest of the storm by inviting the thunder. "So, you're saying that Grant helped your uncle dupe unsuspecting people into buying bad properties as part of a get-rich-quick scheme?"

Trey reddened. "You have a way with words, Rals. To the contrary, I believe he was trying to secure a nest egg for you. Grant knew his job was dangerous. He always worried about what would happen to you if something happened to him. I know it might be hard for you to believe, but Grant was trying to protect you."

Raleigh crossed her arms, feeling that she could ward off Trey's words by doing so. "Protect me by leaving behind a house of...unsavoriness? Trey, this simply *cannot* be true."

He looked at her helplessly.

Raleigh blew out a breath. "Okay, fine. Let's say Grant was doing this. Were the lots sold? Did any of the buyers come back and sue your granduncle? What happened to all of the profit? I have this house, but I certainly don't have a fat bank account that Grant left behind."

Trey frowned. "You don't? But he said..." Her brother-in-law hesitated.

"What did he say?" Raleigh demanded.

"He—he didn't say anything specific. I just knew that he was putting money aside for you in a brokerage account with some big investment house."

Why are you covering for your brother, Trey Bishop? Raleigh wondered.

"As for the buyers," he continued, "as soon as the lots were sold, Uncle Peetie made sure that he cleared out of St. Clements Bluff, shut down their post office box, and cleaned up their online presence."

This was sounding more and more fantastical. Raleigh knew her husband, and this didn't sound like him at all, not even one little bit.

"Why are you just telling me this now? You never said anything to me before," she said, hoping her accusation pierced him.

"No," he replied quietly. "Grant swore me to secrecy. Mom and Dad didn't even know. He was my brother, Rals. And he had this grand cause of taking care of you, which was hard to find fault with."

Raleigh could find fault with plenty in this situation. "I don't understand why you wanted to buy the place, knowing what Grant was doing with it."

"Truthfully, Rals, I saw it as beneficial to us both. You couldn't possibly use such a big place—at least not for the foreseeable future—and I have use of it now. I thought—hoped—you might sell it at a reasonable price, and I could keep it in the family."

"So, you're telling me about it now, hoping I'll decide to sell it to you to eradicate the memory of what happened here?"

"God, no," he said, holding up his hands in defense of himself. "Rals, please don't be angry with me."

More moments passed while Raleigh struggled to shift her understanding of whom she knew her husband to be.

"What about the elaborate furniture upstairs?" she asked. "Did that have something to do with the scheme?"

Trey shrugged. "I don't know. I don't think so. Grant never spoke of it to me. As far as I know that furniture has always been in the house. You may be correct that it had something to do with the Underground Railroad."

Raleigh stood and brushed away a tear of frustration. She didn't believe this of her husband, but what the heck?

"What do I do with this information, Trey? Go kick Grant's headstone? Burn down St. Clements Bluff? How do I carry this around with me?"

Trey rose as well. "I'm sorry, I'm so sorry. I shouldn't have said anything." He tried to hug her but it was awkward, and Raleigh quickly disengaged from the bearer of such rotten news.

Why Trey decided to bring this up now had her questioning his motives too. There was probably more to it that she just wasn't seeing. "I just…need to be alone."

He nodded. "I understand. You, know, the more I talk about this, the more I think that Barb might not like to live in a home with such a dark history. Forget I ever suggested anything about buying it, okay?"

Raleigh knew that her brother-in-law was attempting peace at all costs.

With assurances that she forgave him and that she would call him soon, Raleigh got him out of her house. Alone again with Lindbergh, she began once more missing her sister. But not knowing when Salem would return, she decided it was time for more coffee.

With a fresh carafe made, she poured a cup and started pacing around her downstairs to simply *think*. Lindbergh followed behind her dutifully so that the only sounds in the house were his panting and his nails clicking on the flooring.

The past ten years ran through Raleigh's mind like a film at 1.4 speed. Meeting Grant, their courtship, their marriage, her career, their friends, Christmases and family events, vacations…then his death and the aftermath…and now Grant's supposed betrayal.

Trey had to be wrong about Grant conducting any illicit activities. Perhaps Grant's brother had completely misunderstood whatever it was Grant was doing. Trey was such a carefree spirit that it was easy to imagine him not actually paying attention to something complicated. If anyone was involved Raleigh would've thought it to be Trey, not Grant. And that made absolutely no sense either. *Sigh.*

Salem noisily entered through the front door, her heels tapping as she entered the living room. She was dressed in a Barbie outfit—pink and closely hugging her frame. "I see it's time for coffee. Must be an hour ending in 'o'clock.' Hope you don't mind that I borrowed your white shawl. Mike loved it."

Salem was wearing the item in question, a snowy faux fur wrap that just covered the shoulders. Raleigh had purchased it as part of a Cruella de Vil costume one year. Grant had gone as a Dalmatian pup, much to his friends' uproarious enjoyment.

She nodded acquiescence at her sister as it was pointless to protest at this point. "I'm sure he did."

Not hearing the sarcasm in Raleigh's voice, Salem said, "He really did. He said I looked like a snow princess."

With that, Salem went to the kitchen and came back with a dog treat. She tossed it to the ever-alert

Lindbergh, who deftly caught it in his jaws. With that, Salem said goodnight and retreated to her room.

Raleigh sat down on the sofa, deliberately ignoring her sister having rifled through her closet. Instead, she considered everything about St. Clements Bluff. The secret passageway, the mantel and its contents, the gardener's shed, Magda and Jacky, the bedchamber furniture—

Raleigh stopped so short that Lindbergh bumped into her thigh then sneezed and plopped onto his rear. "Sorry, Mutt Boy, I just had a thought. The house was built in 1823, but the Bishops didn't take possession until 1843. The furniture was built—or at least contracted for—in 1845. The Bishops sold the house to Maritime Shippers in 1861 then regained possession in 1866 after the war was over. It is possible that it has nothing to do with escaped slaves, or oyster pirates, or anything of the sort? Might it have been purchased the first time simply because it was a beautiful property and then the second time for sentimental reasons? Is the furniture just part of that aesthetic? Maybe I've been making sand dunes where there should just be flat beaches."

She strode to the kitchen and dumped her coffee down the sink. "Let's go to bed. We have to get up early," she said to Lindbergh. "It's time I visited Jonson Cabinetmakers again."

CHAPTER 24

"HI, MRS. BISHOP," Derrick Jonson said from behind the counter, flashing Raleigh a huge smile as she entered the cabinetmaker shop at noon on Sunday. "Finally decided you want to sell my furniture back to me?"

Beyond the open doors behind him emanated the high-pitched whines of saws and drills combined with the repetitive clanging of hammers and men laughing and joking. It all worked together to suggest a place that was not just industrious and productive, but happy. Derrick walked to the doors and shut them, reducing the noise level by half.

Raleigh smiled back. "Not exactly. I'm hoping for more information on it."

Derrick frowned. "Beyond the bill of sale?"

"Yes. I'm wondering if you perhaps keep photos of the furniture you build."

"Sure do. You can see them on the wall over there." He pointed to a giant corkboard full of various sized photos arranged haphazardly, each with a thumbtack stuck through it to keep it on the board.

"Our customers give us those so we can see the furniture once it's in place in their homes. But that only goes back I dunno, fifteen or twenty years? As long as I've been here."

Raleigh was disappointed. "You don't have photos of your older pieces, those that might date back to the same era as what's at St. Clements Bluff? I realize there were no cameras when the suite was built, but maybe there would have been a later photo of it in the family home?"

Derrick whistled softly. "That's way back. My dad would know, but..." He paused and rubbed a day's growth of beard on his chin.

Why was he hesitant? "Might I talk to Ezra about it?"

"I don't think so. Dad's in the hospital. Had a heart attack a coupla days ago. Toots is staying with him in the hospital while I take care of things here. Maybe you can talk to him when he comes home."

"Oh, I'm sorry to hear he took ill. I wouldn't have bothered you if I'd known." Raleigh added buying flowers to her mental list of things to do. "I hope he'll be home soon."

"Same here." Derrick rapped superstitiously on the counter. "But this isn't Dad's first dance with Lucifer. He's probably had three or four big episodes in the past decade. He always seems to bounce back. I tell him he's got up and walked away from sicknesses that would have killed an elephant. He doesn't much appreciate when I say that."

Derrick chuckled at the memory, and Raleigh joined him. She was about to apologize for her intrusion when the younger Jonson said, "You can go upstairs and dig around if you like. Dad probably wouldn't mind."

He came out from behind the counter and led Raleigh back up into the loft. He went to one of the old wood file cabinets. "This one hasn't been opened in my memory. As good a place to start as any." He tugged on the handle of the top drawer which was resistant to him but with Derrick firmly jerking on it eventually came away from the cabinet's frame. He shut that drawer, then opened and shut the remaining three drawers for Raleigh, ensuring she would have easy access to what lay inside them.

"Take your time," he said as he returned to his work downstairs.

Raleigh went to work, wishing she had thought to ask about photos the last time she was here. It didn't take long, though, to find an old photo album stashed in the back of the bottom drawer.

She sat at Ezra's desk with it. The album was made of old leather that was mildewed with age and had the distinct musty odor that seemed to attach itself to belongings that had been stuffed away in closets, trunks, or attics for decades.

Raleigh gently opened the album to find that some photos were still surprisingly well-adhered to the fragile black pages. The album wasn't as elaborate as Mutzi's scrapbooks, what with all of the newspaper clippings, old admission tickets, and other ephemera that she collected. But it was arranged with scraps of paper neatly secured to the pages with the photos, identifying in a tidy script what the furniture was and for whom it had been built, as well as which Jonson family member had built it. After some pages, the handwriting would change, as though someone new had picked up the task of documenting it all. But the general layout of multiple pictures accompanied by descriptive information stayed the same.

Raleigh was soon enraptured by the album, which was a trip through the Jonson family's business during the 20th century. It was clear that no matter which artisan constructed the furniture, there was great pride and skill in the effort.

Black and white images of carved armoires, delicately sculpted dining room tables, and even intricately formed tall case clocks passed through her vision. Each photo was taken in its final destination, accompanied by details such as where the owner lived, what room the furniture was placed in, what wood species was used, and sometimes even a mention of what position the buyer held in the community.

She gasped when she turned a page and found the bedroom suite.

There was a single photo of each piece that Raleigh recognized from St. Clements Bluff. However, these later photos were clearly taken within the shop and not in the furniture's final location. Raleigh concluded that the furniture had come back to the shop for additional carvings at some point.

Even more curious was the description that went with each photo, which merely stated, *For Mr. Bishop.*

That was it. None of the flowing detail that accompanied the previous photos she had seen. Raleigh flipped quickly through the rest of the album. Everything else had the same lengthy description contained in the pages preceding the Bishop furniture.

Raleigh closed the album and sat quietly, trying to figure out why the furniture set—surely one of the most exquisite that had ever been built by the Jonson family—merited so little comment in the photo album.

She tidied up the drawers and went back down to see Derrick. She stood back a few moments while an elderly man purchased a can of tung oil and a set of brushes.

Once she was the only patron remaining in the shop again, she put the album on the counter.

"You found something," he said.

"Yes, but I don't know what it means." Raleigh turned the album around so that it was right side up for Derrick and slowly flipped through the pages, pointing out the care the Jonson family had taken back in the day to ensure their work was well documented.

Finally, she reached the two-page spread containing the Bishop furniture order. Raleigh looked at Derrick expectantly. It took him several moments, but finally, his expression registered understanding.

"Nothing here," he said simply.

Raleigh nodded. "Do you know why that might be?"

Derrick frowned. "This was probably done in the early to mid-20th century, Mrs. Bishop, quite a few generations ago. Who can say why this set got no real mention? Although I can see that the writing is the same as what was done, let's see—" He flipped back through the pages. "—for at least ten deliveries before it." He turned pages after the Bishop spread. "And for several after it. So, it wasn't because someone different took over the documentation."

Raleigh agreed. "And maybe it doesn't mean anything, but it's awfully strange, don't you think?"

He nodded. "Maybe Dad could answer it since he knows so much of the family history. Tell you what, as soon as he gets out of the hospital, I'll ask him and then let you know."

Raleigh couldn't ask for more, so she gave him her number and said her goodbyes.

As she turned to leave, Derrick said, "Seems to me as whatever worker who modified that furniture didn't much like Mr. Bishop, wouldn't you say? Like it was a job for money and not for the joy of the project. Yet it was a unique job that any skilled cabinetmaker would have been happy to have. It looks to me as though there was something shifty or no good about Mr. Bishop. No offense meant to your family."

That was Raleigh's thought, as well. "None taken whatsoever."

But she was more puzzled than ever. If the only furniture at St. Clements Bluff was a set that had been modified for a disagreeable member of the family, why had Grant kept it? And why was it the only furniture remaining in the home?

She got back in her car to return to St. Clements Bluff.

As she pulled up in front of the home, Raleigh

noted with alarm that the front door was ajar. Had she somehow forgotten to fully close and lock it the last time she was here? She suddenly wished very much that she had Lindbergh with her.

If there was someone in the house, it might be best to hurry in and surprise whomever it was. Of course, Raleigh's car crunching on the driveway gravel had probably presented plenty of advance notice of her arrival. What if someone was now waiting for her behind the front door?

Raleigh opened up the glove box and searched through it. No flashlight or anything else that she could use as a weapon in case whoever it was had nefarious plans in mind.

She did have Mutzi's thick scrapbook in the seat next to her. That could be a formidable weapon.

She sat in the car for several moments, debating what to do. As she drummed her fingers on the steering wheel, Raleigh started getting angry. How dare anyone just waltz into this house and assume it was perfectly okay to do so? If it was Salem or Trey wandering around in there, surely the sound of Raleigh's car would be an alert to come out on the porch to acknowledge her.

Who the hell was in the house?

Now fueled with growing fury, Raleigh got out of her car and slammed the door with force. The sound echoed in the crisp winter air. As she stormed toward the front porch, the front door swung inward and a person appeared.

It was Magda Raley.

Her tousled hair looked even more disheveled than usual, although she was dressed in her standard fare of cargo shorts and worn Birkenstocks, topped by an old ski jacket. Magda hailed Raleigh with a friendly wave as she stepped out onto the porch.

But Raleigh was now too furious by the intrusion to accept the neighborly greeting.

"What are you doing in my house?" she demanded, striding up the porch stairs and into the house for inspection. Nothing seemed amiss in the entry part of the house, so she walked back to the kitchen.

Magda followed her. "Good Lord, child, I was just looking for Jacky. He does love your Lindbergh, and I figured he must have come over here to play."

Now standing in front of the ancient refrigerator, Raleigh turned to face Magda and said her next words slowly. "And you thought Jacky might have opened the front door and come inside?"

Magda's laugh in response was throaty and loud. "He ain't that smart. Not yet, anyway. No, I just thought I'd come inside and warm up a little. Been walking the woods quite a bit today."

"It's not particularly warm in here."

"Well, I didn't know that before I came in, now did I?" Magda said. "And anyway, the door was unlocked, so it's not like I busted in or anything. You're touchy today."

Raleigh cautioned herself to calm down a little. This was an old, rural part of the county. Maybe everyone just walked into everyone else's house without a thought.

For her part, Magda seemed completely unconcerned with the notion that she had walked into a house that wasn't hers without invitation.

Raleigh took a deep breath. She would have to make extra sure she locked the door when she left. Although she was always careful to lock doors. How could she have possibly forgotten to do so the last time she was here? "I don't mean to be."

"Yeah, no problem. We all have bad days. You've had more than your share of them. Time to go find Jacky."

She joined Magda down on the driveway where the older woman was calling and whistling for her pooch.

After several moments of this, Jacky came loping up to them with a clump of something in his mouth, the sort of thing that a dog would think priceless but an owner would find repulsive.

"What do you have there, boy?" Raleigh asked him. She started to kneel, but Magda stopped her with a hand gesture.

"Jacky, that's disgusting. You get rid of that thing, you hear me?" Magda commanded, grabbing it from his mouth and throwing it away from the house with impressive force toward the woods along the side of the driveway. "Stay here," she said.

Jacky's expression suggested he was unhappy, but he remained at his mistress's side.

"Always picking up nasty things, aren't you, Jacky?" Magda asked of her dog. "Don't know what to do about you."

Magda shook her head, but she glanced affectionately at Jacky. "Time to go home, yeah?"

The woman and her dog wandered away, leaving Raleigh to watch their retreating figures.

With Magda gone, Raleigh retrieved the scrapbook from the front seat and went back into the house.

To satisfy her curiosity, Raleigh walked through the entire upper two floors. Nothing appeared to be disturbed, but how does one "disturb" an empty house?

She went back to the third-story bedchamber. It seemed to her now that if she could examine the scrapbook alongside the strange items in the mantel and the carvings on the furniture, an answer would surely jump out at her to explain Grant's purported involvement in a shady real estate scheme.

Putting the scrapbook on the floor to one side of the fireplace, Raleigh once more opened the mantel, gingerly exposing the hinged levels and bringing them downward. She stood there, staring at all of the random items, willing them to shout an answer at her.

They didn't, of course, so she picked up the scrapbook and then sat cross-legged in front of the exposed mantel with the scrapbook in her lap.

In her examination of the scrapbook this time, she looked at a page, then scanned the contents of the mantel, hoping for an association. She again read the articles on Bishops who had been honored by the community, the piece on Walter Hewitt getting arrested for trying to murder Francis Bishop with rat poison in a jealous rage, and the long obituary on Charles Bishop, who had died in a plane crash during World War I. She hadn't sought out that memorial yet.

Raleigh laughed again over the story of the circus owner approaching the owner of St. Clements Bluff for permission to use the estate's outbuildings for housing animals and P. Bishop expressing outrage over the property being treated like a zoo enclosure.

She paused here. Reminded of the yellowed old clipping that was an amusing room-for-let advertisement she had found in the mantel, she put down the scrapbook, still open to that page, and looked at the mantel's various compartments. The pipe, the burned candles, the spectacles, the pocketknife, and the oyster knife were all exactly as she had left them. Raleigh quickly found the folded piece of newspaper and gently re-opened it, comparing it to the article on the zoo.

Clearly the P. Bishop who had released the ad stating that no zookeepers need apply for the room was the same Philip Bishop who had been interviewed for the circus article.

Was there meaning to the advertisement being stuffed into the mantel or had someone from the past found it as amusing as Raleigh did and thus kept the clipping?

She then re-read the scrapbook's 1935 story about the various historic properties in the county that could be visited. St. George Manor, Kip Hewitt's place, now held new meaning for her.

Raleigh flipped back several pages. The 1913 story about St. Clements Bluff being a stop on the Underground Railroad was very flattering about the Bishop involvement in that effort. The subsequent story on historic properties to visit didn't even mention the fact that St. Clements Bluff had been an important part of the Underground Railroad. That was odd.

Was it possible that it had been discovered after the first article was written that the property had not actually been part of that network of stopping places for runaway slaves? That was a crazy thought, though. If the secret tunnel wasn't for the escapees, and according to Pop would have had nothing to do with the oyster wars, then what in heaven's name was its purpose?

Because it surely hadn't been used as an illicit hideout for mistresses, of that Raleigh was confident.

Back to the mantel contents she went in search of an item that might relate to either of the two articles. Her imagination ran wild. The candle stubs might have been used for light in the tunnel passageway, but she knew it was simply not possible that candles that old would have survived hundreds of years intact.

The pocketknife might have been carried for defense against a slave catcher, as weak a weapon as it would have been.

Hmmm. The oyster knife could have been used as a weapon, as well. She pulled that back out and examined it again, practicing thrusting and stabbing at the air with it. It had a little blade on it, but it was compact and easy to hide. Yes, a definite possibility that it was a defensive weapon. She tucked it into her coat pocket for more examination later.

Daylight was waning. It was time to go. Raleigh was disappointed that her plan of comparing the scrapbook to the mantel items had not been particularly illuminating.

She walked back outside, and this time Raleigh deliberately locked the door and pocketed the key in her coat with the oyster knife.

I locked the door last time, I'm certain of it.

Had Magda innocently found her way into the house… or had someone else been there first?

CHAPTER 25

RALEIGH SPENT MUCH of Sunday evening dusting, scrubbing, mopping, and vacuuming. She even went through Grant's side of the closet and pulled out some more of his clothes and put them in bags for charity. It made the closet neater without removing his presence.

Having a fresh-smelling home made her feel better as she readied herself for her first day back to work since her husband's death.

She even went through her side of the closet, picking out and returning several ensembles to the rack before deciding upon a long-sleeved dress with a ruched collar done in bold splashes of red, black, and yellow.

Might as well go back in style and in Maryland state colors.

Salem brought home a takeout dinner from a local Chinese restaurant. She was animated and happy as she gushed over Mike's musical talents, Mike's guitar collection, and Mike's affinity for Harley Davidson motorcycles.

"He's going to take me for a ride tomorrow afternoon when he's done working for the day. He's an engineer on the naval base and works on some super-secret aircraft project."

Raleigh quickly buried the specter of Grant going down in his aircraft by tipping back her plastic container of egg drop soup and drinking directly from it.

At least Salem was content again, which made Raleigh's life easier.

It was still dark the following morning when Raleigh took Lindbergh for a quick walk around the block, then told him to behave while she was gone. His expression was one of total confusion at Raleigh walking out the door with a travel mug of coffee just as light was beginning to break.

She planned to arrive at the museum before anyone else and was relieved to see that hers was the first vehicle in the parking lot. Rather than walking into a building full of people, Raleigh preferred to get to her desk, get organized, and sift through what was sure to be a mountain of e-mail, if the most recent pile of mail in her chair was any indication of how much had happened in her absence.

She pulled up to the familiar old building, which had started life in a historic old farmhouse, then had seen enough strange family renovations and commercial additions to be of archaeological interest in and of itself.

Within an hour, she had dusted her office, separated her mail into two piles of magazine-type publications and regular mail, replaced a lamp bulb that had died, and performed a first-level scan of her electronic inbox. With most of the junk, spam, and no longer relevant e-mails cleared out, she could more fully concentrate on important communications.

First, though, she needed more coffee. Flipping up light switches in anticipation of her co-workers soon arriving, Raleigh went into the museum's small but well-appointed kitchen, located in the original part of the house. One of the grants managers, Tammy, was manic about cleanliness, so the shared kitchen was always spotless.

Raleigh felt warmth radiating through her to know

that Tammy was clearly still employed by the museum. Opening a cabinet, she found her personal bag of French Roast exactly where she remembered it being.

She glanced at the bulletin board while her coffee brewed. All of the notices employees had posted for personal items they were selling, business cards for local services they recommended, and other communications were neatly arranged on the board with blue thumbtacks. Tammy liked blue and ensured that no other color dared creep onto the board.

Everything was feeling familiar and safe.

Raleigh returned to her office with her cup and stood behind her desk to do a more thorough inspection of months' worth of mail. She had hardly started when Tammy herself entered her office.

"Oh my word, it really is you! I can't believe you're back! Why didn't you call? Bert didn't tell me anything. I would have cleaned your office for you. I would have—" Tammy was always breathless, despite her pint-sized stature.

"No need to worry about me," Raleigh said, coming around her desk to hug the other woman. "I'm okay, I really am. Well, I'm mostly okay."

Tammy was at least in her fifties but looked ageless, with gorgeous red hair that tumbled around her shoulders and nearly flawless skin. "Really? I'm glad. Still, you should have let me know. I could have had your office deep-cleaned. Oh! Was your coffee stale? I can have Regina order more if you need it. What about—" Tammy was getting breathless again.

"Coffee is great." Raleigh picked up her mug and tapped it before taking a sip to prove it.

Tammy smiled in relief.

"My plan today is to get through the mail. Are we still doing Monday morning team meets?"

Tammy rolled her eyes. "Of course. Bert can't function

without his Monday morning meets. See you again in the conference room."

With Tammy gone—and undoubtedly announcing Raleigh's return to everyone—Raleigh went back to work on her mail. She had months of national historical magazines and the St. Mary's Quarterly Historical Review to catch up on, but that could wait. A variety of catalogs offered locking display cases, pedestals, hanging track systems for artwork, reader rails, archival supplies, and security barriers. Raleigh loved going through these sorts of catalogs and imagining new exhibits, but these, too, would have to wait.

The regular mail was a typical assortment of conference ads, continuing education offerings, and archivist society membership renewals. Some of these she tossed into the trash unopened, while others she opened and set aside for further review.

One envelope, though, caused Raleigh to stop, tendrils of unease creeping up her back.

It was handwritten to her at the museum's address, in the same script as the bizarre letter she had received at St. Clements Bluff, informing her that the home might burn down one day soon.

This envelope was equally as thin, clearly containing a single sheet of paper.

Was someone trying to intimidate her? She couldn't imagine why.

She sighed and picked up her letter opener. Before she could remove the letter, Tammy popped in. "Bert's here. Conference room in five."

Raleigh debated for only a moment before deciding to slide the letter into her top desk drawer. It was better to go into the meeting for the first time in a year without having been unsettled by a second contact with an unknown antagonist.

Raleigh was gratified by the welcome she received

from her co-workers in the conference room, all of whom raised their coffee cups at her entrance. Bert seemed genuinely pleased to see her. Raleigh imagined he was probably unsure whether she would actually show up.

This week's hot topic was the museum store. The manager—who had been ordering to excess so that the stockroom was piled up with unsold merchandise—had just quit and taken the best shop worker with him to a big box retailer. They strategized how to staff the store between the remaining shop staff and museum volunteers until someone new could be hired.

Despite this bad news regarding the shop, Raleigh found herself falling right back in love with her job. This was much better than sitting at home, staring morosely into the backyard.

Bert asked her to remain after the meeting concluded. When it was just the two of them in the room he said with emotion, "Glad to have you back. It hasn't been the same without you."

If Raleigh didn't know better, she'd think her boss was beginning to choke up a little over her return.

"Glad to be back, Bert. And I'm glad no one tossed out my coffee bag." She smiled.

"Never," he replied, waving a hand for emphasis. "I'd like you to meet with the St. Mary's City archaeologist who headed up that old Yaocomico village dig to get a better idea of what they have and what they want to put on loan to us. I'll give you a budget and you can re-arrange the entire pre-historic room as you wish."

St. Mary's City was Maryland's first capital, settled in 1634. Long ago abandoned for Annapolis, today it was a remarkable indoor-outdoor museum.

"Thanks, Bert. I can't wait to work on it. Also..." Raleigh paused. Should she mention the letter sitting in her desk? No, she might be wrong about the envelope's contents and then she would feel foolish if she showed it to him. There were plenty of self-righteous idiots out there who believed it their mission to intimidate others, and that was true whether you lived in a city or in small coastal areas.

She recalled a time at the museum when the board of directors had decided to procure a post office box for collecting regular mail, rather than having it delivered to the museum so that if the museum were closed on off days there wouldn't be an unsightly collection of material outside the museum doors.

A citizen had started an ironic letter-writing campaign against it, insisting that the museum had always kept the same address, and what was the point of moving it now, and what secrets were the museum hiding by changing a perfectly good address, and so on for months until the resident wore out his ire.

"A frequent flyer," Bert had observed dryly about the man.

In fact, Raleigh was feeling more and more like these letters were likely from someone who was like the museum's 'frequent flyer' and just didn't have it altogether.

Raleigh didn't allow herself to stay on that train of thought. "Also, I'd like to invite you to see St. Clements Bluff this week. Say, Wednesday afternoon?"

Bert agreed to it enthusiastically. Raleigh raised her coffee mug at him as the others had done to her earlier and returned to her desk.

She sat and stared at the envelope for several moments, unhappy about what she might find inside.

Finally, though, she picked it up and shook the single piece of paper onto her desk. It was another short missive.

Raleigh,

Your husband was a liar and your house was built on a lie.

It is impossible for you or any decent person to live there.

The truth can only come with purifying fire. You have been warned.

This time the note was unsigned. Presumably, the writer was no longer "a friend."

A LIGHT SNOW was falling as Raleigh arrived at St. Clements Bluff two days later to wait for Bert so she could tour him through the estate.

Lindbergh whined and snuffled against the passenger door window as the house came into view.

"Jack isn't here today, Mutt Boy," Raleigh said. "You're stuck with just me. Your Aunt Salem is too busy with Mike these days to hang out with us."

Lindbergh bounded out of the car behind Raleigh as she slid out of the driver's seat. He almost knocked her over in his zeal to run to a spot near the cellar door and begin digging.

Leaving him to his doggie detection, Raleigh made her way gingerly up the stairs to the front door. The falling snow was light but wet and there was no point in slipping and falling with no one around to notice.

The door was securely bolted this time, she had made sure of it after Magda's visit. Raleigh entered the house, which seemed chillier inside than it was outside. With all of these fireplaces, she really needed to see about getting some firewood stacked outside. She also needed to be sure to leave a tap running in the kitchen to be sure the pipes didn't freeze. It might even make sense to—

The sound of Lindbergh barking brought her out of her mental list making. Returning to the front door, she saw a truck pull up next to her vehicle.

It was Derrick Jonson.

Raleigh stepped onto the porch and Derrick came to the bottom of the stairs. Lindbergh followed him, no longer barking. Obviously, he had assessed the man as being of no further danger.

"Mrs. Bishop," he said in greeting. "Hoped you might be here."

Had he already talked to Ezra Jonson about the furniture photos in the old album? Raleigh had to presume that meant the elder Jonson was already home and recovering. It also meant she might be about to receive news to help her put at least part of the Bishop riddle to rest.

"Good to see you," she replied. "Would you like to come inside out of the snow? Although, I have to tell you, it's not any warmer inside than it is out here." She crossed her arms and shivered to emphasize how cold she was.

"No, I'm not staying." Snow was collecting on his wool cap and his shoulders. Perhaps the weather was changing for the worse.

"I just wanted to let you know that, well, that my dad died early yesterday morning." Derrick's eyes reddened at his own words but, other than that, he showed no emotion.

Raleigh was shocked. "I am so sorry! I thought he would surely—you said he always managed to—oh, what terrible news about your father."

Her words felt clumsy in her mouth. Was this the bumbling manner in which people had spoken to her in the aftermath of Grant's death? Probably.

Derrick looked down at the ground for several moments and then back up at her. "Yeah, he always did pull through. Except this time. I never got a chance to talk to him for you, though. He was sleeping a lot the past coupla days and then yesterday he just didn't wake up."

Raleigh firmly tamped down memories of her own grief. This was Derrick's moment of personal pain. "What can I do for you?" she asked.

"Nothing. Just wanted you to know." Derrick started to leave but turned back. "I expect you could keep searching and find out what is wrong with the furniture set. I'm kind of thinking I might not want to buy it back from you anymore if it's got some kind of evil attached to it. I, er—" He hesitated. "I also need to apologize."

"Apologize?" What could the cabinet maker have to be sorry for?

"Yeah. I might not have been completely honest with you on something. I told you I wanted the furniture as a nice sample in our shop. But really, I need it for…I needed to…". Derrick reached up with one hand and rubbed the back of his neck.

Why was he so uncomfortable? Raleigh waited patiently.

"You see, we've got some debts. Not the shop, but Toots. My brother hasn't always made the best decisions in the world, and now he owes money all over the place. That furniture would be valuable to the right buyer. Truth be told, Mrs. Bishop, I would have sold it straight away to take care of Toots."

Derrick cast his gaze at the ground. "But it wasn't right for me to deceive you on my intent. And, like I said, I'm not sure I want the furniture now. No use paying for bad decisions with bad resources, you know?"

Raleigh was overwhelmed with sympathy. "Don't give it another thought. I do understand that we want to do what we can for family. Again, I'm sorry about Ezra."

Derrick accepted her condolences with a nod and left.

Oblivious to the weather now, Raleigh stood on the porch, watching Derrick Jonson drive away.

Two losses. Not only an opportunity to learn more about Grant's secret life, but another life extinguished. She shivered again and called Lindbergh, who was once again worrying over something he had dug up.

"C'mon, Mutt Boy, you don't need to be slipping around in the snow." Lindbergh trotted up to her, proudly carrying something unidentifiable in his mouth.

She bent down to see what he had, but as she reached out her hand, the dog turned away, unwilling to share his prize.

"Is that how you're going to play it?" Raleigh said. "Fine. Bring it inside with you."

She opened the door and he stepped over the threshold, his tail wagging in pride.

"You're a doofus," she said to him warmly, which only caused him to wag harder.

With the door closed behind her, Raleigh took Lindbergh's collar as she knelt. "Now show me what you've got."

She could almost swear he looked mad, but he dutifully dropped his catch at her feet.

It was a grimy, knotted rag, covered in bits of dirt and plant debris. No, wait, it was a toy of some sort. Something Grant had bought him for play during their visits to St. Clements Bluff? No, it was—

Raleigh felt another of those uncomfortable chills that were occurring far too often run up her spine.

It was a cloth doll, handmade by the looks of it. And someone had painted red circles around the wrists and a jagged red line around the neck.

Worse, as primitively constructed as the doll was, Raleigh recognized her face and hair painted onto the wood knob that formed the head. Also unmistakable was the tiny mole painted on the doll's rough jawline.

CHAPTER 26

RALEIGH WAS REELING. It was positively ridiculous to think that she was holding a tiny wood-and-cloth bundle made in her image. Yet she couldn't shake the thought that someone might have tried sticking pins in it in order to—what? Frighten her? Kill her? Up until now, she hadn't really thought someone wanted to do her harm.

Whoever it was had either dropped it or literally handed it to Lindbergh, who had then buried it.

Don't be foolish, she thought. *There is a perfectly rational explanation for this.*

She thought back to Magda throwing something that Jacky had found. Had it been the item Raleigh now stared at?

Surely whoever was sending her nasty notes was behind this further intimidation. Well, these high school threats didn't scare her. The feeble attempts only heightened her curiosity and fervor to know the truth.

She hoped Bert would arrive soon so she could show it to him. He would certainly say something comforting and logical.

Holding the distasteful doll between two fingers of one hand, she went into the kitchen and put the doll in the center of one length of the countertop and contemplated it.

She was in the middle of thinking that maybe someone had simply painted it with no specific model in mind and that the mole was just where some paint had splattered when there was a loud knocking at the front door, followed by the sound of it creaking open and a booming "Helloooo?" filling the air.

It was Bert Mattingly, thank goodness.

Tucking the doll into a kitchen drawer, Raleigh went out to meet her boss, taking him through the entire house and showing him the mantel before taking him through the secret tunnel to the gardener's shed and back to the main house. All the while, she spoke profusely on every theory she had on the place, as well as on what she had discovered in Mutzi's scrapbooks and the Jonson photo album, finally falling silent as they walked back into the front door of St. Clements Bluff.

With a lack of furniture in the place, Bert sat heavily with a grunt near the bottom of the stairs while Raleigh stood in the entry hall, fighting the urge to pace.

Despite the chill in the air, Bert was sweating profusely from all of the walking and climbing. "This is quite a place. I have to say, though, the most impressive thing is that secret tunnel. I imagine the Underground Railroad folks would be very interested in that. I'm sure we can get some experts in here to determine whether St. Clements Bluff should be added to the official route."

He stretched out his thick legs and removed a handkerchief from one of his pants pockets, using it to dab at his forehead and neck.

"If you get it on the official route, that makes it a much simpler thing to have it named a historic site, if that's what you want. Of course, you could also..." Bert paused.

Raleigh raised an eyebrow. "What?"

"You could let the museum purchase it. If you don't have it placed on the historic register, but put it under the county's auspices, the rules about what can and cannot be done to it get so much easier. We could have it running as a county historic property in no time, and you could have a tidy nest egg toward your future life."

Raleigh had been to enough budget meetings to know exactly what the museum's finances were. "Even if I sold it to the museum for half its value, there is no way the museum could afford it. I would need to donate it, which I am not opposed to—"

Bert waved his moist handkerchief in the air in dismissal. "After what you've been through, you should have some recompense. We could swing it."

Raleigh shook her head in frustration. "Bert, there is no way the board of directors would allow the museum to devastate itself financially for this house."

"Well, there are options," he said, slowly lumbering up to his feet now that he had cooled down. "For example, perhaps I could purchase it from you myself and then sell it back to the museum in a few years after a sufficient number of fundraisers. A few banquets, quilt raffles, and craft shows would help out. Plus, the museum could apply for some state grants toward it."

Raleigh didn't like the sound of this at all. Why was Bert volunteering to risk his own money on this property?

Without offering any commitment she said, "Since you mention craft shows, I'd like to show you something."

She led him to the kitchen and opened the drawer containing the doll.

He glanced down at it, then back at Raleigh, his expression puzzled. "What am I looking at? An old rag doll?"

Raleigh patiently pulled it out of the drawer and tried to neaten it on the counter as well as she could. Recognition dawned on Bert's face before he frowned, once again looking confused. "Do you think the face is meant to resemble you? The green eyes, the blonde hair?"

He had instantly come to the same conclusion she had.

She pointed down at it. "Isn't that even my mole? Or is it just spattered paint?"

Bert picked up the doll to examine it but seemed to change his mind. He quickly put it back in the drawer and closed it.

"Raleigh, this could be serious. Don't laugh, but perhaps there are malevolent spirits after you, trying to force you from this house."

Whatever reaction she had expected from Bert, it surely wasn't this. When had Bert become an adherent of voodoo magic and superstitions?

"Really? You think I should leave?"

He shrugged. "Better safe than sorry, as the saying goes. If someone—or something—doesn't want you there, maybe it's best to divest yourself of it as quickly as possible."

If Raleigh didn't know better, she would think her boss was trying to drive her out of her newly-inherited house. She could no longer contemplate it, for Lindbergh entered the kitchen and began whining. Raleigh glanced over at the dog and saw that he was suddenly in some sort of distress.

"What the—?" She started, rushing down and kneeling next to him. "What's wrong, Mutt Boy?"

He was now foaming at the mouth and trying to vomit.

"Did you eat something bad? Drink something?" Thoughts of old news stories on how people would put out antifreeze to kill neighbors' pets flashed through her mind.

But then a worse thought entered her. *Was that stupid doll coated in something poisonous?*

"It's okay, boy, you'll be alright. We just need to get you to the vet." With a strength she didn't know she possessed, she managed to pick Lindbergh up and scurry out the front door.

By the time she got Lindbergh into her vehicle and drove away, she realized that at some point Bert had left without a word.

"So, Lindbergh is going to be okay?" Kip asked, reaching down and scratching the dog behind the ears.

Kip had texted her with an unusual invitation, which Raleigh had accepted with both curiosity and trepidation. It seemed very strange to allow a man to pick her up from her home, even if Kip had proved himself harmless. And interesting. And possessing an intoxicating scent.

Besides, she needed to talk to someone about the doll.

"Yes, the vet said he had clearly gotten into something. It could have been a rotted animal carcass or a poisonous plant of some sort."

Lindbergh sat panting on the floor of the kitchen as Raleigh and Kip talked, shifting his attention from one to the other, depending on who was talking.

"He's a tough pooch. I'm sure he's not going to let a little mischief take him down," Kip said. "Right, boy?" he asked, looking at Lindbergh in mock seriousness.

Lindbergh thumped his tail against the floor twice. Raleigh could have sworn Lindbergh seemed to be smiling at Kip's admonishments.

The dog probably missed a male presence as much as she did.

"Ready to go?" Kip asked, rising from his chair.

Raleigh hesitated. "I—um..."

Kip sat down again. "What's the matter?"

Raleigh sighed. "You're going to think I'm crazy, but something very strange happened yesterday."

"You mean besides your scare with Lindbergh?" Kip leaned against the back of the kitchen chair as if settling in for a story.

"It happened at the same time as Lindbergh getting sick, actually." Raleigh proceeded to tell him about Lindbergh presenting her with the primitive doll.

Kip leaned forward in complete attention. "Can I see it?"

She retrieved the doll from the shoebox she had shoved it into before stuffing it into the bottom of the coat closet. Refusing to even touch it again, she held out the box and removed the lid.

Kip said nothing for long moments while he stared at the partially chewed thing lying against the tan cardboard.

Finally, he looked up at Raleigh. "I have to admit, it does sort of look like you. I've read about this sort of mystical practice but have never seen evidence of it. If indeed it is a little voodoo doll of you."

"I guess Moll Dyer would not approve of such witchcraft," Raleigh said with a weak laugh. "I showed it to Salem. She thinks someone has a very sick sense of humor."

Raleigh also made her sister vow to *not* share any of this with their mother. Good Lord, that's all she needed was for Mom to make a sudden visit and worry them all to death.

"I don't approve, either." Kip gently took the box from Raleigh and replaced the lid, then set the box on the kitchen table. "I hope a sick sense of humor is all this is."

Raleigh hoped so, too. "Let's walk to the edge and back, shall we?" he said. "I'm not going to ask something as stupid as, 'Who would want to hurt you?' because we have to assume you don't know anyone whom you believe would actually desire you harm."

Raleigh shook her head as she sat down.

"Therefore, if this is someone trying to scare you, we can divide our suspicions into two camps." Kip held up the index and middle fingers of one hand. "First, it is a person completely unknown to you who somehow has a beef with you, St. Clements Bluff, or perhaps your late husband. But since it is impossible to determine who that might be, we go to the second option."

Kip put down his middle finger. "Meaning that it is a person you know whom you believe to either be your friend or to have a neutral view of you but who is angry at you for some unknown reason. Tell me about Grant's family." He put down the other finger and once again leaned back in his chair and looked at her intently.

"His family?" Raleigh repeated. "That's ridiculous. They took me in and made me one of their own years ago."

"Uh huh," Kip said, maintaining his stare. "So, there is the brother, Trey, and by extension, his girlfriend, Barbara. Any anxiety, anger, or jealousy across the three of you?"

"Of course not!" Raleigh exclaimed. "Trey has always been like a brother to me. He worked harder than anyone to get me out of my depression after Grant died. He was probably a little bit in Grant's shadow—since Grant was the respected flyboy—but they always got along. Except that..."

Kip waited expectantly.

"Trey told me that—that Grant had used St. Clements Bluff as a base for some shady investment scheme with some now-dead uncle of theirs. It's complete rot, of course." Raleigh filled him in on Trey's conspiracy theory and having explained it all to Kip she was even more certain it was completely ridiculous.

She took a deep breath.

"I guess there's more," she said. "Trey did ask me whether I would consider selling St. Clements Bluff to him as a wedding present to Barb. He thought it would be a good place to raise children. But then he came back and said he no longer wanted it. That the house's history might not sit too well with Barb."

Kip nodded. "He wouldn't be the first man to get cold feet on a purchase. What about Barb? Do you get along?"

"Other than being aware of how very besotted Trey is with her, I barely know her." In fact, Raleigh hardly knew anything about Barb other than her being a nurse at the hospital.

"So, no reason for her to resent your presence in Trey's life?"

"I can't imagine why. I've been kind to her, and I've never spoken a bad word against her to Trey."

"So…" Kip pursed his lips. "What about your in-laws?"

"Mutzi and David? That would be even more ridiculous than Trey wishing me harm. They've grieved at least as hard as I have."

"Is it possible that they somehow blame you for Grant's death?"

"Blame *me* for an aircraft mishap?" This was getting ridiculous.

Kip held up a hand. "I'm sorry, that was stupid. We are just trying to figure this out."

Raleigh closed her eyes briefly. When she opened them, she offered Kip a smile. "I know, you're just trying to help. And I suppose I need all the help I can get right now."

"Then let me propose this." Kip cleared his throat as if in discomfort over his next words. "Is it possible that David—and possibly Mutzi—know the story that Trey told you about Grant and the scheme, and they are now interested in getting you out of St. Clements Bluff? Getting you out of there would ensure you do not give the house over to the museum, which might expose the home's past not as a part of the Underground Railroad but as part of a scandalous scheme that would be the talk of the county for decades if it were discovered?"

Raleigh considered her in-laws, two of the kindest, gentlest people she had ever known. The image of Mutzi's wedding ring rolling around on her shrunken finger arose in her mind, as well as the aroma of her baking and Pop's great love for his wife's cooking.

Would they be mortified if such a thing were to come to light? Certainly. But…

"If any member of Grant's family was upset about the situation, I can see no reason why he or she wouldn't just come to me to discuss it. It's got to be someone else," Raleigh said firmly.

Kip nodded again. "Then who is left that you know?"

"My boss, Bert, has been very supportive of me. He even met me at St. Clements Bluff to look it over. Although—"

Should she tell Kip about Bert's offer? She supposed she wasn't speaking ill of her boss to do so.

"Although he did say something a little…odd. I told him I was seriously considering giving the property to the historical society so that it could eventually be opened to the public. He offered to personally put up interim money to help get the property transferred to the historical society without my having to wait for payment. I told him I would just donate the house, but he insisted that I be compensated for it."

"You didn't think it odd that he would be willing to personally risk a substantial amount of his own money?"

"Well, these sorts of transfers can take forever." Just hearing the tone of her own voice, Raleigh wasn't buying it and knew Kip wasn't, either.

He replied, "Very generous of him to possibly tie up his own capital for an unknown period of time." It was difficult to know if the comment was sarcastic or not.

But Bert didn't have a reason to do anything cruel to her, did he?

She didn't respond, so Kip continued. "There is Magda Raley, your new neighbor. There is also—forgive me—your sister, who is rather new on the scene. Any sisterly quarrels there?"

"We are sisters. Of course, there are quarrels. But why would Salem care about my ownership of an old house? Besides, she is only in town for a short while, presumably to cheer me up, although I think she continues to stay mostly because of Mike. No one you are bringing up has any reason to drive me out of St. Clements Bluff by frightening me."

"Even Magda?"

Raleigh shrugged. "Like Barb, I hardly know her. She's a little peculiar, but I've never had any sense that she wishes me harm. Although…"

She told Kip about Magda being inside St. Clements Bluff when Raleigh had arrived on a recent visit. "It was strange at the moment, but I imagine lots of people down here just walk into one another's homes, so I chalked it up to that."

"What's more concerning is that the door was seemingly unlatched when you know you had locked it."

Except that Raleigh wasn't sure about anything anymore. "I'm pretty sure I wouldn't have left it unlocked. But maybe I did?"

"It's possible." Kip's tone suggested that although it might be possible, it was unlikely. "Who else are you around on a regular basis?"

"Not much of anyone. I was friends with the other military wives but after the…accident…we all drifted apart. Some of them left the area. I haven't spoken with any of them in a long time. Other than that, I've just returned to work and come into contact with my co-workers again."

Always knowing the perfect time to interrupt whatever Raleigh was doing, Salem came noisily through the door, singing a Christmas carol of all things. Salem stopped short when she entered the kitchen and saw Kip sitting with Raleigh.

"Oh, you have company," she said. Salem had several grocery bags in her hands, which she hefted onto the kitchen counter. "Mike was telling me how much he loves prime rib so I thought I would give it a go. You don't mind, do you?" Salem seemed to be pointedly avoiding Kip.

"Enjoy yourself," Raleigh said. It had been so long since she'd cooked anything that she wasn't sure the gas range would even fire up.

Salem began unpacking her groceries. "You're both invited," she said. Clearly, they were not.

Kip grinned. "No prime rib for me. Or your sister. She's going to help me serve oysters during happy hour tonight at Simpson's in Hollywood. My family takes care of their oyster bar on live music night once a month."

"I see." Salem's lips were a tight line as some sort of storm passed across her features, then cleared. "Be careful, Raleigh. Shucking oysters can be dangerous."

CHAPTER 27

RALEIGH ENJOYED SELLING oysters more than she had anticipated. Kip had a long, iced display case set up at the rear of the bar, and they worked from behind it.

Kip had tied a thick canvas apron around her and given her equally thick gloves to wear before placing an oyster knife—just like the one from the mantel but newer—in her right hand.

"You'll thank me later," he said in response to her mild complaint that she felt like she was wearing a baseball mitt on each hand. "The oysters stay on ice, and these will protect you from the cold."

Patrons drifted into the bar, some to play keno, some to drink whatever was on tap, and others to do both. Soon she and Kip were doing a brisk business with oysters, pulling and preparing them to order, either in raw preparations or running them back to the kitchen for the bar's staff to grill, bake, fry, or sauté.

The bar's patrons became raucous as the evening went on, cracking loud jokes and teasing one another. Eventually, Kip and Raleigh were drawn into the frivolity. It was like a big family reunion of strangers and friends.

The family quality became intense, however, when Raleigh noticed an older woman enter the bar and stride purposefully toward the oyster case.

"You must be that gal, Raleigh," the woman said without preamble. She reminded Raleigh of a stereotypical old farm woman, in stocky shoes and a shapeless floral dress over her spare frame, her graying hair pulled back in a severe bun that coordinated well with her disapproving expression.

"Yes, ma'am, I'm Raleigh Bishop," she said. "Who might you be?"

"Good evening, Mother," Kip said from next to her. He had just looked up from where he had been digging up oyster shells from down in the case and arranging them artfully on top of the ice.

"Raleigh, this is my mother, Doreen Hewitt. Mother, this is, as you've observed, Raleigh Bishop." He nodded the introductions.

So, this was Kip's mother, who had endured his father's infidelities. The years had not been kind to the woman. She had a pinched expression on her face, as though life had been both difficult and disappointing to her. As it likely had been.

Raleigh imagined that Kip must resemble his father, for she could see little of his mother in his face. Hopefully, the similarities ended with facial features.

A patron came up and asked for grilled oysters. With his gloved hand, Kip picked six large shells out of the display case, dropped them in a plastic bag, and promised to deliver them to the man's table. The patron happily handed over cash to Kip, who placed it in his apron pocket and headed off to the kitchen, leaving Raleigh alone with Kip's mother.

The woman seemed to be performing a very hard appraisal on her from behind narrowed eyelids, leaving Raleigh to wonder whether she should try to engage in conversation or just stand still and let the critique complete its course.

"*I* usually do this with Kip, you know," were Doreen Hewitt's next words. Doreen leaned over and found another apron on a shelf beneath the display case. As the other woman tied the apron on she added, "Not much room for three back here."

Raleigh nodded, understanding now that she was apparently an intrusion on mother-son time. "I think Kip was just trying to help distract my mind from daily life." She offered the older woman a smile. It was not returned.

"Your husband died in a crash," Doreen said flatly. It was startling, people typically couched it in sympathetic terms. It was as if Kip's mother was trying to needle her.

"Yes," Raleigh replied as evenly as she could. "About a year ago."

"Men leave one way or another. Heart breaks just the same."

Or maybe Doreen simply had a coarse personality.

"Oystering used to be a much easier business," the older woman said, completely changing subjects. "We sold to restaurants as far away as Baltimore back in the day. But there's too much commercial competition anymore."

Raleigh knew from an exhibit in her museum that oystering was far from an "easy" profession, what with the ever-changing restrictions on when and where oysters could be harvested, the daily quantity limits, and the relatively short season of roughly November through March of each year. But she nodded pleasantly to Kip's mother.

Doreen Hewitt continued. "Kip struck the deal with Willie Simpson to sell oysters on Happy Hour nights during the winter. It's some extra money that he uses toward boat maintenance, and he doesn't have to harvest too many of them."

Kip seemed to have many responsibilities, including his mother. In Raleigh's view, he accepted it all with ease.

Raleigh attempted to lighten the mood. "Kip says you

named him for Rudyard Kipling, an author you admire. My mother loves Florence Nightingale, so she named me for the city I was born in and my sister, Salem, for the city in Oregon where she was born."

Doreen did not seem to register any understanding, so Raleigh added, "Because Florence was also named for the city where she was born. 'Florence' wasn't a woman's name until after Nightingale became famous."

"I see. So, that's some kind of bond you and my son have?" Good heavens, the woman was prickly.

Raleigh wasn't sure whether to respond or not so she chose to stay silent. Another few patrons came up with orders. Kip returned briefly and took two bags of oysters to the kitchen to be fried in cornmeal batter for them.

Standing here with his mother was starting to make the evening seem very long.

"Kip says you might live in that old place, St. Clements Bluff." Doreen was veering onto another course again.

"Maybe. I might give it over to the historical society to open it up for visitors since it appears to have been a stop on the Underground Railroad. I haven't completely decided yet." Raleigh had the feeling this was Doreen's actual target of conversation.

"Our family's been in the county a long time. As long as your husband's," the woman said, brushing a loose tendril of hair away from her face with her forearm. "I'm sure my son told you about St. George Manor and how it was used to break my heart."

Raleigh nodded silently.

"Don't let the same thing happen to you. I'm not saying your husband was taking women there. I'm saying that generations of Bishops who have lived there have always been saying one thing and doing another. Managing to look like upstanding members of the community while being shysters on the side. Do you understand what I'm saying?"

Was this reference to the supposed land scheme? "I'm not sure," Raleigh said slowly. "I understand that Peter Bishop may have been involved in selling some properties that had been condemned as—"

Doreen waved a gloved hand. "All the locals knew about Peetie. People do that kind of thing all the time. But there have always been other rumors about that place. It might have been on the Underground Railroad back in the day, but it may have been used for other sorts of human transport in the later years, you know?"

Raleigh hated the shiver of fear that seemed to be running up her spine frequently as of late. "Are you saying St. Clements Bluff was used for some sort of human trafficking operation?" The idea was preposterous. Kip's mom obviously watched too much TV.

Doreen shrugged. "Child, I don't know what's gone on there over the years. Enough prominent Bishops to keep it covered up. But there were always…stories. Lord, I was once up at the fair in Charles County and overhead someone gossiping about goings-on. And that's a good fifty miles away. So, what I'm telling you is, if there was bad stuff happening there in the past, it might be going on in the present. You don't want to get yourself caught up in it, hear?"

Before Raleigh could respond, Kip returned once more to take up his post behind the display case. Doreen stopped talking as she turned her attention to customers. The three of them spent the rest of the evening mostly in silence, which gave Raleigh plenty of time to think.

Was Kip's mother warning her…or threatening her? And if it was the latter and push came to shove, whose side would Kip take?

CHAPTER 28

"WHAT'S SHE DOING with the place?" Doreen Hewitt asked the following morning when Kip dropped off two iced buckets full of the remaining oysters from the previous evening.

"Don't know," he said curtly as he dumped the contents of both buckets into the sink on the back porch.

His mother joined him at the sink. As he ran water over the sink's contents to melt the ice and expose the oysters, she began picking out individual oysters and tapping on their shells. Those shells that tightened up were an indication that the oysters inside were still alive. Those that did not respond contained dead oysters and she threw those back into the bucket.

"So, you took her to St. George Manor, didn't you?" she asked with the air of someone who already knew the answer.

"Yeah, I took her over there. Thought she might benefit from seeing the similarities."

With the ice now melted, Kip now used the water to rinse off the oysters, giving them a second cleaning before freezing.

"I suspected you had, and she confirmed it when I suggested as such to her." Doreen Hewitt shook her head. "Nobody benefits from that. You shouldn't have told her. You never listen to me, son. What happens if Mrs. Bishop decides to start rumors about what happened to me?"

Kip shook the water away from another oyster shell

and placed the shell on the counter. "She's not that type and it's all water under the bridge now. Nothing for you to fret about."

Doreen Hewitt always needed to worry and prod things along, as if she were perpetually trying to catch a fish with her bare hands. She could never realize that most situations in life were more like putting down crab pots. You put them down where you think they might be successful, then you walk away and let time and bait do their jobs.

"Don't worry, Raleigh Bishop isn't going to do anything harmful." He said it with finality, hoping the subject was now closed.

Together, they arranged single layers of shelled oysters in freezer bags. Kip's mother dated them, and they stacked the bags in the freezer.

Kip had learned long ago that while it was tempting to shuck the oysters first, and thus be able to store fifty times more oyster meat in the same space as one layer of shelled oysters, the flavor greatly degraded once they were shucked.

It was worth the flavor for the oysters to remain shelled until just before cooking.

With the work done, Kip said his farewells to his mother.

She was unable to let it go. "I still think you should—"

"Everything is fine." He picked up the bucket of dead oysters to take with him. In the water they would go as food for this year's crabs, who would adore the tasty offal and become plump and tasty themselves on it.

His mother's eyes narrowed to slits, always a sign that she was starting to simmer in anger. "I told her that rumors about the Bishops had reached up into Charles County."

Kip set the bucket down. He could only imagine what Raleigh's reaction had been to hearing that from his mother. "Why would you do something foolish like that?" he asked in exasperation.

"Son, you always think that you know better than me and that I'm willing to be controlled. I assure you I'm not." Doreen Hewitt crossed her arms to emphasize her point.

Kip shook his head and picked up the bucket of spoiled oysters to resume what he was doing. He hated to reprimand his mom but good heavens she had an imagination. "You know that's all hearsay at this point. Cops never arrested anyone and the so-called investigation of it all has been going on for years now." Kip was certain there was nothing to it.

Kip had a fishing buddy who knew the Charles County sheriff, so Kip knew they'd been doing surveillance on a few places, but nothing had come to fruition except the county's gossip mill. *That* had been full steam ahead like a freight train.

"Well, son, just trying to give your girl a heads up. Better safe than sorry, I say. I wish someone would've given me a heads up about your father, may he never rest in peace."

Here we go again. His parents' infidelity was why Kip had waited so long before even proposing to Helen. Which made him immediately think of Raleigh. She was the first woman after Helen that he couldn't get off his mind, unlike Raleigh's sister. He shook his head in pity for any future husband of Salem's.

He needed to get out of this house. Doreen could drive a man to drink, and Kip had seen enough boozers wreck jobs and relationships to make him avoid that fate at all costs.

"Where're you going? I need you to move a few pieces of furniture for me. I was trying to redecorate to some 'fang shuee' that's supposed to help my back, and I think I injured it further trying to move that dang end table."

"Mom, it's feng shui, and why didn't you just call me in the first place to help you? Let me take this to the truck, then I'll be back and you can show me what you want to move." Sometimes he just wondered if she created things for him to do just to have him around.

Kip retreated to his thoughts. Doreen had liked Helen, and he knew his mother was long past her patience in wanting grandkids. Did Raleigh want kids?

He got the traps into the truck, then walked back inside to help Doreen with her blasted end tables.

There had to be an expiration date when a child became an adult and didn't have to do chores.

Raleigh set her freshly poured mug of coffee on her desk as she sat down at her computer with a photocopy of one of Mutzi's scrapbook pages next to her.

She had come into work an hour early so she could search through the museum's artifact collection for the old lantern that Teeny Bishop had been holding in the article about his having won a museum award for donating it. Raleigh had no idea how the lantern could possibly be significant, except that her imagination suggested the lantern might have something to do with the house. She envisioned a previous Bishop guiding escaping slaves through the tunnel with it. Or using it to signal ships in the river that escapees were ready to board. It seemed as good a research point as any.

The digital inventory management system was wonky, plus the museum's storage places were stuffed to the rafters with items that had clearly never been sorted and thus inventoried, so when she didn't immediately find the old lantern in the system, she didn't automatically assume it wasn't in the museum. It would require a physical search to determine that the lantern wasn't actually there.

She took a few more gulps from the cup to ensure she had sufficient caffeine for the job, then began her search. She started with the neatly organized storage rooms—which unfortunately turned up nothing—then moved on to the old home's enclosed porch, which ran the length of the house. Items here had never made it into one of the more modern parts of the museum, for reasons unfathomable to Raleigh. It was as if the contents of the porch were of no importance to anyone and had been left here to become victims of heat, cold, and damp.

She made a mental note to suggest to Bert that inventorying the porch and properly storing its wares be her next job, not setting up the Yaocomico village re-creation, much as she would prefer the creative work of the exhibit.

The two overhead lights provided inadequate illumination, but the sun's rays were starting to break on the horizon, so Raleigh figured that despite the quantity of old items stacked up against the windows, it wouldn't be long before she had plenty of light to work in. It also made her realize that co-workers would likely be showing up soon, so she needed to act quickly.

As methodically as she could in this room stacked high with boxes and with shelves placed randomly throughout, Raleigh began digging.

To her utter surprise, she had hardly started on the set of shelves nearest the door when she found it.

Well, not the lantern itself, but the next best thing.

There was a large round spot on a lower shelf where something that had been there a long time had been removed. In the round spot lay an index card with faded block handwriting on it. Raleigh picked up the yellowed card and held it up to the light.

> *Lantern, ca. 1852. Assumed to have been used to guide escaped slaves to the Potomac River and on to freedom. Donated by Thomas "Teeny" Bishop, 1915.*

Beneath that, in a different, more recent handwriting, it read,

On loan to D. Bishop

Raleigh's mind was awash with questions. Why would the museum loan an artifact out to a citizen? Why wasn't there more identifying information here about who had removed the lantern and why? Moreover, who was "D. Bishop"?

She silently cursed the museum employee who had never inscribed the removal date. Now she had no idea when it had been taken and figuring out who did it would be difficult.

Raleigh suddenly felt as if the wind had been knocked out of her. What if "D" Bishop was David Bishop, her father-in-law?

No, that was impossible. He probably knew nothing about the lantern other than possibly having glanced at it in the scrapbook. He wouldn't have a use for it. He—

"I thought I saw the lights on in here when I pulled in!" It was Tammy, as ridiculously perky as ever. "You're quite the early bird. What are you looking for? Can I help?"

Raleigh was caught off-guard. She hadn't realized how much time had passed. Indeed, the sun was well up now. "Oh, I was just—" She considered making an excuse then decided to just be frank.

"Do you know anything about the lantern that used to be stored in this spot?" she asked, pointing at the shelf with one finger while handing Tammy the card with her other hand. "And do you know whether it was loaned out recently or not? I cannot believe how sloppily the transfer was made."

Tammy glanced down at the card in her hand. Raleigh's co-worker frowned and looked up at her. "Why are you looking for it?"

"It's—it's an old family piece of my husband's, and I recently came across an article about it having been donated here in the early 1900s. I couldn't remember it ever being on display, and I wanted to see this piece of Grant's family history." How easily the deceit was forming in Raleigh's mouth these days.

Tammy pursed her lips. "You know Bert won't be happy that you are disturbing the artifact storage without a directive to do so. You probably shouldn't even be in here. Bert won't be happy," she repeated as she dropped the card back onto the shelf.

Gone was the bubbly little redhead and in its place was strict schoolmarm. What nerve had Raleigh plucked?

"Sure. I'll go see him as soon as he gets in," Raleigh said, confused by Tammy's rapid change in demeanor.

Tammy nodded toward the door as if ordering Raleigh out, then followed Raleigh out and firmly shut the door behind her. "I'm sure Bert will be here soon," she said in finality.

It was as if Raleigh was an errant pupil being disciplined for having been caught digging in the teacher's desk.

Feeling chastised but not quite understanding why, Raleigh tried to forget her interaction with Tammy and get back to her projects. But she was further confused when her boss was cagey and evasive about the lantern.

First, he claimed to not know anything about it, but under Raleigh's further questioning, he said, "I think it went on loan before I got here. Is it that important?"

Raleigh's boss—the museum's director—was unclear

about the status of St. Mary's Historical Museum's artifact collection?

"So, we aren't sure where it is?" she asked.

Bert cast his gaze downward briefly but then looked back up at Raleigh, his fleshy lips curving up in an uncertain smile. "I'm sure I can figure out where it is. Presumably, it isn't critical to your research into the history of St. Clements Bluff."

It wasn't for Raleigh to criticize her boss, despite how odd his behavior was. Her next move would be to ask her father-in-law if he was the Bishop who had checked out the lantern and, if so, why he had done so. Or perhaps Pop knew who had the lantern. If, as Bert suggested, it was even relevant to her research.

"Meanwhile," Bert continued, "have you given more thought to what you intend to do with the house?

Raleigh had the sensation of being pushed into something. "Bert, I can't say that I've made a decision in such a short time."

He held up a hand. "No, no, of course not. How rude of me. That reminds me, how is your dog? Did he eat something bad? Dogs always do that. I didn't mean to leave abruptly; I just figured you needed to take care of your dog so I should get out of your way."

He was changing the subject too quickly. "Lindbergh is fine. The vet said he had definitely eaten something bad. By the way, someone recently suggested to me that there have always been rumors in the community about how St. Clements Bluff was used. That although it was on the Underground Railroad, it might have also been used as a passage for other, more nefarious, reasons."

"Like what are you thinking... something with drugs?" Bert pinched his face at the mention.

Raleigh shrugged. "I don't know. Or smuggling people."

"That sounds a little over-the-top, Raleigh. I'm sure the authorities are monitoring our community for smuggling of any kind and knowing their bloodhound ways I don't think I'd worry myself over that."

"True. Apparently, no one knows what may have been going on there but that there were always rumors among the old-timers."

Bert laughed gently. "Raleigh, you can't possibly think your husband was involved in anything like that. I could swallow a devious land scheme, but not wholesale trafficking of humans. Come on, you know that Grant wasn't involved in that, right?"

Raleigh nodded feeling properly chastised and guilty for even pondering this. Shame on Doreen for even putting this crazy thought into her head. "Right. Grant would have never—"

"Of course not. So then, the best thing to be done is to get rid of the place so that more formal investigations can take place before it is opened to the public. You don't want to find those things out after you've promoted it to the public as having only had a noble purpose, right?"

Bert was behaving in far too pushy a manner for Raleigh's liking. It was probably the land, being on the water, that would bring a pretty dollar if put up for sale. But Bert claimed he would use it for historical reasons, or so he'd said. And with the house's unsavory past, why was he so interested in it? Something didn't add up.

THE SUN WAS quickly sinking on the horizon when Raleigh left work for the day. Hoping that Lindbergh could wait a little longer for her to get home and walk him, Raleigh drove straight to her in-laws' home.

Soon she was alone at the kitchen counter with David Bishop as Mutzi was out grocery shopping.

Raleigh attempted to address a wide range of topics, from possible malfeasance at St. Clements Bluff to the hidden tunnel to the missing lantern.

As when they had had dinner together not long ago, David Bishop seemed a little confused. "So, what is it you are looking for? A flashlight?" He scratched his head over his ear as if that might spark a memory.

"A lantern," Raleigh said patiently. "Teeny Bishop donated it to the museum, but it was put out on loan to a 'D. Bishop.' Was that you?"

"A lantern. A lantern. Hmmm..." Raleigh's father-in-law gazed into the distance beyond Raleigh. "Why would I have an old lantern?"

Raleigh was alarmed. Was he showing signs of dementia? Or was he being purposely obtuse? Or worse, hiding something?

Finally, a switch seemed to flip in David Bishop's brain, and he returned his gaze to Raleigh. "Yes, yes, of course! I borrowed that lantern."

"You did? Where is it?"

He frowned and clouded over again as he considered her question. "The man wasn't too happy about my having it, but the lantern had to be taken for good purpose."

"Good purpose? What good purpose?" Good God this was getting to be bizarre.

"They say the animal trainers had to be helped." David Bishop slid away from his stool at the kitchen island and went to the refrigerator. He pulled out a soda, opened it, and took a long gulp from the red can.

Raleigh felt mildly panicked. "Pop, what are you talking about? What animal trainers?"

He put the can down on the counter. "The ones that take care of the German Shepherds," he said, looking at Raleigh as though she were an idiot.

"Okay...where is the lantern now?" she asked, veering off his nonsensical statement about animal trainers and dogs.

"It's providing the light for the trainers and the shepherds." He drank the rest of his soda in several long gulps, burped loudly, then placed the can in the sink.

Raleigh wasn't sure how to respond. Nothing he was saying made any sense.

Fortunately, Mutzi returned home before the silence between Raleigh and her father-in-law became too uncomfortable.

"Honey, can you unload the car?" she asked her husband.

While David wandered off to do his wife's bidding. Raleigh quickly sketched out her conversation with him for her mother-in-law.

Mutzi smiled sadly. "I know. I think Grant's death has affected Davey more than anyone realizes. He seems to be slipping. It's been going on for months. Did you notice it when we had dinner?"

Raleigh nodded.

"It's like he mentally fades out for a short period but then comes back as strong as ever and you believe yourself to be losing your own mind. What can I do?"

Raleigh had no idea how to comfort Mutzi other than to go to the woman and embrace her warmly. Mutzi was even thinner than she had been the last time Raleigh saw her.

Perhaps it was time to forget about the past and just focus on moving forward in the present. Except the past refused to leave Raleigh alone.

However, something Pop had said sparked an idea within her. As she hugged her mother-in-law, Raleigh let her imagination drift into wild places and several ideas started to interlock with one another, like the gears inside an old clock. Had the answer to St. Clements Bluff been staring her in the face this entire time?

She said a quick goodbye to Mutzi, and as she headed out the door she waved to Pop, who was managing several bags of groceries.

Raleigh sped off to home to walk Lindbergh and then return to St. Clements Bluff with the Bishop scrapbook.

What had dawned on Raleigh was that the truth was much, much worse than she could have ever imagined.

CHAPTER 29

KIP WAS WAITING for Raleigh in the driveway, as she had called him and asked him to meet her at the estate right away.

He opened her door so she could exit the car. "What's the big mystery?" he asked as he took the scrapbook from her arms.

"I think I understand what has happened with this house—why Grant wanted to keep it a secret and why someone doesn't want me here."

"Who is that someone?" Kip shut the car door and hefted the scrapbook under one arm as they walked toward the front porch.

"That's the detail I'm not quite sure of yet." Raleigh sounded evasive. She knew more than she was letting on. He had to admit he was glad she reached out to him; he felt like they were getting closer and that was a good thing in his book.

Kip followed Raleigh into the house and up the stairs to the bedchamber, where she selected an oldies music channel on her phone and placed the unit on the floor so they could have some background noise in the still of the house. Elvis Presley's "All Shook Up" blared out happily. Kip placed the scrapbook next to the phone.

The furniture still stood proudly in the room, a testament to history. Kip watched as Raleigh approached the bed, stepping over one of the side rails and kneeling at the headboard once more. She ran her fingertips over the various scenes of people in chains, people seemingly being hanged, and the official entering through a door while several figures cowered behind a wall of some sort. It was as though something from the headboard transferred to her hand, for she shivered.

Kip stepped over the frame and joined her, gently putting an arm around her shoulder. "It's almost as if someone was telling a story on the furniture."

Raleigh silently nodded her head.

She wasn't often at a loss for words. "You okay?" he asked, squeezing her shoulder, then dropping his hand to his side.

"I'm fine," she replied, turning and offering him a wan smile. "I think you need to see something."

Kip followed her as she stepped out of the bed frame and went to the fireplace. In front of his disbelieving eyes, she pulled out the mantel, which was arranged in a complicated stair-step mechanism. Raleigh moved backward as she brought the section in her hands gently down to the ground.

Kip gasped. "Incredible. Who made this?"

Raleigh shrugged. "I think it might date back to the mid-19th century. The house was built in 1823, but I don't know if it was part of the original build or a later addition."

He watched in fascination as she went through the various compartments and showed items to him. Kip reverently examined each one and replaced it in whatever compartment from which Raleigh had removed it.

She seemed to struggle with one item that was tucked tightly in its compartment. Reaching elsewhere, she pulled out an old oyster knife and pried the item out, careful not to destroy it.

"What is that? A letter?" Kip asked.

Raleigh didn't respond, but instead unfolded the scrap

of paper and held it out with trembling fingers. Kip took it and read it aloud. "'Room to Let. Second floor in quiet farmhouse on large, private property. Rent payable the first of each month. No animals; zookeepers inappropriate; sobers only.' Plus, a phone number to call P. Bishop, whom I presume was some distant uncle or cousin of your husband's."

He grinned as he handed the ad back to Raleigh. "I guess they could refuse service to anyone in those days."

Raleigh pushed the paper back to him. "Read it more closely."

Kip scanned the page and then read it aloud again. "I don't understand. What do you see?"

Raleigh sighed as she went to his side and pointed down at the ad. "No. Animals. Zookeepers. Inappropriate. Sobers only."

"Speaking slowly does not make the words have new meaning, Raleigh." Was she having a mental breakdown?

Raleigh shook her head in frustration, unwilling to speak the horror aloud. "Look at the first letter of each word."

He glanced down at the paper again. "N. A. Z. I… Oh!"

He recoiled and the brittle old ad fluttered to the ground. They stared at it together. Kip half expected it to burst into flames.

They were both silent for several moments, staring down at the aged, sepia-toned advertisement. Instead of the usual chill in her, the room suddenly felt hot and stuffy to Kip, and he found it difficult to breathe.

"What the hell happened here?" he asked in wonder. "I thought this house was on the Underground Railroad. Instead, they had Nazis visiting? For what? Tea and cakes?"

Raleigh pitched out a theory. "I know. I'm just as shocked as you. But here's what I believe happened. Grant's ancestor had indeed placed the house as a stop on the Underground Railroad. I'm not sure how many instances there are of Railroad safe houses in St. Mary's, but this would have been a welcome addition, I'm sure, what with its location directly on St. Clements Bay. Anyone coming from the south or east could have had respite here, then taken a boat under cover of night from here to the Potomac River, then to Washington, D.C., and on to points north. The stairs and tunnel behind this fireplace would have made for a quick escape route if any slave catchers came onto the property and knocked on the door."

She fell silent but Kip quickly prompted her. "What does that have to do with the Nazis a century later?"

"It would seem that the Bishop family had two sides to it, the side to which Grant belonged and a side that was on the wrong side of the tracks, if you'll forgive the railroad metaphor. Lots of them getting in trouble, spending time in jail, and the like."

Kip shook his head. "I guess sometimes behaviors and attitudes really do run through family lines."

"It's hard for me to imagine. Grant and his side of the family have always been such upstanding citizens with no blots at all on them," Raleigh said.

No doubt that knowledge made everything so much more difficult for Raleigh to accept.

"The Underground Railroad largely ended after President Lincoln signed the Emancipation Proclamation," she continued. "Thus, the entire escape setup would have been rendered unnecessary at that point. Then, of course, Maritime Shippers had it for a short period, but then I imagine the property just returned to being a typical rural farmhouse once Philip

Bishop was living in it––and for some reason developed an affinity for Nazi officials fleeing Germany for South America. You know, I had it in my head that the old oyster wars were somehow related to this home, but it wasn't the oyster wars that was significant, it was the Second World War."

Kip was silent, letting Raleigh finish twirling out her theory. As implausible as it sounded, he also had the sense of puzzle pieces falling into place.

"I believe Philip Bishop was somehow the recipient of pro-Nazi propaganda—there was more of it in this country than people realize. Knowing he had a perfect location, he must have somehow managed to connect himself to a group helping the officers escape justice."

Now Kip spoke up. "Yes, I remember reading in school that thousands of Nazis fled via so-called ratlines to countries like Brazil and Argentina, which turned a blind eye to Nazi war crimes. But…didn't they typically go first to Spain or Rome, then make their way to South America?"

"I bet if we looked at a map, we'd find that Maryland was a good halfway point for them. Perhaps a ship to the Port of Baltimore, then a combination river and overland escape route to Miami or Galveston, then another ship to Rio or Buenos Aires. The U.S. was still very rural and there would have been very little technology for tracking anyone. It would have been a fairly simple thing to just melt away."

"True. It's not like there were slave catchers by then. But I don't know, Raleigh," Kip added. "These things you mention are all possible, but until you find proof—if you even want to go down that rabbit hole—I would really keep this under wraps for now. It's quite an accusation and not only puts a cloud on your family but the community too."

"Good point." Raleigh nodded at him as the strains

of "It's Now or Never" floated across the room. It was apparently Elvis Retrospective Day on the channel.

Raleigh retrieved the scrapbook from the floor and handed it wordlessly to Kip. He flipped through the pages, frowning as he began putting together much of the Bishop family history. "And I thought my family had skeletons clacking and jangling into each other in the closet. The Bishops make the Hewitts look like our entire family tree is ready for canonization." He hoped his tone would lighten the mood in the room, which had suddenly become somber and heavy.

"Grant must have been horrified when he put it all together. I imagine that—that—" She was suddenly blinking back tears.

"What is it?" Kip asked softly, looking up from the scrapbook.

She sniffed and brushed away a single drop coursing down her cheek. "I imagine that Grant figured it all out and was torn between not humiliating his family and knowing that there was historical significance to this place. That that significance would be important to someone like me. So, his best option to not embarrass his family was to keep St. Clements Bluff hidden away until after his death, which should have been decades away, but he hedged his bets by entrusting it to me in case he should die early. Which, unfortunately, was exactly what happened."

"What about the furniture?" Kip asked gently, attempting to steer her away from her current thought track.

"The Jonson family certainly made it, but I think that some of the later carvings were memorials to the Nazi escapees who made their way here and couldn't speak English. The furniture told a story for them."

Kip waved a hand over the various trays in the mantel. "So, all of these things likely belonged to Nazis who passed through the house," he said, hardening his features at the appalling knowledge he was gaining. "Well, your theory explains much, but it leaves a lot wanting. I mean, that may explain the past, but who is sending you threatening letters? What's with the dramatic voodoo doll? Why was Lindbergh poisoned, if he indeed was? Most importantly, who is trying to take you away from me?"

His voice broke at that. Curse his body for showing that much emotion. Now Raleigh would think he was as mushy as a molting blue crab. What an idiot. He had leaped square into the "just friends" column.

To his surprise, though, Raleigh leaned against him. He instinctively turned and slid his arms protectively around her. It felt like a warm cocoon of peace amid so much turmoil to just stand there with her. It felt right. Then "Can't Help Falling in Love" wafted around them, and Kip swayed gently against Raleigh.

He was transported back to the Rex, where they had danced like this, and he had felt the first true stirrings of longing since Helen's death. Today, though, the feeling was deeper. More intense. He wondered fleetingly what Raleigh's husband would think of this. Would he be glad for it? Or would he want to strangle Kip with his own two hands?

But he tamped down those thoughts, instead wrapping his arms tighter around Raleigh and enjoying the comfort of her embrace.

"Like a river flows…" Elvis crooned. At those words, Kip, overcome by his emotions and not caring what happened next, paused, tucked a finger under Raleigh's chin, and lowered his face to hers.

Her lips against his were as soft and questioning as could have ever imagined. Kip forgot everything around him and deepened the kiss, becoming first exploratory and then more demanding.

It had been so long since—

"Well, well, isn't this adorable?" A chuckling male voice had joined them.

Kip broke away from Raleigh and turned to find Trey Bishop standing there.

CHAPTER 30

"TREY! WHAT ARE you doing here?" Raleigh said, mentally cursing Trey for interrupting the sweetest moment she had had in a long time. "And what is—" she stopped.

Trey held the old oil lantern that Teeny Bishop had donated to the museum. The wick was lit and a small flame glowed orange behind the glass.

"—what have you got there?" she finished. He held it up, oblivious to her irritation. "Isn't it great? Dad gave it to me. Said he found it in the attic and I should keep it for him. It seemed like a more appropriate source of light than a flashlight for being here."

But Pop had told Raleigh that—

Trey continued. "But I guess you two preferred the shadows. Didn't expect to find you here, Rals. I was surprised to see your car and Kip's in the driveway. What are *you* doing here? More investigative work, perhaps? How can I help?"

Trey looked beyond Raleigh and Kip at the open mantel, which was difficult to miss. "What the hell is that?"

"I stumbled into it," Raleigh said, reluctantly stepping completely away from Kip to show him. "It's quite a treasure trove."

Trey set the lantern on the floor and walked to the mantel. He examined items in the compartments almost reverently, particularly spending time cradling the

Bakelite pipe. "Amazing what's in here. All part of the Bishop history."

His attention was diverted by the old advertisement that had dropped to the floor. He reached down for it and brought it back up to read it. He frowned and seemed to read it again, slowly.

"This is weird," he said.

Raleigh retrieved the scrapbook and flipped to the article about the circus in Leonardtown, handing it to Trey to read.

Trey chuckled as he looked over the amusing article. "My ancestors really didn't like circus folk, did they? I can't believe I've never seen this before. Mom gave this to you?" He handed the scrapbook back to Raleigh.

"Yes. Do you see the connection between the article and the advertisement for the room to let?" Raleigh carefully put the scrapbook back down next to her phone. Elvis was now happily describing how he wanted to be led around in "Let Me Be Your Teddy Bear." How ironic that Elvis was describing that he didn't want to be a ferocious zoo tiger or a lion for his intended, but instead just a cuddly little bear.

"What do you mean?" Trey asked.

Once more, Raleigh emphasized each of the words that spelled out to whom the advertisement was secretly intended.

Trey's mouth gaped. "Really? But...what does it mean?"

Raleigh explained her theory about St. Clements Bluff being used as part of a post-war ratline.

"How fiendishly clever," Trey said, laughing. "Shocking that the other side of the family was this smart, right? Do you mind if I take this?" He was already folding it back up and tucking it into his front jeans pocket.

"I suppose I could—" Raleigh began.

"So, what else do you have? This is a truly exciting revelation. The Bishops are certainly infamous." Trey rubbed his hands briskly together. Raleigh sensed that it wasn't the chill in the air as much as it was anticipation that caused him to do so. It was vaguely disturbing, especially since Trey seemed to get great joy out of the news that some of his ancestors were conducting heinous crimes.

"You certainly seem to find this amusing," Raleigh said.

"Amusing? Of course not. It's actually gratifying to see proof of what Uncle Junior Bishop told me had happened here in the late 1940s under Philip Bishop's care. I had thought perhaps they were just stories, but now it's obvious that they were true. It makes my work that much more important."

"Your work? What do you mean?" Raleigh felt a shiver starting at the base of her spine. Kip seemed to sense it, for he placed a protective hand at the small of her back.

"My work helping freedom fighters from overseas. Uncle Junior and I set up a secret routing for them—sort of like the Underground Railroad—and we had been working together on it. Uncle Junior had promised to give St. Clements Bluff to me in his will, but he never changed the will before he died, so Grant inherited it. Sort of put a stop to the work, you know? Grant wasn't very understanding."

Raleigh was confused. "Grant wasn't very understanding? That you were helping people from other countries in a quest to be free?" That didn't sound right. Grant bled Navy blue and would have jumped at the chance to help others achieve freedom.

"I know, it seems crazy. He had an issue with my calling the people freedom fighters. He called them terrorists." Trey shook his head.

What? The shiver was making its way up Raleigh's back. "Are you saying," she said slowly as she processed what her brother-in-law had just told her, "that you were aiding enemies of the United States in fleeing justice?"

Kip jumped in. "What the hell is wrong with you?"

Trey smiled condescendingly. "Rals, you don't understand," he said, ignoring Kip. "There are many misunderstood and persecuted freedom fighters overseas. We have to do all we can to help them. Like the slaves and then the Third Reich officers this house helped all those years ago, this can be a safe place for the freedom fighters being pursued by our military."

Raleigh could hardly believe what she was hearing. "Trey, are you equating escaping slaves with murdering Nazis and terrorists? Do you hear yourself?"

Trey gazed at her with pity. "Rals, do you hear your *own* self? Anyone fighting for freedom is worthy of saving. You only focus on what history and journalists tell you which people are wholly innocent or have done some great evil, but there is always another side to the story. It is our responsibility to help those seeking a better life. It's the American dream. You are far too caught up in details."

"You're going to jail forever, my man," Kip said. "You're a traitor. You deserve a firing squad."

Trey offered Kip his pitying gaze. "I'm afraid that's not true on all counts. No one will ever know what I've told you."

Raleigh didn't like the sound of that, either.

CHAPTER 31

"TREY, HAS IT occurred to you that you believe you are releasing these people to make their way to South America, but that they are probably just making their homes here in this country?" Raleigh shuddered to imagine how many terrorist cells Trey was responsible for creating. Rogue organizations were probably delighted with how easily they were able to dupe him into helping them reach various parts of the U.S.

Trey was completely unconcerned by Raleigh's statement. "If they feel safer in the U.S., that's fine. You see, the freedom route starts here, at St. Clements Bluff. Isn't that amazing?"

When Raleigh didn't respond, Trey seemed irritated. "I don't think you understand that this house is now in its third century of helping the oppressed secure new lives for themselves. If authorities weren't so narrow-minded about what constitutes 'freedom,'"—Trey rolled his eyes dramatically—"this house would be the most celebrated one in the country. Far more so than if you just gave it to the historical society so that they could brag about one single piece of the house's illustrious history."

How had Trey become so maniacal without Raleigh ever noticing it? But Grant had noticed, and if not for his untimely death, Trey's scheme would have been halted long ago. How distraught Grant must have been at his brother's brazen criminality.

Raleigh tried once more. "Surely you realize that this

goes against everything Grant believed in and worked for. You aren't just betraying your country, you are betraying your brother. You are a traitor and will suffer a traitor's fate."

Trey flicked the fingers of one hand dismissively in her direction. "No such thing will happen. My plan is beautiful in its simplicity. The freedom fighters come in at the Port of Baltimore aboard whatever merchant ship will take them. Then they transfer to a day cruise down to St. Clements Island, ostensibly to tour the island. But instead of getting back onto their boat, they slip into a little craft I have waiting by the pier. You know how crowded the island can get with visitors. Nobody pays attention to who is getting into which boat. Then I bring them here to St. Clements Bluff to wait until the next safe house is made available. They travel by land until they reach the southern border, and then they can melt into any number of countries down there. It's easy-peasy money that is creating a tidy little nest egg."

Trey was grinning broadly now, warmed up to the idea of his own brilliance. Raleigh realized that Trey was experiencing the "need to confess" that all of the crime shows featured whenever the culprit was caught. Trey was proud of what he was doing and needed others to know about it.

He continued. "My greatest achievement was last October during the Blessing of the Fleet. The island was packed with visitors. I was able to return three times to pick up freedom fighters without a single soul noticing it. Made sure all twelve of them got to various safe houses and over the border by year's end."

Kip spoke up. "You used an event like the Blessing of the Fleet to carry this out?" His voice brimmed with disgust.

The annual blessing event featured all manner of entertainment, food, arts and crafts, and evening fireworks. The blessing commemorated the decades-old tradition of blessing the fleet of boats used by local watermen. No wonder Kip was so angry.

Trey shrugged, seemingly unconcerned by Kip's fury. "What other occasion around here provides such good cover?"

Raleigh sensed Kip flexing his fist against her back as his breathing became deep and audible. Elvis also seemed to be angry, as he began belting out how someone was nuthin' but a hound dog. Trey reached down and picked up the lantern and whistled along with Elvis for a few moments. But he stopped, his need to confess apparently not yet fully satisfied.

"Authorities always assume the freedom fighters will fly in, thus my plan—with a more complicated land and water routing—enables them to travel unnoticed. Uncle Junior taught me that trick. Except Grant learned about it. Like you, he didn't understand at all. He swept through and cleaned out the house except for the furniture in this room. He thought it might have high resale value and would provide for you in the future. What a waste."

Raleigh seized on what he was saying. "This furniture. There are scenes that I took to represent officials looking for escaped slaves. But are some of them actually—?"

Trey grinned ear to ear. "Yep. Uncle Junior said that later generations carried on the carvings to depict how various people were saved through this house. Through this very room. Uncle Junior said the armoire was specially built for signifying specific messages to the poor German officers who spoke little English. Can you imagine? All of them passing through here on their way to freedom? In fact, look at this."

Trey stepped over to the armoire and held the lantern up to illuminate the carvings on the piece. "Look at that." He pointed at a vignette that seemed to be an official standing on the other side of a wall a group of people hid behind. "That was to show the escapees that they should hide behind the wall in here if the authorities should show up. It still makes me speechless with awe. I never told Grant about the armoire, though. I figured he would have chopped it up for kindling if he'd known. Like I said, he had no vision for what Uncle Junior and I were doing. Nor do you, it would seem."

Raleigh was aghast. Trey had known about the furniture all along.

"Maybe if you'd had the insight I do, you would have felt differently," he said. "I will admit, you were quite close on one point. Maritime Shippers did use St. Clements Bluff for both blockade running and as a camp for oyster pirates who were dredging close to the Maryland shore. During the Civil War, the owner of Maritime Shippers was caught by the Union Navy as he attempted to run tobacco to the neutral port of Bermuda for eventual shipment down to Florida. With his primary ship seized and facing ruinous debt to buy his way out of prison, he sold St. Clements Bluff back to my family for pennies on the dollar."

Trey picked up the lantern. "You had to be all high and mighty about the property. 'Grant would have wanted it this way.' 'The property should be open for the public.'" Trey mimicked her in a high-pitched voice. "I was continuing Uncle Junior's improvements to the place, like replacing a rotted ladder in the tunnel. Why couldn't you just sell me the place and be done with it? Move back to your parents or run off with him"—he wagged the lantern in Kip's direction—"and let the Bishop name continue on without you?"

Watching the lantern sway back and forth jogged Raleigh's memory of her conversation with Pop. He had said the lantern was 'providing the light for the trainers and shepherds.' What had that meant, given that Trey was in possession of the object?

"Did your father truly give you the lantern?" Raleigh asked. "Or did you steal it from his attic?"

"This?" Trey held the lantern up to look at it. The glow from it eerily lit up his expression. Raleigh noticed for the first time that he had beads of sweat on his forehead. "Why would I steal it? I told Pop I admired it because it reminded me of Uncle Junior, and I wanted to place it back here at St. Clements Bluff, where it belonged. So, he gave it to me. Told me to be careful of the lions and dogs, but that was just some crazy talk of his."

But Raleigh realized it wasn't. Her father-in-law must have known about the old room-to-let advertisement and what it said about no zookeepers, which he had translated into "trainers" and "lions," and the shepherd reference was to German shepherds, or German officers.

The mind's ability to convolute thoughts was remarkable.

"Grant never held the shady real estate meetings, did he?" It was almost a relief to realize that Trey had surely lied about that as he had lied about many things.

"Nah. Grant wasn't interested in that plan. But they happened anyway without my brother's knowledge. What's the old saying? 'What he didn't know didn't hurt him.'" Trey chuckled at his wit.

Raleigh willed herself to remain calm and make no comment to that.

"Was the little voodoo doll your handiwork?" she asked, certain of the answer.

Trey considered the question. "Sort of," he said, which was a curiously non-definitive answer for someone who was so proud of his evil work thus far. "It didn't work, though, did it? Because you weren't scared away. The letters didn't chase you away, either."

"What if I would've gone to the authorities? That could've been a problem for you."

Trey laughed loudly at that. "Geez, Rals, you're such an idiot. Fuck no, they wouldn't have led back to me or anyone around here."

She didn't stop and accused Trey. "I suppose you were the one who tried to poison Lindbergh."

"Nah, I would never do that to Grant's pooch," Trey said with an air of hurt at being accused of harming an animal. "He must have gotten into something."

The irony of Trey's words was suffocating. He would aid and abet terrorists but found it abhorrent that he was accused of hurting a dog.

But she had no time to question him further, for he moved on to another topic. "By the way, that obnoxious neighbor of yours—Maggie or Margery—she's been entirely too interested in the house. I've seen her snooping around more than once, and it has caused me no end of inconvenience. She'll have to be dealt with."

Bless Magda for trying to look out for me, Raleigh thought before trying to steer Trey away from the thought. "What do you mean, 'dealt with'? Magda doesn't know anything, right?" She hoped she didn't sound desperate.

"I suppose not. But she needs to stop being so nosy." He laughed, and the sound was low and guttural. "There's really only one way to handle people who can't mind their business. Once I'm done here and take care of her, I've got a boat to catch."

"Trey," Raleigh said tentatively. "What's that supposed to mean?"

He didn't respond. Raleigh realized she still had the oyster knife in her hand. She slowly brought her closed hand up behind her back and tucked the knife into her waistband Kip stepped directly behind her and she felt him slide the knife back out of her waistband. He bent and whispered to her, "The lantern is dangerous."

Raleigh wasn't sure what Kip intended to do but offered him cover by making a last-ditch effort to reason with her brother-in-law. "What about Barb? You adore her. What is she going to think about all of this?"

Trey paused for only a moment. "Barb's fine. She and I will be very happy together. But that's enough about her. I need to make you both understand that I refuse to be stopped in my work. It is my crusade, if you will, to rescue those persecuted for their beliefs."

Trey's expression was strange as if he was both present in the room and yet somewhere else at the same time. The day was starting to fade into twilight outside, shadowing his face, which was only illuminated now by the lantern.

"So, I need you to sign the house over to me, of course," Trey said flatly. "It's the only way."

Kip slid just slightly to one side of her. To distract Trey from noticing Kip's movement, she spoke again, hoping she didn't sound desperate. "But you told me you didn't want the house. That it seemed cursed, and you wanted to give Barb a different house to raise your children in."

Even in the fading light, she could see Trey roll his eyes. "Really, Rals? You think I meant that? Please don't be intentionally stupid. I can only—"

At that moment, Kip moved fluidly toward Trey and attempted to grab the lantern. Despite the encroaching darkness, Trey reacted swiftly to the movement and brought the lantern up with a grunt, his intent clearly to connect the heavy metal with Kip's head. Kip thrust an arm out and blocked the attempt. Trey held a death grip on the lantern, though, and brought it around once more to fend Kip off.

This time it cracked against Kip's shoulder, causing him to spew a string of obscenities at Trey, who laughed. It also caused Kip to release the oyster knife, which landed across the room, leaving Kip without a weapon.

Undaunted, Kip balled up his fists and lunged at Trey. The men tussled, with Trey swinging the lantern again and again and Kip trying unsuccessfully to tackle him.

While the men fought, Raleigh edged around them and dropped to all fours, seeking out the knife, which was difficult to find against the dark carpet with only the wildly moving lantern providing minimal glow.

Finally, Raleigh's fingers found the bulbous wood handle and she seized the makeshift weapon. As she rose to help Kip, she heard another loud crack and was just able to see Kip fall backward to the floor with a sickening thud.

"No!" she screamed. Her outburst was loud enough that Trey was startled for a moment. Raleigh ran full tilt at Trey and threw herself against him. He grunted as they both tumbled to the ground together, with Raleigh landing on top of him.

Trey had dropped the lantern and it now lay on its side, oil spilling onto the carpet and the flame's glow growing larger.

"You stupid cow," Trey muttered. "You stupid, stupid b—"

But Raleigh had had enough. "You're a snake, you know that?" she whispered as she quickly plunged the oyster knife into his chest as hard as she could and pushed herself away from him. It sliced beneath his skin much more easily than she had imagined the blunted blade would. Trey howled in agony, but Raleigh realized quickly that the blade of the oyster knife was not long enough to do any serious damage.

Trey must have realized it, too, for he stopped howling long enough to pull the knife out of his chest. Another string of obscenities flowed out of him along with the blade, but still he rose unsteadily to his feet with the knife in his hand as Raleigh backed away.

"That's your own stupidity then, Rals. They say you should never wound a snake, you should always kill it," Trey said in a calm voice, as if he was unaware that Kip lay on the ground bleeding, he himself had a stab wound, and a corner of the Turkish carpet was beginning to seriously flame up, sending an acrid odor into the room.

"Trey, you've got to stop this now," Raleigh said, trying to match his calm voice but certain she was failing. *Was Kip okay? Was he even alive?* She could only vaguely see his prone figure in the room. The carpet flame was getting larger, and the smoke was making it difficult to breathe. "You've still got time to avoid punish—"

"Of course, I have time, Rals. I have all the time in the world. It is *you* who lacks time." Raleigh heard a clunk as the oyster knife hit a wall across the room and then clattered to the wood floor beyond the carpet's edge. "You really shouldn't have stabbed me like that. Very rude." Trey's voice was still eerily peaceful.

Raleigh took several short breaths and glanced around desperately for anything she could use as a weapon. The glow from the flame lit up Trey's frightening visage as he took a step closer to her.

She could only think of one thing to do. With energy she didn't know she had, Raleigh ran away from the burning carpet and toward one of the windows. If she could just toss a length of drapery out the window and use it to slide down and break her fall, she might be able to quickly get help and—

Crack!

The blow was so swift and complete that Raleigh didn't really feel any pain. It was more like her vision filled with the light of a thousand stars and she went completely deaf.

As she fell face first to the ground, she was struck by how incongruous it was that the familiar opening of

"Suspicious Minds" lilted out on her phone over the sound of the crackling fire and Trey's laughter.

"I'm sorry, Kip," she whispered, and then she was gone.

CHAPTER 32

RALEIGH BLINKED AWAY moisture. It was raining. No, the dripping was too uneven to be rain.

She shivered from cold. She had to get out of this strange drizzle. But as she worked to assemble her foggy thoughts, she found that her body was not cooperating. It was impossible to feel anything.

Other than the blinding pain behind her eyes.

Maybe she was dead, and this was what it was like to pass into the next world, she thought. Extraordinary discomfort before facing eternal judgment

Wait, what was that? It sounded like the distant blare of sirens.

Suddenly she felt a moist tongue lap across her face.

"Raleigh, are you conscious, girl?" came a voice from somewhere above her.

Raleigh's tongue was thick, and she wasn't able to make it work to form words.

"I think you are. You'll be all right."

Raleigh slowly opened her eyes and found Magda's concerned expression filling her vision. "What am I—where did—is Kip—?" It was impossible to form a complete sentence, and she closed her eyes again.

Magda didn't respond, and when Raleigh opened her eyes a few moments later, Jacky was breathing heavily over her, with doggy spittle dripping on her face.

She put out a hand to him, and he licked her palm.

"Good boy," she whispered and went unconscious again.

RALEIGH WAS ONLY at the edge of awareness of what happened next. She was lifted off the ground by a strong pair of arms that held her close as she was moved swiftly away from wherever she had been. Leaves crunched from down below where she was. The distinct odor of charred wood was everywhere, settling over her like a blanket.

There were voices all around her, too. A male voice came from next to her, deep and comforting. A woman's voice—Magda? No, Salem.

Raleigh drifted in and out of consciousness but finally sensed she was in a bed. It was much warmer here. Beeps, whirrs, and dings replaced the sound of leaves below feet, and there were strange new voices. They seemed to be talking about her and occasionally probing her head.

She moaned in pain at the pressure against her skull and went out again.

CHAPTER 33

Two months later.

IT WAS STILL surreal to Raleigh what had happened in the aftermath of the fire. After dragging himself off the ground, picking Raleigh up, and taking her to the safety of the outdoors, Kip had attempted to run back into the house to get Trey, but the inferno was too great by then, leaving Trey to be physically consumed by the house that had already mentally taken possession of him. Kip said Trey stood in the window of that bedroom, smiling as flames took him.

Kip had then gone back outside and, despite bleeding profusely, had picked Raleigh up and carried her to where emergency vehicles were waiting. Magda told her that he had collapsed himself as soon as the ambulance doors had safely ensconced Raleigh inside, and he was tucked into a second ambulance and underwent an overnight observation at St. Mary's Hospital.

Raleigh had remained at the hospital for several days. Bert Mattingly was, as always, very understanding and simply held her job open until she had completely recovered at home a month later. It was almost silly now that she had been suspicious of someone who had only had her good interests at heart. But then she'd thought Trey had her best interests at heart too, so she wouldn't be too hard on herself.

Raleigh had thrown herself back into her work and had completed the Yaocomico village exhibit in record time. It was scheduled to be unveiled next week.

As soon as a somber memorial event for Trey had concluded, Barb Costello had abruptly left Maryland, telling Raleigh on her way out that, "There is no state too far away for me to escape the humiliation of what Trey did."

Raleigh had tried to convince Barb to stay, to not leave her job and friends, but Barb was adamant that she would be forever tainted in the community by Trey's actions.

In their own way, Pop and Mutzi must have felt stained, as well. Mutzi had come to Raleigh with an offer.

"Davey and I talked about this on one of his good days," Mutzi said over a Saturday lunch at the Rex. "We would like to compensate you for St. Clements Bluff."

"Compensate me?" Raleigh took a sip of strawberry lemonade. She was trying to kick her coffee habit, a battle she was largely losing. The sugary drink made her mouth pucker. What she would give for a cup of brain-jolting java.

"Yes, we want to pay you what the fair market value would have been for the home if it still stood. You've been through a lot, honey, and we want to help you."

Raleigh felt tears welling up in her eyes. "Mutzi, thank you. That is the most generous offer I have ever had. But I have an insurance settlement."

Mutzi shook her head as she stabbed at a grape tomato in her salad. "That's not the same. Insurance will never compensate you for all the pain and loss you've experienced. That house was worth far more than just its replacement value. It was something Grant had cared about. And Trey completely destroyed—" Raleigh's mother-in-law sobbed back tears.

Raleigh smiled sadly. "Mutzi, all of the money in the world won't make me feel better about Grant's death. But I don't want you to feel guilty about anything that happened. You aren't responsible for Trey's actions, although I'm sorry he got caught up in something so terrible."

Mutzi continued to push for some sort of reparation for Raleigh, but Raleigh refused to even entertain the idea. In fact, Raleigh tried to make light of it. "Truly, I'm the one who owes you compensation. Your scrapbook was lost in the fire and that, too, was worth far more than its replacement value."

Mutzi gave her a weak laugh. "I'm glad it's gone. To think, all of those clues in it and I never even realized it. Mercy."

Magda had enjoyed some minor celebrity in the community, as she started hanging near the St. Clements Bluff entrance and offering curiosity seekers information on the events that had occurred. She became sort of a self-appointed tour guide, walking passers-by past the house's ruins, down to the old shed, and showing them where the tunnel entrance was. But as the news disappeared from the local papers, so did the number of curious onlookers. Magda soon returned to her quiet life with her dog.

After Raleigh visited each of them, both the Charles County and St. Mary's County sheriff's departments had, along with help from the Coast Guard, started to more diligently monitor their shorelines for any other misguided fools like Trey Bishop who might think to carry on his work.

Derrick Jonson had come by the property to verify for himself what he had read in the news. "So, the bedroom suite really was incinerated?" he asked Raleigh as he surveyed the pile of debris. "Good riddance, I say. No need for that to be living on. Can build you another set if you like."

But Raleigh agreed with him that it was probably just

as well that the furniture was gone and refused his offer as she had refused Mutzi's.

Salem was the biggest surprise in Raleigh's life, insisting on moving permanently to St. Mary's County. Raleigh hadn't realized how serious her sister had become with Mike.

Raleigh had agreed to let Salem stay with her, and Salem had accepted, quickly finding a job as a budget manager for the Navy. It wasn't as glamorous as what she was used to, but Salem seemed willing to go all in on Mike and make the career sacrifice for him.

"Mom texted and asked if you were annoying me," Raleigh had told her sister. "So, you better be nice so I don't report you."

"*Moi?*" Salem had asked, with mock horror on her face. "Why, Sisso, I am the most adoring of siblings, the most considerate, the most generous, the most—"

"Okay, okay, stop," Raleigh had said, throwing up her hands. "I'll tell Mom you are the sole reason I am feeling better if you'll quit with the theatrics."

Salem had posed again, this time with an exaggerated, pouting expression. "You mean I'm not? You're saying there's someone else who can even come close to having my soothing voice? My comforting shoulder? My—"

Raleigh had tossed a sofa pillow at Salem, who had easily caught it with a giggle.

Raleigh's sister had only been there a few weeks when Kip made the most surprising offer of all.

"Just sorta thinking that maybe you could let Salem have this place to herself and you could, you know, find your way over to St. George Manor. It could use a woman's touch. Maybe even children's laughter one day," he said, his cheeks reddening as he suddenly became very shy.

Now that was a bona fide offer Raleigh could accept.

CHAPTER 34

Seven years later.

RALEIGH HEWITT STOOD at the island inside the renovated kitchen of St. George Manor, attempting to recreate a thin bread made of flour and corn, from an old Piscataway tribe recipe. She was failing miserably. Did it need more salt?

Cooking had become a hobby for her over the past few years, after being at home on bed rest prior to delivering Amelia had gotten her hooked on watching various food channels. She'd had the idea of trying to create dishes eaten by the natives who had inhabited St. Mary's County long ago, with varying levels of success. Her ultimate plan was to develop a museum program to teach historical cooking skills but with a twist to model it after popular cooking classes around town that offered libations and music alongside the learning experience. Raleigh's historical cooking classes would be aimed at couples and groups of friends.

She vaguely noticed the sound of the home's front door opening. Replacing the front door had been just one of many renovations made to St. George Manor, to also include a complete kitchen renovation and completely dismantling and then walling up the house's secret staircase and tunnel. Not only had it made Doreen happy, but it had swept away any sense of previous wrongdoing from the house. It had also seemed to give Derrick Jonson the same sense, for he commented after delivering the final load of their new maple kitchen cabinets that he felt as though he had somehow atoned for his family allowing itself to be swept up in the wood carving and inlay at St. Clements Bluff. "I know none of my ancestors would have agreed to all of that long-term carving if they'd known what it would eventually be used for, but it still felt like a blot on our reputation."

Lindbergh, now too old to get too excited about much anymore, softly woofed from the living room but didn't bother padding out to see who was coming in.

"Sweetheart?" came Kip's voice from the front of the house. "I picked up the mail."

Tiny feet stomping from the front door to the kitchen made Raleigh look away from what she was doing.

"Mommy, Mommy! Daddy let me check the mail! All by myself." Amelia held up a small bundle of envelopes and catalogs. Several pieces fell to the ground, but it was difficult to notice the mess past the winsome smile of her impish eldest child.

"Nice job," Raleigh said, taking the pile and placing it on the counter.

The badly-made bread was now completely forgotten as Kip entered the kitchen and gave her a kiss. "Have you hit on the right dish for the hearth and home event?" he asked.

"Maybe," Raleigh replied. "I don't know how these celebrity chefs whip something out of thin air when I can barely cope with a recipe in hand. But I'll keep trying. I don't want to disappoint Bert."

Bert had been sheepish in the aftermath of the fire, admitting that he had loaned the lantern to David Bishop but immediately regretted it. Then, feeling defensive, he had been unable to just admit to Raleigh having done so and instead tried to make up for it by risking much of his life savings in his offer to buy St. Clements Bluff.

Raleigh had been more than happy to forgive and forget where Bert was concerned.

"Well, in your defense, you are dealing with recipes and ingredients that are a few centuries outdated." Kip never failed to be in her corner.

"Mommy, it's time to read the mail," Amelia insisted as her father swept up the errant pieces and put them on the island's countertop to join the rest of the mail.

"Of course," Raleigh said, wiping her hands on a kitchen towel and addressing the pile. "What have we here? A catalog from the toy company? That sounds like complete rubbish." Raleigh pulled open the trash bin cabinet and held it over the trash can that lay within it.

Amelia's eyes became saucers. "Nooooo!" Raleigh's daughter exclaimed in dismay.

"Hmmm." Raleigh pretended to be thoughtful. "Well, I'm not sure there's any use for it, but if *you* would like to look at it..."

Amelia snatched the catalog and ran happily from the room.

Raleigh and Kip shared a knowing smile. By the end of the evening, Amelia would likely have folded down the page of every toy she liked and then suggested that the list to Santa be started right away, to be sure he didn't run out of her favorites in the next four months until Christmas.

"How did it go with Charles?" Raleigh asked her husband.

"You know my mother. Very happy to have him for a weekend to spoil him. But I ask you, how many toy cars does an eighteen-month-old need?"

Doreen Hewitt had surprised Raleigh by proving to be a very doting grandmother who constantly requested time with one or the other of her grandchildren. It was as if the next generation's arrival made her forget all of her dead husband's sins and gave her a new reason to live. Contrary to Raleigh's initial impression that Doreen Hewitt hated her, it was really just that she was an overprotective mother, trying to ensure that Kip never suffered from a woman what she had with her husband. Especially given Kip's previous heartbreak.

"And the spoiling will continue when Salem comes next month to spoil Amelia for a week," Raleigh said. "I do question our sanity in allowing my sister to teach our daughter shopping skills at such a young age."

Kip shook his head. "We have to give Salem some room for error. I think our daughter gives her a sense of purpose. And there's no doubt how much Salem loves her."

Salem was—surprisingly—still alone. She and Mike had seemed to be quite serious for a couple of years, but then The Two Mikes were offered a recording contract, went on tour, and the relationship fizzled. Salem had been devastated and subsequently moved back to North Carolina and entered a series of short-term relationships that seemed to leave her pained and exhausted.

So, Raleigh's sister had immediately concentrated all of her affections on Amelia when she was born. Amelia had soaked in all of that love and attention and returned it to her aunt tenfold. Of course, it helped that Salem seemed to have a direct line to Santa and was able to secure much of Amelia Hewitt's list for her each year.

Raleigh turned her attention back to the mail, sorting it into piles of bills, catalogs, and advertisements. As she got near the end of the pile, she paused over a thin white envelope that the post office had forwarded from the St. Clements Bluff address.

It was addressed to "Mrs. Raleigh Bishop" in blue ink with no return markings.

It was written in that same familiar script.

Raleigh's heart began racing in a way that it hadn't in several years.

"What's wrong, honey?" Kip asked. "You look like you've seen a ghost."

Raleigh swallowed. "I think I have." She held up the envelope.

Kip looked at her quizzically. "I don't understand. Looks like you got a letter from someone who doesn't know we got married. I'm surprised the post office forwarded it here after all this time."

She nodded slowly. "This is the same handwriting used on the letters I used to get. The ones accusing Grant of terrible things."

Now Kip was concerned. "But those letters were written by Trey and he's…gone. I'm sure you're mistaken."

Raleigh's fingers trembled as she tore open a short end of the envelope and shook out a single sheet of folded paper. It lay on the counter for several moments before she had the nerve to pick it up.

The words swam before her eyes.

Raleigh,

I'm sure you never thought you would hear from me again. If it weren't for my current circumstances, you certainly wouldn't be.

They say that people have an overwhelming need to confess their sins, that the guilt weighs down like a boat anchor. But they forget to tell you that that guilt rests easy on the shoulders until there is an outside force to push it down.

In my case, you should be happy to know that I don't have much longer. Disease has no pity for anyone, and what's coursing through my kidneys right now will see me visiting St. Peter not long after you receive this.

So, I may as well tell you that everything Trey did was because of me. Oh, he certainly had the idea for St. Clements Bluff, but Trey didn't have the complicated wits required to execute a plan. He needed me for that.

Trey was a bit of a fool, but he was a compliant fool.

How relieved I was that Trey died in the fire so he could never again mention my name. His death was like a gift fallen from the sky. I took it and ran back to my home state where all of my old friends and neighbors embraced me for having lost my darling fiancé.

I know what you're thinking. How could a nurse have done such a thing? Well, just because I'm a nurse doesn't mean that I don't have desires. Or ambitions.

I had both in large quantities.

And all I had to do was write a few letters. Oh, and sew a stupid little doll.

The letter went on like this, confessing to multiple sins without ever actually apologizing for anything.

Raleigh hadn't realized that Kip had come behind her and was reading over her shoulder. She became aware of him as he put a hand on her neck and gently massaged her. "So, it wasn't really Trey," he said quietly. "If we had figured things out sooner, maybe we could have somehow stopped him before he went too far."

Raleigh shook her head. "No. Trey was an adult and responsible for himself. No doubt Barb was influencing him into doing her will because he was so besotted with her. But he cannot be absolved of blame. He knew what he was doing, and it was all his idea to begin with."

She closed her eyes and the memories of all of Trey's deceit came flooding back. The pretense of caring for Raleigh, the lies about St. Clements Bluff, the lies about Grant.

"What a shame, though," Kip said placing a kiss on the back of her head. "This was all so unnecessary."

Raleigh opened her eyes and re-read the letter. The shock was wearing off a little and she was able to absorb the other woman's words a little better.

"Barb is wrong, you know. I'm not happy at all to know she's dying. David and Mutzi will be sad to hear the news, I'm sure, although at this point, I doubt David will even remember who she was." David Bishop had few lucid days anymore, but Mutzi continued to care for her husband personally, refusing to see him placed in assisted care.

Raleigh picked up the envelope and glanced at the upper left-hand corner. "As always, no return address so no way to reach out to her."

"She obviously wants it that way," Kip said, taking the envelope and letter from her and adding them to the other trash in the bin.

"It's not us Barb needs to apologize to. It's Trey," he said. "And hopefully soon she will have that opportunity. All we can do is honor the dead as best we can and continue to live."

At that moment, Amelia came bounding back into the room, the toy catalog already in near tatters. "Daddy, what day is Christmas again? Does Santa check his calendar every day to make sure he can make all of the toys on time?"

Kip knelt down and addressed her question seriously. "Santa has a whole team of elves watching the time for him. Santa has never, ever missed his Christmas deadline. Which is on December 25th. A long time from now, young lady."

Amelia gave her father a suspicious look, as though she didn't quite believe Santa could be that organized with just elves to assist him.

But in the way of young children, Amelia noticed one of her picture books laying on a chair. She reached up to place the catalog on the counter then retrieved the book and wandered back out of the kitchen.

Continue to live, indeed, Raleigh thought. She intended to live as fully as possible with her husband and children.

Raleigh knew that Grant would be happy to know she was finally content.

AUTHOR'S NOTE

THIS IS A work of fiction. Although I make references to certain locations that do exist at the time of publication—such as Patuxent River Naval Air Station, the Old Jail, the Rex, and Tudor Hall—most locations are completely fictional or are based on the types of places located in my beloved St. Mary's County.

To my knowledge, there were never any ratlines passing through St. Mary's County, nor have there been terrorist cells in the area.

However, it is true that St. Mary's County residents were arrested and jailed for helping escaping slaves in the 19th century.

St. Mary's County is the birthplace of Maryland. Born of the idea of George Calvert, the First Lord Baltimore, it was settled as a place of religious freedom. The first Catholic Mass in Maryland was said on St. Clements Island in March 1634. Since then, St. Mary's County has continued to be an eyewitness to many important events in American history.

In July 1776, residents were shocked by the arrival of a fleet of seventy-two British ships making an unexpected appearance off Point Lookout. The ships were seeking provisions, fresh water, and recovery from a smallpox outbreak in the fleet.

The St. Mary's County militia was having none of that, however, and harassed the British landing parties until the fleet's commander, Lord Dunmore, decided it was best to find somewhere else to serve as a base of operations.

The British were back during the War of 1812,

continuously raiding and invading the area, which was a convenient location from which to launch assaults on Washington, DC.

Although no Civil War battles took place in St. Mary's County, there was high sympathy here for the South. Smugglers—or blockade runners—were constantly dodging through the Union's Potomac Flotilla. Additionally, the Union established a prisoner of war camp at Point Lookout, where the Chesapeake Bay meets the Potomac River, and held over 3,000 Confederate prisoners there. Most of the old prison camp has now been eroded by water.

The oyster wars were a series of disputes between legal watermen and oyster pirates in the Chesapeake Bay and the Potomac River from the Civil War era through 1959.

The establishment of the Patuxent River Naval Air Station in the 1940s had a lasting effect that is still felt today. During World War II, the Navy formed a flight-testing center at what is now affectionately known as "Pax River" or just simply "Pax." Extraordinary technological advances have been made at Pax River, with such recognizable aircraft as the Harrier, Tomcat, Osprey, and Super Hornet being tested here. It was also at Pax River's Test Pilot School that the nation's first astronauts—including John Glenn, Alan Shephard, Scott Carpenter, and others—were trained.

Unfortunately, the waterman and farmer populations have decreased over time. Today, St. Mary's County's largest employer is Pax River. However, the area still retains a rural feel and attitude. It's the only place I know where you can stand in a field full of cows and listen to the roar of fighter jets overhead.

It's a great place to call home, and I feel privileged to live here.

Although it would be nice to think that the creation

of a novel is entirely due to the author, it really does take a small army of people to bring a book to fruition.

Thanks to the small army that has helped bring this book into your hands: Sue Grimshaw, my lovely book editor; Arleigh Rodgers, copy editor; Kim Killion, book cover designer; Jenn Jakes, book formatter; and Marnye Young, audiobook narrator. All are consummate professionals whom I feel blessed to have found.

In my personal life are countless people who have been supportive of my writing through the years, but here I will mention three.

First is Mary Oldham, who is a human idea factory of plot lines and publishing strategies. We may live on opposite coasts, but I consider her a dear friend.

Someone else who has been invaluable to me is Michelle Cormier, who has done everything from keeping me company at book signings to being a shoulder during tough times. All for just a glass of wine as payment!

Finally, and perhaps most importantly, is my best friend of over thirty years, Mary Russell. Mary is my webmistress extraordinaire. She stays right on top of everything, updating my site every few days and ensuring I've got the latest technology "stuff" that makes my site, *www.ChristineTrent.com,* run well. She's also got a great creative flair. She, too, works for wine.

Thank you, ladies, for being such great friends and partners in my writing career.

Ecce Agnus Dei.

OTHER BOOKS BY CHRISTINE TRENT

THE ROYAL TRADES SERIES
The Queen's Dollmaker
A Royal Likeness
By the King's Design

THE LADY OF ASHES MYSTERIES
Lady of Ashes
Stolen Remains
A Virtuous Death
The Mourning Bells
Death at the Abbey
A Grave Celebration

FLORENCE NIGHTINGALE MYSTERIES
No Cure for the Dead
A Murderous Malady

SHORT STORIES & ANTHOLOGIES
A Death on the Way to Portsmouth (eBook only)
A Pocketful of Death (The Deadly Hours)
Mrs. Beeton's Sausage Stuffing (Malice Domestic Presents Murder Most Edible)

About the Author

CHRISTINE TRENT IS the author of the *Royal Trades* historical series, the *Lady of Ashes* historical mystery series, and several other historical novels.

St. Clements Bluff is the first in a new series, The Heart of St. Mary's County, set in her beloved, wonderfully history-rich home community in Southern Maryland.

Visit her at *www.ChristineTrent.com*

Printed in the USA
CPSIA information can be obtained
at www.ICGtesting.com
JSHW021938280723
45594JS00002B/29

9 781944 745301